TOM CLANCY UNDER FIRE

This Large Print Book carries the
Seal of Approval of N.A.V.H.

Tom Clancy
Under Fire

Grant Blackwood

THORNDIKE PRESS
A part of Gale, Cengage Learning

GALE
CENGAGE Learning·

Farmington Hills, Mich • San Francisco • New York • Waterville, Maine
Meriden, Conn • Mason, Ohio • Chicago

GALE
CENGAGE Learning®

LIBRARY OF CONGRESS CATALOGING-IN-PUBLICATION DATA

Blackwood, Grant.
   Tom Clancy under fire / Grant Blackwood. — Large print edition.
   pages cm. — (Thorndike Press large print basic)
   ISBN 978-1-4104-8081-1 (hardback) — ISBN 1-4104-8081-X (hardcover)
  1. Ryan, Jack, Jr. (Fictitious character)—Fiction. 2. Intelligence officers—United States—Fiction. 3. Missing persons—Investigation—Fiction. 4. Large type books. 5. Political fiction. I. Clancy, Tom, 1947-2013. II. Title.
PS3602.L3259T66 2015b
813'.6—dc23   2015016932

Published in 2015 by arrangement with G. P. Putnam's Sons, an imprint of Penguin Publishing Group, a division of Penguin Random House LLC

Printed in the United States of America
1 2 3 4 5 6 7 19 18 17 16 15

Tom Clancy Under Fire

1

TEHRAN, IRAN

Be careful how you spend your time. You never get it back.

Of all the lessons he'd learned from his father, this one truly resonated with Jack Ryan, Jr. — no small feat, as he'd received the advice as a teenager with little more on his mind than girls and football games. *Go figure,* Jack thought.

In this case, with his lunch appointment predictably late, Jack was playing a round of "watch the watchers," a game introduced to him by John Clark. His location, Chaibar, an outdoor café on a quiet Tehran side street, made the game more challenging. Nestled in the courtyard garden of a renovated villa, Chaibar was full of couples and small groups seated at wrought-iron tables. Jack caught glimpses of muted flowered murals behind potted plants and hanging vines. Overhead, boughs cast the courtyard in dappled sunlight. While most of the murmured voices were speaking in Arabic or Persian, Jack also caught snippets of French and Italian.

The premise of "watch the watchers" was a simple one: He's in the field for Hendley Associates, aka The Campus. He's under surveillance. But by whom? If you're largely unfamiliar with the nuances of casual Iranian interaction, how do you spot that one pair of eyes paying too much attention to you, or someone whose mannerisms are out of sync with the surroundings? With this checklist in mind, Jack studied faces, body language, banter between this couple, or forced banter among that group.

Nothing, Jack thought. None of Chaibar's patrons set off alarms for him. In real life, a good thing; for the purposes of this game, not so much.

If Hendley Associates, aka The Campus, were in fact what it seemed, a privately held arbitrage firm, Jack's game would have been one of fantasy, but The Campus's true purpose went much deeper, as it sat squarely in the grayest of areas in the espionage/counterterrorism world — an off-the-books intelligence group answerable only to the President of the United States. Where the CIA was a bazooka, The Campus was a stiletto.

"Pardon, sir. Another coffee, please?"

Jack glanced up. His waitress was a petite twentysomething woman in black-rimmed glasses, her hair completely covered by a light blue scarf. Her English was heavily stilted.

She wore no niqab. Perhaps Kamran Farahani wasn't simply giving lip service to his administration's moderate platform. Hell, even a year ago Chaibar might have been subject to a police raid; to the previous government, coffee shops were incubators for youthful subversives.

Jack glanced down at his empty cup. The shop's version of coffee made a Starbucks dark roast seem like weak tea.

"No, thank you, two is enough for me. Hopefully my guest will . . ."

As if on cue, over his waitress's shoulder, Jack saw a man with wild, curly black hair walking into the courtyard, his head turning this way and that. There was no mistaking that mop.

"Here he is," Jack told her, raising his hand to get the man's attention. "Give us a couple minutes."

"Of course, sir."

The man walked over to the table. Jack stood up, the iron legs of his chair scraping on the cobblestones. They shook hands.

shared a quick bear hug, then sat down.

"Sorry I'm late, Jack."

"I'm used to it. What would a lunch be with an on-time Seth Gregory?"

It had been that way since high school. If the movie started at seven-twenty, you told Seth seven o'clock.

"Yeah, yeah. It's my only failing. And if you believe that . . . How's the coffee?"

"It bent my spoon."

"Puts hair on your chest."

"How've you been, Seth?"

"Sharp stick, my friend, sharp stick."

Jack smiled. This was Seth's standard response to such questions. Translation: Doing better than if I had a sharp stick in the eye.

"Glad to hear it."

"I've been here before; I know what I want. The *asheh gojeh farangi* — that's a tomato stew with onions, meat, peas, spices. Delicious. Huh . . . still no alcohol on the menu, I see."

"That might take longer. Farahani can't shock the old guard too much, too quickly."

The waitress returned. They both ordered the stew. "And we'll share a basket of barbari bread," Seth added. The waitress collected their menus and disappeared.

With elbows on the table, Seth reached

across and gave Jack's hand a couple of gentle slaps. "Jack, you look good! I've missed you. How ya doing?"

"Never better."

"I was surprised to get your call."

"I was thinking we'd have lunch the next time you were in the States. I had no idea you were in the area."

Seth shrugged, waved his hand. "How's the family? Olivia? And El Presidente . . . Il Duce?"

"Fine, all fine."

Jack had to smile, and not just because Seth was one of the few people who called Sally by her given name and refused to call Jack's father by his correct title, but because this exuberant and near-frenetic questioning was pure Seth Gregory. His friend not only was the quintessential people person, but also suffered from ADHD — emphasis on the "hyperactivity disorder" part. Seth had struggled in school. Jack had been his unofficial tutor.

Jack had always sensed an undercurrent of sadness behind Seth's gregariousness. Despite having known the man since St. Matthew's Academy, Jack always felt there was a part of Seth he kept hidden not only from the world, but from Jack as well. Jack had few friends at St. Matthew's, as most of

11

his classmates had either shunned him as the stuck-up Golden Child of then CIA bigwig Jack Ryan or had been intimidated by the ostensibly lofty circles in which "Spy Boy" orbited. Of course, neither scenario had been true, and Jack had spent his first year at St. Matthew's trying to prove so, to no avail. But Seth had accepted Jack for who he was — an awkward teenager just trying to find his way like everyone else. Looking back at that time, Jack knew Seth had saved him from withdrawing into himself and spiraling into self-isolation. Seth didn't give a shit who Jack's father was, or where he lived, or that he rubbed shoulders with foreign royalty and heads of state at grand dinner parties. In fact, invariably, Seth's only question about such affairs had been whether there'd been any hot girls at the event and whether Jack had hooked up with any of them in some über-secret room at Langley.

Jack had always regretted not telling Seth how much his friendship had meant to him. Perhaps now was the time. Before Jack could do this, Seth continued his rapid-fire interrogation. Sometimes having a conversation with him was like being in the middle of a verbal tornado.

"What's going on with Olivia?"

"Sally?" Jack replied. "You haven't heard? She's an astronaut."

"What? Oh, that's very funny, Jack. You're quite the commode-ian."

Jack laughed. "Man, you're still saying that? It wasn't even funny when we were fifteen."

"Oh, it was funny, and you know it. So: Sally?"

"She just finished with her residency at Johns Hopkins."

"Underachiever, that one. Are you still at that place . . . that financial group?"

"Hendley Associates."

"Right. Making tons of money?"

"Doing okay," Jack replied. The true answer was yes. Though the investment side of Hendley Associates was merely a cover for The Campus, Jack and his cohorts had in fact made hundreds of millions playing the world's markets. Of that revenue, only a fraction paid their salaries. The rest funded the off-the-books intelligence organization.

Seth said, "And how about —"

Jack laughed and raised his hands in mock surrender. "Enough, Seth. You're wearing me out. Tell me about you."

"Still consulting. Been on contract with Shell for the last eighteen months. I was based out of Baku until about eight months ago, when they moved me here."

After high school Seth had snagged a Gus Archie Memorial Scholarship to the University of Illinois at Urbana-Champaign's College of Engineering. Now, apparently, he was parlaying that into big bucks.

"I like it in Tehran, actually. My condo's within walking distance of here. Great place."

"What's your specialty?" asked Jack.

"Mostly looking at drilling rigs and refining plants. It's a nice gig. I spend most of my time in Central Asia."

"Dicey areas." *Especially the two "stans" from which the Emir, aka Saif Rahman Yasin, sprang,* Jack thought. Helping to nab that son of a bitch had been not only damned satisfying, but also Jack's first foray into the world of field operations.

Seth said, "We get good training and plenty of security when we need it — Blackwater-type guys, mostly retirees from U.S. Special Forces. Nice guys. I'd hate to get on their bad side, though."

A sentiment most bad guys share after receiving a visit from Navy SEALs or Army Delta Force, Jack thought.

"Got any investment advice for me?" Jack said.

14

"No. And you wouldn't listen if I did," replied Seth. "You're a straight arrow, Jack, and you know it."

Jack shrugged. "True enough. Plus, I've got a healthy fear of the SEC."

Their food came and they ate. Jack followed Seth's lead, tearing chunks off the barbari bread and mixing it into the tomato stew. It was delicious and filling.

"I was sorry to hear about your dad," Jack said.

"Yeah. I got your card, thanks. Sorry I didn't say anything."

"How's your mom doing with it all?"

"It's been three years. Looking at her, you'd think he died last week."

"It's understandable." Seth's father, Paul, had died of a sudden stroke. Seth's mother had found him in the study. She'd never fully recovered.

"Man, I don't know what to do for her," said Seth. "My sister, Bethany — you remember Bethany, right? — lives about an hour north of her in Georgia. She took her to the doctor, who gave her some kind of prescription — Lamictal, I think."

"Mood stabilizer and antidepressant," Jack said. Half expecting Seth to have jumped to another subject, Jack was surprised he was being forthcoming with such intimate details. "How long has she been on it?"

"A couple weeks."

"If it's going to start helping, it'll be any time now."

Seth smiled. "The benefits of having two doctors in the family, huh?"

"Yep. Osmotic knowledge, I suppose."

Seth dipped a chunk of bread into his stew, then popped it into his mouth. "So, what brings you to Tehran?"

"Scouting. Iranian markets are starting to open up. If Farahani keeps his course, there's going to be a boom. Hendley needs to be ready."

While this was true and was certainly part of the reason for Jack's presence in the country, this was primarily an intelligence-gathering junket. While poring over the new media outlets blossoming in Iran was informative, there was no substitute for what John Clark, Hendley's new operations chief, called a Mark I Eyeball inspection. It was a Navy term, Clark had explained. "Walk the streets and talk to people. Best tool in a spook's arsenal." So far Jack had neither seen nor heard anything to suggest Iran's new president was anything but what he seemed — the first true moderate to hold office since the 1979 revolution. Whether he'd last was anyone's guess.

Jack put that question to Seth: "You've been here awhile. What's your take on all this?"

"Hell, Jack, I don't know. I came here for the first time after the election. I can tell you this much: Nobody's been anything but polite to me. I get dirty looks occasionally from some of the graybeards but that's about it. No one's ever called me 'imperialist Satan,' if that tells you anything."

It does, Jack thought. Before Farahani took office, Seth would have had minders on his tail every moment he was outside his apartment. That would've been the best-case scenario. And with no reports of SAVAK-style crackdowns on the population, the fact that Seth — an American, of all things — could walk the streets unmolested suggested most of Iran's citizenry was on board with Farahani's reforms.

Ceaseless miracles, Jack thought.

They chatted for another hour and shared half a dozen cups of mint tea from a silver samovar the size of a small terrier until finally Seth glanced at his watch. "Shoot. I gotta go, Jack, sorry."

Seth stood up. Jack did the same and extended his hand. Seth grasped it and then did something he rarely did: He held Jack's

17

gaze. "Really good to see you, man. I mean it."

"You too, Seth." Jack hesitated. "Everything okay with you?"

"Yeah, why wouldn't it be? Hey, listen, my apartment's about fifteen minutes from here." Seth gave him the address. "It's right off Niavaran Park. If you're ever back in town and need a place to crash, it's yours. Just use the key. There're steaks in the freezer."

"Thanks, man, that's —"

"Travel safe, Jack."

Seth turned and walked away, disappearing through a vine-wrapped arch.

Key . . . what key? Jack thought. He sat back down and reached for his teacup. Sitting beside it was a bronze key.

"What the hell was all that about?" he muttered to himself.

Edinburgh, Scotland

As the only member of her team to have spent time in the United Kingdom prior to the start of the job, Helen was unsurprised by the blitz of blinking lights and cacophony of voices filtering through the van's half-open windows.

Yegor braked hard and the van lurched to a stop as a young man and woman, clearly

18

inebriated, stumbled past the front bumper. The woman raised two fingers at Yegor and called, "Tosser!"

Helen saw Yegor's jaw pulse with anger, but he did not respond, and instead waited for them to pass before easing the van forward. On either side of the street, similarly intoxicated youth staggered and weaved along the sidewalks. On the passenger side, outside Helen's half-open window, a pub's door burst open, issuing a stream of drunks and pulsing dance music.

"What's a tosser?" asked Yegor.

Someone who desperately needs a girlfriend, Helen thought with a smile. "I'll explain later," she said.

"This is amazing. What are all these places?"

"Pubs," Helen answered.

"All of them?"

"Pretty much. This is just one area. This is Rose," Helen said. "It's the most popular pub street for students."

"All of these people are students from the university?"

"Most of them."

"How do they function in the morning?" asked Yegor. "Don't they have lectures to attend?"

Helen smiled at this. Ever the pragmatist,

Yegor wasn't so concerned about the immorality he was seeing but rather how it affected the revelers' study habits.

"Coffee," she answered. "And other things, I suspect."

In the backseat, the other two members of the team, Roma and Olik, sat with their foreheads nearly pressed against the rear windows, their eyes agog. Where they came from, public displays like these were punishable by imprisonment. Or worse.

Of course, Helen reminded herself, Roma and Olik were men, and sheltered ones at that. Most of their astonishment probably stemmed from the sea of exposed female skin passing before their eyes. Not to mention the physical intimacy couples showed each other on the street. *Snogging* was the term here. At home, neither of these were seen outside the bedroom of a husband and wife.

Olik leaned over the front seat's center console and said, "And this is an important school, you say?"

"One of the most prestigious in the world," Helen replied.

There were a few seconds of silence. "And what exactly are the admission requirements?"

Helen chuckled, as did Yegor, who said,

"Get ahold of yourself, Olik."

Roma, however, muttered, "Whores, all of them. Every one of them. They should be whipped."

This comment didn't surprise Helen. Of the three men on her team, Roma, a last-minute addition, had been the only one chafing under her leadership. He was a zealot, and he thought like one. Theirs was a business of dispassion; Roma didn't understand that. The man bore watching. Sooner or later she would have to put him in his place.

They drove for a few minutes before turning onto Castle Street. Here, too, the sidewalk was lined with pubs and restaurants, though these were more subdued, geared to those students who disliked the "meat markets," she knew. *Is that the correct term now, "meat markets"?* she wondered. She would check. Standing out was a hazard to be avoided.

"My contact says her favorite spot is called The Stable," she said.

"Like for horses?" asked Olik.

"Like for university students," Helen answered. "There it is, Yegor, ahead on the left."

"I see it. Olik, Roma, look for her car. A red Mini Cooper with white hood stripes."

"How does she afford such a vehicle?" asked Roma.

A gift from Daddy, Helen thought but did not say. "Never mind that. Just keep your eyes open."

Yegor slowed the van. Moments later, from behind them came the impatient honking of car horns.

"A little faster, Yegor," Helen said, and he pressed the accelerator slightly. It wouldn't do to be stopped by the police.

"Wait, I think we just passed her car," said Olik. "On the right."

Helen glanced in her side mirror. "Yes, that's the one. Keep going, Yegor."

Yegor sped up, then turned left onto Frederick Street, where he found a parking space a block away from a petrol station. He put the van in park, shut off the engine, and checked his watch. "Now what?"

"Now we wait," replied Helen.

Now we build a pattern.

2

Jack sat bolt upright in bed and looked around. *Just someone at your door, Jack. Relax.* As much as he loved fieldwork, especially the high-adrenaline stuff, it did tend to put you in that zero-to-sixty mind-set.

He exhaled and rolled his shoulders, then his neck. Hotel pillows never agreed with him.

The knock on the door came again, polite but insistent. Jack checked the nightstand clock. Six in the morning. He rolled over, got to his feet, donned his terry-cloth robe, and headed for the door. "Who is it?"

No answer, but another knock.

"Who is it?" Jack repeated a little more firmly. There was no peephole. Isn't that against fire code? It was in the United States, at least.

"Mr. Jack Ryan?" The man's accent was English.

23

Jack didn't respond.

"Mr. Ryan, my name is Raymond Wellesley. May I speak to you for a few minutes?"

"About what, Mr. Wellesley?"

"Your friend Seth Gregory."

This got Jack's attention.

Wellesley said, "This is perhaps a matter best discussed in private."

Ease up, Jack. If by some fluke there had been a coup overnight and these were in fact the Shah's SAVAK back from the dead, he was screwed anyway. Plus, that kind of visitor didn't knock.

Jack unlocked the dead bolt, swung the latch, and opened the door. Standing before him was a short, middle-aged man with thinning brown hair. He wore a tailored dark blue British-cut suit. Savile Row, Jack decided.

"Mr. Jack Ryan, yes?" said Raymond Wellesley.

"Yes, come in."

Wellesley stepped through the door and strode across Jack's suite to the sitting area beside the balcony windows. He carefully lowered himself into one of the club chairs and looked around as though checking for cleanliness.

Jack shut the door and walked over.

"Apologies for the early hour," Wellesley said. "Pressing matters, I'm afraid. Good heavens, I'm sorry, would you care to see some identification?"

"Please," Jack replied. Something told him he was about to be handed a nondescript business card.

He was right. The card read:

RAYMOND L. WELLESLEY
FOREIGN & COMMONWEALTH OFFICE
KING CHARLES STREET
LONDON SW1A 2AH
UNITED KINGDOM
RLW@FCO.GOV.UK
+44 20 7946 0690

Though Britain wasn't due to reopen its Tehran embassy for another few months, something told Jack that Raymond Wellesley wouldn't be the type to have an address here anyway. Wellesley's business card told him nothing except the man was probably not in fact an employee of the FCO.

Jack slipped the card into the pocket of his robe and said, "You mentioned Seth Gregory. Is he okay?"

"Curious word, *okay*. Lends itself to all manner of interpretation, doesn't it?"

Wellesley's accent was not just British,

Jack decided, but what he'd come to recognize as Received Pronunciation — RP or BBC English. Nonregional and indistinct. Apparently, Jack thought, he'd absorbed something from meeting the panoply of British diplomats that had visited the White House during his dad's first term. RP was standard dialect among higher-echelon people at the Secret Intelligence Service, an "old boy" tradition that hadn't changed since the First World War.

Wellesley added, "Whether Mr. Gregory is 'okay' is something I was hoping you could help me with."

Jack felt his heart quicken slightly. *What the hell is going on?*

Jack said, "Answer my question, Mr. Wellesley."

"As far as we can tell, your friend is alive and well. You had lunch with Mr. Gregory yesterday, did you not?"

"Yes."

"Do you know where he is now?"

"No, I don't."

"What did you discuss during your lunch?"

"How much I was hoping to get a predawn visit from the FCO. And here you are."

"I encourage you to take my questions seriously, Mr. Ryan. We're affording you a courtesy we might not otherwise extend."

The message was clear, or at least he thought so: If he weren't *that* Jack Ryan, this talk probably wouldn't be even remotely cordial.

Jack stepped around the club chair and took a seat opposite Wellesley.

"Would you like some coffee?" he asked.

"No, thank you. I can't stay long."

"Mr. Wellesley, Seth is a friend of mine. We've known each other since high school. I'm here on business and I asked him if he'd like to have lunch and catch up."

"What did you discuss?"

"Family, old times, Iran's new government, and a bit about work."

"What kind of work does he do?"

"He's an engineer with Shell."

"Is that what he told you?"

"Yes, that's what he told me. You have reason to believe otherwise?"

"I can't discuss that."

"Why are you looking for him?"

"I can't discuss that, either, but if you can help us find him, we would be grateful."

"I'd trade gratitude for equity," Jack said. "Give me a better idea what's going on and I'll see what I can do."

Raymond Wellesley pursed his lips and stared into space for a few seconds. "Very well. But not here. Are you free this afternoon?"

Is Wellesley suggesting my room is bugged? Jack wondered. It seemed unlikely, but he'd learned early on to never mistake probability with possibility.

"I can be."

Wellesley stood up and drew another business card from the breast pocket of his suit. With a silver pen he scribbled on the back of the card, then handed it to Jack.

"Meet me there at two o'clock."

As had been drummed into him by Ding Chavez, Hendley's senior operations officer, Jack arrived by taxi an hour early for the meeting, then got out and walked the ground, familiarizing himself with the neighborhood around the address Wellesley had given him, the upscale Zafaraniyeh district in northern Tehran. Always know your egress — or, in Ding's SpecFor-influenced vernacular, "Know your GTFO plan": Get the Fuck Out.

According to the travel websites Jack had consulted, Zafaraniyeh was home to mostly Iranian and expatriate millionaires. Behind tree-lined sidewalks, the apartment façades were done in Pahlavi style, a circa-1960s mix of traditional Persian and modern

European.

A light rain began to fall. Jack opened the umbrella the hotel's concierge had suggested and continued down the damp sidewalk. The few passersby he saw, mostly Europeans in casual sport coats and trousers, offered him a perfunctory smile. The locals were a mix of men and women, the latter wearing no headscarves at all, simply nodding. No smiles. Neither friendly nor unfriendly. A good sign, Jack knew. He had chosen his attire in hopes of blending in.

At one-fifty, Jack made his way to the correct address, an apartment fronted by granite columns and a line of neatly trimmed squared hedges. He climbed the steps into the tiled foyer and found the intercom panel. He pressed the button labeled *VII.* A moment later a voice said, "Come up, Mr. Ryan."

Good guess or foresight? Jack thought. *Assume the latter, Jack.*

The foyer's inner door let out a soft buzz. Jack opened it, stepped through, and followed the carpeted runner to the elevator, an old-style accordion-gated elevator that took him to the seventh floor and another tiled foyer. As the gate parted, a door across from him opened, revealing Raymond

Wellesley.

"Early is punctual," he said. "A man after my own heart. Come in."

Jack followed Wellesley inside and down a short hallway to a spacious room decorated in what Jack could only describe as gray, with furniture and decor that were neither British nor Persian, neither colorless nor vibrant. A perfectly forgettable safe house with furnishings that came with the place, Jack thought.

He stopped at the entrance of the room and looked around. To his left a pair of hallways led back to what he guessed were bedrooms; to his right was an alcove mini-bar. Standing beside a sectional couch area in front of the windows was a second man of medium height, with dark cropped hair and a heavy beard. His face was deeply tanned, as though he spent more time outdoors than he did indoors.

Wellesley said, "Jack, may I introduce Matthew Spellman."

Spellman stepped around the couch and extended his hand. "Matt."

"Jack Ryan."

"Coffee, Mr. Ryan?" Wellesley asked.

"Thanks."

They settled into the sitting room, Jack taking a wingback chair, Spellman on the couch opposite him. Wellesley poured Jack a cup of coffee from the carafe on the low table between them, then joined Spellman on the couch.

Jack raised his mug in a half-toast. "To Anglo-American cooperation."

"Let's hope so," Wellesley replied.

Having already guessed Wellesley was SIS, Jack surmised Spellman was CIA. Whatever Seth Gregory had done or was suspected of doing, his friend had attracted some powerful attention. Jack was tempted to take a hard line, to demand answers, but he knew it would get him nowhere, not yet. Moreover, aggression might only pique their interest in him. Better to let his hosts make some progress on their agenda.

"Just so there's no misunderstanding," Spellman began, "we know who you are."

"And who am I?"

"First Son of President Ryan."

"And if I wasn't?"

"Please, Mr. Ryan," said Wellesley. "We're not thugs. What's your business in Iran?"

"Market scouting. I'm with Hendley Associates. We do —"

"We know what Hendley does. But why are you here, in Iran?"

"I told you. Market scouting. President Farahani's move toward moderation may open things up to foreign investment. If so, we want to get ahead of that."

"Makes sense. Heck, maybe I should get some stock tips from you," Spellman said with a chuckle.

"How long do you plan on being here?" This from Wellesley.

Good cop, bad cop, Jack thought. Though Hollywood had made the technique a cliché, it was tried-and-true. Spellman and Wellesley were giving him a mild form of it now — affable cop, slightly testy British bobby.

"It's open-ended," he replied.

"How well do you know Seth Gregory?" asked Wellesley.

"We're old friends from high school."

"When was the last time you were in touch with each other?" Spellman asked.

Intentionally covering already plowed ground, Jack thought. "Yesterday, at lunch. But you know that."

Wellesley said, "Before that, is what he means."

"E-mail, to set up the lunch." *You know that, too.*

The questioning continued for another ten minutes, Wellesley probing and reprobing the nature and depth of Jack's relationship with Seth. They were setting a baseline and looking for inconsistencies. Aside from interjecting bits of lighthearted humor to keep Jack on the roller coaster, Spellman said nothing, but simply sipped his coffee and studied Jack's face.

Finally he said, "Do you know where he is?"

"Have you checked his apartment?"

"Yes," said Wellesley. "Have you been there?"

"I don't even know where it is."

"Pardis Condos, off Niayesh Expressway."

Jack recalled his still-spotty mental map of Tehran. The Niayesh Expressway was nowhere near Niavaran Park, where Seth had claimed his apartment was located. *What the hell is going on?*

Jack shook his head. "I haven't been there."

"I went there after our meeting this morning," said Wellesley. "He's not there. In fact, it looks like he hasn't been there for quite some time."

"He travels for work."

"We know that," Wellesley replied, with a tinge of exasperation in his voice.

It sounded genuine. Perhaps a button Jack could push later if necessary.

"Did you two talk about his work?" asked Spellman.

"Only in passing. He consults for Shell."

Jack watched for a reaction from either man, but got nothing but impassive gazes. He said, "Guys, I don't know what to tell you. You seem to know more than I do about what's been going on with Seth. Are you going to explain what's going on? Come on, give me something."

Wellesley let out a sigh. Spellman set his cup on the coffee table and leaned forward, his elbows on his knees. "We think Seth's gotten himself into trouble. We want to help him."

"Listen, I don't even know who you are, but I've read enough John le Carré novels to make a guess. You don't have to tell me all your secrets, but if Seth's in trouble, I need to know what's going on."

"No, you don't," replied Wellesley. "I suggest you —"

Spellman raised a hand to cut off his colleague. "Hang on a second, Raymond. Okay, Jack, that's fair. I'm going to stick my neck out. Don't chop it off, okay? I got kids to feed." Spellman gave him a sheepish grin.

Jack found himself not disliking Spellman — which was probably the point, he reminded himself.

"I'll do my best, Matt."

"We've had an op going for the past year

or so. Seth's been running it for us, but it's got nothing to do with Iran. Something else. After you two had lunch he was supposed to come here for a sit-down, an update meeting. When he didn't show, we checked his apartment. He hasn't been staying there. The super said he's been collecting Seth's mail for almost a month." Spellman hesitated and glanced at Wellesley, who gave him a slight nod. "He's also taken some money — our operational fund. And we think he left the country."

Damn it, Jack thought. Spellman wasn't kidding; Seth was in deep trouble. Was Seth, his old high school buddy, what he seemed to be? *Too many questions,* Jack thought.

Jack almost forgot to ask the next obvious question, one he knew they wouldn't answer but one a civilian would certainly ask: "What do you mean, 'op'? You mean operation? What kind? To what end?"

Spellman gave him another disarming smile. "Sorry, that's need-to-know stuff. Suffice to say, we're the good guys."

"You're kidding with this, right? This can't be real."

"This is quite real, Mr. Ryan," said Wellesley. "You'll agree the circumstances don't look good for your friend. Of course, all this could be a misunderstanding —"

35

"Crossed wires," Spellman added.

"— which is why it's imperative we find Mr. Gregory."

"No, hey, I get it," said Jack. "All I've got is his cell-phone number and e-mail address, but I'm guessing you've got those, too."

"What are they?" asked Spellman. Jack recited them and Spellman nodded. "Yeah, those are right."

"I don't believe Seth would do something like what you're talking about. You're suggesting he's a traitor, a spy."

"People change," Spellman replied.

"That's not the Seth I know."

"You're familiar with the apple-tree aphorism, I assume?" said Wellesley.

"What, about one not falling far from the other? What the hell does that mean? Are you talking about Seth's dad? He worked for the Department of Agriculture, for God's sake."

"Of course."

Jack stood up. "I've told you everything I know. If I hear from him, I'll tell him to call you. For the record, I think you're wrong."

Spellman and Wellesley stood up as well. The American said, "Hang on, Jack . . ."

"No, I'm done." Jack headed for the door. Wellesley called, "Mr. Ryan."

Jack turned around.

"If you're lying to us, or you try to reach out to your friend behind our backs, we'll know about it. If that happens, your father's influence will only go so far."

"Are you threatening me?"

The SIS man was doing just that, Jack knew, and he wasn't particularly surprised by it, given the alleged stakes. Still, the natural reaction of his public persona, Jack Ryan, Jr., First Son and workaday financial analyst, would be one of outrage and fear. *Give them what they expect.*

"I told you what I know. Seth and I had lunch for about an hour. End of story."

Spellman raised his hands in surrender and stepped around the couch. "Hey, Jack, you're probably right. We just need to find him, that's all. You're his friend and you probably want to protect him. I'd feel the same. But you really don't want to get in the middle of this. Just get ahold of us if you hear from him. Use the e-mail on Raymond's card. And don't go hunting for him, Jack."

Raymond Wellesley said, "Very good advice, that."

As soon as he stepped out onto the street, he took a deep breath, trying to wrap his head around what had just happened, then started walking. The cool spring air felt good on his face.

God damn it, Jack thought. *Can't be. Not Seth.* Spellman's warning about not getting involved had barely registered with Jack. *Not help Seth? No way.* The question was, Where the hell should he start?

As crazy as the man had been, James Jesus Angleton, Cold War CIA spyhunter and raging paranoid, had gotten it right when he assigned the Yeats line "wilderness of mirrors" to the world of intelligence and espionage. The fact that Jack could still remember the poem was either a testament to or an indictment of his Catholic-school upbringing.

Jack's next thought about the meeting would have made Angleton proud: *Are Raymond Wellesley and Matthew Spellman who they claim to be? And if not, who are they? And if . . .*

Stop, Jack commanded himself. Those kinds of spiraling questions would drop him squarely down the rabbit hole. He needed facts. He needed a foundation he could stand on.

First: Know who he is dealing with.

Second: Find Seth Gregory before Wellesley and Spellman did.

3

Short of spending weeks tailing Spellman and Wellesley and trying to build a profile on each man, Jack had only one way of knowing their pedigrees. Tap into The Campus's resources. But as there was no remote log-in portal to Hendley's intelligence gold mine, he had to call in a favor.

Twenty minutes after he left the Zafaraniyeh apartment, the wheels were in motion.

Jack spent the rest of the afternoon killing time, then had a dinner of lamb khoresh in the hotel restaurant, followed by two cups of espresso, before leaving and walking two blocks south, where he caught a taxi and set out for Niavaran Park.

The sun was setting when the taxi dropped him off at the park's tree- and streetlight-lined southern entrance. As Jack made his way north deeper into the park he could hear strains of what sounded like Persian pop music and laughing. Improbably, Niavaran Park was not only the former home of the last shah of Iran, Mohammad Reza Pahlavi, but also currently a public library and a roller-skating rink and teenage hangout. Jack resisted the urge to go watch the spectacle and made his way through the park to Pourebtehaj Street, the park's northern border. From there, Seth's apartment — the one Wellesley and Spellman didn't know about — was a five-minute walk to the east.

The apartments here were built in the fifties, old but well-kept brownstones with fresh white paint and neat grass strips lining the sidewalks. Seth's building was in the middle of the block. Jack walked to the far end, where he found a coffee shop. He took a seat near a window with a view of the building and ordered a cup of decaf tea.

He started watching.

Twenty minutes later, after seeing only a trio of people out and about — two of them walking dogs, the third hurrying to catch a bus on the corner — Jack felt his phone vibrate in his jacket pocket. The screen read *Gavin*.

Gavin Biery's official title at The Campus was director of information technology, but he was also an information scrounger without equal. He hadn't hesitated when Jack asked him to do an unofficial search into Wellesley and Spellman. He'd said nothing about Seth Gregory.

"Hey, Gavin, what's up?"

"We've got sleet here. That's what's up." Gavin wasn't a fan of the outdoors, or weather, or things that didn't involve computers, for that matter.

"Sorry to hear that. What've you got for me?"

"Raymond Lamont Wellesley and Matthew Spellman both look legit. They've got pretty vanilla titles, but you'd expect that. Wellesley is Foreign Office, no department or division named, which says something in itself, and Spellman is Department of State, Political Affairs, European and Eurasia.

"But once I dug a little deeper I started hitting layers of stuff that reeked of backstopping," said Biery, referring to administrative details used to bulwark a cover identity. "I'll keep digging."

"No red flags?"

"Not so far. I'll step lightly. Are you in trouble, Jack?"

"Just being overcautious. Probably nothing. Thanks, Gavin."

Jack disconnected.

He nursed his tea for another twenty minutes until satisfied the block was clear, then paid the tab and walked outside, across the street, and up the brownstone's front steps. The outer foyer door was unlocked. He stepped through. Unlike the building's nondescript façade, the foyer was pure Persian, with blue-and-white mosaic floor tiles and pristine white walls. He stood still for a few moments, listening, then took the stairs to the fourth floor and into the hallway. It was empty, lined on both sides with four apartment doors; Jack heard no sound filtering through them. He felt a prickle of apprehension on his neck. In an American apartment hallway you'd at least hear faint television noise. Different culture, Jack decided. He walked down the hallway, past Seth's apartment door, number 406, and stopped at the fire exit, where he again stood still, listening. If he'd collected a tail here, they had two choices: wait until Jack emerged from the building again or come find him. Jack sat down on the windowsill, his back resting against the roman shade, and waited.

Hurry up and wait. It was a phrase both Clark and Ding had used many times. In both the military and intelligence work, patience was an indispensable virtue.

He waited ten minutes, then gave it an extra five minutes for caution's sake, then returned to Seth's door, pressed his ear to the door for a few moments, then inserted the key and turned the knob and stepped through. He turned the dead bolt back into place with a soft snick. Save the moonlight coming through a pair of windows on the other side of the room, the space was dark.

Jack thought: *Gloves. Should have brought gloves.*

In the corner of his left eye, he saw movement — a shadowed figure rushing down the side hall. Jack spun on his heel to face the charge. In rapid fire, Jack's brain dissected the incoming attack: probably no gun, or the man wouldn't be trying to close the gap; the man's arms and hands were tucked close to his body, so probably no blade or blunt object. This kind of blind rush suggested Jack's arrival had surprised him.

Now Jack's brain switched to autopilot. He let the man cover a few more feet, then dodged right, off the line of attack, spun on his heel again, and twisted his body, slashing at the passing man with his elbow, catching him on the back of the head with a glancing blow. It wasn't enough. The man turned, hunched in a fighter's stance, and

43

lashed out with a Muay Thai–style kick. His shin landed hard on Jack's left thigh. Jack immediately felt his quadriceps muscle go numb. The kick wasn't one of desperation reaction, Jack realized. His attacker had skill.

He stumbled backward, trying to regain his balance, trying to transfer weight onto his good leg, but the man charged again, backing him toward the windows. A back full of glass shards would end the fight, he knew. He sidestepped, a half-stumble, then took a step forward, ducked under the straight right punch from the man, then slammed his own right hook into the man's ribs. The man staggered sideways. Jack's damaged thigh felt dead. He wasn't going to win this standing up.

He pushed off with his right leg and crashed into the man. Together they fell in a heap on the floor, the man pinned beneath Jack. The man turned onto his back, encircled Jack's waist with his legs, and pulled his head down against his chest. *Shit.* The man had Brazilian jiu-jitsu, too. If Jack didn't extricate himself quickly, he'd no doubt find himself in a rear naked choke. Lose standing up, lose on the ground. *Do something, Jack.*

The man slammed an elbow into Jack's temple. Bright light flashed behind his eyes.

He felt his body swaying sideways, saw blackness creeping into his vision. Knowing more strikes would be coming, Jack bracketed his head with his forearms, absorbing blows until he could right himself. He jerked back, breaking the man's grip, then snapped his torso downward. His forehead smashed into the man's cheekbone. Jack heard the soft crunch. The man shoved his arm up, palm-striking Jack's chin. Jack felt the man's fingers clawing up his face toward his eyes. He jerked his head sideways and broke the man's grip.

Don't let up, Jack thought. *Finish him before you go out.*

He lifted his head again, brought it down again, then once more. Before his assailant could recover, Jack reached down blindly, grabbed the man's ears, and slammed the back of his head against the hardwood floor. Then twice more until the man went limp.

Gasping, Jack rolled off the man and scooted sideways, disentangling himself from the man's legs, and craned his neck until he could see down the hallway from where the man had charged. Thankfully, there was no one there; he was in no shape for another fight. His head throbbed and he could hear the rush of blood in his ears.

Half conscious, moving on instinct alone,

Jack crawled over to the man, flipped him onto his belly, and pressed his left knee against his neck. The man didn't move, made no sound. The hardwood beneath his head was slick with black blood. Jack reached down and felt the man's throat for a carotid pulse. It was there, steady and strong.

Good, Jack thought. While he'd killed before and accepted the necessity of it, he'd never liked the feeling. It always made him mildly queasy — a good thing, John Clark had told him: "When it has no effect on you, either when it happens or later, when you're alone with your thoughts, you got a problem." That admission from a man like Clark had surprised Jack, and he'd wondered if Hendley's operations chief was becoming more reflective in his golden years. Of course, *golden years* wasn't a term he ever uttered in Clark's presence.

Jack realized his left thigh was twitching uncontrollably. He sat down on his butt, scooted himself backward over the floor, then began kneading the quadriceps muscle until finally the quivering subsided. Damn, that kick had been unlike anything Jack had ever felt. A second one would have dropped him. Time to do some Muay Thai training, Jack thought absently.

Think, Jack. Had his attacker been surprised by his arrival, or had this been an ambush? One way to find out. Jack crawled to the man and frisked him. There was a wallet in the back pocket; Jack pulled it out and stuffed it into his front waistband. On the man's right hip was a paddle holster; inside it, a nine-millimeter semi-auto. Jack ejected the magazine, found it full, then eased back the slide and saw there was a round in the pipe.

Surprise, then, Jack thought. If this had been an ambush, the man would have been waiting, gun drawn. Even so, he'd had time to draw down on Jack. The man had probably panicked. Good dumb luck for Jack.

"Who the hell are you?" Jack muttered to the unconscious man. A question for later.

He withdrew the nine-millimeter and stuffed it into his jacket's side pocket.

Jack pushed himself to his feet, limped over to the windows and drew the shades, then back to the door, where he flipped on the overhead light. Save a floor lamp in one corner, the room was empty. Jack walked over and unplugged the lamp, then jerked the cord free and used it to bind the man's hands.

Jack made his way into the kitchenette off the main room and turned on the range hood light. He found a glass on the counter and filled it with water from the sink, drank it, then another. His hands were shaking. He put down the glass and clenched his fists until they were steady again.

He opened the mostly empty freezer and found a bag of frozen carrots. With it pressed against his thigh, he headed down the short hallway, where he found a bathroom, empty except for a bar of soap in the shower, a hand towel, and a toothbrush and a tube of toothpaste sitting on the edge of the sink. In the medicine cabinet he found a bottle of what looked like Iranian-brand ibuprofen. He downed four of them, then inspected his face in the mirror. A half-dollar spot on his forehead was bright red and his right cheekbone was swollen and scraped. Could be a lot worse, Jack knew. He turned on the faucet, splashed water on his face, then wiped it once with the hand towel.

At the end of the hall was a bedroom containing a camping cot, a folding chair, and a card table with a flex-neck lamp clamped to its edge. The single window was covered by blackout curtains, their edges taped with silver duct tape. Only a ribbon of light showed through the center. In the corner sat a two-by-two-foot floor safe, its door closed.

"Nice digs, Seth," Jack whispered. "What the hell are you up to?"

Why had his friend abandoned his real apartment for this spartan bolt-hole? According to Spellman, Seth's mail had been piling up for almost a month. Providing that was when Seth had moved here, what had prompted it? And why had Seth given him the key? It certainly wasn't so Jack would have an alternative place to lay his head. Seth had wanted him to come here, to find something — most likely whatever was inside that safe.

Jack crossed to the safe, knelt down, and tried the handle. It was locked.

Unbidden, Seth's final words at Chaibar café popped into Jack's head: "There're steaks in the freezer."

"Clever boy," Jack muttered.

He stepped out of the bedroom.

And froze.

At the end of the hall stood a man; he was pointing a gun at Jack's chest.

"Not a sound, or I'll put you down."

The man's accent was American. His face was covered by a balaclava. *Quiet bastard,* Jack thought. Was he dealing with one of Matt Spellman and Raymond Wellesley's

49

men? If not, this was a hell of a coincidence.

The man held a semi-auto affixed with a noise suppressor the size of a soda can. With a suppressor of that size, a shot would be softer than a paperback book being slammed on the floor. Jack's heart started to pound.

"Hands up," the man said.

Jack raised his hands.

The bag of carrots he'd had pressed to his thigh hit the floor.

The man asked, "Did you kill him, that one out there?"

"Not quite."

"Bloodied him up a bit, though."

"Him or me. Friend of yours?"

"Shut up. I ask, you answer."

If these two men were partners, this one was giving nothing away.

"You got his gun, yeah?" the man said. "Face away from me and pull it out — two fingers on the barrel, nice and slow, put it on the floor."

Jack turned away from the man and, as he pulled out the nine-millimeter, sucked in his gut, then hunched forward slightly, edging the wallet down the front of his pants. He knelt down, repeating the undulation motion, then, hoping the wallet was out of view, laid the gun on the floor.

"Turn around and kick it over to me," said Balaclava.

Jack did so. The nine-millimeter spun across the hardwood floor and bounced to a stop at the man's feet. His own gun never wavering, Balaclava knelt down, picked up the gun, and stuffed it into his waistband.

Jack thought, *I'm still alive.* That was both very good news and very bad news. Something told Jack this new player wasn't the kind of man you wanted to spend any alone time with.

"Listen," Jack said, "I walked in here and that guy attacked me. That's all I know. Let me go and —"

The man chuckled. "Not happening, pal. Walk toward me. Careful or I'll put one in your knee, got me?"

"Got you."

Hands raised, Jack walked down the hall. The man maintained his distance, backstepping until he and Jack were in the main room.

"Stop there."

The man stepped to the door and flipped off the overhead light. The room went dark, save what little light filtered out from the kitchenette.

"On your knees, ankles crossed."

Jack hesitated, considering his options.

There was almost no chance he could close the gap. The man could put three rounds into Jack before he took two steps.

"Best not to think about it too much," the man said. "Do what I say and maybe we'll get to be friends."

Jack knelt down.

The man walked to the unconscious figure on the floor, knelt down, and pressed his fingers to the man's throat.

"Still alive?" Jack asked.

"He is. Good luck for you."

"Maybe he's got identification —"

"Damn, man, shut your mouth. You're not exactly a quick learner, are you?"

Jack shrugged.

"Turn around, face away from me."

Jack shook his head. "If you're going to kill me —"

"Nah, see, I'm more of a face-to-face guy. We're going to have a nice private chat. How you come out the other end will depend on your answers. Turn around."

Jack's heart was in his throat. He had no choice. He was going to turn around either of his own volition or because he had a bullet in his knee. *Shit, is this where it ends?* he thought. Again he quashed the impulse to charge the man. Jack guessed this man's idea of a chat was going to involve a lot of pain and blood, but it might also buy him some time. Either way, at the end of whatever was coming, Jack was going to end up dead. *Play for time, then.*

The man groaned, rolled his eyes. "Oh, come on, man —"

He fired a round into the floor before Jack's knees. Wood chips peppered his thighs. He squeezed his eyes shut. *Son of a bitch.*

"— you're testing my patience. Turn around. Last warning."

Jack maneuvered himself so he was facing the windows.

Footsteps clicked on the wooden floor behind him.

He felt something slam into the back of his head. Then nothing.

4

Jack felt his body lurch upward. His head banged against something with a dull thunk. He opened his eyelids slightly; waves of pain radiated across his head and pulsed behind his eyes. He squeezed them shut again, took several deep breaths, until finally the pain eased. What had happened? *Ambush . . . Balaclava Man.*

The floor beneath Jack was shuddering, emitting a crinkling sound. Jack's brain started assembling pieces: He was moving. Inside a vehicle. He opened his eyes again and scanned his surroundings. A small panel van, white walls, tool racks holding spools of wire and hand tools. An electrician's van. *Remember that,* Jack thought.

He was lying on a plastic tarp, feet toward the front seats, his head resting on the driver's-side wheel well. His jacket was gone, leaving him in only a polo shirt. Jack rocked slightly onto his butt and could feel his back pocket was empty.

They'd taken his wallet, which contained his Virginia driver's license, personal credit cards, hotel room key card, and his hybrid satellite cell phone. None of these would lead his kidnappers anywhere of value. As did all of The Campus's operations officers, Jack practiced good digital tradecraft: In addition to having his phone AES-256 password-protected, Jack religiously cleared his call history, discussed nothing over instant messaging or e-mail that was confidential or extraordinary, kept nothing but innocuous contacts in his address book, and aside from Hendley's main line, there were no numbers on his speed dial; the rest he'd committed to memory. In short, his phone was as gray as could be — as was his room at the Parsian Hotel Azadi. Still, if they realized he was Jack Ryan, Jr. . . . Like it or not, Jack knew he was a high-value target.

The tarp he lay on was a bad sign. It suggested they were going to start working on him here. It wouldn't do to have the van's interior bloody. His hands were bound before him with a thick zip-tie, but not his ankles. Better news.

From the front seat a voice said, "Check

on him." Jack recognized the voice: Balaclava.

Jack shut his eyes. Through his lids he sensed a flashlight beam pass over his face. The beam went dark.

"Still out," came the reply.

This voice Jack didn't recognize, but the accent was American, a rough New York one. Jack felt certain he'd broken the nose of his assailant in Seth's bolt-hole, but he heard no trace of it in this man's voice and his head was covered in a dark wool beanie, which could be covering any scalp laceration. In Seth's apartment Balaclava had seemed both interested and disinterested in the man Jack had taken out. His kidnappers were American, and Wellesley and Spellman had warned him not to get involved. Was this their response?

"How far?" Balaclava said.

"Two miles. Take a left on this road up here. There are headlights behind us."

"The ones from the Shomal?"

"I don't know. Can't tell. Shit, maybe —"

"Relax. It's probably nothing."

After a few moments, Jack heard the soft tick-tock of the van's turn signal, then felt the vehicle turning. He opened his eyes and craned his head backward. Upside down, through the van's rear window, he caught a glimpse of the moon; as the van finished the turn, it slid from view. The tires began crunching slightly. They'd turned onto a gravel road. Were they outside Tehran? This, too, was a bad sign: dark, isolated road, hands bound, lying on a tarp-covered van floor.

Shomal, Jack thought. The name sounded familiar, and Balaclava's use of *the* suggested a highway or freeway. Jack tried to recall his mental map of Tehran, but he drew a blank.

Doesn't matter, he thought. One thing mattered: He had to get out, make a break. If they reached their destination with him inside this van, he was finished. How far would he get, though? The hell with it. Better to die running than lying down.

"Did they make the turn?" asked the American.

"No, it kept going. We're okay."

Not so fast, Jack thought.

He curled his legs until his knees touched his chest, took a deep breath, then mule-kicked the driver's seat. Balaclava lurched forward, his head smacking the steering wheel. The van skewed to the right, wheels thumping on the road's berm.

"Get him, get him," Balaclava yelled.

Jack spun on his butt, curled his legs

again, and kicked the back doors. Knowing it would take more than one try, Jack kicked again, grunting with the effort, then again and again, until finally the rear doors burst outward. The thrum of the tires and the red glow of the taillights filled the interior. The van veered left. Jack bounced off the side wall.

He rolled onto his side, got his feet under him, and stood in a half-crouch. His head banged against the van's roof. He felt a pair of hands on his hips, pulling him backward. Headlights flooded the interior. A horn began honking. How close, Jack couldn't tell. With his eyes squinting against the glare, Jack twisted sideways, broke free of the hands.

"God damn it . . . !" the American shouted. "Get back —"

"Grab him!" called Balaclava.

Jack curled himself into a ball and heaved himself out the doors.

He hit the road hip-first. The impact jarred his spine and knocked the air from his lungs. He barrel-rolled over the road, stones gouging and scratching his arms, his eyesight filled with snatches of dark sky, dirt, tall grass alongside the road, and headlights. Behind him an engine roared.

Tires skidding. A gust of air buffeted him as the car swerved around him. Jack felt himself plowing through grass, then down an embankment. He stopped rolling, faceup and staring at the sky. His stomach filled his throat and his eyesight sparkled. He rolled onto his belly, got his bound hands beneath his chest, and pressed himself up, then onto his knees. Down the road he saw the van's brake lights flash as it skidded to a stop amid a cloud of dust. Thirty feet behind, the trailing car was also sliding to a stop.

Damn, Jack thought. *Frying pan to fire.* Now he had at least three pursuers to elude.

The van's driver's-side door swung open and Balaclava hopped out.

Jack got to his feet, started to turn to run. He stopped.

The trailing car's engine revved, veered sideways around the van, its nose aimed at Balaclava, who flung himself back into the van. The car plowed into the open door; it tore free and skipped over the car's hood and roof in a shower of debris. The car skidded to a stop, the reverse lights came on, and it backed up until it was even with the van. As it passed, out the passenger window came a trio of orange muzzle flashes.

"What the fuck?" Jack muttered.

Spewing a rooster tail of gravel, the van

surged forward, its rear doors banging open and shut. The brake lights went dark and faded into the dust cloud.

The car kept backing up, picking up speed, then did a J-turn and skidded to a stop across the road from Jack. The car was black, a Mercedes E-Class.

From the driver's window a female voice shouted, "Get in!"

Jack didn't move.

"Get in before they regroup and turn around!"

No choice, he thought.

Half stumbling, half running, Jack crossed the road, went around the car's rear bumper, then opened the passenger door, threw himself inside, and slammed the door shut. A moment before the dome light went dark and the car sped off, Jack glimpsed long black hair, and manicured nails on the steering wheel.

With the car's headlights off, the Mercedes's powerful engine ate up the gravel road until they reached the intersection. The woman turned left onto pavement. In the flash of headlights Jack glimpsed a square, white-on-blue sign: a single number *3.* The woman floored the accelerator and within seconds the speedometer swept past 140 kph.

In silence they drove on, the woman's eyes flashing between the windshield and the rearview mirror. She was in her mid-thirties, with large black almond eyes, high cheekbones, and an ever-so-slightly hooked nose. She was Iranian, Jack guessed, but he'd detected little trace of a Persian accent, rather a mix of British and something else.

"It's probably not a good idea to jump out of this one, yes?" the woman finally said. "You would end up a red smear."

"Everything's relative," Jack replied. He glanced over the seat through the back window. There were no headlights.

"They won't catch up," she said. "They don't have the horsepower."

The question is, Jack thought, *am I better off with this woman?*

As if reading his mind, she said, "You're safe. I am not with them."

The conviction in her voice was genuine, Jack decided.

"There's a penknife in the glove compartment," the woman said.

Jack opened it, dug around until he found the knife, then used it to saw through the zip-tie securing his hands. He rubbed his wrists; they were slick with sweat-diluted blood.

"Your car is going to need some bodywork."

"I have another. How do you know Seth Gregory?" she asked.

"Who says I do?"

"You went to his apartment building. You had lunch with him."

This surprised Jack; his countersurveillance skills were solid, yet he'd missed her tailing of him. "How do you know Seth?" he asked.

"Answer my question." A little steel in her voice.

"We're old friends."

"What high school did he attend?"

"Saint Matt's — Matthew's — Academy. Your turn: How do you know him?"

"Seth and I worked together."

Something told Jack this woman wasn't with Shell Oil.

The woman slowed the car, turned right onto another paved road, then accelerated again. Through the windshield Jack could see the lighted skyline of what he assumed was Tehran.

"What's your name?" she asked.

"We don't know each other well enough yet." Jack thought for a moment, then said,

"How long did Seth spend in the Marines?"

The woman sighed. "I do not like dancing. In case you've forgotten, I just rescued you."

"Answer my question."

"He tried to join after college — University of Illinois, by the way — but he wasn't eligible. He wrecked his knee playing football and had to have it rebuilt. Three times. He still wears a brace and needs cortisone shots."

It was the right answer. The military disqualification had nearly crushed Seth, so badly had he wanted to serve. In fact, Jack had flown down to Illinois in hopes of cheering him up. It had worked, but only a bit. For Seth, being turned down for service would be a regret he never got over.

"He also tried to join the Coast Guard, but they denied him, too." She turned toward him and said, "Satisfied?"

While her knowledge of Seth's background wasn't definitive proof of their relationship, it would have to do. "I'm Jack."

"Jack Ryan? Seth has spoken of you."

Thanks a lot, Seth. He waited for the follow-up from her — "*The* Jack Ryan, son of President . . ." — but she only took her right hand off the steering wheel and clasped his in a firm grip. "I'm Ysabel.

Ysabel Kashani."

Having spent time in Russia in his early days with the CIA, John Clark had learned his share of Russian. One of his nuggets of teaching wisdom was *Doveryai no proveryai* — trust but verify, a phrase used to great effect by Reagan during INF treaty negotiations. A proverb, Clark had told Jack, that could also be applied to intelligence work.

Jack decided he would trust Ysabel to a point. How he would verify her bona fides was a question he couldn't yet answer. Nor did he know what exactly he'd gotten himself into. Either way, he could use an ally.

They drove in silence for fifteen minutes until reaching the northern outskirts of Tehran. Jack asked, "Is this the Shomal?"

"Why do you ask?"

"I overheard the driver."

"It's the Tehran-Shomal; outside the city it becomes Freeway Three."

"Any idea where they were taking me?" Jack asked.

"You mean aside from a shallow grave?" Ysabel replied. "No idea."

"Do you know who they are?" Even as the words left Jack's mouth, the word *wallet* popped into his head. In the commotion, he'd forgotten about the second American's wallet. He patted his crotch; the wallet was still here. Thank God for bad frisking technique.

"Do you need some alone time?" asked Ysabel.

"Funny." Jack pulled out the wallet and opened it.

Ysabel glanced over. "Where did you get that?"

"Off one of them back there."

"What about yours?"

"They've got it."

Inside the man's wallet was a driver's license and two credit cards. He stuffed it into the back pocket of his khakis. "Where are we going?" he asked.

"My apartment. We need to talk. Plus, you're a mess. Your arms, your face . . ." She grimaced and said, "You look awful."

Jack checked his forearms; below the sleeves of his polo shirt, his arms looked like they'd been worked over with a belt sander.

"It'll have to wait. I need to go back to Seth's."

"Why?"

"Steaks."

Ysabel paused, then with a flash of revelation in her voice, echoed Jack: "Steaks."

Ysabel picked her way through the city, taking a circuitous route to Seth's apartment, skillfully doubling back and traversing alleys until she seemed satisfied they weren't being followed. She had tradecraft, Jack realized.

"Who taught you?" he asked.

"Seth. Just a few things, really."

She pulled to the curb a block north of Seth's building and across from the café in which Jack had sipped tea earlier that evening. The café was closed, its wraparound windows dark. The Mercedes's dashboard clock read 12:09. Almost three hours since they'd taken him from the apartment. He and Ysabel sat in the darkness, listening to the car's engine tick as it cooled.

After ten minutes of watching, Jack said, "Nothing. You?"

"No. This is a bad idea, Jack."

"I don't see how my night could get any worse. There's something I need in there." *Providing it's still there,* he thought.

"We," Ysabel said. "*We* need."

"Slow down. We're not quite there yet," Jack grumbled.

66

"Suit yourself. Let's go."

Three minutes later they were standing before Seth's apartment door. Ysabel reached into her shoulder bag and pulled out a hammerless .38-caliber snub-nosed revolver.

Jack opened his palm and whispered, "May I?"

"Why?"

"Please, Ysabel."

She frowned at him for a moment, then placed the revolver in his hand.

Key, he thought abruptly. He patted his pockets. He said, "Damn, the key. They must have taken it."

"Hold on," Ysabel murmured. She rummaged in her purse and came out with a bronze key. "Try this."

Jack took it. "Where'd you get this?"

"Seth gave it to me along with the one to his Pardis condo. I assumed it was for something there. It's worth a try."

Jack slipped the key into the lock and turned it; the dead bolt slid back. Using the knuckle of his index finger, Jack swung open the door until the knob touched the inner wall. The room was dark, the window shades still drawn. The attacker he'd left unconscious on the floor was gone, but the blood smear where his head had lain was still there.

Jack waited a few beats, then peeked left around the jamb. Nothing. With the revolver at waist level and tucked close to his body, he stepped into the apartment. Ysabel followed, then shut the door and locked it. On flat feet, Jack walked into the kitchenette, cleared it, then went down the hallway and cleared the bathroom and bedroom in turn.

He returned to the main room to find Ysabel staring at the blood. "What happened here?" she murmured.

"I got ambushed."

"Did you kill him? Was he one of the men from the van?"

"No, and maybe. Follow me. The quicker we're out of here, the better. Don't step in the blood. Keep track of what you touch."

"Worried about fingerprints?"

"Habit. By the way, why do you have a gun?"

"Protection. Rapes are rising in Tehran. The lure of uncovered hair and all that nonsense."

They walked back to the bedroom. Jack crossed the room, adjusted the curtains so the center slit was closed, then turned on the card-table lamp. Jack handed Ysabel the folding chair. "Against the front door."

She returned a few moments later and pointed at the safe and said, "What the hell is that?"

"When was the last time you were here?"

"Two weeks ago, with Seth. It wasn't here."

Jack knelt by the safe. The hardwood floor around its gray steel bottom lip was scarred and gouged. The marks were new. Balaclava Man and his partner had been trying to get to the bolts securing the safe to the floor. If they wanted the contents that badly, they'd be back with heavier equipment.

"Steaks," Ysabel said.

"Steaks."

They returned to the kitchenette. Jack clicked on the range light, opened the freezer, dug around, and came up with four steaks wrapped in white butcher paper. He dumped them on the counter. Together they began unwrapping the meat.

"I found it," Ysabel said.

Jack stepped closer to her, their shoulders touching. Written on the inside of the wrapping in black marker were a string of digits: 37-42-51. Jack folded the paper, stuffed it into his pocket. They rewrapped the rest of the steaks and returned them to the freezer.

They walked back to the bedroom, where Jack dialed in the safe's combination, then depressed the lever. With a dull click the door swung open. Inside was a six-inch-thick brown accordion folder. Jack pulled it out, then inspected the safe's interior: nothing else.

"Let's go," he said.

After using the bathroom hand towel to wipe down all the surfaces they'd touched, they stepped out into the hallway and locked the door.

To their left, the stairwell door banged open, then clicked shut.

At a trot, Jack and Ysabel headed to the fire exit at the end of the hall. Jack placed his hands on the red-striped press bar, said a quick prayer, then pushed. No alarm sounded. They stepped through and Jack eased the door shut. They stood still.

After a few moments, below them came the echoed clicking of footsteps on the concrete stairs. Jack stepped to the handrail and peeked over. Two floors below, a figure stepped onto the landing and turned onto the next set of stairs. In his right hand was a semi-auto.

Jack turned to Ysabel and pointed up the next set of stairs and placed his index finger against his lips. She nodded, then started upward. Jack waited until she reached the next landing, then followed. They climbed upward, Jack occasionally glancing over the rail to check the man's progress; he was on the third-floor landing.

Jack and Ysabel reached the sixth and uppermost floor. Down a short corridor lit by a dim ceiling bulb was a steel door — the roof access, Jack hoped. Jack pointed to it, then made a key-turning gesture to Ysabel, who nodded, then padded down the hall. After a few moments, she turned and nodded, then opened the door. The hinges let out a rusty squeak.

Ysabel froze. Jack froze.

Silence.

Footsteps pounded on the stairs below, heading upward.

Mouthing "Go, go, go" to Ysabel, Jack followed her out the door and onto the gravel roof. He hesitated, then stepped back inside and tapped the barrel of the revolver against the light-bulb. It shattered. The corridor went dark. He stepped out onto the roof and swung the door shut behind him, catching it before it latched, leaving it open a crack.

Jack whispered to Ysabel, "Walk to the edge of the roof and face away from the door. Tuck your hair into the back of the jacket. Whatever happens, don't turn around."

To her credit, Ysabel didn't hesitate and did as Jack ordered.

Jack pressed himself against the wall beside the door. He drew the revolver from his belt.

A few moments passed. From the corridor came the crunch of glass.

Silence. A few more moments passed.

The door swung open, then a voice called, "Stop right there." New York accent. "Hands up."

Ysabel raised her hands.

Jack kicked the door shut. It crashed into the man, who bounced off the door frame, then stumbled into view. Jack took two steps forward and toe-kicked the man in the side of the knee. His leg buckled and he dropped to his hands and knees, stunned. His gun bounced across the gravel and came to rest a few feet away.

While Jack would've liked to have his own Q&A session with the man, it wasn't feasible.

He cocked his leg to his chest and heel-kicked the man in the right ear. With a grunt he dropped face-first into the gravel.

Jack felt a flash of guilt, then quashed it. While the childhood "Play fair" rule was still a part of his psyche, there was no such thing as a fair fight, not out here, and not with guys like this.

Jack leaned over the man; at the back of his head the hair was matted with dried blood, and his left cheek was swollen and the bone around his eye socket was squashed, all souvenirs from their earlier fight in the apartment. One mystery solved.

He turned to the door and eased it shut. Ysabel walked up, knelt down, and checked the man's pulse. "He's alive."

And having a really shitty night, Jack thought. "Search him."

She did so, then said, "Nothing. Jack, you used me as bait."

"They wanted me alive, they'd want you alive, too. Find the fire escape, will you?"

"Don't do that again without warning me," Ysabel said, and walked away.

Jack picked up the man's gun, a nine-millimeter, stuffed it into his jacket pocket, then grabbed the man by the collar, dragged him to the door, and positioned him across it.

"Over here, Jack," Ysabel called. She stood at the far corner of the roof.

He trotted over to her. She whispered, "I don't see anyone."

"After you," Jack said.

5

Twenty minutes later they reached Ysabel's building, an eighteen-floor high-rise in a fashionable garden neighborhood off Vali Asr Street. Inside the apartment Jack found the decor a mix of minimalist modern and traditional Persian, with a sunken seating area and a gourmet kitchen with stainless-steel appliances. The carpet was a cream berber. The wall nearest Jack was dominated by a floor-to-ceiling bookcase; at first glance, all the books looked like either classical literature or history, some of them rare.

Ysabel walked through the space, turning on floor and table lamps while Jack stood at the balcony's French doors, gazing out the windows at Tehran's lighted skyline. Below was a tree-lined lake rimmed by what appeared to be gas lamps. Jack kept Ysabel in the corner of his eye until she walked up and stopped beside him.

"That's Mellat Park," she said. "Beautiful,

isn't it?"

"Very."

In each hand she held a square glass a quarter full of amber liquid. She handed him one; the ice cubes tinkled softly.

He said, "Ysabel, just for curiosity's sake: This apartment . . . your Mercedes . . . Are you rich?"

"My father is."

This gave Jack pause. Was all this a lark for Ysabel, an adventure to break up the monotony of wealthy leisure? He hoped not. Then again, during his dad's first administration he'd faced the same kind of bullshit, so he had no business making any assumptions about Ysabel.

"Iranian fathers like to dote," she said.

"I see."

"Don't judge, Jack."

"I didn't say a thing."

"It's in your voice."

Jack took a sip from the glass. It was ice-cold Scotch; it burned his throat, then settled warmly in his belly. He asked, "Aren't you Muslim?"

"Partially lapsed."

"Daring girl."

"Only in private. Tehran is changing, but it's going to take a while until one can walk down the street with a bottle in a brown paper bag."

"Hopefully the changes will stick."

"I'll drink to that." She took a sip from her glass, then gestured to the park below. "It used to be called Shahanshahi Park — Park of the King of Kings — before the revolution," Ysabel said. "I suppose Khomeini thought it sounded too . . . shah-like."

Jack glanced sideways at her. "I'm sorry about the roof. I shouldn't have used you like that."

Is my regret because she's a woman? he wondered. No, if it'd been him and Ding or Dominic on that roof . . . well, that comes with the job. Ysabel hadn't signed up for this — at least not to that level. Even so, she'd handled herself well. Hell, she'd probably saved his life.

"Apology accepted," she replied. "Just don't do it again. Why did you have me face away from the door? And why the hair?"

"So he didn't see your face and, if we're lucky, couldn't tell you were a woman."

"Ah."

"Thanks for the rescue on the road, by the way. The chance of me getting more than a few hundred yards was slim."

"Something tells me otherwise."

"I noticed your accent. There's only a hint

of Persian in there." Despite himself, Jack found it alluring, exotic.

"I'm mostly a product of the West. I went to Leysin American School in Switzerland, then Cambridge — politics and international studies."

"Educated in the decadent West," Jack said. "How did you pull that off?"

"My father was a doctor. And he sat on the Tehran city council for many years. He was a politician through and through, knew how to walk the tightrope and gather favors." Ysabel paused and smiled. "Plus, behind closed doors even extremists like Khomeini liked having our children educated in the West — the idea being we absorb all the imperialists' knowledge then return home and use it to glorify Iran."

"And have you?"

"Hardly. I teach at the University of Tehran. For whatever reason, our department was immune to politics — and Sharia, if you can believe that. Okay, that's enough interrogation, Jack —"

"I wasn't —"

"Let's see to your arms before you start bleeding on my carpet. And your eye is almost swollen shut — not a good look for you."

She led him down a hallway to a spacious

bathroom done in earth-toned tile. She told him to sit on the toilet, then turned on the sink faucet, let hot water fill the basin, and dropped in a washcloth.

"You don't have to do this for me," Jack said.

Ysabel smiled, then wrung out the cloth and handed it to him. "So presumptuous . . . I'll get the first-aid kit."

She disappeared and Jack could hear her rummaging in the hall closet. She returned with a clear plastic case.

Teeth gritted against the pain, Jack finished wiping the dirt from his forearms until only raw red abrasions were visible. She handed him a towel, which he used to blot his skin dry.

"Painful?" she asked.

"Yes."

She pulled a small spray bottle from the first-aid kit and said, "Arms, please." Jack extended them and she sprayed them. He winced. "Other side," Ysabel said, then repeated the process on the insides of Jack's forearms.

"Lift up your shirt," she ordered.

"What?"

"Do as I say, Jack."

He lifted his polo shirt. She examined his torso, gently probing various spots with her index finger.

"Why Ysabel?" Jack asked. "That's not Persian, is it?"

"My mother was second-generation American — a fiery Andalusian, or so my father tells me. I have her to thank for my dual citizenship, I suppose. She died when I was two."

"I'm sorry."

"Such is life."

Her words were breezy, but there was none of it in her voice, Jack noted. To have little more than secondhand memories of your mother couldn't be easy.

Ysabel finished her examination of his torso and said, "Just a few bruises. You're lucky. Of course, the van wasn't going all that fast."

"Still pretty daring, I think," Jack said with mock indignation.

"Okay, Indiana Jones. How's your vision? Any nausea?"

"No. I've got a hard head."

"In more ways than one."

Ysabel doused a gauze pad and dabbed first at his cheekbone, then his forehead. She leaned back, examined her handwork with pursed lips, then nodded. "Better. Meet me in the kitchen and I'll get you an ice pack."

"I'll be okay."

"Jack, if they're looking for you, a black eye like that might make it easier. You can shower if you'd like, there's a robe on the door hook. I'll make us something to eat. We have a lot to talk about."

A huge understatement, Jack thought. He'd already started compiling his list of questions.

Freshly showered and wrapped in a white terry-cloth robe — a man's size, Jack noted — he joined Ysabel in the kitchen, where she was reheating a casserole dish in the microwave. She pointed to the counter, where a pile of four pills sat. "Ibuprofen."

"Thanks."

"Feel better?" asked Ysabel.

"Much. Should I be expecting company?" Jack grabbed the lapel of his robe and wagged it.

Ysabel smiled. "Nosy."

"I've had enough surprises for one night."

"The owner won't be coming back."

Am I wearing Seth's robe? Jack wondered.

The microwave beeped. Ysabel opened the door and, using a pair of oven mitts, lifted the casserole dish out. She placed it on the counter and began spooning the food into bowls. *"Khoreshteh qiemeh bademjoon,"* she said. "Persian eggplant stew. You'll like it."

Jack carried their bowls to the dining nook and sat down. Piled in the middle of the mahogany table was the accordion folder they'd found in Seth's safe, along with the wallet and nine-millimeter Jack had taken from his attacker.

"I haven't looked at them," she said, sitting down. She laid a blue gel ice pack beside his bowl. Pressing the ice pack against his cheekbone with his free hand, Jack took a spoonful of the stew; the meat-like chunks of eggplant tasted of turmeric and onion. "You're right, it is good."

"So ask your questions, Jack," she said.

Not sure where to start, he took a moment to gather his thoughts.

"Did Seth have a car?"

"That's your first question?" Ysabel replied with an amused smile. "No, he didn't. He used taxis and buses."

"When did you start following me? After I left Chaibar?"

"Yes. Seth told me you two were having lunch. It was the first time I'd seen him happy in weeks."

"Nice disguise, by the way. You looked ten years younger."

"Thank you. I think."

Jack was only mildly surprised Seth hadn't

recognized Ysabel — if she wasn't lying about them knowing each other, that was. To compensate for his ADHD, Seth tended to block out everything except whomever he was talking to at the time. Clearly, Ysabel knew this.

"But why the surveillance at all? Why follow me?" If Ysabel had picked him up at Chaibar, it meant she'd been staking him out for almost thirty-six hours and had followed him to his meeting with Spellman and Wellesley.

Whatever her role in all this, she was dedicated.

"Why not follow Seth?"

Ysabel said, "For a while now I've suspected he was in trouble and not telling me. Plus, Seth is . . . cagey, especially lately. He would have spotted me."

"If he was — is — in trouble, why would you expect him to tell you?"

"We're friends, Jack. And, yes — just friends."

"Not my business."

"But you were wondering about it."

"That's not the whole truth, though, is it? You're more than friends. You're working together."

"After a fashion."

"That's not good enough."

Instead of answering, Ysabel asked her own question: "What were you doing at that building in the Zafaraniyeh district?"

Jack was getting annoyed with the thrust-and-parry, but he decided it might break the stalemate. "I was meeting a man named Speidel."

Ysabel let out an exasperated sigh. "Spellman, Jack. Matt Spellman."

"Right, sorry."

"Seth was reporting to him."

Interesting that Seth had shared Spellman's name with her; in the *Spy Rings for Dummies* manual, sharing a handler's name was taboo. Why had Seth done it? Did she also know about Raymond Wellesley? He said, "Spellman thinks Seth has done a runner — along with a lot of money."

"He's right about the former. The money I don't know about."

Jack decided to gamble: "You were part of his network, weren't you? An agent." It was a logical guess; if Seth was reporting to Wellesley and Spellman, it suggested they were his handlers. Handlers handled agents. The fact that it was a direct conduit with no cutouts told Jack that Seth was overseeing the network. But what was he, an agent or a CIA operations officer? And what was the purpose of the network? Something to do with Iran? *So many damn questions,* Jack thought. He hated having to play catch-up.

"Who were the men who took me?" he asked.

"I don't know. But I did get the van's registration plate." She closed her eyes for a moment, recalling, then recited it for him.

"Could they have gotten yours?" Jack asked.

"Doubtful. They were too busy diving for cover. Their plate might be useless to us, though — unless you want to ring Spellman."

"We're not doing that. I might have a way."

"From your vast array of financial contacts?" Ysabel said with a smile.

"Yep. I think it was an electrician's van."

"It was. I caught a snippet from the placard on the side — Yazdi something. I'll see what I can find."

Jack said, "You knew nothing about Seth's Niavaran apartment? Or about the keys he gave you?"

She shook her head. "As I said, I assumed they were both for Pardis. I'm just guessing, but maybe he thought I'd be able to track down his bolt-hole if things went bad — and if it was important enough."

This was plausible, Jack decided. By leaving Ysabel initially ignorant of the bolt-hole,

84

he might have been trying to protect her.

"Okay, one more question —"

"Thank goodness."

"Was Seth really working for Shell?"

"I don't know."

While Ysabel's answers weren't proof positive she was on Seth's side, Jack's gut told him she was on the level.

He had his ally. Provisionally. *Goddamn espionage,* Jack thought. He'd stepped into this world of his own volition, but it had come with a price: Outside your inner circle, trust was a rare thing; of course, the actions of his former girlfriend, Melanie Kraft, hadn't helped matters. Though she'd had her reasons — objectively good ones — he still considered her turning on him as a betrayal.

Enough, Jack.

Ysabel said, "Shall we check our booty?"

"Pardon?"

"Our spoils. The folder and wallet."

The wallet contained two credit cards and an IDP — International Driver's Permit — all issued to a David Weaver. The address on the IDP was 4711 Hardesty Street, Albany, NY 12203.

"What a perfectly ordinary American name," Ysabel noted.

"Very."

The International Driver's Permit was a nice touch, Jack thought. Standards for IDPs were often inconsistent from country to country. Jack suspected they'd glean little of use from digging into David Weaver. Still, he'd have Gavin check. No doubt Weaver's partner, Balaclava, was also equipped with an IDP.

Jack said, "Spellman wasn't alone when I met with him. He was with a Brit named Raymond Wellesley."

"I've never heard of him. So, British and American handlers, American kidnappers. Quite a coincidence, yes?"

"No coincidence at all."

Wellesley and Spellman had taken off the gloves: Jack's status as First Son had earned him no latitude at all. And as Jack had no intention of leaving Seth on his own, his relationship with Wellesley and Spellman had been bound to sour. Now it was out in the open. Oddly, Jack was okay with that.

Also, he preferred to live outside his dad's shadow — as well as outside his aegis. Of course, Ryan Senior had no control over the former, but fortunately, Jack's dad had so far resisted imposing the latter.

A more pressing question for Jack was what to do about The Campus. He'd found himself neck-deep in a CIA-SIS operation. Gerry Hendley and John Clark would want to know about it. Later.

Much would depend on what was inside Seth's mystery accordion folder. Jack pulled it toward him, unwound the elastic band closure, and opened the flap. Ysabel scooted her chair around the table until she was shoulder to shoulder with Jack.

"This is like Shab-e Cheleh," she said with a tinge of giddiness. Seeing Jack's confused expression, she explained, "Think of it as Persian Christmas. In the West you celebrate the birth of the son. Here we celebrate the rebirth of the sun — the Winter Solstice."

"You're a font of fascinating trivia," Jack replied.

"You have no idea. Open it."

Jack did so. Inside was a stack of legal-sized loose-leaf paper, at least five hundred sheets, he guessed. He shuffled through the ream. All the pages had a faded, old-style typewriter font. In Cyrillic.

The date on the first sheet was 4 Май 1963.

Ysabel said, "I don't suppose you read Russian?"

"Only fair." This was a slight understatement, but not far from the mark. Though his grasp of the language had improved dramatically, for some reason he had a hard time getting Russian to stick in his brain. "That middle word is *May.*"

Yet more questions, Jack thought. The biggest being: What the hell were they looking at? Aside from Gavin Biery, Jack had access to no one who could faithfully translate the document, and he sure as hell couldn't fax the damn thing. Such a task wouldn't escape Gerry's notice, and Jack wouldn't put Biery in that kind of spot. He'd have to give it some thought.

"None of this looks familiar?" he asked Ysabel. "Seth never mentioned something like this?"

"Never."

"Do you know anyone else in the network?"

"Only one — code-named Ervaz."

"Is that a Persian name?"

"No, I don't think so. I've got an e-mail address. It's bad form, I know, for me to know even that much, but I suppose I'd become Seth's 'right hand,' as it were. I've never tried contacting Ervaz. Should I?"

"We'll do it together."

Unbidden, Raymond Wellesley's "apple tree" comment popped into Jack's head. "Ysabel, did Seth ever talk about his father?"

"Are you testing me again, Jack?"

"No. Genuine question."

"Yes, he did, quite a lot. He said his dad — Paul, I think — died of a stroke a few years ago and that his mother was having a hard time with it."

"Nothing else?"

"Uhm . . . His father worked for the government. Something to do with farm-ing."

"Department of Agriculture."

"Yes, that was it. You know, one thing always struck me when Seth talked about his father: He always seemed" — Ysabel paused, searching for the right words — "more bitter than sad. Almost scornful sometimes."

"About what specifically?"

"The death, I assumed. I remember because it seemed an odd reaction. Why do you ask?"

"Something Wellesley said — that Seth hadn't fallen far from the tree."

"Strange. Then again, if this Wellesley is who you think he is, those types like to play mind games, yes?"

"True." If so, had Wellesley been trying to plant doubt in his head about Seth, or was there something to the comment?

"Jack, you haven't asked me what Seth

had me working on. Why?"

The question had been on Jack's mind.

"That's a morning-cup-of-coffee question," he said. "Where am I sleeping?"

6

Jack downed the dregs of his coffee and set the cup on the counter, where Ysabel scooped it up and headed back to the French press. She returned with the second cup, and they walked to the sunken seating area and sat across from each other.

Outside the balcony windows, the sun was fully up, and yellow rays streamed in, casting sharp shadows across the carpet. Jack turned his face to the warmth and let it soak in.

"Your eye looks better," said Ysabel. "How do you feel?"

"Like I went five rounds with Chuck Liddell."

"I don't know who that is."

"Never mind. So, when and how did Seth recruit you?"

"About eight months ago. The truth is . . . we were a little more than friends."

The admission took Jack by surprise. "You

were hooking up."

"What? Oh, yes, I guess that's what you would call it. Purely physical. Does that shock you?"

"Not particularly. Where did you meet?"

"At Chaibar, as a matter of fact."

"So he seduced you."

"It was genuine, and mutual. I could be wrong, of course. We broke it off after a month but stayed friends. He's a good man."

MICE, Jack thought. The most common reasons for someone cooperating with a foreign agency fell within the acronym MICE — Money, Ideology, Compromise, or Coercion — but the umbrella was bigger than that: ego, excitement, disaffection, personal ties, sex . . . Though it seemed this last one may have been Seth's original method of recruitment; the relationship had ended quickly, but Ysabel's cooperation had not. Ideology, then?

"Why did you keep working for him?"

"I didn't start until about two months after we broke it off — after I joined the research group," Ysabel replied. "It has no name, really. It's just a bunch of us academics. We talk about Russia."

"When you and Seth met, did you know about this group?"

"No, I got the impression it had just been founded."

If Ysabel was right, perhaps Seth's relationship with her had been genuine, and her joining the group just dumb good luck for him.

"Tell me about this research group. What's the context?"

"The new leadership in Moscow — what they want, what they might do next and where. It's all brainstorming, really."

"Who runs it?"

"My department head at the university — Dr. Pezhman Abbasi."

"One day out of the blue he just asked you to join?"

Ysabel nodded. "We're very close, he and I, like grandfather and granddaughter. He hired me at the university."

"So you report to him; who does he report to?"

"I don't know that he does, Jack. You don't understand, it's all just intellectual 'what if' games. Many of the departments do it — econ, history . . . Sometimes what they come up with becomes part of curriculum. Jack, we weren't gathering intelligence."

In fact, coopting private-sector academic groups was a common tool for intelligence agencies. Raw, puzzle-piece intel can get you only so far. What a nation or group was capable of told only part of the story; how that nation or group intended to use those capabilities was the real prize, and getting to that often took out-of-the-box thinking.

Before Jack could explain this to Ysabel, she said, "Ah, I see what you're getting at. We may have been feeding someone? The VAJA, yes?"

Ysabel was no dummy, Jack thought. "Could be."

VAJA was the acronym for Iran's Ministry of Intelligence, Jack thought, and ostensibly the latest, kinder-and-gentler incarnation of the SAVAK, Shah Reza Pahlavi's ruthless secret police.

Ysabel said, "I feel foolish for considering this. You don't think Pezhman is involved in —"

"At this point, I don't think anything," Jack replied. "So you were feeding Seth your notes from the group. Tell me about it."

"Yes. He never said why he was interested, but I knew who he was, Jack, and I knew he was working for the U.S. You've heard the old Persian proverb: 'My enemy's enemy is my friend.'"

"Isn't that Arabic?"

Ysabel smiled. "A tragic misattribution.

Anyway, both Iran and your country should fear Russia. Plus, officially, I'm half American. If a few notes from a think tank would help the common cause, then so be it."

Ysabel was right: The direction of Russia's foreign policy was troublesome. Its president, Valeri Volodin, had already invaded Crimea, eastern Ukraine, and Estonia — though he'd been pushed out of the latter, something that seemed only to strengthen his ultranationalist tendencies.

Jack doubted Ysabel's research group at the University of Tehran was the only one the VAJA had launched. *Do the Iranians know something the United States doesn't? Is this what Seth's network was chasing?*

"I assumed I was only working on my own small part," said Ysabel. "Whether there were more than myself and this Ervaz, I don't know."

Jack went silent, trying to assemble pieces, to find the right thread to tug that might lead him to Seth. He said to Ysabel, "Write down the e-mail address for Ervaz. I need to make a call."

"You can use my —"

"No, I need a pay phone."

"There's one down the block. I've got a prepaid calling card."

■ ■ ■ ■

Jack got dressed, jotted the serial number of David Weaver's nine-millimeter on his palm, then left the apartment. He found the pay phone on the corner outside a small convenience store fronted by crates of fruits and vegetables. An employee was sweeping the sidewalk. He nodded and smiled at Jack.

Jack used Ysabel's card to dial The Campus's main switchboard. It was late afternoon there. After five rings, Carly, Hendley's most recent intern, this one from Towson University, answered.

"Evening, Mr. Ryan. You caught me going out the door."

"I won't hold you up. Is Gavin still in?"

"What do you think?" she said, laughing. "I'll transfer you."

The line went silent, then buzzed twice. Gavin Biery picked up and said, "Still alive, Jack?"

"And kicking." Jack hesitated. Dragging Gavin into this was going to put the man into a tough spot, but unless he was willing to give up on Seth, he had no choice. He would fall on his sword with Gerry later. "I need a few more favors."

"Shoot."

96

"I need you to brick my phone. I lost it."
Jack paused, then changed his mind. "No, scratch that. Track it."

"Can do. You want a cloned phone?"

"What?"

"We've got a cloud. We back up all your phones and tablets whenever you're in the building. You didn't get the memo?"

"I guess not."

"By the way, those are some nasty pictures in your photo album."

"I don't have —"

"Kidding, just kidding. Yeah, I'll set up a trace on your old phone. Whenever it's powered up and on either Wi-Fi or roaming, I can track it. I'll get a duplicate headed your way."

"Give me a different number, though."

"Can do. You're at the Parsian Hotel?"

"No, send it to Ysabel Kashani, 1214 West Sedaqat, Tehran. Signature required. I'm going to buy a disposable cell phone. If I give you the number, can you switch it to the number of the stolen phone?"

"Sure, no problem." Gavin paused. "Jack, maybe you should let Gerry know —"

"I know. I'll put him in the loop." The question was: When? Jack probably should have already done this.

"What else?" asked Gavin.

"Monitor my credit cards and get me some new ones."

Though Jack doubted his kidnappers would be stupid enough to use his cards, it was worth a shot.

Gavin asked, "Did you get mugged, Jack?"

"More or less. Next: I need everything you can give me on these two e-mail addresses." Jack recited the Yahoo! and Gmail addresses Ysabel had given him. "Next: Look into a guy named David Weaver." Jack also recited the address on Weaver's IDP, as well as the man's credit-card numbers and the nine-millimeter's serial number. "It looks like a SIG Sauer P226, but there are no markings and no logo."

"Got it. Next?"

Jack gave him Dr. Pezhman Abbasi's name and particulars. "He's at the University of Tehran. Whatever you can get on him." Jack was tempted to ask for the same check on Seth, but he decided to hold off for now. "I've also got an e-mail for you to track." He gave him the address for Ervaz. "Finally, I need you to run a license-plate trace. Can you do Iran?"

"Might take a bit longer, but I think so."

Jack gave him the van's plate number, as well as the partial wording on its side placard, then said, "Thanks. I'll call you back."

Jack hung up, then went into the convenience store, bought a prepaid cell phone, then returned to Ysabel's apartment to find her sitting at the dining table.

Jack asked, "When did Seth give you Ervaz's name and contact info?"

"About a month ago."

This was about the same time Seth abandoned the Pardis condo, the one Spellman and Wellesley knew about, for the bolthole off Niavaran Park. "Did he say why he wanted you to have the name, when you should use it?"

"No. His brain was always going a mile a minute. He'd jump from one subject to the next. Sometimes I could barely get a word in. Sometimes it was like I wasn't even talking."

"That's the ADHD," Jack replied.

"That explains a lot."

"Think back: Did his move to the bolt-hole coincide with something you gave him from your group?"

"Well, the group met once a week and I reported to Seth after each one, so it's hard to say. He never showed much reaction to anything I gave him." After a moment of silence, Ysabel stood up and headed down the hallway toward the bedrooms. "I'm going to have a shower."

Jack removed his disposable cell phone from its blister pack, powered it up, then called Gavin and gave him the new number. Five minutes later the screen blinked with a text from Gavin: THIS NUMBER SWAPPED TO YOUR OLD NUMBER. Jack punched in Seth's number and texted: IT'S JACK. CONTACT ME AT THIS NUMBER, ASAP.

Next he jotted a list of follow-ups on the pad:

— Make contact with others in network. Have Gavin track.
— Look into Dr. Pezhman Abbasi? Name, VAJA point of contact?
— License plate, van. Place of business?
—Translate doc from Seth's safe.
— Info: David Weaver. Gun serial number?
— Who owns: Spellman/Wellesley safe house; Seth's apartments?
— Spellman/Wellesley. Meet again? Confront?

Of these last two items Jack was uncertain. Digging into the ownership of the safe house would probably reveal nothing but a front, and the probing wouldn't go unnoticed. He decided to back-burner this.

As for another meeting with Spellman and Wellesley, if in fact his kidnappers belonged to them, a second visit to the Zafaraniyeh district safe house might land him on the tarp again. Still, wanting to know if they'd heard from Seth was exactly what a friend would do.

And it might be worth the risk to gauge their reaction to his injured face — and to an unexpected visit.

After trying unsuccessfully to leave Ysabel at her apartment, Jack gave in and they took her second car, a dark blue Range Rover, to a nearby men's clothing store and Jack bought a few changes of clothing — khakis, button-down shirts, and a windbreaker — before heading to the Zafaraniyeh. Ysabel parked three blocks away from Wellesley's apartment, under a blooming linden tree.

Jack patted his side pocket and felt the reassuring heft of the nine-millimeter, then climbed out and shut the door.

"Remember," Ysabel said through the open side window, "one call and I'll be there."

"Another drive-by strafing?"

"I have my methods."

In a short eight hours Jack had learned that Ysabel Kashani was beautiful, smart, independent, and resourceful. As allies went, he couldn't have hoped for more. *Too good to be true?* he wondered. If Ysabel wasn't what she seemed, he hoped he would find out sooner rather than later.

"Give me thirty minutes, then start calling. If I don't answer, call this number" — Ysabel powered up her phone and Jack recited Gavin Biery's cell-phone number — "and tell him everything."

"Starting with where you are."

"Right."

"Good luck."

Jack walked the three blocks to Wellesley's apartment building and pressed the call button for the correct apartment. Wellesley answered: "Yes?"

"Jack Ryan."

"Come up."

The door buzzed and Jack went through. When the elevator doors parted on the seventh floor, Wellesley was waiting. He led Jack into the apartment and offered him tea, which Jack declined. They sat down in the seating area before the windows. Spellman was nowhere in sight.

"Where's Matt?"

"Elsewhere. Good heavens, Jack, what on earth happened to your face?"

Wellesley's surprise seemed genuine enough. Which meant nothing.

They were on a first-name basis now, Jack noted. He took a moment to gather his thoughts. What he was about to say might permanently change the game. Whether he answered Wellesley's question truthfully or with a lie, the SIS man's reaction might tell Jack much. He decided on the former; it was the best way, he hoped, to maintain his babe-in-the-woods status with Wellesley and Spellman.

"Someone grabbed me last night. There were a couple of them."

Wellesley leaned forward. "What? Where?"

"Seth's apartment. Not the Pardis condo. A second one."

"Go on."

"I woke up in a van. I managed to get away from them and . . ." Jack touched his forehead and frowned. "I don't remember much after that. A woman picked me up and then I . . . Well, I guess I did something pretty stupid."

"Which was?"

"I went back to Seth's apartment."

"Why?"

"There was a safe in there. At lunch, Seth asked me to get it for him. I went back for it, but the safe was open. There was nothing

103

inside, so I left."

This was the weakest part of Jack's story. While the man on the roof had neither seen Jack's face nor heard his voice, the incident might in Wellesley's eyes be too coincidental. Jack's hope was that the SIS man assumed he was lying out of self-protection.

"Why didn't you tell us about Seth's other apartment?"

"How could I know you were who you claimed to be? Anyone can make up a business card. It means nothing."

"Good point," replied Wellesley.

"I have to ask, Raymond: I leave here and a few hours later I'm kidnapped. It looks bad."

"I understand." Wellesley lowered his head in thought, slowly rubbing his thumb over his chin. "But I can assure you, Jack, it wasn't me."

"You? Or you and Spellman."

Wellesley didn't reply. "Just be careful from now on, Jack. I can get you some protection if you'd like."

"No, forget it."

"If you change your mind, call me. And you should go to the hospital and have your head seen to."

"Have you heard from Seth?"

"Sadly, no. As I said, we're quite

concerned. Did you try to contact him?"

"I texted him. I haven't heard anything back. Listen, I have to be honest: I can't believe he's on the run with your money. That's not the Seth I know. Could someone have taken him?"

"Perhaps, but we have no evidence of that. We think he left of his own accord."

"Any idea where he might have gone? I could take a leave of absence from Hendley and —"

"And what, Jack? Hunt for him like you're in a Ludlum novel? Jack, I do admire your dedication to your friend, but you need to let us handle this. Go about your business. Inform us if Seth makes contact. That's all you can do."

They stood up and shook hands. Wellesley walked him to the door and said good-bye.

Jack returned to Ysabel's Range Rover and climbed in.

"Did they buy it?" she asked.

"It was just Wellesley. I think so, but that's one cagey bastard. And if he was behind it, he deserves an Oscar."

Jack's disposable phone trilled. It was a text message. The screen read: IT'S SETH.

Jack typed: WHERE ARE YOU?

OUT OF TOWN.

SAFE?

Y, came Seth's reply. FIND WHAT I LEFT FOR YOU?

Y.

WATCH YOUR BACK. WILL CALL LATER.

The screen went blank.

Edinburgh, Scotland

The place Helen had found for them, a run-down, side-alley garage with a cramped, two-bedroom flat above it, was private enough, but was filthy and stank of motor oil.

As Olik sat on the ratty plaid couch watching television, Helen finished cleaning the kitchen and putting away groceries, then started cooking lunch — beans and toast and grilled tomatoes, a UK staple, apparently. A good leader fed her troops, she thought.

From below came the honk of a car horn.

Helen said, "Olik, go."

Olik headed down the stairs. Helen leaned over the railing and watched as he lifted the main door's crossbar and swung open the double doors. The garage's interior was lit by a lone fluorescent light suspended from the rafters. Outside, the alleyway's cobbles were wet with rain.

The van rolled inside and Olik shut the doors. Yegor shut off the van's engine and climbed out, as did Roma.

"I have it," Yegor announced with a smile.

Yegor trotted up the stairs, shrugging off his coat as he went.

"Did you have any trouble?"

"Very little. The students have lockers. When she went to lunch, I jimmied the door to hers. No one saw me." He drew a small notebook from his back pocket and handed it to Helen, who scanned the pages.

"Class schedule, dormitory room number, appointments . . ."

"There are only a few here."

"The rest would be on her phone," Yegor said. "I'm surprised they write anything down these days."

"Which dormitory is she in?"

"Chancellors Court."

"Good," Helen replied.

She walked to a nearby cupboard, opened the top drawer, and pulled out a map of the university's campus. She laid it on the kitchen table and traced her finger over the legend until she found Chancellors. "Right here. It's part of the Pollock Halls complex. We need to see it up close. We'll go when it's dark."

7

"How do we even know it was him?" Ysabel said.

They were back at her apartment, again watching the sunrise streaming through her balcony windows and enjoying a cup of her nuclear-powered coffee. Jack had slept fitfully, half hoping for an update call from Gavin Biery while his brain worked the "Seth problem." Jack wanted to move, to take action, but the smart course was to do nothing until he got Gavin's results.

"We don't," Jack replied. "If it wasn't him, it means someone's got him. Or at least his phone."

"If that's true, and they were asking about what we found in the safe, it means you might have been talking to the men who took you. Oh, that reminds me . . ."

Ysabel got up, walked to the credenza behind her couch, opened a drawer, then returned with a fifteen-inch MacBook Pro and sat back down. When the laptop booted up, she started typing. After a minute she said, "The van's placard was real enough — Yazdani and Son Electrical Contractors. The address is in an industrial part of town, on the east side — Ehsan and Tenth Street. Should we go?"

Jack considered this. While they weren't going to find Balaclava and his partner loitering about in Yazdani's offices, it was a lead. Seth's trail was growing cold.

They drove Ysabel's Range Rover to a public parking lot a half-mile from the Yazdani address, then got out and hailed a cab. As the car pulled to the curb beside them, Ysabel said, "When we get there, I'm going in alone."

"No —"

"It's better this way. Trust me."

Jack hesitated. "Okay, but call me and leave the line open."

"Worried for my safety, Jack?"

"Yes."

"That's sweet. Let's go."

The cab took them into the industrial district, two acres of streets lined with cracked sidewalks, sliding security gates, and warehouses fronted by faded red and green awnings and signs in Persian/Farsi.

The driver pulled up to a strip of warehouses and stopped.

Ysabel said something in Persian to the driver, then climbed out and headed for the door to Yazdani's office, dialing as she went. Jack's phone rang. Ysabel said, "Can you hear me now?"

"Very funny."

Ysabel slid the phone into her purse, opened the door, and disappeared inside.

After a minute of silence Jack heard her talking to what sounded like two men. The conversation quickly turned into an argument, Ysabel and the men talking over one another in rapid-fire Persian until finally only one man was replying to her questions, his voice softer. They spoke for another couple of minutes, then Ysabel emerged from the office. She got in the taxi, said something to the driver, and the car pulled away. Jack opened his mouth to speak. Ysabel shook her head slightly.

Once back at her Range Rover, Jack said, "Well?"

"Two men, both Persian. The owner — Vahid Yazdani — and an employee, maybe his son. They were old-school, angry that a woman was in their shop, wearing no head-scarf and being shockingly assertive."

"Sounded like you set them straight."

"Those types are bullies at heart, Jack. Push back and they usually back down. Plus, I'm well dressed — wealth has some social currency. Anyway, Yazdani claims the van was stolen two nights ago. He informed the police, but nothing has come of it."

"Dead end," Jack muttered.

"Not at all. While I was storming and ranting, I peeked out the back door. There's a fenced storage area behind the shop. The van was there."

"You're sure?"

"There was a bullet hole in the door. Right where I put it."

Halfway back to Ysabel's apartment, Jack's phone trilled. It was Gavin Biery.

"Your phone should be there this afternoon," he told Jack.

"That was quick."

"We aim to please. I've got some info for you."

With his phone braced between his shoulder and his ear, Jack pulled out his pad and balanced it on his knee, pen at the ready. "Shoot."

"First, there's no activity on your credit cards. Second, the van's license plate belongs to an electrical contractor —"

"Yazdani and Son. I was just there. The

van was there. The owner claimed it was stolen."

"On paper, they look legit. I also checked out Dr. Pezhman Abbasi. Age seventy-two, been teaching at University of Tehran for thirty-plus years. No red flags, no criminal record, no interesting affiliations.

"Now, this David Weaver guy is interesting. The Albany address on his International Driver's Permit is bogus; it's actually a store that offers short- and long-term P.O. boxes."

"How the hell does that work? Isn't that something Homeland Security keys on?"

"More the Postal Inspection Service, but yeah. I'll keep plugging, but I wouldn't hold my breath. As for Weaver himself, I drew a blank. No Social Security number, no credit history — all the standard stuff, nothing. The guy stinks of special ops."

"And his gun?"

"Now, that's really interesting. It's not a SIG Sauer, but an Iranian knock-off called a Zoaf PC9. The serial number is actually a version of what's called an NSN — NATO Stock Number. In this case, it's a DMC — Domestic Management Code. The two-digit country code makes it an export to the UK."

Raymond Wellesley's homeland, Jack thought. *Too obvious, an oversight, or a coincidence?* The black-market handgun business was booming, as it always had been. Heavy weapons were tougher to smuggle, especially after 9/11, but not so with handguns. Iranian or British or otherwise, the nine-millimeter's origin was proof of nothing. Interesting, though, that it led directly back to Wellesley.

"What the hell are you into, Jack?" asked Gavin.

"I've already asked myself that more than a few times. Tell me about my phone."

"It's powered down now, but it was on, briefly, yesterday morning. The best I could do was a rough location. Somewhere between — and I'll try not to butcher these names . . . Enghelab Road, Rashid Yashemi Street, and Vali Asr Street."

Jack said, "Hold on a second," then asked Ysabel: "The area of Enghelab Road, Rashid Yashemi Street, and Vali Asr Street — mean anything to you?"

"Of course. That's the neighborhood where Seth's apartment is — not the bolt-hole, his real one. It's on the other side of Mellat Park, about a mile from mine."

"Good work, Gavin. What time was Seth's phone on and for how long?"

"About thirty seconds or so, at 10:09."

"Thanks. Talk to —"

"Hang on, Jack. At exactly the same time,

113

your stolen phone powered up, and it stayed on for the same duration."

Someone had hijacked his old phone.

Twenty minutes later they were back at Ysabel's apartment.

"Your phone? How is that possible?" she said, pushing open the front door and laying her purse on the kitchen counter. "Is that even doable?"

Jack closed the door behind them.

"It's doable." The Campus had done it before, and Wellesley and Spellman would have access to their own sophisticated tech nerds. "Assuming my phone was actually pinging from Seth's Naseri Street apartment, somebody's laying a trap." He had to also assume they'd seen the earlier text exchange between him and Seth, though it would do them little good.

"You think they want the folder we got from Seth's safe?"

Jack nodded. "It's a good bet. Let's see if we get an invitation."

Jack's new phone arrived mid-afternoon. He pored over his notes, trying to make sense of the glut of information he'd amassed over the past two days, and occasionally checked his e-mail; earlier he'd sent a curt "Contact me" e-mail to Ervaz, the other agent Ysabel knew about. He'd received no reply.

Jack wasn't sure of his next move. Irrational though it was, he felt he had a lot of leads, and no leads at all. Wellesley, Spellman, Yazdani and Son, Balaclava Man, David Weaver, Seth/ Not Seth texting him, and a pile of papers in Cyrillic that was clearly important to both Seth and . . . whoever.

Jack briefly considered going to Pardis and sitting on it, but decided against it. And while he couldn't be sure the text had come from the apartment itself, Jack's gut told him it had. Such a move made tactical sense. They knew he was looking for Seth, so why not lure him there with exactly that?

How could he turn the trap to his advantage? Contingencies, countercontingencies, evasion, and escape . . . It was a chess game with the highest possible stakes, and no matter how well pre-plotted your game, something would go wrong. Something always went wrong. What mattered is what you did about it. And with whom. He was mostly convinced that Ysabel was who she claimed to be, and she'd so far proven herself reliable, but part of him wanted to leave her behind. Was this sexism or overprotectiveness? The latter, he decided. He'd have to get over that. Ysabel was in this because she wanted to be. Plus, with him overprotectiveness tended. to precede attachment, which tended to precede deeper feelings — in his case, a sequence that often happened prematurely. It was a complication he didn't need right now. It'd be so much easier if she were unlikable.

Back to work. He opened Ysabel's laptop, brought Google Maps up in the browser, then located the neighborhood around Pardis Condos and started putting the streets and building to memory. This would be their ground. They had some advantage: the bad guys would assume they'd be walking blindly into the trap.

A thought occurred to him. "Ysabel, can you do me a favor?" She walked up. He wrote a couple of items on the notepad, tore off the sheet, and handed it to her. "Can you get this stuff?"

"I think so, yes."

"Should be able to find it in a military surplus store, if you have those here."

"What's it for?"

"An experiment."

Once back from her errand, Ysabel spent the rest of her afternoon cooking in the kitchen and listening to her MP3 player, hair tied in a ponytail, humming as she moved among the simmering pots, stirring and tasting and adding spices. She was trying to keep her mind occupied, Jack suspected. Though her romantic involvement had ended with Seth, clearly she cared about him.

And here they were, Jack thought, sitting on their hands and playing house. At this thought, Jack smiled. Despite the circumstances, he didn't entirely mind the feeling. *Careful, Jack.*

He got up from the dining table, stretched his arms, and rubbed his hands through his hair. He called to Ysabel, "Scotch?"

She removed her earbuds. "What?"

"Scotch?"

"Please."

He poured two glasses and joined her in the kitchen. He handed her a glass and she took a sip. Jack said, "When do we eat?"

"This?" she replied, gesturing to the pots. "Tomorrow. It's a complex recipe requiring great patience. Tonight we're having last night's leftovers again."

"*Khoreshteh qiemeh bademjoon?* Persian eggplant stew."

"Very good, Jack."

"Iranians have a thing about stew, don't they?"

She laughed. "We do." Slowly the smile faded from her face and she said, "This feels wrong somehow, you know, enjoying ourselves while Seth is . . . out there. We should be doing something."

"I feel the same. Right now there's nothing to do but wait."

"Well, I'm not a fan. Just so you know."

At eight-fifteen Jack's prepaid cell phone trilled. With Ysabel peering over his shoulder, he checked the screen:

AT PARDIS CONDO.
YOU KNOW WHERE?

Jack said to Ysabel, "Get your coat."

"You're not going to reply?"

"If I can track them, we have to assume they can track us. We don't want to get a knock on your door. I don't suppose you have binoculars, do you?"

"No, but Mr. Hamdi next door does. I'll go get them." Ysabel left.

Jack pulled out the prepaid cell, powered it up, and typed, OFF NIAYESH, RIGHT? APARTMENT 12?

RIGHT. COME ASAP. BRING STEAK. — S.

118

Jack disconnected and then from the table grabbed the product of Ysabel's shopping trip, a silver bag about three times the size of Jack's disposable phone. He put that and his cloned phone inside and sealed it shut.

"What exactly is that?" she asked.

"It's called a Faraday bag. The plastic I asked for is ESD, electrostatic discharge material. Specifically, MIL-PRF-8170 —"

"Just tell me what it does, Jack."

"In theory? It blocks all outgoing signals. If they're tracking us, this might make it impossible."

"Let's hope."

"How close is Seth's building to Mellat Park?"

"It's southeast of here, about a mile. Right across the street from the park's west entrance. What've you got in mind, Jack?"

"We're going to kidnap a kidnapper."

8

Once they were out of Ysabel's apartment garage, Jack instructed her to drive south along Vali Asr Street, skirting the eastern edge of the park. It was fully dark and both sides of the street were lined with yellow sodium-vapor lamps. The traffic was light; Jack saw only a few cars, most of them headed south toward the expressway. When they reached Niayesh they turned west and joined the flow of merging cars.

"We need a place to park, away from Seth's condo," Jack said.

"I'll find something."

After about half a mile, Ysabel said, "That's it, out your window."

Jack looked right and saw Pardis Condos, an eight-floor tower overlooking the lighted entrance of the park. Ysabel drove for another hundred yards, then turned right onto a short bridge spanning a canal, then turned left into an empty warehouse parking lot. A fluorescent security light flickered anemically over the warehouse's garage door. She doused the headlights and shut off the engine.

"This won't draw the police, us parking here?" Jack asked.

"No. Many park visitors park on side streets at night."

Jack raised the binoculars Ysabel had borrowed from her neighbor and zoomed in on the park. Just inside the park's entrance he could see a tiered fountain underlit by amber lights; stone benches circled the flagstone clearing, itself hemmed in by trees.

"What's the plan?"

Jack detected a tingle of excitement in Ysabel's voice. He said, "I'm going to call whoever I've been talking to out on that bench to the far right of the fountain." He handed Ysabel the binoculars. "You see it, with the branches overhanging it?"

"I see it."

"When you see someone approach it and sit down, drive across Niayesh, then down that side street —"

"Rajaei Boulevard —"

"As soon as you pull onto it, shut off your headlights and find a spot directly opposite the bench. What do you make the distance . . . fifty yards?"

"About that. I can get there in less than a minute, I think."

"Good. If anything goes wrong, if I get taken, drive away. Slowly, headlights off, until you reach the next major cross street, then go back to your apartment, wait four hours, then call that number I gave you."

"Gavin?"

"Right. Tell him everything and sit tight."

Jack pulled the Faraday bag from his jacket pocket, removed his disposable phone, then powered it on and texted, MEET ME AT THE FOUNTAIN INSIDE THE PARK'S ENTRANCE. SIT ON THE FAR RIGHT BENCH.

A minute passed before the reply came: WHAT'S GOING ON?

NERVOUS, Jack replied. JUST DO WHAT I ASK, SETH.

OKAY. FIVE MINUTES.

Jack powered off the phone and returned it to the Faraday bag.

"I don't like this plan, Jack," said Ysabel.

"No plan is perfect," he replied. "You work with what you've got, and this is what we've got right now."

Ysabel hesitated, then sighed. "Good luck."

Jack climbed out, walked across the canal

bridge, then west, back down the Niayesh Expressway, until he reached a crosswalk leading to Rajaei Boulevard, then waited for a break in the traffic, and trotted across the street and onto Rajaei. In contrast to the expressway, Rajaei was quiet, its tree-lined sidewalks devoid of pedestrians and dark, save a faux gas lamp spaced every twenty yards or so. The sound of the expressway faded as Jack continued north.

To his right he glimpsed the fountain's amber lighting through the darkened trees. When he drew even with the fountain, he turned left and stopped beneath the low-hanging boughs of an oak tree.

He drew the nine-millimeter from his left jacket pocket and pulled back the slide an inch to expose the glint of brass in the gun's pipe. He released the slide and returned the weapon to his pocket.

Keeping to the deepest shadows, Jack picked his way through the trees toward the fountain, his eyes scanning left and right until he reached the tree directly behind the bench. Beyond it, the fountain gurgled softly, the amber spotlights casting swirling shadows on the underside of the fountain's tiered basins. To Jack's left, down the broad paved entrance to the park, he could see the lighted lobby doors of Seth's condo building.

He checked his watch. Three minutes had passed since he'd sent the text. In the next two minutes he'd have an answer to one of his worries: Would whoever was on the other end of the text messages assume Jack was in fact expecting Seth? Jack hoped so. If not, they'd likely be setting up their own ambush or at least scouting the area, which would take more than the five minutes Jack had given them.

Sixty more seconds passed.

A figure emerged from the condo's lobby, crossed the street, and trotted up the steps to the park. It was a man, Jack could see from the build and gait, but he was wearing a hoodie. The face was in shadow. The man angled right so he passed directly under the streetlamps, his head tilted downward, hands stuffed into the hoodie's pockets.

Son of a bitch, Jack thought. He took a deep breath, let it out, then drew the nine-millimeter from his pocket and thumbed the safety to the off position.

The man reached the entrance to the fountain's clearing. He stopped, looked around.

Come on, come on . . .

The man continued forward, his boots

echoing on the flagstones, then sat down on the bench.

Jack said, "If you move, I'll put a bullet in the back of your head. Nod if you understand."

The man nodded.

"Are you being covered?"

The man shook his head.

"Say it."

"Does it matter? You're going to do what you're going to do."

This wasn't Seth, Jack realized, but rather Balaclava.

"How did you know?" the man asked.

"Stand up, stay facing away from me, and take your hands out of your pockets."

"You're making a mistake, son."

Jack repeated his order.

Balaclava stood and removed his hands from his pockets.

"Keep your hands out to your sides. Turn around and pull off your hood."

The man did as instructed.

Balaclava was in his mid-thirties, tanned, with black hair and a mustache. In Iran, he would blend in, Jack decided.

"Walk toward me."

Balaclava stepped around the bench and into the trees. Jack backed up, nine-millimeter on the man's chest, until they were deeper in the shadows. Jack ordered Balaclava to drop to his knees, then to his belly, which he did. Jack stepped forward, then knelt down, left shin jammed against the man's neck, the nine-millimeter pressed between his shoulder blades. With his left hand Jack frisked him, having him roll slightly onto his side to check his front pockets. Balaclava was carrying neither a weapon nor a wallet, but in the hoodie's right-hand pocket was a phone — Jack's phone.

"Now what?" said Balaclava.

"Now we go someplace quiet and talk."

"You haven't the stomach for it."

"We'll see," Jack replied. The truth was, he'd never had to make that decision. Though the battery-cables-and-pliers routine looked sexy in Hollywood movies, torture usually produced sketchy results at best. Then again, it had worked on Saif Rahman Yasin — the Emir — but it had been ugly and the image of Yasin writhing on the table was never far from Jack's mind.

"Stand up," Jack ordered. "We're heading west toward Rajaei. You lead. If you run or turn around —"

"I know the drill."

"Walk."

They headed through the trees, Jack trailing ten feet back, his eyes scanning for movement in the trees and occasionally glancing over his shoulder. There was no one. That wouldn't last, though. Unless Balaclava was working solo, without David Weaver, someone would have seen Balaclava disappear into the trees. If the cavalry wasn't already coming, it soon would be.

When they reached the sidewalk Jack saw Ysabel's Range Rover parked across the street. *Good girl,* Jack thought. She'd parked in the dark spot between two streetlamps. The Range Rover's engine started. Ysabel's face was illuminated by the dashboard's blue glow.

Jack and Balaclava started across the street.

Ysabel rolled down her window and said, "Any —"

The top of Balaclava's head exploded into a red mist.

Dead where he stood, Balaclava dropped to his knees, then toppled onto his side in the middle of the road. His left leg twitched spasmodically. Blood gushed from the man's head wound and began puddling beneath his torso.

"Down!" Jack rasped. "Ysabel, down!"

She ducked out of sight.

Jack resisted the urge to run for the Range

Rover and instead turned on his heel and sprinted back across the sidewalk and into the tree line, where he stopped and crouched down.

"Where are you?" Jack muttered. Jack was stunned, his brain racing to catch up with what just happened. The shot had been little more than a muffled crack — not the sound of a handgun but rather a suppressor-equipped rifle. Where was the shooter? Logic suggested somewhere from Seth's condo, somewhere high up. No other firing angle made sense. Either way, he couldn't stay here. As quiet as the shot had been, he had to assume someone had heard it and called the police.

"Ysabel," Jack called.

"I'm here."

"I'm coming to you. Be ready to move. No matter what happens, stay as low as you can."

"Hurry, Jack, the police will —"

"I know."

Jack didn't give himself a chance to think, but stood up and walked back toward the street, his head turned right so he could keep the condo in view through the trees. When he was six feet from Balaclava's body and directly opposite Ysabel's Range Rover, he stopped and looked right again. At the end of the block, around the edge of an oak tree, he could see the corner of the condo's roof, two hundred yards distant. If the sniper was still around, that's where he would be.

Jack dashed forward, leapt over Balaclava's body, and ran for the Range Rover's rear bumper. As he reached it, he glimpsed a red dot reflected on the Range Rover's window to his left. A bullet thunked into the rear corner post. Jack ducked down, kept going. Another round smacked into the curb to his right. Jack reached the sidewalk and jumped onto it. His toe caught the curb and he sprawled face-first onto the pavement.

Out of the corner of his eye, six inches away, the red dot appeared on the pavement.

Done, Jack thought numbly. *He's got me.*

He heard a pop, then another one. The red dot skittered across the sidewalk, then leapt wildly into the trees beyond.

Jack pushed himself to his knees, got his feet under him, and dodged left, behind the shelter of the SUV. He opened the passenger door, crawled inside, then slammed the door behind him.

Ysabel slammed her foot against the gas pedal, jerked the wheel left, and the SUV surged ahead and down the street.

Edinburgh, Scotland

It had taken time, too much time, Helen thought, to find a pattern, and it had nothing to do with precautions their target took. In fact, they'd found the young Amy traveled with no bodyguards and usually strolled the Rose Street area with only an entourage of giggling and frequently drunk girls. Whether any of her friends knew Amy's true identity Helen didn't know, but they were certainly aware of the depth of the young woman's pockets. The professional part of her brain didn't care one way or another, but the maternal part, small though it was, hoped Amy's friends were genuine. Being far from her homeland and among strangers was an experience Helen knew very well. Even with training and preparation, it was a lonely existence; for a nineteen-year-old Muslim girl trying to fit in here . . .

Helen pushed the thought from her mind. They had a job to do.

She turned in the van's passenger seat and said to Roma and Olik, "Are you clear on what's to happen?" She didn't need to ask Yegor, who'd been with her for all but two of these jobs.

"Clear," Olik replied.

"Roma?"

"I'm not an idiot," he grumbled, eyes star-

130

ing out his window. "I know what to do."

"If you were an idiot, you wouldn't be here," Helen replied, hoping the compliment would mollify him. He was an idiot, but she was stuck with him.

"Just watch for my signals. If you don't see the abort sign, go ahead with it. Don't hurry, and keep calm. Do it as we rehearsed." Helen checked her watch. Ten minutes.

"Let one of us come with you," Yegor said.

"No. I'll arouse no suspicion if I'm on my own."

Helen climbed out, waited for a gap in the cars, then crossed Princes Street and started down Frederick. Behind her, Yegor pulled the van away from the curb, its red taillights fading quickly in the low mist clinging to the ground. Helen pulled the sequined French military ball cap — the current and inexplicable fashion trend among the university students — closer over her eyes.

If not for the honking of the cars and the hissing of bus brakes, she could imagine herself back in Victorian Edinburgh, such was the architecture. More buildings than not seemed to have frozen in their medieval forms, with turrets, alleys fronted by sally port entrances, and moss-trimmed stonework.

Put her fellow pedestrians and revelers in period garb and the scene would be almost perfect.

The Mexican restaurant, Chiquito, was just a block away, and it took Helen less than two minutes to get there. Chiquito had only recently become a regular stop for the girl, every Monday, Wednesday, and Friday night from seven-thirty until eight forty-five, with two of her girlfriends.

Amy had been naughty, Helen's surveillance had revealed. The girl's newest boyfriend or hookup — one could never tell anymore, not even the kids themselves, she suspected — was, Robby, a thirtysomething busboy at Chiquito who apparently could make time for Amy only after his shift and before he went home to his wife and kids. Having spent time tailing Robby a day earlier, Helen didn't understand the allure, but clearly Amy did. She seemed content with taking whatever time he allowed her.

At seven twenty-five, Helen passed Rose Street and stepped inside the dimly lit plexiglass bus stand. The next bus was due shortly.

The minutes ticked by.

"Evening," a man standing beside her said. "Chilly tonight."

132

"Piss off, wanker," Helen shot back, her chin tucked into the cowl of her anorak.

"Hey, I'm just being friendly."

"I said, 'Piss off!' "

Helen suspected the man was simply making conversation, but apparently "Piss off, wanker" was a perfectly acceptable response to unwanted attention on Rose Street. It seemed rude, she thought, but when in Rome . . .

"Sorry," the man muttered.

Down the block toward Chiquito, Helen heard a trio of raucous giggles and immediately recognized one of them as belonging to Amy. She had a nice laugh, natural, not the mush-mouthed cackles many of her friends let out when drunk. Tonight Amy was with the most obnoxious pair, Margaret and Tera.

Helen glanced left and saw Amy, flanked by her two friends, walking toward the bus stand. As they passed, Helen stepped out and followed. Amy was wearing a thick red cardigan against the chill. *That makes things even easier,* thought Helen.

When they reached Princes Street the group disappeared around the corner, heading east. *Good,* Helen thought. *Sticking to schedule.* She slowed her pace, letting them gain some distance, then also rounded the

133

corner. Fifty feet ahead, Amy and her friends were walking, shoulders pressing, talking and giggling and occasionally sidestepping to avoid collisions with fellow bar-goers.

At the next intersection, Hanover, Amy and her friends stopped at a bus stand. Helen kept walking, passed them, and hurried through the crosswalk to the other side, where she stopped, got out her cell phone, and pretended to make a call.

Across the intersection, Margaret said in a lilting Scottish accent, "Do you have to go, Ames? Stay with us. We'll go to Voltaire!"

"No, sorry, this is the only time we get to see each other."

"Yeah, right. Well, don't do anything I wouldn't do."

"You do everything, you slag — what're you talking about?" said Tera.

"Hey, that's not nice!"

"Then what's it gonna be tonight, Ames?" Tera asked. "Need to borrow a condom?"

"God, no," Amy shot back. "We haven't done that yet."

"Yeah, I know what you're doing," Margaret said. "It's all nice for him, but has he reciprocated? You know, south of the border . . ."

"Stop, Margaret, you're awful."

"I'm just looking out for you, girl."

"I have to go. Your bus will be here soon. Text me, let me know you got back to Pollock safe," Amy said, and the three of them exchanged cheek air-kisses.

As they parted, Helen pocketed her cell phone, then recrossed the street, passing Amy halfway across. Hurrying now, Helen headed down the block until she saw a break in the traffic, then jaywalked to the other side of the street and onto a gravel path leading into the tree-lined Princes Street Gardens. She glanced left and saw Amy in her red cardigan step onto the sidewalk and head in Helen's direction.

Helen kept going and soon was on the curving path that led past the garden-keeper's cottage. On either side of the path, green tulip leaves were poking from the soil. The sounds of the cars on Princes Street faded until all Helen could hear was the hissing of tires on the wet pavement.

Helen glanced over her shoulder. Amy was thirty feet behind, her face illuminated in the glow of her cell phone's screen as she double-thumb texted someone — Robby, Helen assumed, letting him know she was on her way.

Their "snog spot," as Margaret had dubbed it on Amy's behalf, was the decidedly unromantic roof of a toolshed beside some railroad tracks; above these, atop a lush hill a quarter-mile away, sat the decidedly romantic Edinburgh Castle.

The path straightened out. Ahead, Helen saw the van sitting on the maintenance road that bordered the railroad tracks. Yegor had positioned the vehicle perfectly, bisecting the path leading to Amy's snog spot so she would have no choice but to go around the van.

Helen slowed her pace and started rummaging through her purse until Amy passed her on the path and started across the maintenance road. As she did, Helen upended her purse. Its contents spilled onto the gravel.

"Oh, bloody hell," Helen cried, putting a little sob in her voice. "Of all the damned nights!"

Amy stopped and turned around. "You all right?"

"My boyfriend, that wanker . . ." Helen replied.

"Here, let me help," Amy said, and started walking back to Helen.

Yegor, climbing from the van's driver's-side door, was already striding across the road to Amy, the flour-sack hood dangling from his left hand. Suddenly, Roma came around the rear bumper and charged toward the girl. His face was a mask of anger.

Despite herself, Helen called, "Yegor, grab him!"

Amy stopped in her tracks. "What?"

Yegor grabbed at Roma's shoulder as he passed, but it was too late.

Amy had stopped in her tracks. "Yegor? Who's —"

She turned around.

"No, Roma!" Helen screamed.

Roma was already swinging, a right haymaker hook that caught Amy squarely in the jaw. Her head snapped around. She stumbled sideways, trying to regain her balance, but Helen, already rushing forward to catch Amy, saw the light go out of her eyes. She landed in a pile in the street. Roma was still charging, closing in on her inert form. Helen stepped in front of him and he skidded to a stop. She shoved him backward. "You fool!"

At the van, Olik was climbing out the rear doors.

Helen said, "Yegor, check her. Olik, get over here. Roma, you get in the passenger seat."

Roma didn't move.

"Do it!" Helen barked, and Roma stalked off.

Helen looked around and saw no one. Yegor and Olik were kneeling next to Amy. Helen asked, "Is she alive?"

"Yes," said Yegor, relief in his voice.

"Put the hood on her and get her in the van."

9

TEHRAN, IRAN

"What just happened, Jack?" asked Ysabel. She shrugged off her purse and let it drop to the floor, then tossed the binoculars and her keys onto the counter and walked to the sideboard, where she poured a glass of Scotch.

Jack clicked the door shut behind him, then leaned his back against it and closed his eyes. He took a deep breath, then another. It felt good to be . . . home. It wasn't quite the right word, but Ysabel's apartment had become not only Jack's base of operations, but his safe house as well. So far, no one knew of this place.

Ysabel said, "I saw his . . . His head just —"

"I know."

"Who was shooting at us?"

"I don't know."

"What —"

"Ysabel, stop. Let me think." He paused

139

for a few moments to orient his thoughts. "Do you have a washing machine in here?"

"Yes."

Jack headed for the bathroom, calling over his shoulder, "We should both shower and wash our clothes."

"Why?"

"Blood particles get everywhere, Ysabel." Jack had no idea whether the Tehran police were sophisticated or dedicated enough to look for such forensics, but he was taking no chances. The idea of ending up in an Iranian prison — which was the best-case scenario — held no appeal at all.

After they were both showered and their clothes were in the washer, they settled into the sunken living room, Ysabel with her second glass of Scotch, Jack his first.

He took the nine-millimeter from his jacket pocket, as well as the Faraday bag holding both his phones, and placed them on the table.

Ysabel sat in the chair opposite the couch, her legs curled beneath her and a glass pressed against her chest with both hands. Her eyes were vacant.

"Were we followed, do you think?" she murmured.

It was a good question. Jack had been

careful to check for tails and they'd pulled into Ysabel's apartment garage just as the police sirens began converging on Mellat Park. Though it seemed doubtful anyone had gotten the Range Rover's license plates, Jack couldn't be sure.

"Tomorrow morning you're going to call the police and report the Range Rover missing," he said.

Ysabel's eyes went wide. "Jack, that's crazy."

"That's what an innocent person would do. If someone reports it being near the scene of the shooting, you need to be disconnected from it."

"They'll ask a lot of questions."

"All of which you'll have answers to. We'll talk it through. They won't be able to make the connection between you, Seth, and the Pardis condo. You'll be a victim of a crime, nothing more. Where's the closest sketchy area?"

"Sketchy?"

"Run-down, away from things."

"Uh . . . there's a bunch of vacant lots beneath Velayat Bridge about three kilometers from here." Ysabel stood up, collected her MacBook from the credenza, and then, after it was powered up, showed Jack Velayat Bridge on Google Maps.

Jack scrolled around on the map, then tapped the screen. "Take your Mercedes and meet me a block south of this bus stop in about twenty minutes."

After popping the Rover's ignition with a screwdriver and tearing out the wires, Jack parked it beside a pylon beneath Velayat Bridge, then doused the seats and dashboard with a bottle of Ysabel's nail polish remover, set the interior ablaze, then ran the quarter-mile to where Ysabel was waiting for him. Forty minutes after leaving the apartment, they were back.

"What time would you normally go out in the morning?" Jack asked.

"I guess about eight, for breakfast."

"Then follow that routine. Walk down to the garage, look for your car, then call the concierge and report the theft."

"What will you be doing?"

"Making myself scarce."

"Who was that, the one that died?"

"One of the men who kidnapped me," Jack said. "I'd named him Balaclava. And don't ask me who or what or why, Ysabel, because I don't know. I need to sort it out."

Ysabel took his admonishment in stride, simply nodding. She downed the rest of her Scotch — her third one — then gave him a sloppy half-grin. She was tipsy, bordering on drunk. "I'm glad they didn't shoot you, Jack. That would have been a bad thing."

Despite himself, Jack laughed. "Me, too."

And why aren't I dead? he thought. Jack replayed the events in his mind. The sniper had him dead to rights. The slightest adjustment to that red laser dot would have put Jack's skull in the crosshairs. The two pops he'd heard before the red dot went wild had come from a handgun; of that Jack was certain. Someone else had been on that roof with the sniper. Who was Jack's guardian angel and why had he interceded?

"You're far away, Jack," said Ysabel. "What are you thinking about?"

"I'm wondering why I'm alive."

"What?"

"Nothing."

Jack opened Ysabel's laptop, brought up the chat window, and entered Gavin Biery's cell-phone number and typed: IT'S JACK. YOU THERE?

A few moments passed before Gavin replied: IF THIS IS JACK, HOW OLD IS MY CAT?

Jack smiled. Gavin enjoyed what he called "all that spy nonsense." Jack indulged him occasionally. He replied, PEEPERS DIED TWO WEEKS AGO.

GOOD ANSWER. WHAT'S UP?

I GOT MY HIJACKED PHONE BACK. CAN YOU DO ANYTHING WITH IT? REMOTELY, I MEAN.

DEPENDS ON WHAT THEY DID TO IT. WHERE IS IT?

POWERED OFF AND INSIDE MY HOMEMADE FARADAY BAG.

WHY BOTHER WITH IT?

I MIGHT BE ABLE TO GET THROUGH TO SETH — THE REAL ONE.

LET ME SEE WHAT I CAN DO. POWER IT UP. WATCH THE CLOCK. IF YOU DON'T SEE THE SCREEN FLASH TWICE IN THE NEXT SIXTY SECONDS, POWER IT DOWN AGAIN AND PUT IT BACK IN THE FARADAY.

Jack removed the phone from the bag and turned it on. He watched the screen. Only ten seconds passed before the screen double-flashed.

Gavin typed: GOT IT. IT MIGHT TAKE SOME TIME. NO GUARANTEES. BACK TO YOU ASAP.

As Jack closed the chat window, Ysabel's laptop let out a chime.

"New e-mail," she said.

Jack called up the e-mail window. "It's Ervaz," Jack said.

"Really?" Ysabel climbed out of her chair and sat down beside him. "What's he say?"

144

"Basically, 'Who the hell is this?'" Jack typed in: FRIEND OF SETH'S.

SETH IS MISSING.

I KNOW. I'M TRYING TO FIND HIM.

GIVE ME PROOF THAT YOU ARE HIS FRIEND.

I CAN'T, Jack replied. I DON'T KNOW YOU, DON'T KNOW ANYTHING ABOUT YOU AND SETH. HELP ME FIND HIM. HE'S IN TROUBLE.

The reply took sixty seconds to arrive: MAYBE. HAVE TO THINK. I WILL GET BACK TO YOU.

Jack closed the laptop. "Now we wait."

"Now we sleep," Ysabel replied with a yawn.

As planned, Ysabel left the apartment at eight a.m. Jack rode down in the elevator with her. When the doors parted on her parking level, she said, "I'll call you when I'm done."

"Right. Use the cloned phone number."

He took the elevator down to the ground level, left the garage, and wandered into Mellat Park. It was another rainy day. Sheltered under one of Ysabel's umbrellas, Jack strolled the path around the park's north end, resisting the impulse to head south to where Balaclava had been gunned

145

down the night before. The police might still be canvassing for witnesses, and that was a list Jack didn't want to be on. Even so, he eventually needed to get into Seth's condo, as well as onto its roof. Unlikely though it was, perhaps the sniper and his guardian angel had left behind something useful. It seemed unlikely Seth had been keeping anything of value in his condo, but it was still a stone Jack wanted to turn over.

He made his way to the shores of Mellat Lake, where he found a canvas-covered vendor stall. He bought a cup of coffee and a bag of bread crumbs, then picked his way through the trees to the waterline, where he crouched down. The rain pattered softly on the umbrella. A pair of ducks spotted him and paddled over, squawking and turning small circles until Jack tossed them some bread crumbs. Clearly they'd been through this routine hundreds of times.

For the second time in as many days Jack wondered what he'd gotten himself into. The murder of Balaclava had changed everything, and not just in terms of violence. Jack's gut told him Balaclava had been taken out by one of his own, perhaps by his own partner, David Weaver, perhaps by a player Jack had yet to meet. If so, someone was deeply and dangerously invested in whatever Seth was doing here — so much so that Balaclava had been deemed better off dead than talking. Who had made that decision? Spellman and/or Wellesley were the obvious choices, but Jack was reluctant to buy into that answer. Spellman was American, like Jack, and Wellesley was from the UK, America's closest ally. What would drive one or both of these men to order last night's ambush? And who'd saved his life?

Jack found a nearby rock, set it between his feet, then drew his disposable cell phone from the Faraday bag and laid it on the ground. He took the rock and smashed the cell phone into several pieces, then shoved the debris into the water.

Jack's clone phone trilled.

"Hello."

"It's done," Ysabel said.

Jack dumped the rest of the bread crumbs into the water, watched for a moment as the ducks gobbled them up, then shoved the bag into his pocket and started walking.

"You were right," Ysabel said a few minutes later. She was standing in the kitchen. She poured him a cup of coffee. "They asked a few questions, but seemed nonchalant about it. They said someone would get back to me."

"Good. If they'd already found your Range Rover and connected it to the shooting, you'd be in an interview room talking to a detective right now."

"They will find it eventually, though."

"Probably today or tomorrow. Unless they're incompetent, they'll see the bullet holes, make the connection, then process the car for prints —"

"But yours are all over it."

"I'm not in their system," Jack replied. *Not in any systems, unless you've got a lot of horsepower,* he thought. Working at Hendley had more than its fair share of perks, as did being the First Son. Then again, if he was arrested and they had prints on file, none of that would help him.

"After they're done with the Range Rover," he went on, "they'll come back to you and ask more questions. Just stick to your story. You probably won't get your car back for a while, as long as the murder's unsolved. Call your insurance company and report the theft."

"How do you know all this stuff, Jack?"

He shrugged, took a sip of coffee. "How do you feel about getting into some more trouble?"

"What kind? Man getting killed in front of me, or something else?"

"Tonight I want you to go see your boss, Dr. Abbasi. We need to know who he's feeding your think tank's info to. What do you think?"

"That's no trouble. If I approach the subject in the right way, he'll give me the name. And what kind of trouble will you be getting yourself into?"

"That depends on whether Yazdani and Son's office has an alarm system."

Having decided Ysabel's Mercedes was safe to use, Jack told her to take it for her visit to Abbasi.

Jack utilized Tehran's surprisingly uncomplicated subway and bus systems to make his way to the city's eastern outskirts, where he got off and walked the remaining distance to the warehouse complex where Yazdani's office was located. After completing a surveillance circuit of the surrounding blocks and finding the area deserted and quiet and so far devoid of patrolling police cars, Jack made his way around the back of the warehouse to the weed-entangled hurricane fence enclosing Yazdani's rear lot. Through the fence he could see the van Balaclava and Weaver had used to kidnap him.

Jack stood still, watching and listening for

ten minutes. Nothing moved. He picked up a handful of pebbles and spent another few minutes lightly pelting the building's aluminum wall and the side pedestrian door until satisfied no one was about.

From under his arm he took a blanket Ysabel had given him, tossed it onto the fence's barbed-wire topper to form a drape, then scaled the fence, wriggled himself over the blanket, then hopped down. He tugged the blanket free, then walked to the side door. Lacking any lock-picking tools, Jack had already decided on the blunt approach.

He clicked on his penlight and scanned the enclosure until he found what he needed, a rusted leaf spring from what he assumed was one of Yazdani's vans. He draped the blanket over the doorknob and slammed the leaf spring into the knob. He stopped, listened for thirty seconds, then repeated the process. On the fourth strike, the knob tore free and hit the ground with a metallic thud. Jack scooted the knob out of the way, then stuck his finger into the hole and swung open the door.

Inside, the garage's walls were lined with steel shelving holding plastic bins and pegboard tool racks. To his right, up a set of short steps, was a glass-enclosed office. Through the windows Jack could see the milky glow of a computer monitor against the back wall.

Hurrying now, Jack scanned the interior for an alarm panel, first beside the pedestrian door, then beside the front door, then finally in the office. He found nothing.

Yazdani's computer system was ancient, with an IBM tower, a mouse the size of a double deck of cards, and a clunky fourteen-inch monitor. The upper right corner of the screen was taped to the housing with a strip of grimy duct tape. To the side the dial-up modem blinked green and amber.

"Time to upgrade, Mr. Yazdani," Jack muttered, and sat down. He pulled on a pair of thin leather gloves and went to work. It didn't take long. Neither the computer nor any of its files were password-protected. On the downside, most of the files were written in Farsi.

He called up the computer's accounting program and took photos of the bank records, expense reports, and balance sheets for the last three months. Next he photographed the Web browser's history, then its cached files, before turning his attention to the e-mail window. He scrolled down until he reached the day of Ysabel's visit, but found nothing but what appeared to be routine e-mails, some personal, some to suppliers and contractors around the city.

"Damn," he muttered, then immediately thought, *Trash.* Too many people thought sending a file to the trash was the same as deleting it. He hoped Yazdani was one of those people.

He clicked on the trash icon and again scrolled down to the correct date. There were eighteen messages. Jack checked each in turn until an address caught his eye. This one was in English: info@hamrahengineer ingarch.com. He scanned the messages: SOME WOMAN . . . HIT HER CAR . . . WHAT SHOULD I DO WITH THE VAN . . . And so on. Jack photographed the entire exchange.

At the bottom of each message from Hamrah were a name and an address:

FARID RASULOV, SHIPPING MANAGER
HIGHWAY E19
ARCHIVAN, AZERBAIJAN
(+994 25) 491 79 12

"Gotcha," Jack murmured.

10

"What's the saying?" Ysabel asked. "Never meet your heroes?"

Jack had returned to the apartment to find her sitting on the balcony, sipping a cup of tea. He'd joined her and together they watched the lights of Mellat Park below.

"Why? What happened?" Jack replied.

Ysabel sighed. "Dr. Pezhman Abbasi, my beloved mentor and kindly grandfather figure, has been taking kickbacks."

"Explain."

"Some investment firm based in Mashhad — the Bayqara Group — hired him as 'consultant.' Apparently, our think tank is about looking for opportunities in the Russian Federation."

Jack didn't reply immediately. This was unexpected, and probably nonsense. Given the nature of Russian–Iranian relations, unless the Bayqara Group was working behind multiple front companies, it seemed unlikely

Moscow would permit such investments. After the business in Crimea, eastern Ukraine, and Estonia, President Valeri Volodin's policies had grown even more insular.

The question was whether the Bayqara Group was barking up the wrong financial tree or was itself a front for someone else — such as Iranian intelligence.

Wheels within wheels, Jack thought. Before long he'd have to start flowcharting this crap.

"When did Bayqara approach Pezhman, before or after he set up your group?"

"After. It started out as just an internal thing, like all the other ones at the university."

So how and why did Bayqara get interested in it? Jack wondered.

"Why did Pezhman tell you all this?"

"Guilty conscience, I imagine. He wanted to get it off his chest and I asked the question. His wife is sick. Terminal cancer. He's been taking her to any clinic or doctor he can find, and that costs a lot of money."

"Lucky for him the Bayqara Group happened along."

"My thought exactly. And yes, before you ask, I told him to tell no one about our chat. He will."

"How can you be sure?"

"I just am."

"Who's his contact?"

"I wrote it all down on the pad on the dining room table. Suleiman something," Ysabel replied, gesturing over her shoulder. "All Pezhman had was a cell-phone number. Tell me what you found at Yazdani."

"A lot of stuff for you to translate." Jack told her about the e-mail between Yazdani and Farid Rasulov of Hamrah Engineering. "Your visit stirred up a hornet's nest — at least on Yazdani's end. You scared the hell out of the guy."

Ysabel smiled. "I have my ways. What's Hamrah Engineering?"

"I don't know. I'll give it to Gavin. What kind of name is Farid Rasulov?" asked Jack.

" 'Farid' is Arabic, but it's also Azerbaijani. 'Rasulov' is Russian, of course, but most Azerbaijani surnames are holdovers from the Soviet days. What do we do next, Jack?"

This question had been in the forefront of Jack's mind since the shooting at Pardis Condos. "Time to pay the piper," he said.

Jack settled into Ysabel's guest bedroom, closed the door, and used his cloned phone to call Gavin Biery. His instructions were

155

curt, and produced nearly immediate results. Ten minutes after his initial call, Jack's phone trilled.

"Jack, it's Gerry. I've got John Clark with me. You're on speaker. What's going on?"

Jack thought, *I have no idea,* but said, "I'm into something in Tehran."

For the next ten minutes, he took them through the last four days, from his lunch with Seth Gregory to his breaking into Yazdani's office. He left nothing out.

There was a long, uncomfortable silence on the phone. Finally, John Clark said simply, "Christ Almighty, Jack."

"Are you safe?" Gerry asked.

"I think so."

"What do you know about this woman?"

Jack gave them Ysabel's particulars, then said, "She's on the level."

"Or not, and she's playing the long game."

Clark said, "What's your gut say, Jack?"

"She's on the level," Jack repeated.

"Then that's what she is, Gerry," said Clark.

Gerry said, "Jack, can you guess what I'm going to say next?"

"Drop it all and be on the next plane out. But I'm not going to do that."

"The hell you aren't!"

This gave Jack pause. Gerry Hendley was

the epitome of even-keeled; his response was anything but.

John Clark said, "Gerry, hang on. Jack, explain, and whatever you do, don't say, 'Because Seth is my friend.' "

That's exactly what Jack was going to say, despite knowing how juvenile it sounded. "Okay, then, let's break it down," he began. "CIA and SIS are running an op out of Tehran; Seth is running the network and he's gone to ground, along with the operational funds; two men, probably Americans, kidnapped me, and last night someone blew the skull off one of those men simply because he might talk to me —"

Gerry said, "You don't know that."

"It's the answer that makes the most sense. Listen, Gerry, I get it: This isn't exactly in our brief, but it's damned close. Let me keep working it."

"Jack, you're putting me in a hell of a spot. If this goes bad, the blowback on us could be —"

"I know."

"What do you want me to say? Come home or you're fired?"

"Your call, Gerry."

"You'd take it that far?"

"I would."

There were a few moments of silence,

then Jack heard John Clark chuckle. "Hell, Gerry, friends is friends. Plus, Jack is right: Langley and our across-the-pond cousins are running an op — in Iran, of all places — and if Jack's right, the thing's in the shitter, or nearly so. Maybe we should know why that is."

"That sounds like a 'them' problem," Gerry snapped, but Jack could hear the tone of his boss's voice softening.

"Never let the plumber who broke your pipes try to fix them."

"That's downright folksy, John," replied Gerry. "Damn, Jack, when did your brass ones get so huge?"

It was a good question, one Jack had never really thought about. A lot had happened since he'd joined The Campus, most of it since he'd started working the ops side of the house: the Emir, India, China, Ukraine, North Korea . . . Somewhere in there, he supposed.

"When you weren't looking, Gerry," he replied.

"Apparently so. What do you need from us to get the ball rolling?"

Edinburgh, Scotland
"How did this happen, Yegor?" Helen said, pacing their loft apartment's kitchenette.

"How could you — you! — get it this wrong?"

Yegor sat at the dining table, his head down, fingers drumming the tabletop. Olik and Roma sat on the couch, the latter watching yet another game show.

"I'm sorry, Helen," Yegor replied. "They look alike, they stay in the same dormitory, have the same first name —"

"Not the same first name!" Helen shot back. "Amelia . . . Amy . . . Not the same!"

"Nickname, then," Yegor replied. "Their friends call them both the same nickname. I'm sorry, Helen. I assumed it was her."

As if on cue, bumping sounds and muffled screams came from the bathroom. Helen said, "Olik, go quiet her down. Gently."

Roma bolted from the couch and headed toward the bathroom. "I'll quiet her." In his right hand a folding knife appeared; he flicked open the blade.

"No! Sit down! You've done enough." The girl's jaw was badly broken and the whole left side of her face swollen and bruised. "Olik, go on."

Grumbling under his breath, Roma returned to the couch and his game show.

Olik disappeared into the bathroom and shut the door behind him. For several moments the thumping sounds grew louder;

then Helen heard Olik murmuring. The sounds lessened, then stopped altogether.

Helen walked over to the couch, her body blocking the TV. "What were you thinking?" she asked Roma.

"About what?"

"You almost took her head off."

"So? She's a whore, a disgrace to Islam —"

"Shut up about that," Helen said, then thought: *As am I, strictly speaking, but here we are.* She loved her faith and loved Allah and the prophet Muhammad, but sometimes the myriad dictates felt like a boot on her neck. Surely that wasn't what Allah intended, was it, for women to feel like this?

Eyes narrow, Roma sat up. "Woman," he growled, "you will not speak to me like this. You should know your place."

Helen stepped closer to the couch, penning him in. "And you yours," she said. "I'm in charge. You knew that when you joined. I've done this before. Have you?"

"What's to know? You grab them, you hold them, you let them go."

"You're an idiot," Helen replied. "You'll do as I tell you."

"I won't —"

Before she could stop him, Yegor was out

160

of his seat and moving toward Roma, shoulders hunched and fists raised. "You stupid bastard!"

Helen raised her arm, blocking Yegor from reaching the couch.

"Do you know what they'll do to us if we get caught?" shouted Yegor. "In their eyes, we'll be terrorists. No trial, no lawyers, just some dark hole the British have dug specially for people like us! Use your head! Helen knows what she's doing. If you want to get paid and get back home, you'll listen to her."

Yegor's words "back home" resonated with Helen. If they failed here, ending up in prison would be the better of their two fates. Her employer, wildly generous though he was, had made plain the price they'd pay for either failure or refusal to do exactly as he ordered. And even if they succeeded, what would await them back home? Almost certainly she and the others would be loose ends that needed tying up.

First, finish the job, she thought.

For several seconds Roma said nothing. Then he leaned back on the couch. "Fine. Now let me watch my program."

"First give me the knife," Helen said.

Without looking at her, Roma dug into his front pocket and handed her the blade.

"I'll want it back," he said.

Olik emerged from the bathroom and walked to the sink, where he began filling a glass with water. Helen joined him. "Well?" she asked.

"I'm going to give her some aspirin. She's in a lot of pain. And very scared. I told her we weren't going to hurt her."

Roma muttered, "Moron. We can't let her go."

"We're not doing that," said Helen.

"Then we have to go for the right girl and make sure we don't mess it up," replied Olik. "Helen, we can't deal with two of them at the same time. It's too much of a risk."

Objectively she knew he was right, but the girl in their bathtub was there because of their mistake, and until now Helen had never had a job go wrong. She'd never killed one, had never tortured one, and had never accepted a contract that had asked for either. What sympathy she felt for the girl was reinforced by . . . what? A commitment of professionalism? The thought was almost laughable, but there it was.

She wouldn't kill the girl.

Even so, Helen knew none of her personal reasons would convince her team, especially Roma, and while she didn't particularly care, this wasn't a discussion she wanted to have again.

"If we kill her, we can't keep the body here. And if we dump her we'll have a constable on every block, knocking on every door," Helen said. "As it stands, that girl is simply missing. The police will assume she's gone off with her boyfriend. It'll be a few days before they start asking real questions, then another day or two before they start hunting for her. By then, we'll be out of the city." Helen looked at each man in turn. "Agreed?"

Yegor and Olik nodded, but Roma never took his eyes off the TV screen.

"Roma, answer me."

"Where I would dump the body no one would ever find it."

He said this with a smug half-smile. Helen felt a chill on her neck. Roma meant it.

"Okay, have it your way," he said. "Let's grab the other one and get out of this place."

11

Jack's answer to Gerry's question was a simple one: All he needed for now was Gavin Biery and his expertise. Gerry agreed, but conditionally. One, Jack would keep John Clark closely updated; and two, any further requests that involved digging into CIA or SIS business must be preapproved by Hendley. Though a few people within the U.S. intelligence community — Mary Pat Foley, the current director of national intelligence, being the most prominent — knew about The Campus, Gerry tried to keep direct contact to a minimum.

Jack was relieved that one of his boss's provisos hadn't involved dispatching Clark, Ding Chavez, or Dominic Caruso to ride shotgun over him. He didn't need hand-holding, and hadn't for a long time, in fact.

"Thanks for bringing Gerry into the loop," Gavin said over the phone. "I was getting nervous about all this."

"No problem. Did he tear you a new one?" asked Jack.

"Nah. Just readjusted mine a bit. So I've got something for you. First, your old phone is clean. Whoever had it put some malware on it, this nifty little code that injected itself in the RTOS —"

"You're giving me a headache, Gavin," Jack said. "Bottom line, I can use the phone?"

"Yep. I ran a quick check on Hamrah Engineering. It's headquartered in Baku; the e-mail you gave me belongs to its Archivan branch. Hamrah is a contractor — one of hundreds — attached to the Parsabad–Artezian railway project."

"Never heard of it."

"It's a plan to run a rail line from northern Iran, through Azerbaijan, Dagestan, then into Ukraine. Moscow is pushing for a branch line in Georgia as well. The project's been going on for twenty years, but half of that time on hold. About five years ago it restarted."

"I'll bet Georgia loves that idea." Given Russian president Volodin's aggression in Ukraine and Estonia, the last thing the government of Tbilisi wanted was a direct line from Russia to Georgia's doorstep.

"Anyway, I'm still digging into Hamrah,

but on the surface it seems to be what it is."

"It isn't. Or someone there isn't." Jack told him about the exchange he'd found between Yazdani and Farid Rasulov.

"I'll be damned. You know that Gmail address you gave me, the one belonging to, what was the agent's name, Ervaz?"

"Right."

"That also links back to Hamrah. The alternate Gmail contact is listed as info@hamrahengineeringarch.com — same as this Rasulov guy's address."

Ervaz and Farid Rasulov were the same person.

"Focus on Rasulov, see what you find," said Jack. "Do the same for a guy named Suleiman Balkhi with a company called the Bayqara Group. They're out of Mashhad." Jack gave him Balkhi's cell-phone number.

"I'm on it."

Jack disconnected, then switched to his main phone and texted Seth: IT'S JACK. URGENT. REPLY.

He waited, staring at the screen, hoping for a quick reply, but none came.

He came out of the bedroom and found Ysabel on the couch, her MacBook on her lap. Before making the call to The Campus, Jack had uploaded the photos he'd taken at Yazdani.

"Nothing so far," she reported. "All of their accounting is done in-house, as is their banking. I haven't found any financial connection to Hamrah. We did, however, hear back from Ervaz."

"And?"

"He's agreed to meet us. I haven't replied yet."

"Where and when?"

"Day after tomorrow, eight p.m., at a farmhouse outside Nemin. It's about four hundred kilometers northwest of here, near the Azerbaijan border."

"How near?"

"Eight kilometers or so."

"And how far from Nemin to Archivan?"

Ysabel studied her laptop's screen for a few seconds. "Twenty-eight."

Jack did a quick conversion in his head: about five miles and twenty miles, respectively. It couldn't be a coincidence Ervaz wanted to meet so close to the border and so close to Hamrah's Archivan branch. Jack mentioned this to Ysabel.

"I agree," she replied. "Okay, so, Balaclava Man used one of Yazdani's vans to kidnap you, and Yazdani is under Farid Rasulov's thumb, a man who shares the same e-mail address as Ervaz. Right so far?"

Jack nodded. "Go on."

"So, ipso facto, Farid Rasulov, aka Ervaz, one of Seth's own agents, is behind your kidnapping."

If true, Jack thought, Seth had even bigger problems on his hands than Wellesley and Spellman hunting for him.

"And just to remind you, Jack, this is the man who wants to meet us in the dead of night in a village in the middle of nowhere," said Ysabel.

"It's all we've got. Reply to him. Tell him we'll be there. Wait . . . Add a dollar sign at the end of the message."

"Why?"

"Just do it."

Edinburgh, Scotland

Hoping to make up all the time they'd wasted building a movement pattern on the wrong Amy, Yegor had spent the previous twenty-four hours tailing the right target. Helen had sent Olik along, wary of how Roma might behave on a campus full of young women no better than whores whose fathers should have long ago killed them to restore honor to their families. Roma was not just an extremist, Helen had come to realize, but one who had little impulse control and even less fear of consequences. Sooner or later, he would get tired of taking orders from a woman. Helen only hoped this job would be over before that happened.

Yegor and Olik returned mid-afternoon, pulled through the double garage doors, and shut off the engine. Helen walked down from the apartment, shut the doors, and met Yegor as he climbed out of the driver's seat.

"She's got a late class today, a lab in the Sanderson Building that goes until eight-fifty. She takes the number twenty-two bus back to Pollock Halls. From Sanderson to the bus stand, four minutes."

Olik said, "We followed the bus twice. From Sanderson to Pollock, between ten and twelve minutes. At night, probably a bit less than that."

"You're sure about this?"

Olik nodded.

"And the route from the bus stop to Chancellors Court?"

Yegor answered, "Fifty meters on a narrow path with plenty of trees."

"Vehicle access?"

"A hundred meters directly north of Pollock, Duddingston Low Road. It heads directly east. Eight minutes after we leave, we'll be in Joppa. This will work, Helen. We should do it. Tonight."

Helen thought for a few moments, then nodded. "Olik, go upstairs and start packing our things. Tell Roma to start cleaning; I don't want a trace of us, or the girl, left behind."

"Right."

Olik trotted up the stairs. Once he was out of earshot, Helen whispered to Yegor, "Watch Roma tonight."

"You had another run-in with him?"

"Just watch him."

At eight-ten p.m. with the sun almost fully set, they left the garage, Yegor behind the wheel, Helen beside him, and Roma and Olik in the rear seats.

Before leaving the garage Olik had made sure the drug had taken effect and Amelia was sleeping soundly in the garage's bathroom, her gag and bonds secure. Once they had the real target in hand and they were clear of Edinburgh, Helen would place an anonymous call to the police and give them Amelia's location. The girl's jaw would heal, as would, eventually, the trauma of what had happened to her. It was better than Roma's solution, Helen told herself.

As she'd instructed, Yegor drove them east to Portobello Bay, then north into Joppa, then Duddingston, where they spent fifteen minutes driving the narrow and winding streets. Yegor and Olik were right, she decided. If the worst happened and they failed to get cleanly away after taking the girl, they could get lost in one of these villages, which might buy them enough time to make their way to the safe house. *Maybe,* she thought.

At eight forty-five she told Yegor to head for the campus.

With Yegor driving slightly under the speed limit, they reached the entrance to the campus, Holyrood Park Road, at 9:00. Helen instructed Yegor to pass it and pull onto the darkened shoulder and shut off the headlights. From the glove box Helen pulled a spray can of synthetic snow they'd picked up at a dollar store. She got out, walked to the front of the van, sprayed the front license plate, then the rear one, then climbed back into the van.

Yegor pulled out, then U-turned onto Holyrood Park Road.

Helen could see Chancellors Court silhouetted against the night sky out Yegor's window behind a screen of trees. Almost all the top-floor windows were lit, some of the curtains open, but most of them closed.

"Her room is on the second floor, third

from the right corner," Yegor said.

Helen saw it; the window was dark.

"She'll be on the bus by now," Olik said softly from the backseat.

"Show me where she gets off," Helen told Yegor.

He reached the intersection and turned left.

"The stand's up ahead on your side," Yegor said.

Three people, all carrying book bags or backpacks, were waiting in the dimly lit stand. *Waiting for the number twenty-two,* Helen thought. She checked her watch: 9:02.

"The path she'll take is directly across from the stand. Coming up on my side now."

"Good," Helen replied. "That will work. Turn right up here."

Yegor passed the bus stand and turned into the parking lot. Out her window, Helen saw a sign that read ROYAL COM-MONWEALTH POOL. She told Yegor to pull up to the curb, then turned around in her seat. "Olik, pick her up at the bus stand and follow her down the path. Don't crowd her. Text me when she's on her way. Understood?"

"Understood."

Olik climbed out and shut the door behind him.

"Back to Pollock," Helen told Yegor.

He made a U-turn, then turned left, heading back the way they'd come, then right onto Holyrood. Helen checked her watch again: 9:04. "Slow down, Yegor."

She didn't want them sitting in the Chancellors Court parking lot for more than three minutes. The one variable they hadn't accounted for was the routes and timing of the university's security patrols. If one happened by at the wrong time, Helen would have no choice but to call it off.

Yegor turned into the Pollock parking lot. Helen craned her neck, looking for pedestrians and parked, occupied cars; there was one of these sitting in front of the lobby to Chancellors Court, some thirty meters away, headlights off and a trickle of exhaust illuminated by the lobby's interior lights. Helen could see no one inside the car. For now. They had to assume the owner would be back soon. She felt her heart rate increase.

Her cell phone vibrated in her hand. The screen read: OFF BUS. COMING YOUR WAY.

To Yegor she asked, "Where does the path come out?"

"Ahead on the right. Almost there."

Yegor followed the road as it curved toward the tree-lined exit of the path. He pulled up to the curb and put the van in park.

Helen's phone vibrated again: *I see you. Twenty seconds.*

She turned in her seat. "Roma, get in the back and be ready to open the doors."

He didn't reply.

"Roma!"

"I heard you."

"Ready, Yegor?"

"Yes."

Helen glanced out her side window and saw a figure emerging from the path; ten feet behind her, the silhouette of Olik. Helen waited until Amy was twenty feet from the van, then opened her door and climbed out.

"Excuse me, miss, I'm looking for Chancellors Court."

Amy, her arms full of books clutched to her chest, stopped.

This was the right girl, Helen realized with relief.

"Oh, you've found it," Amy said.

"Where? Can you show me?"

Amy walked to the rear of the van and stopped at the bumper. Helen followed. Amy pointed toward Chancellors' lighted entrance. "Right there —"

Yegor came around the other side of the van and strode toward Amy, hood in hand.

"Hey, what are you —"

Amy dropped her books and started fumbling in her purse.

Helen pushed her forward as Yegor stuffed a balled-up sock into her mouth and slipped the hood over her head. Amy started wriggling. Helen knocked on the van's rear doors. They swung open; crouched inside, Roma reached for Amy, who began kicking and screaming through the gag. Olik appeared beside Helen and together the four of them began wrestling the girl into the van. She was surprisingly strong. Helen felt one of Amy's arms break free, then felt a blow to the side of her head. "Get her in, get her in," Helen called.

"Hey, stop!" A voice shouted. "Amy!"

Helen heard footsteps pounding on the pavement behind Yegor, and over his shoulder she saw a man charging toward them. "Behind you, Yegor!" Helen rasped.

He turned, but not quickly enough. The man, now running at full speed, tackled Yegor and together they fell in a heap on the pavement.

"Olik, help him," Helen said, as she bodily shoved Amy into the van. Roma grabbed her by the neck and dragged her the rest of the way. "Bitch!" he rasped.

"Don't hurt her," Helen told him.

Behind her, Helen heard a thump, then a grunt, then another thump. She turned. Yegor was pinned beneath the inert figure of the man.

Helen made a split-second decision: "Take him, put him inside."

Olik rolled the man off Yegor and together the three of them lifted him up, manhandled him over the bumper, and rolled him inside. Helen slammed the doors shut.

"Get in," Helen told Olik and Yegor.

She took a moment to look around. She saw no one, but several previously dark windows above the Chancellors Court lobby were lit; in one of them, a curtain slid open.

Helen walked to the passenger door and climbed in.

"Drive."

12

TEHRAN

Jack awoke to his sat phone buzzing on the night table beside the bed. He rolled over and checked the screen: Raymond Wellesley.

"Good morning, Raymond."

"My apologies for waking you so early, Jack."

"No problem. What can I do for you? I haven't heard anything from Seth."

"Nor us, sadly. Might you have time to meet this morning? Come by the apartment and I'll have a hearty English breakfast for you."

Wellesley was back to jovial British bobby. Did Wellesley's use of "I'll" mean Spellman wouldn't be joining them? He hadn't been at their last meeting, either. Did that mean something?

Jack had no intention of stepping onto Wellesley and Spellman's turf. "I'm pressed for time today. Why don't we meet at my hotel, around ten, in the lobby." Though

Jack hadn't been back to the Parsian since the day of his kidnapping, he hoped they didn't know that.

"Very good," said Wellesley. "See you then."

Despite her protests, Jack managed to persuade Ysabel to stay at the apartment and do some research. Ervaz had chosen the ground for their meeting, Nemin, so Jack wanted to know as much about the place as possible. Plus, he didn't want to run the risk of having Wellesley or his people spot Ysabel.

Jack's cab dropped him at the Parsian's lobby at nine-thirty. He went to the front desk, asked if he had either any messages or visitors. He'd had neither. As it had the first time he'd seen it, Jack found the hotel's lobby mildly astonishing, a gallery of khaki and ecru, from the tiled floors, to the row of columns running down the center, to the circular, lighted tray ceilings above. Seating areas with burgundy and brown wingback chairs bracketed by potted palms were strategically placed throughout the space.

Jack took the elevator up to his room, slid the key card, and stood at the threshold. *You're getting paranoid, Jack.* Then again, after the last few days, the feeling was forgivable. He walked in, closed the door behind him. Aside from signs the maid had come in to clean, nothing appeared disturbed. His briefcase, which contained Tehran sightseeing brochures, nonconfidential Hendley documents, and Jack's passport, looked untouched as well.

Jack pocketed his passport, but left the briefcase, then went back down to the lobby. He took a chair in a seating area facing the door. Wellesley arrived in a black Khodro Samand, Tehran's version of a hired Lincoln Town Car, got out, and walked into the lobby.

"Jack, there you are," Wellesley said, walking over, his hand extended.

Jack shook it. "Thanks for meeting me here. No Matt?"

"He's otherwise engaged."

Jack led Wellesley to the Parseh, the hotel's twenty-four-hour café. The hostess gave them a booth in the back. A waitress promptly brought a carafe of coffee for Jack and a pot of tea for Wellesley, then took their orders. When she left, Jack said, "What can I do for you, Raymond?"

"You're not ones for small talk, you Americans."

"Sorry. I've got a busy day in front of me."

"Very well. I'll come to the point. A man

was murdered outside Seth Gregory's condominium the night before last."

The statement took Jack by surprise; without missing a beat, he let the emotion show on his face, then replied, "Tell me it wasn't Seth."

"Jack, please, let's not do this. You know as well as I do it wasn't Seth. You were there. You saw the man die. Had I not put one of my men there, you would be in the city morgue alongside him. Tell me why you went to the park."

"I got a text message from Seth saying he wanted to meet me. When I got there, it was this other man. He told me he was going to take me to Seth. We started across the street, then . . . You know the rest. Who was he?"

Wellesley shrugged, then asked, "Tell me this: Did he have an American accent?"

"Yes. Who sent him?" Jack asked.

"It's very complicated."

"Spellman?"

"Jack, please, I can't answer that question."

"Then tell me how you knew to send someone to Pardis," said Jack.

"You're in over your head, Jack. I told you once and now I'm telling you again: Leave it be. Go home."

"You know I can't do that. Tell me how you knew to send someone to Pardis," he repeated.

"I had you followed."

He said, "You had me followed, or you and Spellman had me followed?"

Wellesley hesitated, then said, "The former. As I said, it's very —"

"Complicated. I know."

"I can't make you stay out of this, Jack, and I can't force you to go home. Instead, do me a favor, if you would: Keep me informed. Night before last didn't have to happen. You could have easily died on that street. If that had happened your father would have been looking for someone's head on a pike — mine, specifically — and he'd damn well get it."

"You're telling me to leave it to the professionals?"

"That's my strong recommendation."

When Jack walked into Ysabel's apartment, she called from the seating area, "The police called. They found my Range Rover. You didn't tell me you were going to torch it, Jack."

"Sorry."

She shrugged. "Insurance will cover it."

Jack sat down on the couch and recounted

for her the meeting with Wellesley. She said, "How much of that do you believe? Could they have been following us?"

"I don't think so, but it's possible. But if they've known all along what we've been up to, why didn't they roll us up?"

"Either way, I think we can safely assume one or the other lured you to the condo."

"Or both. Spellman and Wellesley could still be working together, and Wellesley's just playing mind games. Hell, for all we know, Balaclava's murder could have been designed to scare us off."

"It's a very cold thing to kill one of your own men."

"Or an ally's man," Jack added. "I think last night was proof of that."

Ysabel let out an exasperated sigh, leaned her head back, and wriggled her fingers through her hair. "This is enough to give me a migraine."

"Me, too. Let's break it down. Come on."

They walked to the dining room table and sat down.

Jack said, "Okay, this is what we know, or can reasonably assume."

He started writing on the notepad:

— Seth missing.
— Wellesley/Spellman claim Seth's CIA

and he's stolen operational funds and gone to ground.

— Seth kept bolt-hole apartment unknown to Wellesley/Spellman.

— Seth kept safe in bolt-hole apartment.

— Balaclava/Weaver kidnappers. Have American accents.

— Balaclava/Weaver tried to break into Seth's safe.

— Contents of safe important to Seth. Document in Cyrillic.

— Balaclava and Weaver used Yazdani van for kidnapping.

— Yazdani linked to Hamrah Engineering.

— Seth's agent, Ervaz, is Farid Rasulov, Archivan branch, Hamrah Engineering.

— Balaclava/Weaver took Jack's phone. Used it to pose as Seth and lure Jack to Pardis Condos.

— Balaclava killed outside Pardis condo. Attempt on Jack's life.

— Wellesley implied he's Jack's guardian angel, implied Spellman untrustworthy.

— Ervaz/Rasulov behind Jack's kidnapping.

Jack stopped writing and studied the points. He frowned and shook his head.

"What?" Ysabel asked.

"I don't know. I'm missing something. I

can't put my finger on it."

"It will come to you. But Jack, let's make sure we don't gloss over the last one. Tomorrow night, the man we're meeting in the middle of nowhere is behind your kidnapping."

Hoping Wellesley would assume he was neither stupid enough nor bold enough to go back to the Pardis condo, Jack did just that. After walking a surveillance circuit through Mellat Park and then the side streets bordering the condo, he walked into the lobby, used the key Ysabel had given him to open the inner door, then took the elevator up to Seth's floor, where he got off and walked down the hall. He felt the reassuring heft of the nine-millimeter in his jacket pocket. So far, his experiences at Seth's two residences had been bad, one ambush/kidnapping and one sniper attack. He hoped the third time would be the charm.

He put on his gloves, then slid the key into the lock, pushed open the door, and stepped inside. He drew the nine-millimeter, then went from room to room, clearing each in turn, before returning to the front room.

This apartment was the exact opposite of Seth's bolt-hole, lavishly furnished with thick carpet, leather couches and chairs, Persian tapestries, and a gourmet kitchen in stainless steel.

Jack caught a whiff of something in the air. *Copper,* he thought. He knew the odor. He felt a hollowness fill his belly. *God, no,* he thought. *Bathroom tubs,* he thought. He hadn't checked the —

He strode down the hall to the guest bathroom, then jerked back the shower curtain. The tub was empty. He headed for Seth's master-suite tub and swept open its curtain, the rings rattling on the bar above.

He found himself staring into a pair of milky eyes.

Floating in the half-full bathtub was the body of David Weaver. There was a ragged, golfball-sized hole three inches above his left eyebrow. Someone had put a bullet in the back of his head.

Who? The body showed little sign of decay; Jack guessed he'd died around the same time as Balaclava. The two men that had kidnapped him from Seth's bolt-hole were now dead. Wellesley had taken credit for killing the sniper. Did he mean Weaver?

There was virtually no blood in the tub's water, and Jack saw no signs of blood anywhere else in the apartment, and with a head wound like Weaver's, the place would've been a slaughterhouse. That left one possibility.

Jack left the apartment, walked the four flights to the top floor, and wandered around for a few minutes before finding the roof's access door. Jack opened it and stepped outside.

With his feet crunching on the gravel, he crossed the roof to the southwest corner and looked over the edge. He had a direct line of sight around the edge of the nearest tree, then down onto Rajaei Boulevard, where Balaclava had gone down. Jack raised his arms to simulate holding a rifle, his far index finger as the barrel. He nodded. This was the spot.

Jack stepped directly backward to maintain the sight line, and began scanning the roof. He would find no shell casings, he knew, but if this was where Weaver had died, there might be something. Using the toe of his boot, he began raking the gravel aside.

There.

He stopped and knelt, shoveling gravel with his hands until he'd uncovered a circle three feet in diameter. A patch of the exposed tarpaper was discolored a pale yellow. Jack leaned over and sniffed. He wrinkled his nose. Bleach. In the middle of the patch was a bullet hole. Jack took the pen from his pocket and poked it into the hole but felt nothing.

He put it together in his head: Seconds after Weaver shoots Balaclava, someone kills Weaver himself, then collects the rifle, the shell casings, the spent round embedded in the tarpaper, and Weaver's corpse, then goes down to Seth's apartment, puts the body in the tub, then returns to the roof to dump bleach on the blood pool — all while the police sirens are converging on the area. Had this man sat inside Seth's condo while the police did their door-to-door, or had he calmly left, rifle hidden under his coat?

Whatever the answer, Jack now knew he was dealing with one ice-cold, and well-trained, operator.

Edinburgh, Scotland

Their safe house, a rental cottage on Pettycur Bay, was less than ideal, with a cottage close on their left, but it did have three things Helen had demanded for the operation: a basement, a garage for their van, and a landlord who took cash and considered a handshake better than a contract. Helen had told the old man she would be attending the university next year for her postgraduate degree in art history and that she wanted to spend the summer getting to know the area along with three of her fellow students. The landlord had simply nodded, smiled, and taken the cash.

With any luck, Helen planned to be gone before the next month's rent was due.

"He's a bull," Yegor said, emerging into the kitchen from the basement stairs. Just before the door swung shut behind him, Helen could hear muffled, angry cries from below. "If he keeps this up we'll need chains. You would think he'd be exhausted by now. I know I am."

"Leave him. No one can hear him."

Almost seven hours had passed since they'd trundled the boy and Amy into the van.

After leaving the campus, Yegor had driven the route as he'd practiced several times before, heading directly north to Leith, where he pulled over to wipe the synthetic snow from the license plates before turning onto the coast road. Thirty minutes later they crossed Forth Road Bridge and were headed up the coast, rapidly putting miles between them and Edinburgh.

In the backseat, Olik had sat with headphones pressed to his ears, listening for signs of alarm from either the university security force or the local police. All was quiet. That wouldn't last, Helen knew. Whoever had slid open that curtain back at Chancellors Court had seen something. Whether it had been alarming enough to call the authorities, only time would tell.

Yegor limped to the sink and splashed some water over his face. He gingerly touched the top of his left ear and winced. In going to the ground with "the bull," Yegor's ear had been smashed against the pavement, and the left side of his rib cage was on fire, from either a break or a deep bruise.

"I'll see to those in a bit," Helen said. "Sit, I'm making eggs."

Olik came down the stairs and joined Yegor at the table. In the front room Helen could hear the strains of giggling and vaudevillian music. Roma had found a cartoon network. The man was worrying Helen, more so than before. He was no longer sullen, but simply withdrawn, speaking only when spoken to, and then only in curt replies. This hadn't gone unnoticed by Yegor and Olik, Helen was sure.

"How's the girl?" Helen asked Olik.

"Sleeping. I gave her something."

"I want you to check on her every fifteen minutes. The same with the boy, Yegor."

Yegor nodded.

Olik asked, "What's our next step?"

Helen checked her watch. It was almost four a.m. here, so almost seven in Kizlyar. "I'll make the call in four hours."

13

IRAN

Providing they didn't get stuck in one of Tehran's often-unpredictable rush-hour jams on their way out of the city, Ysabel told him, the four-hundred-mile journey to Nemin would take about five hours. Though the highway speed limits outside the capital were only 110 kph, they were only lightly patrolled by police.

At six p.m. they pulled off the highway and into a gas station on the southern edge of Ardabil, Iran's northernmost metropolis and, according to Ysabel, the home of fine silks, carpets, and the best pizza in Iran.

Jack got out and started pumping gas while Ysabel went inside to prepay and get them something to drink. When she emerged Jack nodded at the gas pump's display. "Translate that for me."

"Nine thousand rial per liter. About a dollar twenty a gallon."

"Wow. Must be nice."

She laughed and handed him a bottle of water. "Jack, you do know where you are, right? We've got a few gallons of oil laying around."

"Funny," he replied, then thought.

He topped off the tank, then replaced the pump nozzle. As he climbed into the Mercedes's passenger seat, his phone rang. It was Gavin.

"What's up?" Jack said.

"Suleiman Balkhi and the Bayqara Group."

"Tell me."

"The group's real, but Balkhi's not — at least, he's not employed there. I triple-checked it. The man might exist, but he's not who he claims to be."

"What about his cell-phone number?" asked Jack.

"It's valid. I've asked Mr. Clark to look into it. Could be Balkhi's with VAJA," Gavin said, referring to Iran's primary intelligence agency.

"My thought exactly."

"One other thing: Gerry looked into Wellesley and Spellman. They're legit. Wellesley's with SIS's Maghreb and Gulf States Division. Spellman is NCS."

The CIA's National Clandestine Service was the new name for the Directorate of

Operations. "Which department?" asked Jack.

"Apparently, he's 'without portfolio,' as the Brits say. Essentially, Spellman's a free safety."

"Okay, keep me posted. Tell Gerry we're headed to a town called Nemin to meet Seth's agent —"

Ysabel broke in, whispering, "Farid Rasulov."

"If you don't hear from me or Ysabel by ten o'clock our time, you can assume things went bad."

Jack disconnected. He asked Ysabel, "How long until we're there?"

"Thirty kilometers, but from here the roads get worse. We're heading into the Elburz Mountains. An hour, give or take."

By nightfall they'd reached Nemin, a town of about ten thousand sitting on a mostly barren plain surrounded by brown hills. At this distance, perhaps a few miles away, Jack could see the slopes and peaks of the Elburz Mountains against the night sky.

Ysabel followed the main road into the city proper. Jack found the architecture surprisingly utilitarian. If not for the occasional Islamic-style façade on some of the shops, he could imagine himself in any small U.S. town.

"I'm nervous, Jack," Ysabel said softly.

"Understandable."

"Let's go back to Ardabil and have pizza."

"You can drop me off near the farmhouse. I'll come find you after it's over."

Ysabel glanced sideways at him, her face illuminated by the dashboard lights. "How could you ask me that?"

"I thought you were serious."

"I wasn't. I was sharing. Now shut up. Check my gun, will you? It's in my purse."

Jack reached behind the seat, pulled out the revolver, and flipped open the cylinder. "You're good," he said, then returned the gun to her purse.

"It won't be enough, that one and yours, if things go . . . Well, you know what I mean."

Jack did, and the answer was no, her revolver and his nine-millimeter probably wouldn't be enough to protect them if they were walking into a trap. While Ysabel's pizza idea did have its appeal, if there was any hope of reaching Seth, it lay at this farmhouse.

"We'll be fine," he said.

When they reached the city center, the Mercedes's navigation system told them to turn right onto Imam Khomeini, which took

194

them southeast, past a sports stadium, then onto an unlit gravel road bordered by drainage ditches half full with standing water. Ysabel drove for another half-mile, then pulled onto the shoulder and doused her headlights. She studied the car's navigation screen for a moment, then tapped a spot with her index finger.

"It's up ahead on the right side. You see the light pole?"

"I see it."

"That's the driveway."

Jack checked his watch. It was 7:20.

He took the binoculars out of the center console, lifted them to his eyes, and panned down the driveway to a clearing, where he saw a ramshackle two-story farmhouse with peeling white paint. Jack zoomed in on it. The windows were partially boarded up, but not the front door. Like most of the buildings in Nemin, the house had a distinctly Midwestern feel to it. Diagonally across from the house stood a barn, and beside it a small shed, before which sat a pair of rusting steel drums.

"I don't see any cars," Jack murmured.

He handed the binoculars to Ysabel. She scanned the area, then said, "I don't see any, either, but that barn is big enough."

A good point, Jack thought. If Ervaz had in

fact arrived early, and not alone, and there were cars inside that barn, then there was little doubt they were walking into an ambush. The problem was, the only way to know for sure was to walk into it.

Jack leaned closer to the car's nav screen and used his index finger to scroll the picture. After a few moments he found what he was looking for. He turned to Ysabel.

"Is your car all-wheel drive?"

Following the waypoint Jack set in the Car's nav system, Ysabel drove past the farmhouse, shut off her headlights, then turned right onto a narrow dirt track shielded from the farmhouse by a screen of trees and overgrown brush. With her eyes scanning the road ahead, Ysabel slowed beside a sloping gap in the shoulder, did a K-turn, and backed onto the dual-rut tractor path. The Mercedes's ground clearance, significantly less than any tractor, scraped on the raised center dirt strip as she reversed toward the tree line. As Jack had instructed, she kept her foot off the pedal, using the hand brake instead to slow the car to a stop.

She shut off the engine.

"Good enough?" she asked.

"Perfect."

"Do you think anyone saw us?"

"If they're in there waiting, probably." That was fine with Jack. If noticed, their stealthy approach to the farmhouse might force the occupants into action. Maybe. This was the part Jack hated most about these situations — the uncertainty. Eventually you had to make a move, and often blindly or nearly so. *Defense rarely wins the fight,* he reminded himself.

He asked Ysabel, "Should I bother trying to talk you into staying here?"

"I wouldn't." She said it with a smile, but there was a set to her jaw that told him she was serious. She didn't like being coddled, and he'd been doing some of that.

"Okay, let's go. If you hear even one gunshot, go back to the car. I'll be right behind you."

"Promise?"

"Promise," Jack replied with his own smile. "Unless I'm shot, that is."

They got out, walked around the edge of the tree line, then headed for the farmhouse's rear wall, some hundred feet away. The rutted, cold soil crumbled beneath their feet, keeping them off balance. With the nine-millimeter carried in the ready-low position, Jack scanned the house's windows and corners, watching for the slightest movement.

"Still with me?" Jack whispered.

"Yes."

They kept moving and were soon standing with their backs pressed against the farmhouse's wall. The lowermost window was a foot above Jack's head. He got Ysabel's attention, pointed at his eye, then at hers, then at the corner of the house to their right. She nodded her understanding. Jack sidestepped down the wall, his eyes moving from the windows above them to the corner he was approaching. When he reached it, he stopped. Behind him, Ysabel gave him another nod and a half-smile. Jack leaned closer to her and whispered, "We're going for the barn. We'll be exposed between it and the house. I'll watch the barn, you watch the house."

"Got it."

"If you see anyone in the windows or anyone comes out the front door, fire a round in that direction, then head back to the car."

"Okay."

Jack led the way down the side wall, peeked around the next corner, saw nothing moving on the front porch, then kept going, turning in circles and scanning for the farmhouse's windows as he stepped into the open. When he saw Ysabel had passed the porch and had eyes on the front of the house, Jack turned his full attention to the barn. Ysabel's gun handling wasn't perfect, but it was solid enough.

Through the barn door's slatting he saw a pair of headlights glow to life, casting striped shadows on the ground. Jack never stopped moving but adjusted his course and headed for the steel drums in front of the shed, where he knelt down, the nine-millimeter trained on the barn doors. He glanced over his shoulder to make sure Ysabel had done the same.

She whispered, "Jack . . . what —"

"Eyes on the house," he whispered, then shouted, "You in the barn! Can you hear me?"

"We hear you," came the Russian-accented reply. "Are you Seth's friend, the one I have been talking to?"

"First things first: How many are you?"

"Three."

"Come out, hands up. Stay in the headlights."

"Yes, yes, we're coming." The man's voice was steady, without a trace of panic. "I'm opening the doors."

Jack heard the squeaking of hinges and the double doors swung open, their bottoms scraping the ground. Dust billowed in the glare of the headlights. Slowly, three figures emerged from the barn. As instructed, their hands were up.

"You on the left," Jack called. "Step into the light."

When the group was ten feet away, Jack ordered them to stop and turn around to face the headlights.

"Which one of you is Ervaz?" asked Jack.

The man closest to him said, "I am."

"Why the dramatic entrance?"

"We wanted to let you know we were here. I thought it better than simply coming out of the doors. I did not mean to scare you."

You failed, Jack thought. He took a deep breath, willing his heart to slow. "How did I end our last e-mail exchange?"

"I don't understand."

"At the end of my e-mail, what did I type?"

"Uhm . . . may I check my phone? It is in my left coat pocket."

"Slowly."

The man reached into the pocket and withdrew a phone. He looked at the screen for a few moments, then said, "A dollar sign."

"Good answer." This was Ervaz.

Behind him, Ysabel whispered, "Very smart of you."

"Thanks. I'm checking the barn. If any of them move, shoot."

Slowly Jack rose from behind the barrels, stepped around them.

"I'm checking the barn," he told Ervaz. "Stay put."

"You still do not trust me?"

"No."

Staying clear of the headlights, Jack walked past the men until he reached the corner of the right-hand door, then peeked around the edge. There was no one. He walked through the barn, cleared it, then reached through the car's window and shut off the headlights.

He rejoined Ysabel at the barrels. He lowered the nine-millimeter to his side.

"Satisfied?" said Ervaz. He was short and stocky, with a goatee.

"We'll see," said Jack. "Where is Seth?"

"I was hoping you could tell me. I haven't heard from him for over a week. That is not like him."

In his pants pocket, Jack's phone vibrated. He pulled it out and checked the screen. It was a text from Seth: WHERE ARE YOU?

Ervaz asked, "Is that him?"

Jack ignored him and typed, TELL ME HOW YOU'RE DOING, SETH. In reply, a trio of question marks appeared on the screen.

Jack repeated his last message, this time in all caps.

Another few seconds passed, then: SHARP STICK, JACK.

Jack smiled. He was texting with Seth, the real one. OUTSIDE NEMIN, he replied. MEETING ERVAZ.

Seth's response was immediate: RUN.

14

Jack felt his gorge rise into his throat. He suppressed it. "No, it's not him," he told Ervaz.

"I don't believe you."

Behind Ervaz, one of the men took a half-step to the right. He was clearing himself for a clean shot-line.

Jack half raised the nine-millimeter in his direction. "Don't."

Ervaz said, "Who are you? What's your name?"

Jack didn't reply.

"Tell me where Seth is."

The man behind Ervaz took another sidestep.

"One more step and I'll drop you!" Jack barked.

Ervaz repeated calmly, "Where is Seth?"

Jack heard the roar of a car engine somewhere to his right. He resisted the impulse to look and kept his focus on Ervaz and his men. To Ysabel, he asked, "Where is it?"

"Coming down the driveway. Fast, one SUV, headlights off. What should we do?"

Jack's phone buzzed again. He glanced at the screen: run!

In unison the men behind Ervaz reached into their coats.

Jack shouted, "Ysabel, get to the house!"

Jack turned slightly right, double-tapped the man behind Ervaz, then adjusted aim, fired a third round at the fleeing Ervaz, then backstepped behind the barrels and crouched. A trio of bullets slammed into the steel lip. Jack felt a sting in his eye. To his right, a pair of headlights came on, pinning him. He glanced that way, saw the SUV's grille twenty feet away and closing fast.

Jack turned on his heel, coiled his legs under him, and sprinted toward the farmhouse. Ysabel was almost through the door. He heard a crash of metal on metal, then a hollow gong as the steel drums scattered. Then three gunshots, followed by two more. Jack reached the door, ducked through, and turned right and pressed himself against the inside wall. He peeked around the jamb.

The SUV had come to a stop, half hidden

in a cloud of dust. From the barn came flashes of orange. Jack saw the driver's door open; then, a moment later, came the chattering of an assault rifle. The gun's muzzle flare lit up the front of the SUV. From the passenger side, another rifle opened up, the bullets peppering the front of the barn.

The rifles went silent. A voice shouted, "I've got two down, two down!"

"Check them!" came the reply.

From the SUV's passenger side, a figure crossed in front of the headlights and disappeared into the barn. After a moment came a lone gunshot, then a second one. The man emerged from the barn.

"They're done," he called.

"Strip them," the man at the driver's door replied, then shouted, "Jack! You there?"

It was Seth.

"I'm here!" he called back, then whispered to Ysabel, "Stay put. Same deal: If there's shooting, run for the car."

"But Jack, that's him. I recognize the voice."

"Just do what I say. I'm coming out, Seth."

With the nine-millimeter hanging at his side, Jack stepped out the front door.

Seth called, "Nice to see you alive, Jack." He turned around, opened the SUV's rear door, and dropped the assault rifle inside.

Jack stuffed the nine-millimeter into his jacket pocket and walked over.

Seth walked up, embraced him briefly, then said, "Sorry about all that. Wow, what a rush, huh?"

"Christ, man, you almost ran me over."

"Better than a sharp SUV in the eye, though."

Despite himself, Jack laughed.

"Hey, you look like hell; looks like you've already been run over once. And your eyebrow's bleeding."

Jack touched the spot with his index finger and felt something hard just beneath the skin. "Splinter from one of the barrels, I think. By the way, Ysabel's here."

"Thank God. I hoped you'd find her, but I wasn't sure. Listen, we gotta get out of here. The gendarmerie out here is on the ball."

Seth's partner came out of the barn and walked over, his assault rifle cradled diagonally across his body.

Seth said, "Jack, I think you've met Matt Spellman."

"Good to see you again, Jack."

15

With Jack and Ysabel following in her Mercedes, Seth led them northeast away from Nemin and higher into the Elburz Mountains until they could see snowcapped peaks appear in the distance.

"Where is he going?" Ysabel said. "We're almost to the Azerbaijan border."

"No idea," Jack replied, but decided if Seth didn't stop before the border, they would. It was time for some answers.

"Jack, is that really Spellman?"

"That's him."

"Then why are we following him? He sent Balaclava and Weaver to snatch you in a van that belongs to Ervaz, tried to kill you at Pardis, then kills Ervaz back at the farm. Are you sure we should be trusting him?"

"No, I'm not, but Seth seems to."

"I'm not sure that means anything anymore," Ysabel whispered under her breath. "I really don't know how you do what you do. I'm starting to think no one is trustworthy."

Welcome to the rabbit hole, Jack thought.

After another ten minutes of driving, Seth's SUV pulled off the road and into what Jack guessed was a scenic overlook. Out his window he could see a steep-sided valley cloaked in fog. Seth and Spellman climbed out; Jack and Ysabel did the same, and the group met at the SUV's hood.

Spellman had left his assault rifle in the vehicle, Jack saw.

"You look great, Ysabel," Seth said, coming around to give her a hug. She backed away from him. He held up his hands, said, "Okay, okay, I understand," then returned to where he was standing.

Seth said, "Jack, you're going to want some answers, I'm guessing."

"Damned right."

Jack pulled the nine-millimeter from his pocket and laid it on the SUV's hood with a dull thunk. He kept his hand on it.

"Easy, Jack. What's —"

"Fuck easy. Spellman, you'd better start talking."

"What's going on, Jack?" said Seth.

"It's okay," Spellman replied. "I can put your mind at ease, Jack."

"Make it good."

"Three nights ago at Pardis Condos," Spellman began, "there were three shots fired. One took off that man's head —"

"Balaclava," Ysabel interrupted.

"His real name was Scott Hilby, he's ex–Royal Marines. After he went down, there were two more shots, one into the rear corner post of the Range Rover. The third one I didn't see. The fourth shot never came. You were sprawled face-first on the sidewalk. You and Ysabel headed north on Rajaei Boulevard —"

Ysabel broke in: "How do you know my name? Seth, you gave him my —"

"After that, I lost you."

"That means nothing except one of your people was there," said Jack. "Along with Balaclava and the sniper."

"I assume you went into Seth's condo?"

Jack nodded.

"There was a man in the bathtub with a hole in his forehead."

"David Weaver," Jack replied.

"Not his real name, I'm sure," Spellman replied. "I don't know what it is. His Albany address is fake."

"Tell me what I found on the roof," Jack pushed.

Spellman smiled at this. "You're sharper than I gave you credit for, Jack. Southeast corner of the roof, about eighteen inches back from the edge, I dumped a gallon of bleach, then covered the blood pool with gravel. There was a hole in the tarpaper, but no bullet."

"Wait a second. You said you dumped it? That was you up there?"

"I've had to wear a few different hats since this thing started."

Matt Spellman was his ice-cold guardian angel. Or not.

"Keep going."

"The weapon Weaver used was a L115A3 Lapua — standard issue for British Army snipers, sans markings. It's in the back of our car, if you want to see it. Satisfied?"

"Mostly."

Ysabel said, "What exactly is 'this thing' you mentioned, Mr. Spellman?"

"Matt. We'll get to that."

Jack asked Seth, "Why did you kill Ervaz?"

"First of all, that wasn't Ervaz. Right now, I just want to make sure we're all friends again."

"That's a bit of a stretch," replied Ysabel. "Do you have any idea what you've put us through? Any idea at all?"

"No, I don't. You can tell me all about it later. We need to get across the border. I've got somewhere safe we can go."

"I didn't bring my passport," Ysabel said sarcastically.

"You won't need it," Spellman replied.

"What's across the border?" Jack asked.

"Someone I want you to meet," said Seth.

Their crossing into Azerbaijan was surprisingly uneventful, a mere twenty-minute drive through a winding mountain pass, then down into a valley. No spotlit checkpoints, no guards, not even a sign to let Jack know they'd left Iran. He kept his eye on Ysabel's dashboard compass, but after the tenth switchback curve Jack gave up.

Finally Seth pulled the SUV onto a short dirt road that opened into a clearing with three rust-streaked Quonset huts and a wooden tower, atop which sat a roofed platform. This place was a forestry service camp, he guessed. Either that or an old border outpost.

He and Ysabel climbed out. The air was much colder; their breath steamed around them. They followed Seth and Spellman into the smallest of the three huts. The interior was lit by a pair of kerosene lanterns hanging from a rafter above a workbench with a scarred and stained top.

The group gathered around it.

Ysabel said, "Seth, do you have a pair of tweezers, a pocket knife? And some alcohol?"

"Yeah, hang on." He walked to a nearby cabinet.

"Jack, sit down on that stool. Don't argue."

Jack did as instructed. Seth returned with a pair of fine needle-nose pliers and a half-pint bottle of vodka. With her index finger under Jack's chin, she turned his face toward the glow of the lantern, dipped the tip of the pliers into the bottle, then into the wound in his eyebrow, and plucked out the splinter. Jack winced.

"Done," she said, then handed Jack the vodka bottle. "Clean it."

She set the pliers aside and turned to face Seth, her hands on her hips. "How did we get across so easily? I thought the border was better guarded than that, and I live here."

"What's with the attitude, Ysabel?" Seth replied. "Why're you mad at me?"

"Because you're an asshole, that's why."

"What?"

Spellman interrupted and answered her question. "Iran's got almost thirty-five hundred miles of border, a good chunk of it with Iraq, Afghanistan, and Turkey. Your new president's got bigger worries than a border with a mostly friendly neighbor."

Jack said, "You said you wanted me to meet someone, Seth. Where are they?"

"He's late. Crossing borders is a little harder for him."

"Tell us what this is all about."

"Better to let our guest get here first," Spellman replied, "but I'll tell you this, Raymond Wellesley ain't a friend of ours."

"Us or America's?"

"Both. Jack, you two had breakfast yesterday. What did he tell you? That one of his men saved you at Pardis?"

"Yeah."

"Think it through. Did he give you any details that he couldn't have gotten from the news?"

"No, he didn't." Jack shook his head, frustrated. Wellesley hadn't offered any details because the two men who could've provided them were dead. "I should have caught that."

"Nah, listen, Wellesley's a master at this and he's been doing it for thirty years. Let me take a wild guess, Jack: He threw me under the bus?"

"Subtly. Weaver's address, the American accents . . ."

Seth said, "And after you almost get killed

Wellesley shows up, the sympathetic White Knight, and hands you a common enemy."

Unbidden, a sentence popped into Jack's head: "You haven't the stomach for it." That was what Scott Hilby had said to Jack moments before the kill shot had come. Not "You haven't got the stomach for it." The phrasing was British. There was no doubt now: Hilby and Weaver belonged to Wellesley.

Jack asked them both, "Did you know they snatched me up?"

"When?" asked Spellman.

"The night after the three of us met. They were at Niavaran Park, trying to get in your safe."

"Shit," Seth muttered. "Did they get in?"

"No."

"Niavaran Park?" Spellman repeated. "Seth, what's he talking about?"

"I have a place you and Wellesley didn't know about."

"Clearly, Wellesley knew about it," Jack replied.

"Do you know where they were taking you?" asked Spellman.

Ysabel answered, "North of the city, up the Shomal Freeway. They were headed east on a dirt road outside Keshar-e Sofla when I caught up with them. Does that matter?"

"It might. Let me look into it."

Jack said, "Tell me about Ervaz."

Seth hesitated, then said, "I don't know who that was back there, but it wasn't Ervaz. Probably one of his heavies. Ervaz is actually a guy named Farid Rasulov —"

"We know that. Hamrah Engineering."

"He's also two other people: Suleiman Balkhi and —"

Ysabel said, "The Bayqara Group. We know that's fake."

"Well, he's none of the above. His real name is Oleg Pechkin. He's SVR," Seth said, referring to Russia's foreign intelligence service.

Jack took a few moments to digest this. The revelation made things both easier and more treacherous. They'd just consolidated four names into one, but that name had also put the Russians firmly on the playing field.

Once again Jack found himself assembling puzzle pieces in his head: Pechkin ordered Yazdani's van be used by a pair of kidnappers supplied by Wellesley, who was working hand-in-glove with Pechkin.

"I've been playing cat-and-mouse with Pechkin for almost a year," Seth said.

"Who's the cat and who's the mouse?"

Seth shrugged. "It's only been in the last

few weeks I discovered he was also Ervaz, and that he was connected to Hamrah."

"And to Raymond Wellesley," Spellman added.

"What's so special about Hamrah, anyway?" asked Ysabel.

"Easy access," Seth replied. "Hamrah does all the Parsabad–Artezian railway project surveys, from Parsabad in the south, all the way north past Makhachkala. With my degree, getting hired was a snap. I can cross the borders like I'm crossing the street."

Jack said, "Get to the point, Seth. What's it about?"

"Self-determination."

From outside came the crunching of tires on the dirt road. Spellman trotted to the hut's partially open door and peeked out. "It's them," he called over his shoulder. "Medzhid and two bodyguards."

Instinctively, Jack put his hand in his pocket and gripped the butt of the nine-millimeter, then changed his mind and pulled his hand back out. Seth saw this.

"You've got to trust somebody sometime, Jack."

"I do," Jack replied, and tilted his head toward Ysabel.

"I'm not setting you up, Jack. Not on my life."

"You've already done that," Ysabel shot back. "Three times."

"Necessities of war."

Before Jack could respond, the hut's door swung open and three men strode inside. Spellman led them to the workbench. As the lead man stepped into the lantern's light, Jack saw he was tall, broad-shouldered, with perfectly styled salt-and-pepper hair and a square jaw. He was, Jack thought, movie-star handsome. Despite probably being in his late fifties, Medzhid looked ten years younger than that.

The man's two bodyguards split up and started searching the hut. Once done, one returned to the door while the second took up position just out of the pool of light.

Seth said, "Jack, Ysabel, I'd like to introduce Rebaz Medzhid, head of Dagestan's MOI — Ministry of the Interior. He runs the country's *politsiya.*"

16

Unsmiling, Medzhid stepped forward and shook Jack's and Ysabel's hands. "Very nice to meet you." His English bore only the trace of an accent.

"One correction to your statement, Mr. Gregory," Medzhid said. "Republic of Dagestan and soon-to-be former federal republic of the Russian Federation. Or perhaps not. Much depends on this meeting."

Jack looked from Medzhid to Seth to Spellman. "You're planning a coup. You're going to try to break Dagestan away from Volodin."

Medzhid nodded. "And hopefully not get squashed in the process."

Absently, Jack wondered if his father had authorized the coup. Probably so. Toppling an entire country, let alone a republic of the Russian Federation, wasn't something the CIA would initiate on its own — at least not under a Ryan administration.

Jack smiled. Here he was, on the ground and in the middle of an operation his own father had sanctioned. And the hell of it was, neither of them would tell the other. One familial hand not knowing what the other was doing.

"Wait," Spellman said. "Rebaz, you said 'perhaps not.' What do you mean? Has something happened?"

"Someone took my daughter, Mr. Spellman. Aminat was kidnapped from her university dormitory two days ago."

Medzhid said this so dispassionately that Jack wasn't sure he'd him heard correctly.

"Damn it," Seth growled.

"How did you find out?" asked Spellman.

"I was approached this morning by a man outside my tennis club. His message was to the point: 'Do not cooperate with the authorities and await further contact. Disobey and we will begin sending Aminat in small pieces to you and your wife. We will begin with her toes and move upward.' "

"Oh, God," Ysabel murmured.

"Did you have him followed?" asked Spellman.

"His parting words warned against that. He showed me a picture of Aminat unconscious and tied to a bed. This is very real, and they are obviously professionals. They knew I go to the tennis club every Thursday morning. They had been following me. The man was calm, self-assured. He has done this before."

"What are you going to do?" asked Ysabel.

"A better question is, Who took her? My enemies or my friends?"

"Hold on," Spellman said. "You're not suggesting this is our doing."

"Until the kidnappers contact me again I have no idea of their goal — to halt my participation in the coup, or to ensure it. If it is the latter, then you two are behind it."

"It's not us," Spellman replied. "You have to believe that."

"I do not have to believe anything. Whatever the truth, I blame you. Either you two are behind this or somehow your actions tipped off the opposition to my involvement. Let me be clear: If Aminat is not returned to me safe and unharmed, our partnership is finished. And if I find you were behind this, I will hunt the two of you down."

Seth said, "Rebaz, you can't do this —"

"I can and I will."

"We've worked too long for this. Three fucking years!"

"All the more reason for you to take Aminat."

Seth turned away, paced in a small circle, then slammed his hand on the table. "You're going to sacrifice the future of your country? You can't be serious!"

Medzhid's hand lashed out, the palm landing squarely on Seth's cheekbone. Seth stumbled sideways, then regained his balance. The bodyguard behind Medzhid stepped forward, hand reaching into his coat. Medzhid held up his hand and the man stopped.

"Do I look serious to you, Mr. Gregory?"

Rubbing his reddening cheek, Seth replied, "Yeah, you do. Okay, we'll get her back. Just don't start rolling back what we've got in place. Please, Rebaz."

"I'll give you one week. And, you'll return with proof you weren't involved in it."

"What're you talking about?"

Jack answered for him: "You take her, then rescue her, and he's in your debt."

"We wouldn't do that," said Spellman.

"One week," Medzhid repeated. "If you find her, give her this so she will know I sent you. It was her favorite childhood toy." He tossed a red-and-yellow polka-dotted thimble on the table. "I will be in Baku. You know the place."

Medzhid turned and strode away with his bodyguards in tow. They disappeared through the door, and moments later Jack heard the car pulling away.

Ysabel murmured, "Seth, what is wrong with you? How could you say that to him? That's his daughter."

"No, it's an entire fucking country," Seth shot back. "This is the real world, Daddy's Girl!"

"You bastard!"

Ysabel started toward him. Jack caught her elbow and pulled her back. "Leave it," he whispered in her ear. "Let's get some air." Jack gently pushed her ahead of him, and they headed out the door. Jack said over his shoulder, "Seth, get yourself together. When I come back, you're going to tell me everything or we're gone."

He and Ysabel walked around the clearing for a few minutes, Jack saying nothing as she cooled off. Abruptly, Ysabel said, "Follow me," then strode over to the fire tower and started scaling the ladder.

"Ysabel . . ."

"Come on."

Jack started after her. At the top of the ladder he climbed through the open hatch and found Ysabel sitting at the edge of the platform, her legs dangling over the edge, her forehead resting against the waist-high handrail. Jack sat beside her.

"That's not the Seth I know," she said.

"Me neither."

"What's happened to him? Do you think he took the girl? Could he have done that?"

Jack wanted to reply, "No way," but now he wasn't sure. "On the upside," he said, "we've got a clearer picture of the field now."

Ysabel nodded. "Thanks for what you said in there — that you trusted me. It means a lot to me."

"You're not a daddy's girl. You've proven that."

Ysabel curled her arm through his and laid her head against this shoulder. "It's cold."

Jack almost said, "Then let's go inside," but he stopped himself. "We'll sit here for a bit."

Jack put her in the car with the heater running, then returned to the hut, where Spellman and Seth were huddled together at the workbench, whispering.

"Matt, give us a few minutes, will you?" said Jack.

"Sure."

Once Spellman was gone, Jack said, "That was a shitty thing to say, Seth."

"She doesn't get it, Jack. We've got a chance to pry Dagestan out of Volodin's grip and Medzhid's going to throw it away for one person."

"His daughter."

"I thought he was tougher than that."

"You're going to apologize to Ysabel."

"Yes, Father."

"You have no idea what she's gone through to stand by you, Seth. Make it right with her."

"Okay, okay."

"I meant what I said, about leaving, so you'd better start talking."

"Where do you want me to start?"

"How about, why didn't you just tell me what was going on when we met at Chaibar? Why the mysterious key crap?"

"I didn't have the time and it would have been a long damned conversation. I knew you'd go to the apartment. I knew you'd figure out the steak thing. I just didn't think Wellesley would move on you — or at least that fast. Was it bad?"

"I woke up on a tarp. You figure it out."

Seth said nothing. No apology, no remorse. Then he asked, "How did you meet Wellesley?"

"He came to my hotel, then later he and Spellman laid it out for me: You've turned and you've gone to ground with the operational funds."

"The first one isn't true. The last two are, but I had good reason. See, I started to get suspicious about Wellesley. Moves I was making in Makhachkala were getting countered. Assets were disappearing, getting run over by cars . . . Matt and I decided to feed Wellesley something that looked juicy, but was actually trivial. Two days later we got a reaction."

"What kind of reaction?"

"One of my people there, a hacker, went missing."

"You burned some kid just to flush Wellesley?"

"Ah, Christ, Jack, not you, too. When are you going to get it through your skull? Shit happens. The point is, after that happened we were pretty sure Wellesley's gone over."

"Pretty sure?"

"Well, we're sure now."

"Why haven't you gone to Langley about all this?"

"Because they'd pull the plug," Seth replied. "I can't let that happen. I can work around Wellesley. I can still pull it off."

Jack suddenly realized the truth of what

he and Ysabel had been going through. "You've been using us as stalking horses," he murmured. "You sons of bitches."

"We figured if you poked the hornets' nest enough Wellesley would make a mistake. He's just that cocky. Now we've got his number, and that he and Pechkin are in it together. We can turn that to our advantage."

"Wellesley knows that we know, Seth. If he hasn't already heard about the farmhouse, he will soon."

Seth scratched his head. "You're right. Oh, well, doesn't matter."

Of course it matters, Jack thought. Seth had tunnel vision. Not only was this not the friend he knew, but it was a Seth he never imagined could exist: cold-blooded, driven, reckless. This couldn't be just about making sure a coup succeeded, could it?

Rather than push this question, Jack asked instead, "Why did Wellesley turn?"

From the doorway, Spellman said, "Differing political agendas." He walked over and leaned his elbows on the workbench. "First thing you have to know, Jack, is that we think Wellesley's just following orders."

"Explain that."

"We — the U.S. — think Volodin is spread too thin, literally and figuratively. After

Ukraine and Crimea and the never-ending Chechnya mess, his political base in Moscow has weakened. If we ever had a chance to pull one of the republics free, it's now. And believe me, Dagestan wants independence. You won't see that on the news, but it's the truth."

Seth added, "Dagestan breaking away may spark a Caucasian Spring. Other republics will follow, and the more democracies bordering Russia, the better."

"And the Brits disagree?" replied Jack. "They think Volodin will invade and the region will plunge into chaos."

"Maybe," Spellman said. "Officially, we're all on the same page when it comes to Russia. But if not, they can't openly oppose us; we're bosom buddies, their closest ally. So they joined the op and put Wellesley in place so he could work it from the inside."

The scenario sounded plausible, but Jack had a hard time believing the United States' closest ally would go as far as partnering with the Russian SVR.

"Wellesley could have gone rogue."

"Also possible," Spellman replied. "Wouldn't be the first time a field operator made his or her own national policy."

"You've got proof that he's turned. Lay it out for your bosses."

"The man's a legend. He's got more intelligence decorations than my shoes have eyelets. Hell, rumor is he's in line for the OBE when he retires," Spellman said, referring to Officer of the Order of the British Empire. "His credibility is impeccable. Even if I can convince Langley to approach the SIS, by the time the smoke clears Wellesley's reputation will win the day and Seth and I will be pulled out."

Which prediction of the coup's outcome is correct, Jack wondered, *the Brits' or the United States'?* Jack didn't know the answer, but he agreed with the theory behind boxing in Valeri Volodin. The man might lose his grip on the government and get pushed out in favor of a moderate. But, as Medzhid had said, would Dagestan get squashed in the process? Volodin wouldn't take kindly to the idea of losing his only two republics along the oil-rich Caspian Sea, and he didn't give a damn what Dagestan's citizens wanted.

Plus, since Napoleon had invaded Russia, Moscow had always preferred having a buffer of satellite countries. In that respect, Volodin was cut from the same cloth as Joseph Stalin.

Seth went on: "And Wellesley's ahead of us, the bastard. He has been for a while. I know we can still make it work, though."

Jack asked, "Did you two kidnap Medzhid's daughter?"

Seth's head snapped up and he locked eyes with Jack. "No. On our friendship, we didn't take her."

Jack believed him. "Then it's the SVR."

"Or a Federation-friendly group in Dagestan," replied Spellman. "There are a few of them, though none of them naturally occurring, if you get my meaning."

"Seth, this isn't just about the coup, is it?" said Jack. "You fed some poor guy to the opposition as an experiment; you served up Ysabel and me to Wellesley. Hell, you even missed seeing that one of your agents was SVR. Tell me what's going on."

Seth frowned and shook his head. "Nothing."

Spellman said, "Bullshit, Seth. Clearly you and Jack go back a long way. Is he right?"

Seth said nothing.

"God damn it, answer me!" said Spellman.

"It's complicated."

"One of Wellesley's favorite words," Jack observed.

"You're not going to like this, either of you."

Spellman said, "Out with it, or I'm sending you home."

"Fine. Jack, you know about my dad . . . the stroke. It wasn't a stroke. He killed himself, shot himself in his study. His brains were all over the fucking wall. Mom found him."

"Why'd he do it?"

"Shame . . . anger. He wasn't with the Department of Agriculture, Jack. He was CIA. They drummed him out — after twenty-two years of service."

Spellman replied, "Wellesley said something about the apple tree. Is that what he meant?"

"I guess. Langley thought my dad had turned traitor, gone over to the Soviets. This was before the collapse. A document went missing from my dad's group and ended up in Moscow."

"Document," Jack repeated. "Was that the one I found in your safe?"

"Yeah."

"What is it?"

"For lack of a better term, it's my dad's coup manual for Armenia. He ran this group for Intelligence Directorate dedicated to drawing up plans and contingencies. They were behind Guatemala, Congo, Brazil, Chile — all of those."

"Wait a sec," said Spellman. "I heard

about them. I thought it was urban legend. They were called 'the golden boys,' as I recall."

"They were real. Langley disbanded them in 1974."

"Why?" asked Jack.

"Dad had been pushing for a coup in Armenia for nine or ten years. His bosses kept shooting him down, saying South and Central America were the safe bets. Armenia was too risky, too close to the Soviet Union. When they went after Argentina in 'seventy-three, they said my dad went off the deep end and tried to sabotage the coup out of frustration or a misguided attempt to get them to listen about Armenia. It's all bullshit. Then they found what they claimed was evidence, that he leaked plans for Turkey and Nicaragua — and Armenia — to the KGB."

"You said 'claimed.' "

"They had nothing," Seth replied. "Nothing except a mistake my dad made when he joined. He lied about his heritage."

Jack felt a sinking feeling in his belly. "He was Armenian."

"Yeah, he emigrated here in 'fifty-three. He had a false passport and birth certificate. His real name was Boghos — Armenian for 'Paul' — Grigorian."

"Christ," Spellman muttered.

"They thought he was a KGB plant. He wasn't. He was loyal."

"Then why the false documentation?" asked Jack.

"He knew they wouldn't take him. He wanted to join the military, but they rejected him for asthma, so he applied to CIA. He just wanted to serve, Jack, and he did. Then they tossed him out."

Jack wondered if Seth recognized the striking parallels between his father and himself: Both had tried to join the military and then, failing that, had joined CIA.

"Langley should have caught this," Spellman said.

"Which is why they didn't prosecute; they didn't want the embarrassment. But what they did was just as bad. They called him a traitor, stripped him of his retirement, his right to vote, kept him under surveillance for the next ten years . . ." Seth's voice broke; he wiped at his eyes. "They hounded him to death."

"I'm sorry, Seth," said Jack.

"Yeah, me too."

Spellman asked, "How the hell did you get hired with your history?"

"Either I slipped through the cracks like my dad or they decided to give me a chance.

What happened with him was half a century ago."

Jack asked, "Did you join with all this in mind, to redeem your dad?"

"I only found out about him a few years ago. My mom told me after he died; in fact, I think my joining CIA pushed him to tell her the story."

"How did your dad's manual end up in the Soviets' hands?"

"I don't know, but it wasn't him. And as far as I know, they never made use of it. You gotta believe me."

Jack wasn't sure one way or the other, and it was irrelevant now. "Where did you get it?"

"Doesn't matter."

"Bullshit," said Spellman. "What's the big deal with this damned thing?"

"I'm using it as the blueprint for Dagestan."

"You're what?" Spellman roared. "That's ridiculous, Seth. That thing is, what, fifty years old?"

"Fifty-two."

"It's obsolete! And it was written for Armenia. Not Dagestan!"

"That doesn't matter, I'm proving that here."

"And in the process, what, absolve Daddy,

soothe your boo-boos? This is abso-fucking-lutely unbelievable!" Spellman stalked away, kicked a pail across the hut. "God damn it, Seth! Do you really think CIA stopped planning coups after your dad got the boot? You've lost it, man. Gone."

Spellman was at least partially right. For Seth to think a coup manual from the early days of the Cold War was viable for today's world meant he was at best unstable; at worst, he'd lost touch with reality. Did he even care about this coup succeeding for its own sake, or was this just a personal mission?

Seth asked, "By the way, Jack, where is it?"

"In a safe place."

Spellman walked back to the table. "It's done. We're outta here."

"Fuck that," Seth shot back. "You go. I'm staying."

Spellman reached into his jacket and came out with a Glock 19. He let it dangle beside his leg. "You want to stay? Fine by me. I'll bury you in this goddamned shed. You're fucking with my career, man."

Jack knew the CIA man meant it. He rose from his stool. "Okay, everybody relax. Matt, put it away."

Spellman turned his gaze to Jack. "Huh-uh. Who are you, anyway? Some financial nerd? Not buying it. You've got some training. You show up, chase all over Tehran —"

"Leave him alone, Matt."

"Shut up."

Jack said, "Matt, you're right. I've got some training, but believe me, we're on the same side. If you shoot Seth, you'll have to kill me and Ysabel, too. Are you prepared to do that?"

Spellman grumbled a curse under his breath, then returned the Glock to its holster. "Just tell me: Who are you exactly, aside from the First Son?"

Jack gave him what he hoped was a disarming smile. "Ask me no questions . . . Let's work this through. Seth, convince us why Matt shouldn't abort this whole thing."

"Because the plan is working. Come on, Matt, you know the pieces we've got in place, you know how long we've been grooming Medzhid. Listen, my dad's plan ain't the standard 'Take the radio station and arrest the president' bullshit. He was ahead of his time.

"Think about it," Seth went on, ticking points on his fingers:

"Medzhid's got a ninety-plus approval rating; the people love him, Avars and minorities alike, Muslims and Orthodox alike. He's become Dagestan's de facto foreign minister; he's made inroads with Tbilisi, Baku, and even fuckin' Grozny. They'll all step up when the time comes. He's got all but a handful of district police commanders on his side, and those he doesn't have are outliers.

"Jack, we know they're going to shut down cell towers and regular Internet as soon as things get started, so we've got the whole of Makhachkala rigged with access hubs that'll be manned and guarded for the duration."

"Hubs?"

"See, we're not so worried that people won't be able to call out of the country. We want to make sure the visuals get out, and since Crimea, Ukraine, and Estonia, Volodin has ordered satellite Internet dishes from the bigger republics confiscated. Medzhid's had no choice but to comply. Our hubs are basically collection centers for uploading videos and pictures. We've got a network of blind agents, and they are their own network, and so on, like a pyramid scheme. After a half-dozen handoffs and cutouts, videos and pictures that get taken on the streets end up at a hub, which then uploads them via satellite Internet. We figure if we can get even twenty percent of the on-the-ground stuff uploaded it'll go viral on

YouTube, Twitter, Instagram, all that. The more live stuff we've got, the less chance of Moscow putting its own spin on things."

"This is where you've lost me, Seth. You said you've based your plan on your dad's manual. Back then, there was no —"

"Semantics, Jack. I'm using the manual as a rough blueprint. He talked about controlling communications, making sure none of it was happening in a vacuum, that kind of stuff. I'm just applying that principle to our technology."

"Got it. Keep going."

"As for crowd control, we've got both online and on-the-ground organizers and a precise timetable with primary and secondary rally points. Two hours after we pull the trigger there'll be a hundred thousand people on the streets, ten thousand cell phones filming it, and hundreds of international outlets airing every one of them. It'll make the Arab Spring look like a . . . like an old ladies' bingo meeting.

"See, Jack, that's what people don't understand: Coups aren't about infrastructure or who's taken over which building. Coups are about people, exposing their shit lives and telling them it doesn't have to be that. It's about hope — and someone they focus that on. That's why we've spent so much time on Medzhid, his image, his message. We're framing the debate so when everything jumps off, the opposition will never catch up."

Jack had to admit that whatever Seth's failings elsewhere, both personal and professional, he was passionate. He was, Jack decided, a true believer.

"While all this is going on, what're the Russian troops in Dagestan doing?"

Seth grinned. "You should really keep up on your reading. Since Ukraine and Estonia, Volodin's downsized the garrison here — sixty thousand to sixteen thousand, and three-quarters of those are stationed in districts along the Chechen border. The ones left in the capital are native Dagestanis. We're guessing they won't turn their guns against their own people."

"You better be right. If not —"

"We're right. See, Jack, Volodin's got a big PR problem and don't let anybody tell you he doesn't care. So far, anytime a republic's even hinted at wanting to break away, his solution has been to send in troops and tanks. The question is being asked in Moscow: If Volodin can't keep the Federation together without using force, maybe he's not the right man for the job. He needs this coup to fail organically."

"What about Dagestan's president?"

"Nabiyev? He's dirtier than Papa Doc Duvalier and he dances every time Volodin jerks his strings. The people are sick of it. He's covered his tracks pretty well, but once we're done with him, his corruption will be out for everyone to see. He'll have ten thousand pissed-off protesters on the doorstep of his mansion."

"Well, none of this might matter," Spellman replied. "You said it yourself: Wellesley and Pechkin are ahead of us."

"Not that far," Seth replied. "They've got bits and pieces, but not enough to stop it, and they don't know the timetable. What's Volodin going to do, roll the tanks south, park them on the border, and wait? Guys, what the hell does it matter if I've got another dog in the hunt? The point is, we can win it."

Jack had to admit Seth's case was compelling.

Spellman said, "You should have told me."

"Don't pull the plug. Please. Let's finish it."

Spellman glanced at Jack. "What do you think?"

"Me? Listen, I reunited the two of you. My part in this is over."

"You don't mean that," Seth replied.

"You've got hundreds of thousands of Dagestanis on your side. You don't need me. But if it makes you feel any better, I'll watch it all on TV and raise a beer when Medzhid's on the throne."

"Actually, we do need you, Jack," said Seth. "If we don't get Medzhid's daughter back and prove we weren't behind it, the whole thing's over before it starts."

"What do you care more about, the coup or making sure this girl doesn't get a bullet in the back of her skull?"

"Come on, Jack. Of course I don't want her to die."

"Then send someone else. You have to have special-ops guys around here someplace. They know how to do kidnap-and-rescue."

"There is no one else," said Spellman. "And Seth and I can't leave, not this late."

"Then call Langley and have them put somebody on a goddamned Gulfstream."

"If I call home they're going to ask me questions I don't want to answer — and I don't want to lie about. Better to ask for forgiveness than for permission."

Seth said, "It has to be you."

Jack sat back down on the stool. *Bad idea, Jack.*

"Where's she go to school?" he asked.

17

Jack pulled to the side of the road and turned on his hazard lights, then checked his phone's screen. Outside, the wind buffeted his Ford Fiesta hatchback. He glanced up, half expecting to see the Fiesta sliding sideways on the road, but saw only the serrated waves crashing against the seawall out his side window. The Firth of Tay, which Jack assumed was Gaelic for "stretch of nasty water," had been raging since he arrived the previous day. On the upside, the sun was out and bright. Jack adjusted the roof visor so he could better see the phone's screen.

"Shit," he muttered. He'd taken a wrong turn three miles back. The signs for Dundee were few and far between, and his phone reception was spotty.

The day before, after following Seth and Spellman east to the Azerbaijani coast to Lankaran, Jack and Ysabel had checked into a motel off the M3 and gotten a few hours of sleep. The next morning, on the way to the Baku airport with a mildly disgruntled Ysabel (Jack had asked that she remain behind to keep an eye on Seth), he'd called home and gotten Gerry, John Clark, and Gavin Biery on the line and prepared himself for yet another uncomfortable discussion.

He laid out what had happened in the last twelve hours, from the ambush at the farmhouse to Seth's revelation about his father's secret past, Oleg Pechkin, and the CIA's plans for the Dagestan coup. Jack ended the story with a paraphrased version of the case Seth had made for not abandoning the coup.

"Well, I'll give him this, it's a solid plan," Gerry said. "Still, your friend sounds nuts. Sorry, but it has to be said."

" 'Nuts' is a stretch, Gerry," said Clark. "He's got some daddy issues, so what? When I was at Langley I met a shit-ton of people that should've been wearing canvas 'Hug me' jackets."

"You're mellowing with old age."

"The point is, it could work. And I think the Brits are wrong. Getting Dagestan out of Volodin's sphere is the smart move. It's worth the risk."

"My concern isn't whether it's worth the risk. The plan looks good in the abstract, but what about in execution? On paper the Bay of Pigs should have worked. Jack, how long do you have to get this girl back to Medzhid?"

"Just under a week."

"Not much time. You'll have to move faster than the police — probably Scotland Yard, given who her father is."

"Also, Medzhid wants proof that Seth and Spellman didn't order the kidnapping."

"You didn't tell us that."

"It slipped my mind."

John Clark said, "If the police get to her first, you can forget about the proof Medzhid wants."

"Okay," Gerry said, "how do you want to go about this — finding one girl in a city of half a million?"

"I need Gavin."

"Shoot, Jack."

"First, find out if the story has broken about the girl. Her name is Aminat. Medzhid hasn't alerted the authorities himself, but I doubt her disappearance has gone unnoticed. Next, get on Facebook, Twitter, Instagram, whatever, and see what her friends are talking about. Finally, see if you can hack into the university's campus security. Look for any reports that jump out at you."

"Like what?"

"Stalking, break-ins, thefts — especially if they came from Aminat herself or they happened near where she lives or hangs out."

Two hours later Gavin called with bad news, or mostly so. If the Edinburgh police knew about Aminat's kidnapping, they were keeping it quiet, which dovetailed with the kidnappers' instructions. This was the good news. The bad news was that if in fact there was an investigation Jack could tap into, the information might be buried deep behind firewalls. If so, Jack was counting on Gavin's open-source data-mining skills being faster than those of the police.

As for Edinburgh University's campus police database, Gavin told him, they had no reports that fit Jack's criteria.

"There is one thing that caught my eye, though. The day before Aminat went missing, a girl named Amy Brecon went missing for about twenty-four hours. After an anonymous call, the police found her tied up in a garage off Kirkgate Road."

"Get me everything you can on the garage."

"Right. Apparently, the girl's jaw was

broken and she'd been drugged. Now, get this: According to Twitter, Aminat went by the nickname Amy."

"Go on."

"Both Amys lived at Pollock Halls, and they look a lot alike. I've seen their Facebook profile pages myself."

"Where can I find her?"

"They transferred her this morning from Saint John's Hospital to Ninewells in Dundee."

Jack pulled into Dundee at seven o'clock and followed the signs to Ninewells, which sat a few miles from the coast north of the airport. The hospital complex was sprawling, with white buildings sitting on 150 acres of lush green lawns. He parked in the main lot, walked into the lobby, and used the lighted information map to find the correct ward. Level 5, ward 17.

A woman in the nearby information booth asked, "May I help you, sir?"

"What are your visiting hours?"

"Eight in the morning until eight at night. You've got a bit of time yet."

"Thanks."

Jack found the elevator banks and took a car up to level 5, followed the signs to ward 17, then walked down the hall to Amy

Brecon's room. As he passed the door, he saw a middle-aged man and woman sitting beside the girl's bed, chatting quietly.

Jack turned around and walked back to the visitors' lounge beside the elevators. He sat down, started paging through a magazine, and waited.

At seven forty-five, Amy's visitors — her mom and dad, Jack assumed — came around the corner and pressed the elevator call button. Once the car's doors closed, Jack returned to Amy's room. The interior was dimly lit and the curtain around Amy's bed was half drawn. Jack gently rapped on the door.

"Hello?" Amy called groggily.

Jack stepped forward through the curtain. The side of the girl's face was yellow and black and still badly swollen.

"Hi, Amy, my name is Jack. I was wondering if I could talk to you for a couple minutes."

"Are you the police?" she asked, through the wires securing her fractured jaw. "I already talked to —"

"Just a few follow-up questions, if that's okay."

"Okay."

Jack pulled up a chair.

Amy said, "You're American."

Jack smiled. "A transplant from Los Angeles. I've got family here, so I decided to get away from the smog. I heard what happened to you. I'm sorry. I know you've been through all this with the other inspectors, but I'd like to go over it once more. What do you remember about that night?"

"Not much. Bits and pieces. The doctors said I had a lot of antihistamine in my system, plus that date-rape stuff."

"Rohypnol?"

"Yes," she replied, then quickly added, "They said I was okay down there, you know, so that's good."

"I'm glad."

"Yeah, so, I remember walking through the Gardens — Princes Street — and there was a woman. She dropped her purse. I heard footsteps, then I was falling. I heard her voice yelling and I heard a couple of names. Funny-sounding ones. Roman, or something like that, and Yegor."

"You told all this to the other inspectors?"

"Yeah. My mum thinks you lot aren't very keen. I was drunk and had drugs in my system, and I was walking on my own. Just a stupid girl being stupid. I guess if I'd been raped, then you'd be more interested."

Amy's eyes brimmed with tears. Jack pulled a tissue from the box on the bedside table and handed it to her. Though he didn't want to believe the police were giving her case the short shrift, there was no way to tell. Similarly, he had no way of knowing whether the police, if in fact they were actively investigating Aminat Medzhid's disappearance, would connect this Amy's abduction to that of Aminat. He needed to reach Medzhid's daughter, and her kidnappers, first.

"I'm interested, Amy," said Jack. "Do you have any memory of the garage where we found you?"

"Just being in the tub where the police found me, and someone giving me water."

"How about the van? Do you remember anything about it? Smells, sounds, snippets of conversation? Close your eyes. Take a few deep breaths."

Amy closed her eyes.

After a bit Jack said, "It's okay if you don't —"

"No, wait. Something about a toll. Someone was arguing — 'no toll' . . . 'used to be' . . . 'February.' I don't know," she said. "I can't tell if any of that's real. Sorry."

"It's okay. Did you just remember this, or did you tell the other inspectors?"

"I just remembered it. Why would someone do this to me? I wasn't raped, my parents didn't get any ransom calls, we're not even rich . . . What was it all about?"

Something far, far outside your world, Jack thought.

What he couldn't understand was why Amy Brecon was even alive.

He drove back to Edinburgh, checked into a motel, slept until six, then drove to Kirkgate Road in the southeastern corner of the city. After several wrong turns on the narrow, winding side streets he found the garage where Amy had been held. It was nothing more than a pair of tall wooden doors set into a graffiti-covered cinder-block wall. The front of it was crisscrossed with blue-and-white police tape and the side door was open. As he passed, he saw a policewoman kneeling, looking at something on the floor.

Following his phone's map, Jack then drove two miles east to a block of row houses that backed up to a cemetery. He slowed, studying the house numbers until he reached number 15. In the front window hung a giant red-and-blue roundel emblazoned with the words *Rangers Football Club.* He got out, walked up the front steps, and pushed the buzzer. Thirty seconds passed. Jack pressed the buzzer again.

"Yeah, yeah . . . hold on," a male voice called.

The door opened, revealing a gaunt elderly man in plaid pajamas. His skin was pale and paper thin. A cigarette dangled from his lips. "Whatya want?" he grumbled.

Instead of answering, Jack pulled a pair of fifty-pound bills from his pocket and pressed them against the glass.

"What's that for?"

"Five minutes of your time."

"What's it about?"

"What happened at your garage," Jack replied.

"Already talked to you. They broke in. Squatters."

Jack tapped the money on the glass and repeated, "Five minutes."

"Ah . . ."

According to Gavin, the owner of the garage, Fingal Cowden, was dirt poor, subsisting on welfare and what sporadic income he gained from renting his garage, and he was also dying of emphysema.

Cowden sat down on the couch.

Jack looked around. The apartment was cramped, with just a ratty couch against one wall facing a thirteen-inch television. The only light came from a floor lamp aimed at the wall. Beneath the lamp was a green oxygen cylinder.

Cowden was miserable, and dying. Jack felt bad for what he had to do next, but he put it out of his mind.

He handed Cowden the bills, then said, "You told the police you hadn't rented it out."

"Right. They broke in."

"You're lying."

"Get out of here!"

Jack pulled another fifty-pound note from his pocket and dropped it on the couch beside Cowden. "I'm not the police, and I don't care that you lied to them."

"I didn't want no trouble. If I'd told them, they would've stuck me in a cell."

"I don't care," Jack replied.

"Who are you?" Cowden said, eyes narrowing.

"Did the police tell you about that girl they found in your tub?"

"Not my tub."

"Did they tell you about her?" Jack pushed. "Her name is Amy."

"Yeah."

"She's in the hospital, badly hurt. I'm a friend of the family. I'm here to find who did this to her." Jack dropped another fifty on the couch. Cowden stared at the bill for a moment, then slowly reached out and took it. Jack said, "Tell me who you rented the garage to."

"You're not the police?"

"No."

"I'm gonna need more than this you gave me."

Jack pulled out another fifty, wadded it up, and dropped it between Cowden's feet. "That's all you're getting."

"Then get outta here —"

"Have it your way. I'm coming back — this time with Amy's dad." This got Cowden's attention. He looked up at Jack. "Who's her da?"

"I'll let him introduce himself. If he comes, it won't be with money. Tell me who you rented the garage to and we're done."

"I don't know who —"

Jack turned and headed for the door. "Twenty minutes," he called over his shoulder.

"Wait! I have a phone number. I can give you that. And a name, the woman who came with the rent money."

"That's it?" Gavin said a few minutes later over the phone. "A phone number and a first name? Helen?"

"Not quite." It had taken another fifty pounds, but Cowden also gave him the

252

make and model of the van. It had been insurance, Cowden had told him, in case the woman did any damage to the garage.

"Pretty weak insurance," said Gavin.

"Have you made any progress on what I got from Amy?"

"Assuming they're even real," Gavin said. "Helen and Roman have a lot of variations from several countries."

"Any of them from the Caucasus?"

"Both of them. 'Yegor' is a variation on 'Igor.' The most prevalent distribution is in Russia."

"How about what she said about the tolls?"

"Still working on it. It could be roads, freeways, bridges, parking lots, and there are a lot of them around Edinburgh, and chat rooms about toll roads in Scotland aren't exactly a big thing. And we're assuming that's where she was when she heard it."

"You can do it. I've got faith."

"Bless you. I've also got something on Helen's phone number. It's a pay phone in Kinghorn. As the crow flies that's nine miles north of Edinburgh. And no, before you ask, I can't get LUDs from the phone. Hey, are you near a decent Wi-Fi connection?"

"I can be."

"I found some video surveillance from the university you need to see."

Jack was back in his hotel room thirty minutes later. He powered up his laptop, then called Gavin, who directed him to a Dropbox account. He gave Jack the log-in and he typed it in.

"I'm there," said Jack.

"I downloaded all the feeds for that night, but the two I want you to see are labeled zero-two-four and zero-two-six." Jack scrolled to the first MP4 file and double-clicked on it. His screen filled with a dim but otherwise sharp black-and-white image.

"I'm watching it."

"That's the CCTV camera just south of Pollock Halls, looking north."

After a few moments, the white top of a bus came into view from the lower edge of the screen. It pulled to a stop beside a lighted bus stand.

Gavin said, "That's the number twenty-two bus. Aminat's on it. She'll get off and cross the street."

The bus pulled away and Jack watched a figure trot across the street then disappear beneath some trees along the sidewalk. "What is that?" he asked.

"A path that leads directly to Chancellors Court. Keep your eyes on the sidewalk. You see him yet?"

"Got him."

A figure jogged down the sidewalk and turned onto the path. "He's in a hurry," Jack murmured. He felt his heart quicken; he was watching something horrible about to happen to Rebaz Medzhid's little girl. In his mind's eye he could see the figure jogging up behind her —

"Okay, now go to the other video," said Gavin.

Jack double-clicked on the file and again a black-and-white image filled his laptop's screen. "What am I looking at?" he asked.

"CCTV at the intersection of Dalkeith and Holyrood Park Road, looking north. You see the building at two o'clock, the one with the lighted top floor? That's Chancellors Court. The path Aminat took is to your right, out of frame."

"We don't have anything of the actual parking lot itself?"

"No. Keep watching."

Jack kept one eye on the video, the other on the running time code at the bottom. Forty seconds had passed since Aminat entered the path.

Fifty seconds.

From the direction of the path a dark, late-model van approached the entrance to

Chancellors Court. It stopped. The right-hand turn signal started blinking. The van slowly pulled out and turned north onto Holyrood Park Road. Jack lost sight of it.

"God Almighty," Jack murmured. From the time Aminat had stepped onto the path to when the van left the scene, barely one minute had passed.

"She was in there, Jack," replied Gavin. "Maybe fighting —"

"Shut up, Gavin."

"Sorry."

"Do you think you can make something out of the license plate?"

"They're local, that much I can tell, but at a distance the CCTV resolution is lousy, so I can't make anything more of the license plate."

"Where does that road lead?"

"A T intersection with roads heading east and west. I'm checking for any traffic stops on those roads, but I wouldn't hold my breath. Whoever was inside that van, they've done this before."

"Can you tell whether campus security made any copies of these vids?"

"There are no duplicates on their servers, but whether they'd forwarded copies to the police is anyone's guess."

Jack hoped not. The video he'd just seen

might lead the police to Aminat before he could get to her. If that happened he'd never make Medzhid's deadline. "Can you wipe the originals from their servers?"

"Yeah, but —"

"Do it."

18

The thought gnawed at his brain: Had he just signed Aminat Medzhid's death warrant? If the police hadn't yet obtained the surveillance videos Gavin had just erased, they might now have no leads at all. Chancellors Court's parking lot looked empty and was poorly lit. Even if there had been witnesses, something told Jack the people inside that van weren't dumb enough to use real license plates, or at least unobscured ones, leaving the police with only a vague description of a vehicle that had been sitting in the lot for less than two minutes.

Of course, Jack had little more than this information. The smart move would be to turn over what he had to the police, pray they find Aminat before Medzhid's five-day deadline expired, then hope Seth could convince Medzhid they had nothing to do with the kidnapping.

Jack dismissed the idea. He would find

her and get her back home.

What happened with the coup was Seth's problem.

Jack spent the rest of the day and all the next morning either pacing around his hotel room, watching the news for reports on either Amy Brecon's kidnapping or the disappearance of Aminat, or driving around the city, going nowhere in particular and hoping his subconscious brain would kick out some angle he hadn't yet considered. He managed to resist the impulse to go to Chancellors Court and start canvassing the occupants, knowing he'd end up sitting in a police interview room, being asked questions he couldn't answer.

Jack awoke to the sound of a news reporter's voice: ". . . police spokeswoman has verified for an STV Edinburgh producer that reports of a missing Edinburgh University student are indeed true."

Jack sat up, found the remote beside his pillow, and increased the volume.

"Though the police spokeswoman refused to confirm whether investigators believe the young woman's disappearance may be the result of foul play, they will be treating the circumstances of the disappearance as suspicious until further notice. The young woman, as yet unnamed, is apparently the citizen of another country, having come to Edinburgh two years ago —"

Jack muted the TV.

The race was well and truly on now.

His phone rang. It was Ysabel.

"Where are you?" she asked. "Are you okay?"

"In a seedy motel in Edinburgh. I'm fine. You?"

"In Baku at the lovely Mirabat Hotel. There are cockroaches in the shower. Seth said he wants to be close to Medzhid. He's also talking about breaking into Hamrah's headquarters. He thinks he might be able to find a lead to Pechkin. I think Spellman's talked him out of it."

"How's Seth acting?"

"Hyper, worse than I've ever seen him. I don't think I trust him anymore, Jack."

He was more than a little ashamed to admit it, but he shared her feelings. While he thought — hoped — Seth wouldn't burn them again, his friend's judgment was still highly questionable.

"I don't blame you," he said.

"One more thing: I found out that meeting, our relationship, was a lie."

"Explain."

"He told me himself. He'd been following Pechkin in Tehran; Pechkin got interested in the Pezhman working group at the university, so when I was brought on board, Seth set his sights on me."

Was his tailing of Pechkin how Seth got involved with Hamrah Engineering, or was it the other way around? It didn't matter, Jack decided. The two were intertwined.

Ysabel added, "I don't really care, actually. The way he told me, it was so matter-of-fact it gave me the chills." She chuckled. "I can tell you this much: He's off my Shab-e Cheleh card list."

Jack laughed. "You have a unique sense of humor, Ysabel Kashani. Do me a favor: Don't let him out of your sight."

Given Seth's obsession with the coup, vindicating his father, and the mistakes he'd already made, Jack wondered what might be unraveling without their knowledge.

Mid-afternoon, his phone rang: Gavin. "I assume you saw the news?"

"Yes."

"The latest is that Scotland Yard's involved."

"Please tell me you didn't call to ruin my day," said Jack.

"It is mostly bad news. I struck out on the van's origin."

Jack had hoped that if Helen had paid cash for the garage, she might have done the same for the van.

"Edinburgh's got too many back-lot dealerships."

"We've got another missing Edinburgh student, Jack, a kid named Steven Bagley. The same night Aminat was grabbed he was supposed to be headed home to London for a wedding. He never got there. Steven and Aminat are Facebook friends. Good ones, based on their posts. Campus security found his car parked a block from Chancellors Court. They must have gotten him, too, Jack."

"Maybe he stopped by Chancellors to say good-bye," Jack replied. "Where did you find this?"

"Bagley's parents called his friends, then campus security. The police will have all this by now."

Jack thought, *Helen and her team didn't intend to take Bagley. He saw something and tried to intervene. Bagley will be a burden to them. Expendable.*

"Start watching for reports of bodies turning up that match his description," he said. "Anything else?"

"I think I've figured out what Amy was talking about with the tolls. Forth Road Bridge used to be toll-free, but the toll was reinstated back in February."

Jack called up Google Earth on his laptop, typed in the bridge's name, and scanned the area. Forth Road led north, away from the city, and across the channel to the North Queensferry. On a hunch, Jack typed in "Kinghorn."

The town was eighteen miles from Forth Road Bridge.

Jack gave Gavin his next set of marching orders and then, sick of sitting in his room waiting, got into his car and headed east, crossed the bridge, then drove up the coast to Kinghorn, more a quiet seaside resort than a town. As tourist season was still three months away, the streets were quiet, with only a few local cars on the main roads. As it had at the Firth of Tay, the wind whipped off the ocean, buffeting the Fiesta and whistling through its window seals.

He knew the trip was pointless, but it was action he could take. If he was very, very lucky perhaps the gods would smile on him and he'd stumble upon a late-model dark-colored van. It wasn't going to happen, he knew, not even in a town as small as Kinghorn.

At sunset he drove back to the motel.

Another twelve hours passed.

"I think you hit pay dirt," Gavin said the following afternoon. "Your boy Pechkin isn't as crafty as he thinks. He deleted his Gmail account, but forgot about Google's mysterious ways."

"Explain."

"Pechkin frequently checked his Gmail account from the Hamrah office in Archivan. He deleted all of the e-mails, and his browser history, but he forgot or didn't realize that Hamrah's website is set up with Google Analytics. It tracks back-end website data — traffic, referrers, conversions, and so on. It also keeps a hidden cache of browser history. Interesting, no?"

"Gavin . . ."

"Okay. About six hours after your shootout at the Nemin farm, someone logged in to Hamrah's computer system, then went straight to a Web-based e-mail site called YourMailStack. Their firewall is for shit. Pechkin e-mailed someone outside the country — someone in Scotland."

Long shot though it had seemed, Jack wondered whether Oleg Pechkin — also playing the roles of Farid Rasulov, Suleiman Balkhi, and Ervaz — might also be pulling the strings of Aminat Medzhid's kidnappers.

"Where'd his e-mail go?" *Say, "An address in Kinghorn,"* Jack thought.

"A cell phone, but it's somewhere where the cell towers are few and far between. I don't have the resources to pin down the signal."

"Shit," Jack replied. Then, a thought: "The NSA would. Give it to Gerry, tell him to get out his favors-owed book. And one more thing: I need a gun."

Their second captive — Steven was the name he'd finally offered Olik — had by the evening tired himself out and now lay sleeping on a blanket in the cottage's basement.

The team sat down at the dinner table for a meal of TV dinners Helen had stocked the refrigerator with. Hunched over, Roma shoveled spoonfuls of pasta and green beans into his mouth. "Not bad," he said. "Perhaps when I get home I will buy myself a microwave oven."

"Good idea," Helen said with a smile.

For whatever reason, slowly throughout the day Roma had emerged from his funk and had started talking and joking with the others, and even asking after the girl's condition.

"I'm sorry about all that," he told the group. "I shouldn't have hit the other girl. It's just that this place, all these people . . . I don't like it here."

"We'll be home soon, my friend."

Helen hoped this was true. Her latest communication with their employer was troubling. Medzhid would not be approached in the manner planned. She and the others were to stay in place and not leave the cottage under any circumstances. Worse still, Aminat's "disappearance" had reached the news earlier than Helen had hoped, and the fact that Scotland Yard was involved told her the authorities were treating the affair as a kidnapping. This had happened much more quickly than she'd anticipated.

Though her team had seen the same news reports, Helen had done her best to assuage their fears. "This was all expected and planned for. We're safe here."

But not Aminat and Steven, she thought, *if she followed orders.*

Yegor said to Roma, "And when we're back we will go shopping for microwaves, the two of us. I know the perfect store in

Lipetsk."

"With your money, yes?"

"Do not push your luck."

Roma laughed.

Helen awoke to shouting and footsteps pounding the kitchen floor below her room. Still dressed as she'd fallen into bed, Helen threw back the covers, reached under her pillow, and grabbed the semi-auto pistol there, then ran for the door. Yegor, emerging from his own bedroom, nearly crashed into her. He backpedaled as she raced to the stairs, then followed.

Taking the steps two at a time, Helen heard a door bang open and then Olik rasping, trying to keep his voice down, "Roma, no, don't —"

Helen turned the corner into the kitchen and saw Olik dash through the open door. From outside came a reedy scream, then the grunting-thump of two bodies colliding. The screams became muffled, but more frantic.

"Shut up!" Roma growled. "Shut . . . up! Shut . . . up!"

With each repetition came an umph of expelled breath.

Helen sprinted out the door. In the driveway a pair of bodies were writhing, indistinguishable from each other in the darkness. Helen saw one of the bodies rise up. Moonlight glinted on the blade of a knife. It plunged downward.

Helen shoved Olik aside, rushed forward, raised the pistol, and slammed it against the back of Roma's skull. He rolled off the body beneath him and started crawling away. Helen took another step and crashed the pistol's butt against his temple. He went down.

"Oh, no, no . . ." Yegor murmured.

Helen turned. Yegor and Olik were kneeling beside Steven. The boy lay on his back, eyes glazed over. The front of his sweatshirt was a patchwork of blood.

Helen's head swirled. She took a breath, refocused on the boy. *Think . . .*

"Get him inside," she whispered. "Put him on the kitchen floor."

With one lifting Steven's shoulders and the other his feet, they carried him toward the door.

"Then come and get this piece of shit," Helen called. "And put him in the basement."

Helen stood, staring dumbly at the boy. The linoleum floor beneath his body was slick with blood.

"Go upstairs and get some towels." She knelt beside the boy and grasped his hand. "It's okay," she murmured. "You'll be okay. Just look at me. That's it . . ."

She kept her eyes on his until they went dark and he stopped breathing.

When the other two returned she told them to pack the blankets around his body to dam the blood.

Helen shuffled to the dining table and sat down. She could feel a haze of panic creeping into her brain.

"Get buckets," she ordered. "Wash the blood off the pavement. Check everywhere. Don't miss even a drop. Olik, when it's done, take a walk around the neighborhood. Look for anyone outside or any lights on."

It took five minutes, the two of them filling and refilling buckets in the kitchen sink until Yegor came back inside and shut the door behind him. He walked to the sink and dropped Roma's knife into it. It clattered against the stainless steel.

Yegor sat down at the table with Helen, neither speaking until Olik returned. "Nothing. No lights, no one outside. I heard no sirens, either."

Helen wondered if it mattered. If the police even knocked on their door and asked anything more than the most rudimentary questions, it was over for them.

"What happened, Olik?"

"I'm sorry, I —"

"Tell me what happened."

"I was in the kitchen, like you told me, keeping watch. Roma was in the other room watching television. I told him I had to go to the bathroom and asked him to cover for me. It was only going to be for a few minutes."

"Keep going."

"When I came back down here, the basement door swung open and the boy came stumbling up."

"Steven."

"What? Yes, Steven. I reached for him, but I missed, then Roma shoved me aside and went out the door after him. You know the rest. It happened so fast, Helen."

Yegor asked, "What do you want to do?"

She stood up, opened the basement door, and started down the stairs. "Both of you stay here."

As she'd instructed, Yegor and Olik had tied Roma to the same pipes against the basement's far wall where Steven had been secured. The room stank of urine and sweat. A lone light-bulb dangled from the center rafter. Roma lay on his side on the blanket.

She walked to him and nudged his foot

with her own.

He didn't stir.

She kicked him in the thigh. He jerked his leg back. His head rolled sideways and his eyes opened. "What happened?" he croaked. "Hey, why am I tied up?"

"You killed the boy."

"He tried to get away."

"How did that happen?"

"Olik went to piss. I heard the kid call up that he had to use the bucket so I went downstairs. The bucket was full, so instead of dragging it to him and getting piss and shit all over me, I untied him and walked him over to it. He broke free, ran up the stairs, and then out the door. I tackled him, but he was strong. He was fighting me. I had to stab him."

Roma's story was plausible, but Helen could hear the lie in his voice. Worse still, his eyes shone with amusement, as though he was replaying the act for his own pleasure. Now Helen was sure: Roma was a psychopath. He let Steven go, told him to run, then chased him down and stabbed him to death. He'd done it because he wanted to do it.

"I didn't have a choice, Helen. He was going to get away. Untie me. This is silly."

Helen turned around and walked back up

to the kitchen.

Roma shouted, "Hey, come on, let me go."

"What did he say?" asked Yegor.

Helen ignored him. She climbed the stairs to her room and grabbed a pillow from her bed and returned to the kitchen.

"What are you doing?" Olik asked.

"Shut up."

She picked up the gun from the dining table and, with the pillow in her left hand, walked back downstairs. When Roma saw her he said, "Are you going to let me —"

"No."

She strode over to him, doubled up the pillow, and shoved it hard against his head.

"Hey, what —"

She pressed the gun's barrel to the pillow and pulled the trigger.

19

Of Jack's two latest requests of Gavin, the gun had been the easier, surprisingly so. Jack's request for an NSA trace of what Jack hoped was Helen's cell phone was a tougher task.

"The gun's coming from some connection of Mr. Clark's," Gavin explained. "Some guy from Hereford, whatever that is."

"Home of the 22 SAS Regiment," Jack replied, referring to the Special Air Service, Britain's elite Special Forces unit.

"Sure," Gavin replied, and then gave him the details.

As promised, in locker 123 at Saint Andrews Street bus station Jack found the weapon inside a padded envelope. It was a noise-suppressed .32-caliber Walther inside a paddle holster with belt pouches containing three spare magazines, each full of what Jack knew would be subsonic rounds.

Jack was pulling back into his motel's parking lot when his phone trilled. "It's under way," Gavin said. "Gerry didn't look too happy about it, but you've got your trace. Providing the phone's not off, we should have a location in a couple hours."

"Good. I'm heading back to Kinghorn."

The trace didn't come in a couple hours, and it didn't come four hours after that. Jack, who'd been sipping coffee and waiting in Kinghorn's only twenty-four-hour coffee shop, left as the sun was coming up and checked into the Carousel Motel overlooking the ocean. Through his balcony windows the sun reflected yellow off the choppy water.

At noon, Gavin texted him a "still working on it" message.

At five, Gavin called. "I'm with Gerry and Mr. Clark."

Clark said, "We've got a hit on the phone. It's pinging somewhere east of the Pettycur coastal road, about a hundred-meter square between Abden Place and Long Craigs Terrace."

"How many houses?"

Gavin said, "Twenty-two. We have no way of knowing which ones are occupied,

274

though."

"Helen paid cash for the garage in Edinburgh and I'm betting she paid cash for their van. Stands to reason she would have done the same here."

"Good point," said Clark. "Gavin, see what you can come up with. Check rental permits versus private ownership, landlords hauled into court for unfit lodgings, pensioners on a fixed income —"

"Why?"

"If you own the house you're not as likely to hand the keys to a stranger with a wad of bills. And poor landlords who take cash under the table are often stingy with repairs and not fans of Her Majesty's tax collectors."

"Ah. Okay, I'm all over it."

Gerry said, "John's going to run the plan with you, Jack."

"I can handle —"

Clark interrupted. "If you find the house you'll probably be outnumbered. And whoever's inside has done this kind of thing before. Fail to plan, plan to fail."

He's right, Jack thought. As much as he wanted to move right now, blindly crashing through whatever door he eventually found would probably get both him and Aminat Medzhid killed.

"Okay, let's walk it through."

Jack waited until nightfall, then parked his Fiesta in a pub parking lot on Nethergate Street, then started the five-minute walk to the target area. If Kinghorn's streets were quiet during the day, they were almost deserted at night. He passed an equally vacant trailer park overlooking the shoreline to his right. When he drew even with Abden Place, which sat back twenty yards from the coastal road, he stepped off the shoulder and down a short grass slope to a paved trail bordered by hedges; through them he could hear the crash of waves. In the distance a buoy bell gonged rhythmically. Across the road sat the line of Abden Place. He counted five porch lights on, but none of the front windows were illuminated.

Jack stopped and texted, IN PLACE.

STAND BY, came the reply. This would be John Clark.

To his left he saw a pair of headlights coming down the road. He backed deeper into the hedge and crouched down. A few seconds later he saw the car pass; on its roof was a light bar.

POLICE. KEEP GOING . . .

The car's engine faded.

Jack waited.

■ ■ ■ ■

His phone vibrated.

SIX RENTAL COTTAGES, Clark texted. TWO ON LONG CRAIGS TERRACE, FOUR ON ABDEN PLACE; OF THESE, TWO BELONG TO PENSIONERS. HOUSE NUMBERS 5 AND 9.

Jack texted, MOVING.

STAY IN TOUCH.

Jack looked left and right down the road, then crossed. On the other side of a strip of grass he reached the sidewalk. The address placard on the cottage before him read AB-DEN PLACE #2, the one to its right, #3. Both porch lights were dark.

Behind one of the cottages a dog yipped twice, then went silent.

Jack started walking, counting cottages as he went. When he drew even with number 5 he saw the porch light was on. He continued on and soon reached number 9, the last cottage on the block. This one's porch light was also lit.

Were the kidnappers more or less likely to leave the lights on? he wondered. On, was his guess. If the group was clever — which Helen clearly was — they'd want to behave as naturally as possible. Occupied homes tended to leave the porch lights on. It was the friendly thing to do.

Jack passed number 9 and followed the sidewalk as it curved around and intersected with Long Craigs Terrace. To his right he could see the fenced backyards of the Abden cottages; running between each one was an alleyway. He walked south until he was back at number 5, then turned down the alleyway. At its end he found himself standing between the cottage and its garage. Gently, Jack opened the side gate and crept down the grass path to the garage's half-glass door. He clicked on his penlight and shined it through the window. Inside was a white Škoda station wagon.

This wasn't proof positive, of course. The kidnappers may have ditched the van they'd used to abduct Amy.

He retraced his path through the alley, then back down the sidewalk until he reached the second cottage's yard, then again took the alley to the front of the house. To his right was the cottage's side door. Through it he heard a soft metallic clink, like a utensil striking metal. The kitchen.

Jack crouched down. His heart was pounding.

He drew the Walther from its holster and then affixed the noise suppressor to the muzzle. Gun trained on the door, he stepped onto the driveway, then sidestepped to the gate. He pushed it open, went through, swung the gate shut, then stepped to the garage door. Hand cupped around the end of the flashlight, he shined the beam through the glass and saw a dark brown wheel well. He panned the flashlight upward.

It was the van.

Behind him the cottage door creaked open.

"I'm taking the garbage out," a voice called.

Jack detected an accent. It sounded Russian.

He retreated down the path to the corner of the garage, circled it, pressed his back against the wall. He brought the Walther up across his body and aimed it at the corner.

The gate banged open against the fence.

Footsteps squished on the sodden grass.

Jack realized he was holding his breath; he let it out.

Come on, go away . . .

The garage door swung open and a moment later Jack heard the soft clunk of aluminum cans and glass on concrete.

The footsteps faded. The cottage door clicked shut.

Jack couldn't tell if the lock had engaged.

He got out his phone and texted, FOUND IT. GOING IN.

He checked his watch: 10:04.

As arranged, if he didn't reestablish contact within ten minutes Clark would push the panic button. This was false comfort, of course, and Jack assumed Clark knew it. Three thousand miles from home, ten minutes or ten hours made no difference.

MONITORING POLICE CHANNELS, Clark replied. WATCH YOUR SIX.

Having already decided kicking in the cottage's front door was a no-go, Jack turned his focus to the side door. This was problematic, however. There was at least one man on the other side of it, in the kitchen. Beyond this, he had no idea of the cottage's layout. He would have to clear the cottage blindly and on the fly.

You know this stuff, he told himself. *Don't hurry it. Watch your corners and your intersections —* He stopped himself. *Get on with it.*

He shifted the Walther to his left hand, swiped his sweaty right palm across his chest, then regripped the gun.

On flat feet he walked back down the path and out the gate. He scanned the length of the driveway and the front corner of the house. Nothing moved.

Down the street the dog yipped again. A voice shouted, "Quiet, Numsy!"

Jack crept to the cottage door. Through it he heard running water, then the clink of a dish. He reached out with his left hand, turned the knob. It was unlocked. He pushed open the door a couple of feet; through it was a round dining table and an arched entryway, through which he saw the flickering light of television playing on the walls.

A loud buzzer went off and a voice said, "No, sorry, Annette. The answer is Dumfries."

To the right of the dining table a wooden plank door was set into the wall. A basement door, Jack guessed.

Using the door as a screen, he stepped inside and peeked around it. A man was standing at the sink, doing dishes under the glow of a pendant lamp; its light reflected off a window above the sink. *Careful, Jack. If he looks up —*

Something on the beige linoleum floor caught his eye. In the floor's indentations were slivers of a brown substance. Dried blood.

Jack crouched down and crab-walked into

the kitchen until the man's body was between him and the window, then stood up. A single shot at the base of the skull would do the trick. He'd never done that before. Then again, he told himself, these people had threatened to send Aminat back to Medzhid in pieces, and Jack had no doubt they meant it. They'd signed up for whatever they got.

Make a decision.

He crept toward the man, who suddenly shut off the water and reached for a towel on the counter beside him. Jack clamped his left hand over the man's mouth, then rapped him behind the ear with the butt of the Walther. The man went limp. Jack caught him and lowered him the rest of the way to the floor, then turned the sink faucet back on.

He turned his attention to the entrance to the TV room. It was empty.

He paced to the basement door and waited for the game show's buzzer to sound again. When it did, he opened the door, revealing a set of stairs. Leaving the door open a crack, he took the steps to the bottom, where he found a dimly lit basement.

Tucked against the far wall beneath some pipes lay an elongated shape beneath a gray woolen blanket.

"Please, no . . ." Jack murmured.

He walked over, took a breath, and jerked back the blanket. Lying on the concrete floor were two bodies. Bloody towels were packed around the edge of the corpses. One man was lying on his side with a bullet hole in his temple; the other, who was younger, lay on his back. His shirt was sodden with blood and his forearms were covered in slashes.

This had to be Steven, Jack thought, but who was the other one? Steven had gone down fighting, while the second man had been executed.

From upstairs came the creaking of floorboards.

Jack froze and listened, trying to gauge their path. In his mind's eye he saw the TV watcher stepping into the kitchen. Jack braced himself for the shout of alarm. None came.

He crept back up the stairs and stopped at the door.

A shadow passed the gap.

"What the hell . . . Yegor —" a voice muttered.

Jack pushed open the door and raised the Walther.

The man in front of him was already turning around. In his left hand was a small semi-auto equipped with a noise suppressor. Jack shot him twice in the chest. Aside from the click-clack of the racking slide, the Walther's report was almost silent. The man stumbled backward, eyes wide with surprise. His legs gave out and he dropped butt-first on the floor. He looked down at the seeping holes in his chest, then at the gun still clenched in his right hand. He started to raise it. Jack took a step forward and shot him in the forehead.

Upstairs, a door opened. A female voice called, "Everything okay?"

This would be Helen.

Shit. Jack didn't give himself a chance to think. He put what he hoped was a Russian-like accent in his voice and said, "Dropped something."

The woman didn't reply.

Then: "Okay. Turn that down, will you?"

The door clicked shut.

Jack walked to the TV room's entrance and peeked around the corner. Carpeted steps led upward to the darkened second-floor landing bordered by a wood balustrade.

Jack found the remote on the couch and lowered the TV's volume.

Two down, but how many more upstairs?

20

He took the steps slowly, agonizingly so, stopping each time one of the treads squeaked, until he reached the landing. Before him was a hallway with four doors, two on the left, one on the right — which Jack could see was a bathroom — and one at the end. All but the bathroom door were shut.

Again Jack forced himself to stand still and listen. This was a failing of his, he knew, the urge to go, go, go; every time he found himself in the field he had to fight against it. His legs were trembling.

He stepped to the first door on the left. It was unlocked; he opened it a couple of inches and looked inside. The bed's covers were jumbled, but it was empty. He moved to the next room and repeated the process. This bed was occupied.

The diminutive shape told him it was a girl. She was turned slightly away from him, her duct-taped right wrist stretched toward the bedpost. Moonlight streamed through the side window and cast a pale rectangle on the carpet.

Jack stepped through and clicked the door shut behind him. Gently he sat on the bed. Aminat jerked awake and rolled over, her eyes wild with panic. Jack clamped his hand over her mouth and, before she could start struggling, raised the red-and-yellow thimble before Aminat's eyes.

"Your father sent me," he whispered. "Can you walk? Just nod or shake your head."

Aminat nodded.

"Are you hurt?"

She shook her head.

Jack pulled a penknife from his front pocket and sliced the tape away, first from her wrists, then from her ankles, all of which were wrapped in thick fleece; someone had shown at least some concern for the girl's comfort. Jack helped her to her feet. She lost her balance. Jack caught her before she bumped into the nightstand and held her until she nodded that she was okay.

He whispered in her ear, "How many are there?"

She held up four fingers.

That meant he had two left to deal with — or not, providing he and Aminat could get out quietly.

"When we're in the hall, follow me. Move only as I do. If I stop, you stop. You're going to be fine, Aminat. You're going home."

She nodded.

"At the bottom of the stairs, we'll turn left, then out the kitchen door. Don't look around. If I say run, you run and don't look back. Head down the driveway, cross the road to a paved trail. Turn right onto that and run as fast as you can until you see lights. Flag down a car or start pounding doors until you find someone. Have you got all that?"

She mouthed *Yes*.

Jack took out his sat phone and texted: HAVE GIRL. LEAVING HOUSE.

ROGER.

Jack handed Aminat his second phone. "Once you're safe, hit speed-dial four. It's a man named John. Tell him who you are. He'll help."

He stepped around her and opened the door a couple of inches. The hall was empty. He turned back to her, put his finger to his lips, then stepped out and headed for the stairs with Aminat on his heels.

Jack heard a thump and the twang of vibrating wood. Aminat cried out. He looked over his shoulder and saw her leaning over, holding her bare big toe. Her face was a grimace.

At the end of the hall the door swung open and a petite figure emerged. *Helen.* She shouted, "Hey!"

Simultaneously, Jack grabbed Aminat's wrist, jerked her behind him, and raised the Walther and fired two shots over the balustrade. One bullet went wide, splintering the door beside Helen's head, but the second hit home. Helen stumbled backward into the bedroom.

Taking steps two at a time, his hand still clamped on Aminat's wrist, Jack rushed down the stairs.

Aminat shouted, "Wait, I can't —"

Her feet slipped out from under her. She landed on her back and slid down the steps, sideswiping Jack's legs as she went. He felt himself tipping sideways. He slammed his left hand against the wall for balance, then vaulted the last three steps, landing astride Aminat, who was trying to get to her feet.

"Stop!" Helen shouted from the top of the stairs.

Jack didn't look back, but instead shoved Aminat into the kitchen. Jack felt something slam into his left hip. The impact shoved him sideways into the entryway jamb. He hadn't heard the shot; Helen had a suppressor as well. A second bullet smacked into the wood above his head. He pushed off and stumbled into the kitchen. Aminat was standing in the open door, looking back at him.

"Go!"

She sprinted out and turned right. Jack ran after her.

He heard pounding on the steps behind him.

He turned, saw Helen in the doorway. He fired, missed, fired again, then dashed outside. Aminat had reached the end of the driveway. *Good girl,* he thought. *Keep going, fast as you can —*

Helen shouted, "Stop, damn it —"

Jack spun on his heel and saw her shuffling across the kitchen floor, gun pointing at him. The side of her blouse was soaked with blood. She fired. Jack ducked left, reached out, and slammed the door in her face. The door buckled outward.

Half limping, half running, Jack headed down the driveway. Aminat was well ahead of him, almost lost in the darkness, save the white of her T-shirt. Jack crossed Abden. Ahead, he saw Pettycur Road. He glanced left and right and saw no headlights. *Just need another sixty seconds,* he thought dully.

He heard the snap beside his ear. Too

close. If you could hear the snap, the round was close enough to touch. He ignored it and kept going. His left hip was growing numb. With each step he could hear the squelch of blood in his shoe.

Despite himself, he glanced over his shoulder. Helen was thirty feet behind, gun extended before her and weaving as though drunk. Her face was deathly white. The muzzle of her gun flashed orange. Jack felt the bullet pluck at his sleeve. *Fuckin' good shot, this one.*

He crossed Pettycur Road. At the shoulder his foot caught the dirt berm and he fell forward and started barrel-rolling down the slope. He crashed to a stop against the hedges. Out of the corner of his eye, he saw Helen appear at the top of the slope. She stopped, looked for him. She spotted him and raised her gun.

Jack rolled sideways, raised the Walther, and fired twice. This time his aim was true. The first round slammed into Helen's thigh, the second into her belly. She folded forward, then pitched headfirst onto the grass and rolled onto her side.

Jack heard bare feet slapping on the paved path, then Aminat was crouching beside him. "You are hurt."

"I told you to run," he said.

"I did. And then I stopped and came back. Should I check to see if that woman is —"

"No, stay away from her. Help me up."

Leaning on her, Jack got to his feet and limped up the slope to where Helen lay. She wasn't moving. Gun trained on her head, he prodded her shoulder with his foot.

She let out a groan.

"Thank God," he murmured. "Aminat, look over the berm and tell me what you see."

Aminat did as he asked. "I don't see anything."

"Pick up her gun and help me with her."

Together they dragged Helen down the slope by her shoulders; her body left a slick of blood on the grass. With Aminat's help, Jack manhandled Helen over his shoulder, then he found a gap in the hedges and pushed through. Another fifty feet brought them to a jumble of boulders at the waterline that Jack hoped would screen them from the road. He laid Helen on the sand. He sat down with his back against one of the boulders.

He got out his phone and texted Clark: OUT SAFE.

CONTACT WHEN CLEAR OF AREA.

Jack stuffed the phone back into his pocket.

Aminat said, "Your pant leg is all bloody."

"Yeah, I need something to stop it."

Aminat raised the hem of her T-shirt to her mouth, bit a hole in it, then ripped free a strip of the cotton. "Where is it?"

"You better let me do it."

"Tell me where."

"Left hip."

Aminat unbuttoned his pants and pulled them down until the wound was exposed. Unceremoniously, she stuck the tip of her index finger into the hole. Jack winced, tried to jerk away. "Hold still," Aminat said. "It's small and not very deep. I can feel the bullet beneath the skin. I need to shove some of my T-shirt inside. It's going to hurt."

Jack gritted his teeth as she jammed the material into the wound. A scream rose into his throat. He swallowed it, breathed through it, and slowly the pain subsided to a sharp throbbing.

Aminat said, "That will do for now, but it should be seen to."

"Exactly how old are you?" Jack asked.

"Twenty-one. You know who my father is, yes? You know where I come from? Not such a nice place sometimes. We grew up fast, my brothers and I."

Helen let out a groan. Her eyes fluttered open. She turned her head, saw Aminat, then looked at Jack.

"I didn't hit her, did I?"

Jack was taken aback. "No, she's fine."

"Please don't take her," Helen pleaded. "She doesn't deserve this."

"Deserve what?"

"Do you have any idea what he has planned for her?"

Jack felt a pit in his stomach. "Who're you talking about?"

"Farid Rasulov. But I'm sure it wasn't real."

Oleg Pechkin, Jack thought. "Aminat's father sent me, not Rasulov."

Aminat said, "He's telling the truth. Who is Rasulov? What was he going to do to me?"

"I'll explain later," replied Jack.

Helen said, "Funny, I've never had one get away before. This is the first time, and it's turned out to be a good thing."

Jack's mind was blank. This wasn't what he expected to hear from a hardened kidnapper who'd threatened to dice up a twenty-one-year-old girl. Nor was her appearance a match: Helen was petite, barely taller than five feet, with a black pixie haircut. *A tough woman,* Jack thought, *to succeed in such a cut-throat business.*

All he could think to ask was, "How many of these have you done?"

Helen took a ragged breath and a bubble of blood appeared at the corner of her mouth. She was bleeding inside, Jack knew. There was nothing he could do for her.

"Thirty-eight. All of them returned safe. I am a saint, aren't I? Rasulov . . . I had a bad feeling about him from the start. The money was very good, but what he asked me to do — I couldn't."

"Who were the two men in the basement?" asked Jack.

"Roma killed the boy . . . stabbed him. So I killed him. He was an animal. He would have killed you too, Amy. You were never going back home."

"Then why not just let me go when the others weren't looking?"

"I was, but I had to think it through. Rasulov would have killed Yegor and Olik when they got home. They are dead, aren't they?" she asked Jack.

"Only one of them. The one in the kitchen is okay."

"Yegor; he's a good man," Helen said with a wan smile. "Make sure the police get him."

"Why?" Aminat said. "You're not making sense."

"I told you: He can never go home again."

Jack decided Helen deserved to know the truth; soon it would make no difference anyway. "Rasulov's real name is Oleg Pechkin. He's SVR."

"Bastard." She coughed and her face twisted in pain. "I should have listened to my little voice. He told us it was a straight ransom job. It wasn't, was it?"

"No," Jack replied. "Helen, I need you to do me a favor. I need you to say all of this on camera. Aminat's father has to know who took her."

Helen nodded. "You'd better hurry."

After she was gone, Jack searched her and found only a cell phone. Then they covered her body in sand and some seaweed that had washed up on shore. Aminat sat staring at the mound. "I don't understand any of this . . . By the way, what is your name?"

"Jack. Your father will explain it all. We need to go."

As if on cue, in the distance he heard the warble of sirens.

"Just sit tight," John Clark said over the phone six hours later. "He'll get to you by tonight."

Jack sat hunched over on the edge of the tub, elbows on his knees, phone pressed to his ear. He was exhausted and his hip had in the last hour gone from numb to pulsing with pain. The long walk hadn't helped matters.

Sticking to the shoreline, they'd headed north away from Kinghorn while the police sirens converged on Abden Place. As they walked, Jack field-stripped Helen's weapon, heaving the pieces into the ocean at irregular intervals. Two miles and as many hours later they found themselves in Linktown, where Aminat, armed with Jack's credit card, got them a motel room.

"Tell him to bring a first-aid kit," Jack muttered.

"Already done," replied Clark.

Gerry Hendley said, "How's the girl?"

"Sleeping like the dead." Through the half-open door he could hear Aminat snoring softly. "As for the long term, she's probably going to need some help."

Back at the shoreline Jack had realized Aminat had either missed hearing or hadn't understood Helen's comment about Roma murdering Steven Bagley. It was a conversation he wasn't looking forward to. As if being kidnapped wasn't enough, now she'd have to grapple with the fact that her friend had died trying to save her.

"You've already sent the video?" Jack said.

"Yes, to Ysabel," said Gavin.

Knowing he wasn't going to be able to

physically reunite Rebaz Medzhid and his daughter before the deadline expired, Jack had tacked onto Helen's video confession a personal message from Aminat.

"What about the second one?" he asked.

Of her own volition Helen had made a second video, this one addressed to her "broker," a man named Dobromir, who had for the last decade negotiated and coordinated her jobs. He would, if shown the video, help Jack track down Pechkin.

"I'm not sure I buy it," said Gerry.

"Dying declaration," Jack replied. He actually understood Helen's motivation: The SVR man not only had hired her under false pretenses, but also had asked her to do something that went against her own sense of — warped though it was — professionalism.

Clark said, "I'm with Jack. She offed one of her own men, for Christ's sake. Besides, Pechkin could be so deep into Seth's plan that it's already scuttled. Better to know that now."

"All right," Gerry said. "Gavin, dig into this Dobromir. You did good, Jack. You got the girl out safe. And yourself."

"I got shot in the ass, Gerry."

Clark said, "Better that than in the head."

"True. Anything on the news about the

cottage?"

"For twenty minutes after you left, the police bands were going nuts, then they went silent."

"A triple murder in a sleepy seaside resort tends to have that effect," Clark observed. "Jack, did you get out clean?"

"If anyone saw us running, it was our backs, not our faces. As long as we're not around when the police expand their canvass up here, we'll be okay."

"Get some sleep. Cavalry's coming."

Though the man wasn't one for small talk, when he did speak, he seemed friendly enough. His accent was British, somewhere in the Midlands.

He tossed a bag of spare clothes on the dresser and then, with Aminat watching from the chair in the corner, had Jack lie on the bed, belly-down. He examined the bullet wound, proclaimed it "a doddle," then jabbed a needle full of lidocaine into the area around it.

"We'll give that a few minutes to set in," the man said.

"This is awkward," Jack said.

"Could be worse. Could've gone straight up your arse."

Aminat let out a blurt of laughter, then

298

whispered, "Sorry."

Jack said to him, "Do I have you to thank for the Walther?"

"You have Mr. Clark to thank. Worked okay for you, did it? Good weapon, the Walther."

It was an odd question. On one hand, he'd used it to kill two people who were trying to kill them; on the other, he'd killed two people with it. This was something he doubted he'd ever get used to.

"Everything's relative," Jack replied.

"A truer word never spoken. It'd probably be best if I take it with me, yeah? Unless you've got plans for it, that is."

"Take it."

"Your car, too. Saw it on the way in. The cops haven't gotten to it, but they will. Right, then: You should be nice and numb now. Hey you, girl —"

"Amy."

"There's a bottle of Keflex in that bag. Make sure he takes them, yeah, or he could be oozing pus down his leg by morning."

"Eww . . . gross."

He returned his attention to Jack's wound. "Okay, go ahead and cry like a bitch if this hurts."

"Get on with it."

The man put a flashlight between his teeth

and aimed it at Jack's hip. "First we clean it, then forceps and red-hot screwdriver. Kidding, mate, just kidding."

21
BAKU

Even two hundred miles from his own capital in a foreign country, Rebaz Medzhid had horsepower. Clearly, Jack thought, reports of Dagestan and Azerbaijan's lukewarm relationship were mistaken. Gerry Hendley had handled the first leg of Jack and Aminat's flight, from Glasgow to Heathrow and then to Istanbul, where Medzhid's private plane, an aging Learjet, took them the rest of the way to Baku.

They were met by Seth, Spellman, and one of Medzhid's bodyguards on the tarmac outside the fenced charter terminal. As one of the bodyguards ushered Aminat into the car, Jack asked, "Where's Ysabel?"

"Back at our motel. She wants to see you," said Seth. "Hey, Jack, you dog, what's going on with you two, anyway?"

Jack ignored him.

Twenty minutes later they reached

Medzhid's hotel, the Four Seasons at the base of Baku Bay. The minister was waiting when the elevator doors parted on the penthouse level.

"My girl!" Medzhid cried, running toward her. He wrapped her in a bear hug and they remained like that, Aminat crying in his arms, for a full minute.

When they parted Jack could see Medzhid's eyes were wet. This was a wholly different man from the one who'd slapped Seth back at the forestry camp.

"Where is he?" Medzhid said, looking around.

"He means you, Jack," said Spellman, stepping aside.

Jack limped forward. With the bullet out, the pain in his hip had lessened enough that the codeine cut the pain to almost nothing. Clark's Hereford friend had recommended a cane for a week or so. Jack said no.

Medzhid extended his hand and Jack took it.

"Thank you, Jack, thank you for bringing my girl home. You are a man I can trust, I see that now." He turned and nodded in turn at Seth and Spellman. "And you as well."

Aminat came forward and hugged Jack, her head pressed hard against his chest.

"Thank you for coming for me, Jack."

"My pleasure," he replied. "I'm sorry about Steven."

"When I get back to Edinburgh, I will call his family. Don't forget to take your antibiotics and to change your dressing."

"Aminat," said Medzhid, "go call your mother and tell her you are safe."

Aminat pulled away and went through the penthouse's door.

"Come in, gentlemen. We have a lot to discuss."

While their boss settled Aminat into one of the back bedrooms, the bodyguards served Jack and others tea from a silver samovar. Once done, they stepped left, to take up their posts, Jack assumed. Medzhid's suite was expansive and bright white, from the carpet to the draperies.

"Wow, I should've brought my sunglasses," Seth remarked.

Jack said nothing.

"Come on, Jack, that's funny. What the hell's wrong with you?"

Before Jack could respond, Medzhid emerged from the hallway and joined them in the seating area. He poured himself a cup of tea, then leaned back in the couch.

"I saw the video. That woman is dead, yes?

I should have had you bring her to me alive." He drew his thumb across his throat. "Her head . . . off."

Jack said nothing. Though he'd probably feel the same hatred if his own daughter was kidnapped, beheading was a vengeance too far for Jack. Then again, it was going to take a strong and brutal man to wrest his country free of Valeri Volodin, and Medzhid seemed to fit the bill.

Still, Jack wasn't sure whether he trusted Medzhid. For starters, he doubted the man's Learjet was government-issue. How does someone who makes the equivalent of $30,000 afford that?

Jack wasn't about to further implicate himself or Ysabel in what had happened at the cottage. It was the kind of leverage Medzhid might use to his advantage.

"Did she give you any information on who hired her?" Medzhid asked.

"No," Jack lied. For now he'd keep to himself their lead on Dobromir the broker.

"And what happened to the other ones?" the minister asked. "They are also dead?"

"Don't worry about them. Worry about Steven Bagley's family."

"Who?"

"He's a friend of your daughter's. He tried to stop them from taking her. He's dead."

"That is very sad. But Aminat will get over it. To business: I had planned to be back in Makhachkala by this evening, but that's now impossible."

"Why?" asked Spellman.

"Four of my district commanders are being . . . fussy. They control the Rutulsky, Akhtynsky, Tlyaratinsky, and Suleyman–Stalsky areas along our border with Azerbaijan."

"What do you mean, 'fussy'?"

"They want more prestigious positions in the new government. Believe it or not, they are actually good, loyal men."

"Clearly, we have different definitions of those terms," Jack observed.

"It's the way of things in my country: If I accede to their demands, I appear weak and they may not follow me when the time comes. If I try to cross in either of their districts, there will be a confrontation. I will win, of course, but they will have lost face and, again, they may not follow me when the time comes. Better to avoid the whole business. Everyone involved will pretend like it never happened. Once I am back in Makhachkala I will assure them their loyalty will be rewarded. That will suffice."

"What's to say they won't up the ante when things get rolling?"

"Because I will have my own people in place down there," Medzhid said with a grim smile.

"This is just fucking great," Seth growled.

"Have faith, Mr. Gregory."

"Forget them. We don't need 'em."

"We do. When the coup begins there will be chaos and our Azerbaijani friends will get nervous about spillover. Having the border districts firmly under our control will reassure them. They will stand with us against Volodin, at least politically."

"Why don't we just use the Parsabad–Artezian? They might not have railroads covered, especially that one."

"They will, trust me."

"Then get aboard your damned jet and just fly to Makhachkala."

Medzhid snorted. "A plane. The man wants me to get a plane."

"So what?"

Spellman answered. "Seth, think it through: You said yourself Wellesley and Pechkin are ahead of us. Who knows how far, or what resources they've got. For all we know they've got operators on the ground. We can't put the linchpin of our plan on a plane and send him into Dagestani airspace."

"Shit, you're right."

Medzhid said, "Forget it, my friend. You just need some sleep." *He needs more than that,* Jack thought.

"Okay," he said. "We've only got one option if we're going to get back into the country: go through Georgia."

Leaving Seth and Spellman with Medzhid, Jack took a taxi to the Mirabat Hotel, which he found overlooking a tire factory and what looked like an abandoned water-slide park.

He'd rapped only once on Ysabel's door when it jerked open. She stood on the threshold for a moment, then smiled and rushed him. They hugged for a bit, then she pulled away, took his hand, and led him into the room.

"I'm so glad you're back," she said.

"Me, too."

"Matt told me you were shot. In the butt."

"Hip, actually," Jack replied.

"Does it hurt?"

"Not as much anymore."

"You'd better let me take a look at it," she said.

"It's fine, Ysabel. It's all stitched up and —"

"Jack, you're not very good at hints, are you?"

"What?"

307

"Hints."

"Oh," he said.

Afterward, they lay together, Jack dozing in and out, Ysabel's head resting on his chest.

"I feel a bit shameless," she whispered.

Jack chuckled. "You are direct, no doubt about it."

"You don't like that?"

"I like it. As long as this isn't a case of combat bonding."

"I don't know what that is," she replied.

"When soldiers share hardships for a while, they form strong ties. Nothing like having bad guys trying to kill you to solidify friendship."

Ysabel sat up on her elbow and looked him in the eye. "Do you really think that's all this is?"

"No, I don't. I shouldn't have said it."

"You're right, you shouldn't have. Jack, what are we going to do about Seth?"

"What do you mean?"

"He's unstable. I don't particularly like what he's become, but I still care about him, and I know you do, too. He's almost . . ."

"Self-destructive. The thought has crossed my mind. There's not much we can do except watch him, try to keep him from slipping any deeper."

She switched gears back to her buoyant self. "I'm hungry. Do you think they have room service?"

They didn't, and given Ysabel's report of cockroaches, Jack was glad for it. They were heading out the door to find a restaurant when Seth texted: WE'RE BACK. ROOM 204.

They walked down the hallway and knocked on Seth's door. Spellman opened it and ushered them inside. Seth was sitting at a table beneath the window, writing on a legal pad.

"You've really put us in it, Jack. You have any idea what a mess Georgia is?"

"Some. You have a better plan?"

Spellman answered, "No. We've got bigger problems anyway. Wellesley's in the wind. His cell phone's disconnected and the Zafaraniyeh apartment has been cleaned out. We have to assume he and Pechkin are on the move together."

"To Makhachkala," Jack said, thinking.

Seth waved his hand dismissively. "Doesn't matter. *Dagestanskaia Pravda* broke a story this morning — it claims Medzhid was involved in the Dagestan mas-sacre."

Jack knew of this, and had seen the videos, something he regretted.

In 1999 a Chechen force of fifty rebels crossed into Dagestan and attacked a small village, which was guarded by twenty-two Russian conscripts; of these, all but nine ran away. All of those who stayed were beheaded by the rebels.

"Involved how?" asked Jack.

"Medzhid was the area's district deputy commander then. He chased down some of the rebels — about fifteen — before they got back across the border. Medzhid's team cornered them in an old mosque in Almak. There was a gunfight, and a fire broke out. All of the rebels were killed."

"The problem is," Spellman went on, "a man from Medzhid's team just came forward claiming it wasn't rebels inside the mosque, but civilians taking shelter from the battle. He says Medzhid firebombed the mosque and that when he discovered the civilians inside, he covered it up."

Jack asked the obvious question: "Is it true?"

"Of course not. In fact, according to Medzhid, no one from his team is still alive; most of them died in the fighting around Karamakhi."

Convenient, Jack thought. Whether for Medzhid or the opposition he didn't know.

"This is Pechkin and Wellesley," said Seth.

"Yes, there was a gunfight, and a fire, but it was only rebels inside."

"We need to get Medzhid back to the capital so he can get in front of the story," said Spellman. "If it's not already too late."

22

TBILISI

Whatever the truth about Medzhid's involvement in the Almak incident, the man had clearly parlayed his current position into a friendship with Dagestan's neighbor to the southwest, Georgia — or at least with the government in Tbilisi. On that count Seth had been right.

Led by Medzhid, Jack and the others stepped down the Learjet steps to the tarmac below, where a trio of olive-drab pickup trucks with black push bumpers and black roll cages over the beds were waiting. Each truck's bed held six armed soldiers in camouflage and gray berets. None of them gave Jack's group a second glance, instead facing away and scanning the airport's perimeter. Special Forces, Jack guessed.

A man in a navy blue suit walked up to Medzhid. "Minister Medzhid, welcome to Tbilisi. General Zumadze is waiting for you. If you'll follow me . . ."

The man led them to a Soviet-era ZiL limousine and soon they were heading toward a hangar on the other side of the tarmac. The ZiL pulled through the hangar's doors and braked to a stop beside a glassed-in office.

Through the ZiL's rear window Jack saw the Special Forces Brigade trucks take up station outside. Beside him, Ysabel whispered, "Are we guests or prisoners?"

"We're about to find out," Jack replied.

They got out and followed Medzhid into the office, where a stocky man in a charcoal military uniform was waiting. "General Zumadze," Medzhid said, "thank you for your hospitality."

The two men embraced and exchanged double cheek kisses.

Medzhid didn't introduce Jack and the others, and General Zumadze paid them no notice.

"Our pleasure," said Zumadze. "My deputy has shared with me your problem. Terrible when you cannot trust your own comrades."

Medzhid chuckled. "I trust them. Just not right now; we'll come to an arrangement. Can you get us across the border?"

"Quickly or safely?"

"The former. And it has to be away from

my border districts."

"I can get you close to the border, but we are having problems with a new Ossetian separatist group — the Ossetian Freedom Brigade — in that particular area. Here, let me show you."

Medzhid and Zumadze walked to a gray steel desk and leaned over a map; Zumadze tapped a spot on it. "Omalo. It's a village in the Tusheti National Park. The OFB has been attacking convoys and stations on GMR East between there and the border."

Spellman whispered to Jack, "Georgian Military Road."

"I've had thirty dead and two helicopters shot down in the last month," said Zumadze. "I am spread thin and I fear military vehicles will only attract the OFB's attention. It is risky, but I think your best chance for getting through is to do so incognito. Once you reach the Yuzhno border checkpoint, you will be safe."

Jack said from his place against the wall, "Omalo to the border is how far, sixteen kilometers?"

Zumadze suddenly seemed to notice he and Medzhid weren't alone. He narrowed his eyes at Jack and said, "You are American. Who are you?"

"Just a guy asking a question. How far is

the border?"

"Nineteen kilometers. But the terrain is mountainous."

Zumadze's answer told Jack something. The Georgian military had completely lost control of a twelve-mile stretch of a major transportation artery, one of its only into Dagestan. Worse still, Zumadze's refusal to provide escort was likely born of survival instinct: If Dagestan's Minister of the Interior were to die while under his protection, he'd likely lose his job. It appeared Medzhid's partnership with Georgia wasn't as solid as Seth had suggested.

"It is a very hard area to patrol," Zumadze said.

"Sounds like it," Jack replied.

"What does that mean?"

"Nothing. General, can you give us weapons?"

Zumadze slapped his hand on the desk, then jabbed a stubby finger at Jack. "Who are you to demand —"

"Forget him, my friend," Medzhid said, flicking his fingers in Jack's direction. "Can you provide us with weapons?"

Zumadze tore his gaze from Jack, then nodded. "Guns I can give you."

Two hours later they were on their way,

moving in convoy formation with one of the pickup trucks on point, another taking the rear, and Jack's group inside a canvas-covered GAZ 4×4 truck. Medzhid's two bodyguards, Anton and Vasim, sat at the tailgate, occasionally peeking through the canvas flaps.

With each passing mile the air grew colder. Jack could feel his ears popping as they moved higher into the Pirikiti Mountains. The GAZ's diesel engine groaned with the strain.

For the tenth time in half as many minutes the truck's tires plunged into a pothole and bounced them off the wooden bench seats. Jack put most of his weight on his good butt cheek, but it didn't help much.

"I'm going to have bruises," Ysabel whispered to Jack. "They'll need seeing to later."

"I'm happy to help in any way I can."

From the opposite bench Medzhid called over the engine noise, "I am sorry about that, Jack. Zumadze is not fond of the West, especially America."

"Clearly."

"Having it appear you are under my thumb makes everything easier."

"Mr. Minister —"

"Rebaz, please."

"Rebaz. How well do you know General Zumadze?"

"Very well. He and I have worked together closely on a number of antiterrorism operations — along with our counterpart in Grozny."

"Does Zumadze know about the coup?"

"No."

"Why are you asking, Jack?" said Spellman.

"Back in Tbilisi, Rebaz told him he's being blocked from entering his own country and he didn't bat an eye."

"Baksheesh," Seth replied. "Institutional extortion. Zumadze has to deal with it himself, I'm sure."

"Indeed," replied Medzhid. "It is a different world here, Jack."

No shit, he thought.

Late in the afternoon they pulled into Omalo. The GAZ's engine shut down. General Zumadze swung back the canvas flaps. "You will stay here tonight. It is too dangerous to drive at night."

Jack and the others jumped out and began stretching their legs. Bundled in a Georgian Army parka two sizes too big for her, Ysabel wrapped her arms around her torso. "It's beautiful here," she said through a shiver.

"Nice place to visit."

"But not live."

The village, which sat in a shallow valley surrounded by rolling foothills, was little more than a scattering of ramshackle saltbox-style homes with tin roofs. Across the dirt road was a fenced pasture full of horses grazing at the spring grass. To the west stood a line of snowcapped peaks behind which the sun was dropping. Jack saw long shadows creeping down the hills toward Omalo. During the winter Omalo probably had little or no contact with the outside world.

At a gesture from Zumadze, two of the Special Forces soldiers jumped down from the nearest truck and trotted toward the house adjacent to the pasture. They banged on the door; when it swung open, they disappeared inside.

Jack led Ysabel out of earshot from the group. "When we get across the border we're parting company with Seth and the others."

"Why?"

"The woman who was holding Aminat —"

"Helen."

"She gave me the name of her broker, a guy called Dobromir. He took the contract for Aminat's kidnapping. Pechkin set it up.

Dobromir lives in Khasavyurt."

"What makes you think he'll cooperate with us?"

"Before she died, Helen made him a video, sort of a last will and testament. If he has anything on Pechkin, he'll give it to us."

"Jack, why am I just hearing about this?" When he didn't answer, she said, "You were going to leave me behind, weren't you?"

"I changed my mind. You don't break up the team in mid-game."

"Very wise of you."

Zumadze called, "May I have everyone's attention!"

Jack and Ysabel returned to where the rest of the group was standing. "A few hours ago the OFB attacked an outpost — in Shenako, two miles to the east."

"How many dead?" asked Medzhid.

"None, thankfully. Two wounded. They will be evacuated in the morning. I must return to the capital tonight, but I will leave Major Asatiani with you. In the morning, he'll see you on your way."

"What about our weapons?" Jack asked.

Zumadze offered him a mocking smile. "Are you frightened? Do not worry yourself. You will be fine."

"Not with that truck. It's got target written all over it."

"That's being taken care of."

From the ranch house, one of Zumadze's soldiers called to him. A man, a woman, and two children slipped past the soldier and headed down the road toward the village center.

Ysabel asked, "Where are they going? We can't put them out of their own home."

"It is just for the night," Zumadze replied. "Follow me. We will get you settled in."

Shortly after nightfall, Zumadze left in one of the pickup trucks.

Major Asatiani spent a few minutes patrolling the area surrounding the house, then assigned two men to the front door and two to inside the horse barn, leaving himself and one more, a private no older than twenty, inside the home with Jack and the others.

As the private started cooking the evening meal, Asatiani sat down at a small table beside the door and began stripping and cleaning his sidearm.

Medzhid turned in early, leaving his bodyguards playing cards outside his door. Jack and the others gathered around the trestle-style dining table on the far side of the room.

"Friendly guy, the major," Ysabel said.

"Most of his kind are," replied Spellman.

"Good in a fight, though."

Jack said, "Seth, yesterday you talked about Volodin rolling tanks up to Dagestan's border and sitting there waiting for the coup to start. What if he does just that?"

"He won't. But to answer your question, if he comes it won't be through Chechnya unless he wants to get bogged down, which leaves him Stavropol to the west and Kalmykia to the north. Between them there are only two major highways into Dagestan — the P215 and the P285." Seth grinned. "They're both two-lane, and they both go over several river crossings."

Seth and Spellman had a plan in place to sabotage the crossings, Jack realized. This coup wouldn't be driven solely by an Arab Spring–like popular groundswell, but also by on-the-ground insurgency warfare. The problem was, if Volodin committed himself to invasion, such tactics would only delay the inevitable.

If Makhachkala didn't go as planned, a whole lot of innocent civilians were going to die.

23

After receiving their weapons, AK-47s with three spare magazines each, from Major Asatiani, they set out in the predawn darkness with the GAZ, now emblazoned with the red-on-white flag of the Red Crescent Society, the Islamo-centric cousin of the Red Cross. Whether this garnishment would mean a damn to the OFB was anyone's guess.

With Jack at the wheel, Ysabel beside him, and Spellman in the passenger seat, they made decent progress for the first hour and then the winding mountain road narrowed, its surface rutted with ice and half-buried boulders. Jack eased up on the gas pedal but still had to fight the steering wheel to keep the truck from sliding onto the shoulder.

Spellman sat with the barrel of his AK resting on the dashboard, his eyes scanning the road ahead. Jack's and Ysabel's rifles were propped between her knees, muzzles down.

"Jack, what was that business about how well Medzhid knows General Zumadze?" asked Spellman.

"Probably nothing. But if I had a friend like Zumadze, I'd be rethinking the relationship."

"What, you thinking he's feeding us to the OFB?"

"I'm not saying that."

"Then spit it out."

"Your plan is partially counting on Georgia backing the coup, and Zumadze won't even give Medzhid safe passage out of his own country."

"Yeah, I see your point. But Zumadze's as savvy as Medzhid; if the coup goes our way, Tbilisi will want to back the winner."

By noon, having covered half the distance to the border, they reached Chero, a village perched on a slope overlooking a river gorge. Jack steered the GAZ through the village, then down a switchback road to the bottom of the gorge, where the road leveled and began following the course of the river. Through Spellman's half-open window Jack could hear the rush of water spilling over boulders. Though directly overhead, the sun's rays didn't fully penetrate the gorge, leaving the road in partial twilight.

The Velcro flap behind the seat tore open and Seth's head appeared in the square opening. "We better pick up the pace or we won't make Yuzhno by nightfall."

"Any faster and we'll go into the river," Spellman answered. "Jack's doing fine."

"We won't be if we get stuck out here. Pick up the pace, Jack."

Seth disappeared and the flap closed.

"Whoa," Spellman called, as Jack rounded a corner. "Slow it down, Jack."

"I see it."

Jack slowed to a stop, the truck's brakes echoing off the gorge's walls.

Ahead a pair of UAZ jeeps covered in what looked like improvised spray-paint camouflage sat astride the road. They were staggered, one ahead of the other, to lessen the chance of a vehicle's ramming its way through the roadblock. Jack counted six men, all bearded, four standing before the vehicles and one behind each one's wheel. They were all armed with AKs.

"The OFB?" Ysabel muttered.

"He'd better assume so," Jack replied.

He glanced in his side mirror, studying the road behind them. Though they'd passed no turnoffs since entering the gorge, a bracket ambush was the smart move. The road was empty. How fast he could drive the GAZ in reverse while being pursued he didn't know.

Seth's head poked through the canvas opening. "Why are we stopping — Ah, shit."

"Sit tight and keep quiet," Jack told him.

"I'll talk to them," Spellman said, and reached for the door handle.

"Bad idea, Matt."

"Better to start out friendly."

Ysabel asked, "Do you speak —"

"Ossete? No, but I've got Farsi, and they're close. And I look the part."

"Barely," Ysabel remarked.

"Can you two cover me?"

"Stay within sprinting distance," said Jack.

Leaving his AK on the truck's floorboard, Spellman climbed out. Jack did the same, but propped his weapon muzzle-first on the running board.

"Show them your hands. And don't smile."

Jack raised his hands and took a step away from the door.

In Farsi, Spellman called to the group and then strode forward a few paces and into Jack's sight line.

That's far enough, Matt.

The men didn't respond. Spellman called out again.

The man standing at the front of the group answered, his tone aggressive.

"He says the road is closed. I told him we're Red Crescent. He doesn't give a shit."

"Tell him we're carrying medicine for the kids in Ibtsokhi."

Spellman did so, but got the same biting reply.

"He doesn't give a shit about that, either."

Suddenly the man pointed his AK skyward and let off a short burst. He shouted at Spellman, gesturing wildly.

Spellman began backing toward the truck. Jack waited until he was in the passenger seat, then climbed in. Through the windshield he could see the OFB leader glaring at them.

"What now?" asked Ysabel.

"We find another way."

Through the canvas divider Medzhid said, "Out of the question. The only other route will cost us a full day. If I'm not back in Makhachkala by morning, the Almak story will be out of my control. Look, there are only six of them and seven of us."

Jack turned to him. "And we're on their home turf, stuck on a narrow road with nowhere to go."

"Ram them."

"We'd never make it —"

Spellman shouted, "They're moving!"

Jack turned back around and saw the OFB men piling into the jeeps. The lead one started speeding toward them, the other one close behind.

Jack jammed the shifter into reverse and hit the gas pedal. The GAZ lurched, then began backing down the road. In the dust kicked up by the rear tires he could see little more than the rock wall flashing by on his left.

"You're on the shoulder," Spellman shouted.

He turned the wheel right. The truck swerved toward the rocks and he adjusted again.

"They're catching up," Ysabel called.

"Matt, when we get around the next corner, you and I are getting out. Ysabel, you're driving. Just keep backing it up and keep your head down."

When the GAZ swung around the bend, Jack slammed on the brakes, shifted it into park. He and Spellman jumped out with their AKs. Jack's bad leg buckled slightly and he stumbled, then regained his balance.

"Go, Ysabel!" he shouted.

The gears crunched and then the GAZ

started reversing.

The lead jeep came around the curve. Jack and Spellman opened up, stitching the vehicle across the hood and windshield. The jeep fishtailed sideways, overcorrected, then vaulted over the shoulder berm and slammed into a boulder jutting from the river. The windshield shattered outward and a pair of men slid down the hood and into the water. The man in the backseat wasn't moving.

Jack, who had been tracking the jeep with his muzzle and pouring fire into the door, stopped and turned back. The second jeep skidded around the corner. It sped up, bearing down on Spellman, who stood in the middle of the road, firing. Jack raised his AK, ready to fire, but the jeep veered left, putting itself between him and Spellman. The side mirror caught Spellman in the side and he stumbled back, bounced off the gorge wall, then slid to the ground.

The jeep turned the next corner and disappeared.

"Spellman?" Jack called.

"I'm good. Go!"

Jack started running as fast as his bad leg would allow. As he approached the bend he heard the chatter of AK fire, then the wrenching of steel on steel. He rounded the corner. Fifty feet away the jeep and GAZ were almost bumper to bumper, the truck still backing up. Its windshield was pocked with bullet strikes, so Jack couldn't see Ysabel. One of the OFB fighters leaned out the jeep's side window and started firing into the truck's grille. Steam billowed from the hood.

Jack dropped to one knee, switched the AK to semi-auto, then took aim on the leaning man and fired twice. The man went limp and folded sideways at the waist, his head bumping over the ground. Jack adjusted aim and put three rounds into the jeep's rear window. Chunks of the glass disintegrated. A rifle barrel poked through one of the gaps. Jack saw a silhouetted head. He fired twice and the head disappeared in a haze of blood spray.

The GAZ slewed sideways. Its back end vaulted over the shoulder. The rear tire plunged into the river and started spinning, sending up a plume of water.

Jack stood, started running again, the AK tucked into his shoulder, firing as he closed the gap. The driver's door swung open and a man climbed out, struggling to clear the muzzle and bring it to bear on Jack. Jack stopped, shot him in the chest, then a second time as he went down.

The GAZ's engine sputtered to a stop, leaving only the high-pitched hum of the jeep's motor.

Behind him, he heard Spellman jog up.

"Let's clear it," Jack said.

They stalked forward, AKs raised. When they were ten feet from the jeep's rear bumper Seth walked down the side of the GAZ. He strode up to the jeep, stuck the barrel of his AK through the window, and fired a short burst, followed by two more. He ejected the magazine, slammed another into the receiver, then leaned down and peered inside.

"They're done," he announced. "Come on, let's get moving."

"Fuckin' hell," Spellman murmured.

It was shortly after ten o'clock when they pulled up to the spotlighted Yuzhno border checkpoint. Jack braked the truck to a stop, put it in park, but left the engine running. He was worried it wouldn't start again.

Before the checkpoint's drop-gate stood four men in Dagestani *politsiya* uniforms. On the other side of the gate an armored personnel carrier blocked the road. Its 14.5-millimeter cannon was pointing in the GAZ's direction.

"That's not very friendly," Ysabel

murmured.

After the firefight, it had taken the better part of two hours before they were back on the road, the first ten minutes of which involved Jack and Spellman jumping down on the jeep's hood until its bumper tore free of the GAZ's. Once done, they manhandled the truck's rear tire back onto the shoulder, then Jack, Seth, Ysabel, and Spellman stood guard as Medzhid's bodyguards went about fixing the GAZ's engine. While the truck's combat-constructed grille had absorbed most of the AK rounds, the radiator hoses were nicked in a dozen places. After expending an entire roll of duct tape and a spool of baling wire, they were moving again.

"I will handle this," Medzhid said through the canvas divider.

He hopped down from the tailgate, then strode to the checkpoint.

The men saluted Medzhid, then Medzhid took one of them aside and started talking. After a few minutes they shook hands and Medzhid walked to the GAZ's passenger window and stepped onto the running board.

"The sergeant has heard nothing more about the Almak story. He will tell no one we crossed. With luck, we will be in Makhachkala before morning."

■ ■ ■ ■

When they reached Buynaksk, thirty miles southeast of the capital, Jack pulled off the highway and into a vacant lot across from a gas station; its fluorescent lights hummed in the darkness.

Jack shut off the engine, jumped down from the cab, and walked around to the tailgate.

"What's going on?" Seth asked.

"This is where we part ways."

"What're you talking about? Who's 'we'?"

Jack said to Medzhid, "Do you think you can arrange a car for us?"

"That is no problem, Jack, but first answer Seth's question."

"We have a lead on Pechkin, a man named Dobromir in Khasavyurt. If it pans out, we might be able to get Pechkin off the field. With him out of the way, your odds improve."

"What lead?" asked Spellman. "When did you get it?"

"Don't worry about it," Jack replied, with what he hoped was a reassuring smile. "This shouldn't take us more than a day, two at the most. We'll find you when we're done."

"Let me send some men with you,"

Medzhid said.

"You need them more than we do."

"Not necessarily untrue, I'm afraid. The Khasavyurt district isn't fully under my control. The commander there, Major Umarov, is Chechen. I suspect he's not quite convinced I'm as politically tolerant as I claim."

Jack read between the lines: If he and Ysabel got into trouble in Khasavyurt they could expect neither help nor acknowledgment from Medzhid. For Dagestan's chief of *politsiya* to be associated with a jailed American and an Iranian citizen on the eve of the coup would be disastrous. And according to Gavin, so corrupt was the government of Khasavyurt that its last mayor had been ousted for aiding terrorism.

Of course, this was only part of their problem. In the past three years Khasavyurt had seen seven bombings and two cross-border raids from Chechen terrorists. In all, ninety-two Khasavyurt citizens had died.

Spellman asked, "Is this worth the trip, Jack?"

"I think it is."

"Okay," said Seth, "go run your errand, then get your ass to Makhachkala. We may have to pull the trigger sooner than we'd planned."

24

KHASAVYURT

Cross-country, the distance from Buynaksk to Khasavyurt was only sixty-five kilometers, but Dagestan's highway system being what it was, Jack and Ysabel found themselves following the GAZ east toward the capital before they could turn north for the remaining eighty kilometers of the journey.

It was eight a.m. before they reached the city and were immediately greeted by signs of the most recent bombing attack, a six-acre patch beside the highway that was piled high with the remains of an apartment block.

"That's what four hundred pounds of explosives can do," Jack remarked.

"How many died?" asked Ysabel.

"Just workers, forty of them. The apartment hadn't opened yet."

"Thank goodness for that."

Despite its bloody recent history, they found

the city quiet and seemingly normal. People starting their day stood on sidewalks, chatting and laughing as they waited for buses. Along the main road, Shamilya, shops and markets were opening for the day, owners hosing down and sweeping the pavement and setting out displays.

Jack stopped at a gas station. As he topped off the car's tank, Ysabel went inside and bought a two-page tourist brochure and map of the city; reliable online versions were nonexistent.

Once they were back on the road Ysabel gave Jack directions, which took them across the Yaryksu River, which inside the city was funneled into a concrete-sided canal. Over the bridge railing the water was brown and sluggish with spring silt.

"Cotton, fruit canning, and wrestlers," Ysabel said, reading from the brochure. "Those are Khasavyurt's claims to fame."

"Wrestlers?"

"Six Olympians. Don't pick any fights, Jack."

"Noted."

Across the river they turned left, then left again onto a frontage road overlooking the canal. On their right was a block of tall, narrow houses with red tile roofs; from each one sprouted a satellite TV dish. Each home was separated by an alley no wider than Jack's shoulders.

"It should be up here, in the middle of the block. Number 4215."

Jack drove past the house, then pulled to the curb.

"How do you want to do this?" asked Ysabel.

This question had been on Jack's mind. They didn't have the time it would take to tail Dobromir and learn his comings and goings. Jack had decided on the direct approach.

"We'll let Helen do the talking," he said, then opened his door.

They walked back down the block to Dobromir's house. Jack pushed the buzzer. Inside, a dog started barking; it sounded big. The door opened, revealing a bald man with a broad face. Beside the man was a dog with thick, shaggy fur and a blunt snout. It growled. The man made a clicking sound with his tongue and the dog turned and trotted away.

Jack said, *"Vy gavarite pa angliyski?"*

"Yes, I speak English."

"Helen sent us."

"I do not know any Helen."

Jack pressed play on his phone and held it before the man's face.

Helen's voice came over the speaker. "Dobo, my love, I'm afraid the job did not go as planned. This man's name is Jack. I told him you would help him —"

Jack shut off the video.

Dobromir asked, "She looked ill. What did you do to her?"

"It's a long story. May we come in?"

Dobromir hesitated for a moment, then stepped aside and let them through into a cramped foyer covered in peeling red stick-on tile. Dobromir clicked shut the door's dead bolt, then did the same to a second and third one at the top and bottom. The door was steel.

"Come," he said, then headed down the hallway.

Ysabel whispered to Jack, "Did you know they were involved?"

Jack nodded.

"What's with the door?"

"Cost of doing business, I guess."

They followed Dobromir to a room lined with overflowing bookshelves. From wall to wall the space was no more than twelve feet; from front to back, thirty feet. A semicircle of three LCD computer monitors sat on a desk against the wall. Dobromir gestured for them to sit on the couch.

"Let me see the video," he said.

Jack cued it up again, then handed him the phone. Holding it close to his face, Dobromir hit play.

"Dobo, my love . . ."

As Helen continued speaking, Jack kept his eyes on Dobromir's face. If this was going to go bad, it would happen in the next thirty seconds.

When Helen neared the end of the message, Dobromir's eyebrows narrowed. "The man that is showing you this, Jack, shot me. But I do not blame him and neither should you. He came to rescue the girl and he was defending her. The man named Rasulov had ordered me to do terrible things to her. Roma killed the boy and he would have done the same to her. I would not have let him, but Jack did not know this. I want you to help him. Dobo, you will always be my one and only —"

Dobromir shut off the video. He handed the phone back to Jack. His face was hard, his eyes cold.

"I want a copy of that."

"Sure. You're taking this very well."

"She did not blame you, so I do not blame you. She was always the boss, my little Helen. And my smarter half."

"We're sorry for your loss," Ysabel said, her eyes brimming with tears.

"It comes with the job. We knew that. I had not heard from her in a couple of days. I was afraid something had gone wrong. Tell me this much: Did she suffer? The truth."

"She was in shock, so not very much."

"Where is her body?"

"We buried her by the ocean."

"Good."

Ysabel asked, "Were you two married?"

"No, Helen did not believe in it. Paper isn't love, she always said. So, Jack: I assume you want to find Farid Rasulov?"

"His real name is Oleg Pechkin. He's with Russian intelligence."

"Motherless whores," Dobromir muttered. "Tell me what he looks like." Jack gave him the description Seth had provided. Dobromir shook his head. "That is not the man I met. True, he was Helen's point of contact, but I never met him. I should have."

"You usually meet people that hire you?" Ysabel said with surprise.

"If they are unwilling to meet face-to-face, they are not for us. And I only take a contract after I have done my homework. I never sent Helen on a job blind."

"Who approached you with the contract?"

"He said his name was Ashworth," Dobromir replied. "He was British."

"Describe him."

"Short, with brown hair, going bald."

Raymond Wellesley, Jack thought. Apparently the SIS man wasn't above getting his hands a bit dirty. Though both he and Pechkin were behind Aminat's kidnapping, they'd compartmentalized their involvement, one of them arranging the contract, the other interfacing with Helen.

"This was never a ransom job, was it?" Dobromir said.

"It was about leverage. They were trying to get the girl's father to cooperate with something he didn't want to do."

Dobromir accepted Jack's vague explanation with a nod. "Bad business. Of course, I know Ashworth is not the man's real name, but I could find nothing else about him. I can give you both their numbers, though, and an address in Makhachkala. It's an apartment building I followed Ashworth to. He did make it easy. I could not see which room he went into."

"Where did you two meet?"

"At a restaurant on Nabetsky Street."

"How far away from the address you've got?"

"Four blocks."

This could be something, Jack knew. Though Wellesley was an old espionage hand, it was human nature to eat and shop close to home, regardless of whether the stay is for the short or long term. Perhaps Wellesley was smug enough to have set up a permanent base of operations in Makhachkala. Where they found Wellesley they would probably find Pechkin.

Dobromir walked to his desk, tore a sheet from a notepad, jotted down the information, and handed it to Jack. He glanced at the two phone numbers: Both had Makhachkala landline prefixes. He committed them to memory.

"Is there anything else I can do to help?" Dobromir asked.

Jack wanted to say, "Quit the abduction racket," but didn't. Too soon. Perhaps Helen's death would be enough for Dobromir to consider retirement. Though he and Helen had never harmed a hostage, it was still an ugly business.

"Maybe," Jack replied. "If I ask, will you make contact with Pechkin?"

"And say what?"

"I don't know yet. I have to think about it."

"I will do you that favor if you do one for me: Bring either Pechkin or Ashworth to me. Both would be preferable, but I will settle for one."

"I can't promise that."

A buzzer sounded from one of Dobromir's computers. "Perimeter alarm," he said, then leaned over the middle monitor. "Someone's here, at the back door. Were you followed?"

"No."

Dobromir tapped on his keyboard and a video feed appeared on the monitor's screen. Jack could see a pair of uniformed men standing before the door, their faces distorted by the fisheye lens.

"Politsiya," Dobromir said. "This cannot be a coincidence."

"We didn't bring them," Jack replied.

"I believe you. Perhaps they will go away."

One of the officers turned and gestured to someone off camera. A moment later a man came into view carrying a handheld battering ram. The other two stepped away and the man swung the ram backward.

From the back door came a muffled thump of steel on steel.

Dobromir turned and said to them with a grim smile, "It seems they are not going away. You two need to go. This way."

He led them through an arched opening between two bookcases, then left down another short hallway. At its end, the back door buckled inward. The doorjamb splintered and chunks of plaster dropped to the floor. Without pausing, Dobromir kept

343

going, then turned left again onto a winding staircase. At the top was a small bedroom containing a trundle bed, a nightstand, and a small writing desk. Fixed to the nearest wall was a short ladder.

Downstairs, the ram pounded into the door again.

"Go through the hatch," Dobromir said. "It will lead you to the roof. Go now!"

"What about you?" asked Ysabel.

"They will search, find nothing, then take me to the station and ask questions. I will be home by suppertime. Do not go back to your car. Take mine." He dug into his pocket and handed Jack a key ring. "It's a blue Volga two blocks west of here."

"Thanks," Jack said.

"I'll be expecting your call."

Dobromir headed back down the stairs. The blows from the ram were coming faster now, one every two seconds.

"Up the ladder," Jack told Ysabel.

She climbed to the top, slid free the locking bolt, then opened the hatch. Sunlight streamed through.

Jack heard a crash, then a bang as the steel door slammed open against the wall. He looked down the stairs.

In rapid-fire Russian the police started barking orders. Over the tumult, Jack could hear Dobromir trying to answer, his voice soothing, cooperative.

Ysabel rasped, "Jack, come on!"

Dobromir appeared on the steps, backing up, his hands raised. The muzzle of a pistol was almost touching his nose. The cop holding it came around the corner, looked up, saw Jack, and shouted, *"Stoj!"*

Dobromir wrapped the man in a bear hug and they began bouncing against the walls. "Go!" he shouted.

Jack put his hand on the ladder rung.

The roar of a gunshot filled the stairwell. Jack looked back and saw Dobromir lying on the stairs with a bullet hole in his sternum. The cop raised his gun and took aim on Jack. *"Stoj . . . stoj!"*

Jack dodged left, grabbed the leg of the nightstand, and swung it around the corner and down the stairs. He heard the smack of wood against flesh, followed by the sound of the cop tumbling down the stairs.

He scrambled up the ladder and out the hatch, then leaned back in and grabbed the locking bolt. Ysabel slammed the hatch shut and Jack slid the bolt into the latch. While the bolt was as thick as his thumb, the hatch was made of sheet metal. It wouldn't hold for very long.

25

"Which way?" Ysabel asked, gasping for breath.

Jack turned in a circle, trying to orient himself. To his left he saw the concrete wall of the canal. That was east. He turned and ran for the other edge of the roof with Ysabel close behind.

He skidded to a stop and peeked over the eaves and down into the alleyway that separated Dobromir's house from his neighbors'. Clotheslines crisscrossed the gap so thickly that they looked like a fishing net. The bottom of the alley was lost in shadow.

Jack backed up a few steps, then leapt to the next roof. Ysabel did the same and they kept running, dodging chimney vents, low-hanging wires, and satellite-dish risers until they reached the last roof on the block.

To the west, Jack heard sirens approaching, growing louder as they converged on

Dobromir's house.

Ysabel said, "Here, Jack."

She was kneeling beside the curved railing of the fire-escape ladder. He walked over. Directly below them was a blue Volga — Dobromir's, Jack assumed. They'd soon know.

A police car, its lights and siren off, rounded the corner at the other end of the block and headed toward the canal. Jack and Ysabel pulled away from the edge until they heard the engine fade into the distance.

"There's no point in waiting," Ysabel said, then started down the ladder.

At the bottom they stood in the alley a few feet behind the entrance.

Jack walked over to the Volga and tried the key in the lock. It worked. "We're good, come on."

They got in. Jack started the car and they pulled away.

They had left their map in their own car, so Jack had only his vague recollection of Khasavyurt's layout to go on. He headed directly west, driving just under the speed limit, slowly but steadily putting distance between them and Dobromir's house. Ysabel sat crouched on the passenger-side floorboard.

"They're looking for a man and a woman," she explained. "Do you think they know about this car?"

"Judging by Dobromir's security precautions at the house, I'd say no. We'll find out."

"That poor man," Ysabel whispered.

With each mile they covered, Jack breathed a little easier, until finally they cleared the city limits and headed into farm country. Both sides of the road were lined with miles of apple groves. Here and there Jack saw farmworkers spraying the trees, many of which were already showing tiny white blooms.

"You can sit up now," Jack said.

Ysabel did so and buckled her seat belt.

They passed a white-on-blue sign with Cyrillic lettering. Beside the label was an arrow pointing straight ahead. Beside the arrow was a green, white, and red flag.

"That's the Chechen flag, Jack," said Ysabel. "We really don't want to go there."

Jack chuckled. "Understatement of the year."

Another mile brought them to an intersection. He turned left and they drove for another ten miles before reaching the next town. The Volga's gas gauge needle was on E. Jack found a gas station. Ysabel went inside, then emerged with a map. Jack finished filling up, then climbed behind the wheel.

"Look, English captions," Ysabel said, the map open against the dashboard. "According to this, we're in Leninaul."

"How far to Makhachkala?"

"About two hundred kilometers. So, a hundred twenty miles. I can't tell how good these roads are, though."

"Ysabel, there's something we need to talk —"

Out his window, Jack saw a police car drive past the gas station.

"Company," Jack said.

The car stopped in the middle of the road, swung right onto the shoulder, did a U-turn, then headed back in their direction.

"Should we run?" asked Ysabel.

"We wouldn't get far. Stay here and do what they tell you. Your name is Julie Smith. Give me your wallet."

She handed it over and Jack got out of the car.

"You're not leaving me, are —"

"I'll be right back."

Jack walked into the station. He asked the female clerk behind the counter, *"Gde naxoditsa tualet?"*

She pointed down a short hall. At the end

349

of it on the right was the bathroom; next to this was the station's back door. Jack opened it, stepped outside, then looked around. There was nothing: no garbage, no debris. He pulled out his passport and wallet, tossed them onto the roof, then went into the bathroom and shut the door. He turned on the water and waited.

He heard a voice shouting in Russian, then the clerk's agitated reply.

Jack opened the bathroom door and stepped out. A cop was stalking toward him, gun drawn and shouting, *"Ruki vverh! . . . Ruki vverh!"* Hands up! . . . Hands up!

Jack raised them.

Outside, the lone police car had been joined by two more, all of them arrayed in a crescent facing the station's front door. One of the officers had Ysabel shoved against the side of the Volga, her hands cuffed behind her. A second one was leaning close to her, whispering.

"Are you okay?" Jack asked her.

"Yes."

The second cop walked up to Jack and in Russian demanded his name. Jack shrugged, feigning ignorance.

"Name," the man barked.

"John Smith."

"Your wife, there, yes?"

"Yes."

"Come with us."

Thirty minutes later they were back in Khasavyurt. Jack and Ysabel were led into a two-story gray cinder-block building fronted by glass windows covered in what looked like anticrime posters. Once through the doors, they were herded past the front counter, an area containing four wooden desks, then left down a hallway whose right side was lined with windowless jail cells with mint-green walls. They were ushered inside and the door banged shut.

"This can't be good for us," said Ysabel, sitting down on the bench. "Where did you put our wallets?"

"The first place they'll probably look after the toilet. We should probably talk about something."

"You mean aside from us being in jail?"

"Back at his house, Dobromir said the police showing up couldn't be a coincidence. He's right."

"Well, we know we weren't followed."

Jack said, "Only five people knew where we were going and who we were seeing. And they were all in the back of the GAZ."

351

26

Two hours passed. Jack heard the clicking of footsteps coming down the hall. A lanky man with a tidy black mustache appeared, carrying a wooden chair. Very carefully, he placed the chair before their door and then sat down. In his right hand were their phones.

"My name is Major Umarov," he said in decent English. "I am the police commander for the Khasavyurt district."

Medzhid's uncooperative underling, thought Jack.

Half expecting Umarov's next words to be "We found your wallets on the roof," Jack was relieved when he said, "Tell me your names."

"John and Julie Smith," said Jack.

"Can you prove this?"

"No."

"Tell me the passcode to your phones."

When Jack didn't respond, Umarov said,

"You are both American, yes?"

"Yes."

"Do you know a man named Dobromir Stavin?"

Jack had expected this question. "We just left his house. He told us to run, so we ran. We didn't know it was the police."

"According to my captain, they identified themselves as police."

"We don't speak Russian," said Ysabel. "We heard banging on the door, then saw the guns. We were frightened."

Umarov gave this some thought, then shrugged. "An understandable reaction, I suppose."

Jack couldn't tell whether Umarov's semi-amiable disposition was genuine or a prelude to something a lot less pleasant. Nor could he be sure Umarov was the one who'd been tipped off to their arrival here. Whoever had burned him and Ysabel could have called any number of sources in the Khasavyurt *politsiya.* One thing was certain: If Umarov disliked Medzhid, their being linked to him would worsen their situation — perhaps dangerously so.

Again Jack chastised himself for sharing with Seth and the others Dobromir's name and location.

Umarov asked, "Why do the two of you

have no identification?"

"We were robbed on the way here, in Gadari."

"I am sorry to hear that. I will have my sergeant take a report. By the way, I do not believe your story about what happened at Stavin's home."

"I see," said Jack.

"Captain Osin claims you shot Mr. Stavin moments after they gained entry to the house."

"We didn't do that," said Ysabel.

"He has sworn to it. He saw you fire the weapon," Umarov replied, pointing at Jack. "And the gun you used was found at the scene."

"He's lying."

"Then you would submit to a test, yes?"

"What kind of test?" asked Jack. He knew the answer, but wanted to hear it from Umarov.

"A lead-barium analysis. It will determine whether you have fired a weapon recently."

To his credit, Umarov at least had the science of GSR testing right. Jack shouldn't have been surprised. Crime-scene television made the test look complicated and dramatic. It wasn't.

"We can at least solve that part of the mystery," Umarov said. "If you are innocent, there's no danger in taking the test."

Jack suspected their permission was irrelevant. Damned if we do, damned if we don't. "Who will be doing the test?"

"I will."

"Go ahead, then."

Once Umarov was out of earshot, Ysabel whispered, "Jack, what are you doing? This is the man Medzhid talked about. If he —"

"They'll give us the test either way. Pass or fail, we'll know whether Umarov's honest or not. If he is, then his captain lied and he'll know it."

"That doesn't mean he'll let us go."

"True," Jack admitted. "But at least we won't be charged with murder."

Umarov returned a few minutes later. In turn he asked each of them to stick their hands through the bars. Umarov swabbed their fingers, palms, wrists, and forearms, then placed each swab in its own plastic vial half-filled with clear fluid. With one in each hand, Umarov shook the vials. The fluid remained clear.

"Is that good or bad?" Ysabel asked.

"For you, good. For Captain Osin . . . very bad. Please excuse me for a moment."

Umarov walked out.

Fifteen minutes later he returned with two

officers, who were frog-marching between them a man in a white T-shirt and boxer shorts. They walked him to the end of the corridor, shoved him into a cell, and shut the door. Umarov walked back to Jack and Ysabel.

"Is that your captain?" she asked.

"Not any longer. He is bad. Dishonest."

"And a murderer."

"That, too. It is sad it came to that. I should have been more diligent." He saw Ysabel's puzzled expression, then smiled. "Let me guess: Here you are in a remote *politsiya* district with a commander answerable to no one and subordinates who are corrupt and incompetent."

"I didn't say that."

"You did not have to."

"You're going to let us go now?"

"Let you go? No. At the very least, you are witnesses. There may be a trial, you may have to testify."

"That could be a problem for us," Jack said.

"Not my concern. Even so, you are foreigners with no identification, found driving a stolen car after fleeing the scene of a crime."

Ysabel said, "Dobromir gave us permission to —"

"Perhaps so. But you might further help your case if you tell me your names. I will give you some time to think."

Umarov left.

Jack awoke to the sound of shouting and grunting. He pushed himself upright and saw Captain Osin being dragged down the corridor by two *politsiya* officers. They disappeared around the corner. A door slammed and Osin's shouts went silent.

"What are they going to do with him?"

"*To* him," Jack corrected her. "Something bad."

Four times throughout the night Osin was dragged from his cell, only to be returned thirty or forty minutes later. Each time Jack saw no marks on his face or body, but the exhaustion was etched into his face, his eyes hollow and red and vacant. This procedure continued throughout the morning, then into the afternoon and evening, until finally Osin didn't return.

With a guard in tow, Major Umarov appeared with their evening meals. The guard opened their cell. Umarov stepped inside, handed them their trays, then nodded for the guard to leave.

Umarov sat down on the bench. "If you run —"

"We won't run," Jack replied, taking a bite of bread.

"Do you have anything you would like to share with me?"

Jack glanced at Ysabel, who nodded. Earlier they'd discussed and agreed on the course Jack was about to take. The best lie is the one closest to the truth. Whether Jack would be digging them deeper into trouble or out of it, only time would tell.

"Our wallets are on the roof of the gas station," he said.

"Thank you for telling me." Umarov chuckled. "Clearly my officers need some remedial training."

"My name is Jack Ryan and this is Ysabel Kashani. I'm American and she's Iranian."

"Interesting. Why were you visiting Mr. Stavin, Jack? May I call you Jack?"

"Sure. How well do you know Dobromir?"

"Not very well. He has a number of parking tickets, but nothing more."

"Do you know his girlfriend?"

"Helen. I've heard her name, but not met her. She travels for work, some kind of sales."

"She died a few days ago," Jack replied. "We came to give Dobromir the news."

Umarov's eyes narrowed. "Is this the truth?"

"It happened in Scotland. She was shot."

Umarov sighed. "That's very sad. And for Mr. Stavin to know . . ." His words trailed off. "How do you know all this, Jack?"

"Helen and I worked together."

"You could have simply called Mr. Stavin with the news."

"She asked us to come," said Ysabel.

"Why did you lie about your wallets being stolen?"

"I told you," she replied. "We were afraid. We saw a man killed in front of us."

Umarov nodded thoughtfully, then walked out and shut the cell door behind him. "I'll have my sergeant go to the gas station."

"You appear to be telling the truth," Umarov said an hour later.

"What now?" asked Jack.

"Well, there's still the matter of assault on a police officer. Captain Osin claims you threw a chair at him."

"It was a nightstand," Jack replied.

"And then there is Mr. Stavin's car. You —"

Ysabel said, "I told you. We —"

"— did have his keys and the car wasn't broken into, so this is a matter for my judgment, I suppose, as is the assault. However, you also misrepresented yourself to a law enforcement officer, which is no small matter."

Jack asked, "What did Osin tell you?"

"He admitted to shooting Mr. Stavin. He said it was an accident."

"Do you believe him?"

"I'm not sure yet."

"What's your gut tell you?"

Umarov thought for a moment. "Based on how you described the scene, I suspect he shot Stavin on purpose."

"As ordered," added Jack. "Did he say why he went to the house?"

"You ask a lot of questions."

"Ten minutes after we show up to tell the man his wife has been killed, you guys show up and —"

"Not us. Captain Osin."

"Right, sorry. Osin shows up and Dobromir's dead. Answer my question, please."

"Still none of your business."

Jack was down to his last card. Even if Umarov released them, they would be returning to Makhachkala not knowing which of the five had betrayed them. He might be able to kill two birds with one stone. He said, "Call Minister Rebaz Medzhid and give him our names."

"Pardon me?"

"Talk to him and no one else. Tell him why we're under arrest."

"So many demands, Jack. You do know you are in jail, don't you?"

"Please, Major," Ysabel said sweetly.

Umarov returned ten minutes later. "The minister has confirmed he knows you, but refused to say how. That troubles me."

"Because you don't like his politics," said Ysabel.

"Politics?" Umarov replied with surprise. "Who told you that?"

"He did."

"Then the minister does not know me at all. I care nothing for politics, or politicians, for that matter — or ethnicity, if that is what he is implying. Of course, that's irrelevant. He is my superior. There is nothing else. He did not seem happy when I told him your names."

"I'll bet," said Jack.

"He told me to give you my full cooperation. First, however, you will answer some of my questions. Did Minister Medzhid send you here?"

"No."

"Is he illegally connected in any way with Dobromir Stavin?"

"No."

"Did the purpose of your trip here involve any illegal activity?"

Jack felt as though Umarov was going through a checklist labeled "Arrest / Don't Arrest." He decided it would be best if he responded in kind.

"No," he replied.

"Finally, are you on Dagestani soil as agents representing a foreign government?"

"No."

Umarov paused, scratched his head. "I believe you. So, what are your questions?"

"The same one as before: Why did Osin go to Dobromir's house?"

"He says that six hours before the raid he got a call from an anonymous source claiming there was a cache of explosives in Mr. Stavin's home. He put the address under surveillance, and when you arrived, he moved in."

"Go on."

"The call came from a telephone number in Makhachkala."

"What kind, cell or landline?"

"Landline." Umarov recited it for Jack.

It was the same as Helen's direct line to Pechkin.

Umarov continued, "He was told to apprehend and hold anyone he found in the house and then call the Makhachkala number back."

"Hold us for whom?" asked Ysabel. "Did he give you a name?"

"No. He might still, but then again he might not even have one."

"Did he make that call?"

"Not according to his phone's history," replied Umarov, "and he wouldn't be stupid enough to use a *politsiya* phone."

"Did he say why he did all this? Why he killed Dobromir?" asked Ysabel.

"My guess is money. Osin's car and apartment are too nice for a captain's salary."

"Was he working with any of your other *politsiya*?"

"No — and that much I am confident of."

"So," Jack said, "where does this leave us?"

"It leaves me facing dozens of hours of paperwork and an internal investigation that I'll have to submit to Minister Medzhid. As for you two, you are free to go."

27

BUYNAKSK

Unsurprisingly, Umarov had refused to release Dobromir's Volga to them, but he was kind enough to give them a ride to Khasavyurt's only rental-car agency, where they rented a 1992 Opel, which got them back to Buynaksk shortly after midnight. Jack drove around until he found a motel with wireless Internet, then got them a room. He wasn't yet ready to go into Makhachkala, not until they could sort friend from foe — or at least had a plan to do that.

While Ysabel went to shower, he called Hendley and got Gerry and John Clark on the line. He recounted their visit with Dobromir, the police raid, and their brief imprisonment.

"Well, the tip-off sure as hell didn't come from our end," said John Clark. "So unless this Dobromir guy burned you —"

"He didn't."

"Or he did and it backfired and then Osin killed him by accident."

"I don't think so."

"Then, yeah, it's gotta be Medzhid, Seth, or Spellman."

"Or one of Medzhid's bodyguards," said Gerry. "Do you have their names?"

"Just Vasim and Anton, no surnames. Actually, I think we can cross Medzhid off our list. He could have ordered Umarov to hold us, or worse. He didn't."

"You might be right, but that's not proof positive," said Clark. "Medzhid may want you in Makhachkala."

"John, he's got more to lose than anyone else."

"You gotta stop thinking logically about this," said Gerry. "A man like Medzhid doesn't get to where he is by being transparent. His kind always have agendas within agendas."

A thought suddenly occurred to Jack: Medzhid had left Aminat in the Four Seasons Baku under the protection of two bodyguards.

"I'll call you right back," he said.

He disconnected, looked up the hotel's number, then dialed it. When the operator answered, he asked for the penthouse suite. After the tenth ring the operator came back on the line. "My apologies, sir. I actually show those guests as checked out."

"When?"

"Late last night."

Jack hung up and called Hendley back. "Aminat's gone."

"Don't hit the panic button, Jack," Clark said. "Medzhid might have moved her."

"Man, I hate this shit," Jack said. "I can see why Seth's dad lost it."

Gavin said, "I heard by the time he died Kim Philby was eating his own hair and dressing up as Napoleon."

"Urban legend," Gerry said. "Jack, you don't have to like it, you just have to do it."

Clark replied, "Hijacking a Navy SEAL aphorism, boss? I'm surprised at you."

Jack said, "Focus, guys. Gavin, I've got a couple telephone numbers I want you to run down: the contact number Dobromir had for Pechkin and the one Captain Osin was supposed to call after the raid."

"Will do."

Clark said, "Jack, first things first: For the time being, you have to forget about Aminat."

"Easier said than done."

"Even if they took her again, she's just a symptom. You need to find the disease."

Find out who's not what they claim to be,

366

Jack thought.

They left Buynaksk the next morning for the hour-long drive into Makhachkala.

Ten miles outside the capital, Jack saw through the windshield a thin column of smoke rising from the city center.

"Oh, no," Ysabel said. "Has it started already?"

Jack pulled onto the shoulder and texted Gavin: FIRES IN MAKHACHKALA. NEWS?

His phone rang a minute later. It was Clark. "We were just going to call you. BBC is reporting mobs in the street. Hundreds of them, maybe more."

"Seth's pulled the trigger early."

"No, Jack. These are anti-Medzhid protesters. They've set up camp outside the MOI headquarters."

They detoured slightly south, then west to Turali, a suburb about three miles down the coast from Makhachkala proper. Jack found a public parking lot above the beach, parked, then texted Seth: IN TURALI. WHERE YOU?

The response came immediately. DOWNTOWN, TWO BLOCKS FROM MINISTRY.

BAD?

VERY BAD, Seth replied. FIND ANYTHING IN KHASAVYURT?

Jack hesitated and glanced at Ysabel, who shook her head. DRY WELL, he replied. THERE'S A RESERVOIR A MILE NORTH OF YOU. ONE BLOCK EAST THERE'S A TRAIN DEPOT. MEET YOU THERE.

When they reached the depot, Seth waved to them from the open driver's window of a black Chevy Suburban. Jack assumed it was up-armored.

"Nice car," Ysabel whispered to Jack. "Do they import Suburbans here?"

"No. At least not to the general public."

"A private jet, a Suburban . . . Must be nice to be Minister Medzhid."

She rolled down her window. The stench of burning rubber filled the Opel's interior.

Seth said, "You'd better leave that here."

"We'll keep it for now," replied Jack. "We'll follow you."

"Suit yourself. When we get downtown, whatever you do, don't get out of your car. And drive slowly. If you hit someone, the mob will turtle that thing."

Seth led them up the coast road for fifteen minutes before turning west toward Makhachkala's center. The plume of smoke

Jack had spotted earlier grew larger through the windshield. Through their half-open windows they began to hear chanting in Russian. Seth turned left, then braked hard, as did Jack. The block was filled with protesters milling about, some holding signs written in Cyrillic, others pumping their fists in time with the chanting.

"Windows up," Jack said. "Lock your door."

Seth's Suburban crept into the crowd and was immediately swallowed by the throng. Moments later, so was the Opel. Fists began pounding on the roof and hood, palms slapping at the windows. A man's face pressed against Ysabel's window, shouting, spittle flying from his lips.

"Oh, that's nice," Ysabel murmured.

Jack couldn't help but smile. "Look straight ahead."

The Opel started rocking from side to side, the engine revving as the drive wheels came off the ground. Jack honked the horn and the Opel's tires thumped back onto the pavement.

Jack's phone trilled. "Yeah, Seth."

"If you get stopped, stay in your car. We'll come get you."

With his foot barely touching the gas pedal, Jack kept the Opel moving forward.

■ ■ ■ ■

After what felt like an hour but was only ten minutes, they emerged from the mass of protesters and found themselves on a street bordered by imposing gray buildings fronted by tall columns. To the right the sidewalk was lined with people sitting quietly, holding hand-painted signs aloft. Heads turned, sullen eyes tracking the Opel, but no one shouted or even gestured.

Seth texted, MINISTRY OF THE INTERIOR ON THE RIGHT.

Ysabel asked Jack, "Why the difference? One block is chaos, the next peaceful. And no police anywhere."

"I have no idea."

After another two blocks and three more turns Seth pulled the Suburban up to a gated parking garage entrance. He rolled down his window, said something to the man in the tollbooth, then gestured to the Opel. The gate lifted and they pulled through.

On the sixth level, they went through another gate, then parked in a pair of spots. A sign above each one bore the yellow double eagle-head emblem of the Ministry of the Interior.

They got out and followed Seth to a bank of elevators, where he swiped a key card through a slot on the wall.

"What is this place?" asked Ysabel.

"Tortoreto Towers. Medzhid's private apartment," Seth said, as the elevator doors parted.

When the doors opened, Jack found himself in a foyer with mirrored walls and a brown tiled floor. Vasim and Anton, Medzhid's primary bodyguards, nodded at Seth but paid Jack and Ysabel no attention. Anton opened the apartment door.

The interior wasn't much different from Medzhid's suite at the Four Seasons Baku, though larger and with windows that spanned the length of the space, through which Jack could see the blue waters of the Caspian Sea. At the far end, two women in light blue pantsuits sat at a long conference table, phones pressed to their ears. Mounted on the wall above them were three forty-two-inch LCD televisions.

"Jack . . . Ysabel," Medzhid called from a sectional couch in the center of the room. He was seated on a stool with a nylon cape draped around his torso. A woman holding a pair of scissors stood behind him.

Medzhid stood up, shrugged off the cape,

371

and walked over to them, hand extended. "So glad you are back safe. Did Major Umarov mistreat you?"

"Not at all," Jack replied.

"What was this business about the shooting?"

"Someone laid a trap for us. They didn't want us talking to Dobromir."

Jack studied the minister's face for a reaction, but he merely nodded and said, "That's unfortunate. Have you found out who did it?"

"Not yet."

"Keep me informed. Seth will show you to your rooms."

"Just one more thing — in private. I need to talk to you in private."

"Of course. Seth, do you mind . . ."

"Uh, sure." Seth walked away.

Jack whispered to Medzhid, "Where's Aminat?"

"Why do you ask?"

"She checked out of the Four Seasons Baku the night after we left for Tbilisi."

"I know. I moved her to another location. She is safe, Jack."

"Who's she with? Do you trust them?"

"With my life."

"Vasim and Anton?"

"All of them. They've been with me for

many years."

Meaningless, Jack thought.

He'd known Seth for decades and Spellman was a fellow American, one of the good guys, and yet they were two of the five people who might have set up him and Ysabel.

Medzhid smiled and clapped him on the arm. "It is kind of you to worry after her, Jack, but all is well."

"Glad to hear it. I need a favor: Can you get Major Umarov to sit on the shooting story for a few days?"

"I doubt I'll have to ask. Until he completes his internal investigation, he'll say nothing. Besides, Khasavyurt has no newspapers or television stations. Now, have something to eat and drink. We will talk later." Medzhid turned toward the conference area and called, "Albina, have you reached Captain Salko yet?"

"No, Mr. Minister."

"Tell his deputy I want the man on the phone in five minutes or I'm coming down there personally."

Jack and Ysabel followed Seth down a hallway to a mini-suite with a kitchenette, a sofa, and a chair. A blond-haired woman in a red miniskirt and a white blouse sat on the sofa, flipping through a magazine. She had impossibly large breasts.

Seth said, "Give us a minute, will you?"

The woman glared at him, then stood up, tossed the magazine aside, and sashayed away.

"Another assistant?" asked Ysabel.

"Not exactly," Seth replied.

"Mrs. Medzhid, then."

"Don't get cute, Ysabel. We didn't pick the man because he's a saint. Rebaz and his wife have an understanding: she has her life and he has his. It works for them."

Spellman walked down the hall into the suite. "Hey, guys, how was Khasavyurt? Get anything useful?"

Seth answered for Jack: "A dry well. Right, Jack?"

"Yep. What's going on outside the ministry? Why is it so peaceful?"

"They're obeying the law, believe it or not," Spellman replied. "As long as they don't damage property or assault anyone, they can actively protest anywhere but on blocks that house government buildings. There they have to mind their manners."

"A half-unruly mob. Strange place, Dagestan."

Seth gestured to a pair of doors on the other side of the suite. "Your bedrooms. Get settled and then I'll bring you up to speed.

Feel free to . . . consolidate, if you want. I'm cool with it."

Jack saw Ysabel's expression change, and he could guess what it meant: Ysabel didn't give a damn whether Seth was okay with "it." To her credit, she simply replied, "Thanks."

Once Seth and Spellman were gone, Jack said, "Everyone seems way too chipper."

"And why wouldn't they be, Jack? Part playboy mansion, part salon. What's not to love?"

And all while mobs are at the gates, he thought.

28
MAKHACHKALA

As he had been doing for the past ten minutes, Jack watched Seth and Spellman talk to and over each other across the conference table, getting nowhere in the process. At the end of the table, Medzhid watched patiently, saying nothing.

"No, no, no," Seth said. "He needs to do more than give one damned speech."

"From the Ministry, Seth. Directly to the people."

"That's a start, but we need him in every newspaper and on every radio and television station."

"But what's the message?" asked Spellman. "How do you spin something like Almak when you're being peppered by questions on live TV?"

"First he flatly denies the allegations, then he reminds them of what started it. Show the pictures of the beheaded soldiers and their crying families. Hammer that until it's the only thing people see in their heads."

Again Jack was stunned listening to this version of Seth Gregory. His PR suggestion was to use gore and despair to take attention away from the allegation. Sure, it would be effective, but it was ice-cold opportunism Jack had never seen in their twenty-plus-year friendship. Was this nature, nurture, or obsession? *Or,* Jack thought, *am I just being naive?* As Seth had said, the stakes here were massive.

Seth went on: "Then he turns the focus to his brave team, now all dead, having sacrificed themselves to protect the homeland, and he will not stand by while their memories are sullied by a lie."

Medzhid said, "Which is the truth."

"All the better. That's the message. We stay on it and never let up."

"Fine, but we've still got the *Pravda* story," replied Spellman. "Right now people believe someone was at Almak and he saw the whole thing — civilians burning to death in a mosque. That's a tough image to erase."

"Not if our imagery is stronger and our message is consistent."

Jack spoke up: "Who's their source?"

"That doesn't matter —"

Medzhid held up his hand for silence and then said, "What was that, Jack?"

"*Pravda* got the story from someone. Who?"

"I told you: They don't have one," replied Seth. "Or they got it from one of Medzhid's team before he died."

"And they've been sitting on it all this time? Almak happened sixteen years ago. Rebaz, were you even on anyone's political radar back then?"

"No. I had no interest in politics. I wasn't known outside my district."

"So someone at *Pravda* gets the story, decides the massacre of civilians in a place of worship isn't newsworthy, and sets it aside."

"Yeah, Jack, we understand the timing of it," said Seth. "It's Wellesley and Pechkin's opening salvo. But this is an opportunity for us. They've moved too quickly. Once we discredit this story, we push ahead."

Ysabel said, "Seth, you're missing Jack's point. Next to President Nabiyev, Medzhid is Dagestan's most powerful politician — probably more so if you're talking about popularity. Does *Pravda* really think Medzhid's not going to come back hard at them? That he's not going to demand they reveal their source?"

"By law, they don't have to do that," said Spellman.

"Actually, there is such a law," Medzhid replied. "If the allegation involves a government official the media must name the source, in private, to a cabinet-level panel and the official has the right to question the witness. Jack's right. Unless they want to be tarnished, *Pravda* must produce its witness. If the person is false, we can prove it; if they are genuine, I can prove they are lying."

"Could there be a witness?" asked Jack.

"I was told all my team died in the war. I had no reason to doubt it, but I suppose it's possible."

"Or there is no one," Spellman said, "and Wellesley found a stand-in."

While Medzhid recalled his team of assistants to the conference area and gave them their marching orders, Jack and Ysabel left the apartment. Seth caught up to them at the elevators.

"Where're you going?"

"Errands," Ysabel replied.

"Are you crazy? It's nuts out there."

"We'll avoid downtown," said Jack.

He turned to press the call button. Seth grabbed his arm. "Jack, what're you holding back? Did you find something in Khasavyurt?"

"Good question," said Spellman, from the

apartment's doorway.

"We may have something, but I'd rather run it down first."

"I'm starting to think you don't trust us," asked Seth. "Why the secrecy?"

"Compartmentalization," Jack replied.

The doors opened and he and Ysabel stepped inside. After the doors closed she asked Jack, "Do we trust them? Any of them?"

"Hell if I know."

"You're smiling. What for?"

"Nothing. Sleep deprivation. I just had the irrational impulse to tie them all to chairs until one of them starts talking."

They took the Opel north away from the parking garage, listening through their open windows as the protesters' shouts slowly faded behind them.

Out Jack's window a tree-covered escarpment topped by a serrated ridge loomed over the city. This was, Seth had told them with a straight face, the eastern face of the Tarki-Tau range.

Since hearing the name, Ysabel had been occasionally repeating it to herself, sotto voce, as though simply enjoying the sound of it.

Jack couldn't help smiling. Such an

interesting woman.

"If I ever get a dog, that's what I'll name him — Tarki-Tau."

"Not if I beat you to it."

"Don't you dare."

The slopes from which the escarpment rose formed a five-mile-long tadpole-shaped knoll, with the head facing north and the long tapered tail curving south and then west, where it merged with the next chain of hills.

Jack found a café and pulled to the curb. On both sides of the streets pedestrians strolled the sidewalks, laughing and chatting. The traffic was heavy but orderly, with no honking of horns. It was as though the city was going about its normal business, save the few blocks surrounding the Ministry of the Interior.

"Not exactly groundswell, is it?" Ysabel observed.

"I agree. If this is the best Wellesley and Pechkin can do, the coup should go off without a hitch."

He pulled his phone from the Faraday bag and dialed Gavin, who looped Gerry and John Clark into the call. Jack brought them up to speed.

"With any luck, we have some time before Wellesley and Pechkin know the ambush in

Khasavyurt went wrong. Gavin, what'd you find out about those phone numbers?"

"Both are landlines, but the addresses are unlisted — I mean *really* unlisted, as in buried. You can't pull off something like that without horsepower."

Presidential horsepower.

"Jack, we've decided it's time you got some backup," said Clark. "We're sending Dom."

"I don't need —"

"He's already on the plane. Tomorrow morning, Uytash Airport, Aeroflot flight 278."

Even as he'd said the words "don't need," Jack knew it wasn't true. Having Dominic Caruso here would be a relief; partially because he was family — cousins — and partially because Dom was a solid operator.

Gerry asked, "What's your next move, Jack?"

"I'm going to ask Raymond Wellesley to lunch."

They drove past the address Dobromir had given them and found the apartment building, two stories, surrounded by trees and a six-foot red-brick wall. The only entrance, a private drive on Chirpoy Road, was blocked by a rolling gate. Beside this was a pole-mounted key-card box.

"That doesn't look like something built for the average Makhachkalan renter," Ysabel said. "Where did Dobromir say he and Wellesley had lunch?"

"On Nabetsky Street."

"Well, that's about four blocks from here. We've definitely got the right place."

"Yes, but is this where Wellesley and Pechkin had set up shop?"

They returned to the Tortoreto apartment to find it bustling with activity. At the conference table the number of assistants had doubled to four, all of them busy working the phones. Medzhid stood by the windows, talking to a uniformed man with black hair and long sideburns.

Seth and Spellman walked up. "We've got trouble," Seth said simply. "Medzhid's —"

"Who's that guy?" Jack asked, nodding at Medzhid's guest.

"Captain Salko. He heads Medzhid's ERF, the Emergency Response Force — essentially, the cream of the *politsiya* crop."

"Has something happened?" asked Ysabel.

"Just playing the what-if game in case Nabiyev makes a bold move."

"What were you saying about Medzhid?" Jack said.

"He's been summoned by President Nabi-yev. He wants to hear Medzhid's side of the Almak story. We're talking about possible responses."

"Well, he can't refuse," Ysabel said. "Unless you and Matt have everything ready to go, that is."

"We don't," Spellman replied.

Jack thought for a moment. "The only move Medzhid has is to demand a hearing so he can confront *Pravda*'s witness. That might buy some time. Does he have enough cabinet-level allies to make it work?"

"Maybe," Seth replied. "Wellesley and Pechkin are behind this."

"Probably, but it's also what the public would expect Nabiyev to do."

Too many moving parts, Jack thought. "There are three possibilities: Nabiyev ignores the objections of the cabinet and denies Medzhid's petition; he either suspends Medzhid or leaves him in place until the panel reaches a decision; or he simply fires Medzhid and throws him in jail."

"If he does that, we're screwed," said Spellman. "It'll take us at least a week to finish coordinating our own protests. And even then, with Medzhid off the field, we can't be sure the *politsiya* district commanders will back a losing horse."

Seth said, "We need to hunt down *Prav-da*'s witness before he can testify."

Ysabel's eyes narrowed. "And do what to him?"

"Jesus, Ysabel. Not what you're thinking. The Almak massacre story is bullshit. Medzhid's innocent. Either the witness is bogus and he wasn't there or he was there and he's been coerced into lying. Either way, we've got to get to him first."

29

MAKHACHKALA

Jack pulled the Opel to the curb outside Uytash Airport's arrivals and sat waiting for five minutes, nodding and smiling at the civilian security guard trying to wave them on, until Dominic Caruso came out the sliding doors, carrying a black duffel bag. Jack and Ysabel climbed out and met him at the rear hatch. Jack made the introductions.

"So you're Ysabel," Dom said. "Heard a lot about you."

Ysabel glanced at Jack. "What have you —"

"He's kidding. Come on, let's get moving before this guy calls the airport SWAT team on us."

As they exited the airport's terminal road, Jack checked his watch. "He's probably coming on," he said. Ysabel turned on the radio and Rebaz Medzhid's voice came over the car's speakers.

". . . allegations are false, and I am outraged that the bravery and patriotism of the men under my command is being tarnished by such accusations. My director of personnel has discovered the name of *Pravda*'s alleged witness, a sergeant named Pavel Koikov, one of the finest I've had the pleasure to serve with and one of the most decorated members of the *politsiya* in the history of Dagestan. I fear that Sergeant Koikov is being coerced and may be in danger. If I find that either of these is true, the full weight of the Ministry of the Interior will fall upon those responsible."

Ysabel turned down the radio. "Well, he followed the script to the letter."

From the backseat, Dom asked, "This Koikov is the one from the Almak massacre?"

"Yes."

"Smart move on Medzhid's part. He's upped the ante."

And put the opposition on notice, Jack thought. Now Wellesley and Pechkin could neither kill Koikov nor allow him to appear before the panel, lest the *Pravda* story fall apart. They'd painted themselves into a corner.

"Now we just need to find him," Jack replied.

■ ■ ■ ■

Jack drove Dom to his motel, a three-star about three blocks from Medzhid's private apartment. By mutual agreement, they'd decided to keep Dom's presence in the capital from Seth and the others for the time being. This was probably overkill, but Jack had decided to be careful with what information he shared with whom, and when.

The three of them got out and walked to Dom's room.

"I'm showering," he announced. "I've got Aeroflot grime all over me. Hey, Jack, we're gonna need hardware."

"I'm working on it."

"And you're going to need to bring me up to speed."

Jack pulled his phone from the Faraday bag and sat down on the bed.

"Are you sure this is a good idea, Jack?" asked Ysabel.

"Not entirely, but Medzhid's just increased the pressure. It's time to turn it up another notch and see if we get a re-action."

Jack dialed Raymond Wellesley's cell phone. The SIS man picked up on the

388

second ring. "Jack Ryan, how good to hear from you. Are you well?"

"Very. And yourself?"

"Well, frankly, I'm a bit worried about you."

"Let's get together and talk about it," Jack replied. He was about to find out — maybe — if Wellesley knew where he was.

"Good," Wellesley said. "How about your hotel, that same coffee shop we met —"

"How about Zolotoy on Petra Pervogo Street?"

"I don't know the place."

"I think you do, Raymond. I'll see you at two o'clock."

Jack disconnected.

Ysabel said, "There goes the gauntlet."

He and Ysabel returned to the Tortoreto. Seth, Spellman, and Medzhid were standing in the conference area, staring at the bank of televisions.

Seth spotted them and walked over. "It's working. The media's banging the drum, asking where Pavel Koikov is and whether he is safe. Medzhid's used it to delay his meeting with Nabiyev until the day after tomorrow."

"How did you find Koikov?"

"He was reported as MIA, presumed

dead. When he turned up alive a few days later outside Karamakhi, someone forgot to amend the report. According to his personnel file he's in his mid-fifties and has liver trouble. Medzhid's got a couple men sitting on his house. He hasn't had any visitors."

"On the way here we passed the Ministry," said Ysabel. "The crowds look smaller."

"Yeah, it'll be all broken up by the end of the day, I'm sure. Whether it was all organic or something arranged by Wellesley and Pechkin, I don't know."

"I've been thinking about that," said Jack. "What if it was a trial balloon to gauge Medzhid's reaction? To see what it will take to derail him?"

Seth was nodding. "Or the coup itself. Very smart, Jack. Either way, we've got our timeline back. We finish getting the rest of the pieces in place and it's a go."

"And while you're doing that, so are Wellesley and Pechkin. Have you thought about that?" said Ysabel.

"Of course."

"What's your dad's manual say?" The sarcasm was plain in Ysabel's voice.

"I've made some tweaks to it. It's not your worry, anyway."

"I'm involved. It's my worry."

Jack knew pushing the issue would get

390

them nowhere. He intervened, saying, "Do you have a few minutes to talk?"

The three of them walked down the hall to Jack and Ysabel's mini-suite and sat down. Jack said, "We need some weapons. And a second car."

"Why?"

"The city's going to boil over when things get rolling. I don't want us out there naked."

"You don't need to be on the streets. We'll sit it out here."

"You said yourself we need to find Koikov," said Jack. "Wellesley might not kill him, but he'll probably hide him away. Once Koikov's safe, he can testify that he was coerced — and by whom. Besides, you don't have the bodies to spare. Get us some weapons and we'll find him."

Seth thought for a moment, then said, "Listen, I trust you guys, but something tells me it's not mutual. Talk to me, Jack."

Jack decided they had nothing to lose by telling him the truth, or at least part of it. "We were ambushed in Khasavyurt. The man we met was killed by a *politsiya* captain who admitted he was tipped off by someone here."

"And the only people who knew you were going up there were me, Matt, and Medzhid. And his bodyguards. Okay, I get

391

it. But it wasn't me. Please believe me. What I did to you guys, using you as bait in Tehran, was wrong and I'm sorry. I wouldn't do it again. Tell me you believe me."

The expression on Seth's face was one Jack hadn't seen since their lunch at Chaibar. This was the old Seth. "I believe you."

"Ysabel?"

She sighed. "I believe you, too."

Jack said, "Somebody in your camp is playing for the other side, Seth, and until we figure out who, we need room to maneuver."

"Yeah, okay, I'll get you weapons. Just don't get yourself killed. Il Duce and Mrs. Il Duce would string me up."

After picking up Dom they drove to Zolotoy restaurant, arriving forty minutes early for Jack's lunch date with Wellesley. Jack and Ysabel parked the Opel in a lot a few blocks away, while Dom, behind the wheel of the Lada compact car Seth had arranged for them, started his scout of the area.

From a duffel bag in the backseat Jack pulled out their weapons, a pair of Ruger nine-millimeter pistols in hip holsters. Dom had his own Ruger; the trio of Beretta ARX noise-suppressed assault rifles Seth had supplied were tucked under a blanket in the

Lada's trunk, along with three hundred rounds of ammunition. Seth hadn't skimped.

"I like my revolver better," Ysabel said, turning the Ruger in her hand.

"We're beggars," Jack replied.

He checked his watch, then texted Gavin: SET?

SET. FIRST CALL AT TWO-TEN, SECOND AT TWO-TWELVE.

At one forty-five they got out of the car. Ysabel kissed Jack and they parted company, her walking down the block, Jack toward the restaurant.

Zolotoy was part Italian bistro, part Russian steak house. Jack stepped through the doors beneath a green awning and was met by a hostess.

"Vy gavarite pa angliyski?" Jack asked.

"Some, English, yes," said the hostess.

Jack asked for a table for two, and she led him to a small booth beside the windows. Dom was already in place, seated at a corner table reading *Dagestanskaia Pravda*. Absently Jack wondered if his friend even read Cyrillic. If not, he was putting on a decent show of it.

The waiter appeared with glasses of ice water and a stainless-steel pitcher beaded with condensation. Jack placed his phone on the table. As he'd hoped, the restaurant's lunch hour had passed and there were only six other patrons, only two of them close by.

Jack's phone vibrated. IN PLACE, Ysabel texted. I CAN SEE YOU. WAVE, HAND-SOME.

He suppressed a smile and touched his ear.

At two exactly, Raymond Wellesley walked in and spoke briefly to the hostess, who showed him to the table. "Hello, Jack."

"Raymond."

A pair of men in black leather coats stepped through the restaurant door. Ignoring the hostess, they took a table ten feet behind Wellesley's chair.

Subtle, Jack thought.

"Have you ordered?" Wellesley asked.

"I thought I'd wait for you."

They stared at each other across the table, the SIS with a half-smile on his face, until the waiter had returned and taken their orders.

"Cards on the table," Jack said.

"Agreed. Jack, what are you doing here? You have no idea what you've got yourself involved in."

"I have some idea."

"I assume Seth and Matt are here as well?"

"Not here, but around. Raymond, why are you trying to derail all this? The outcome will be good for everyone."

"Not if our Moscow friend does what we expect he'll do."

"He won't." *I hope,* Jack thought but didn't say.

Wellesley shook his head sadly and chuckled. "American hubris. You never consider the potential blowback. I thought your father was smarter than this."

"I can't speak for him, but you're wrong. We've calculated the odds just as you guys have. It's a gamble worth taking. And this is something the people here want."

"Want?" Wellesley repeated. "Desire can be manufactured. These people don't know what they want until they're told."

"You take a dim view of 'these people.' We don't."

"That's irrelevant. It will fail, what you have planned."

"I guess we're going to find out."

Their food arrived. Once the waiter finished arranging the dishes and was gone Jack said, "That was some cold business back in Tehran. Luckily for him, Scott Hilby never knew what hit him. What was it, you were afraid he might talk to me?"

Wellesley said, "Jack, are you trying to play James Bond again? You're hoping to get a recorded confession for something I wasn't involved in?"

Jack pushed his phone across the table to Wellesley. The phone's screen read 2:09. "Check for yourself."

Wellesley waved his hand dismissively. "You're smarter than that. By the way, does your father know you're not a . . . Remind me of your title again. Arbitrage specialist?"

Jack glanced at his watch: 2:10. No call. *Come on, Gavin, give me something.*

Jack didn't respond to Wellesley's question, but instead asked his own: "You haven't heard from David Weaver, have you?"

He saw a flicker of doubt in Wellesley's eyes. "I don't know who that is."

"He knows who you are. Apparently, he and Hilby were close. You ordering him to blow off the top of Hilby's head is eating him up inside."

Jack glanced at his watch: 2:12.

Wellesley said, "You're lying. Otherwise I would have already been called home."

"Not if what you're doing isn't sanctioned. I think you're out here trying to set national policy."

Wellesley's cell phone chimed. He finished

chewing the piece of chicken in his mouth, said, "Excuse me, please," then pulled the phone from his inner suit pocket. He studied the screen for a few moments, typed a reply, and then returned the phone to his pocket.

"Jack, since Nine-Eleven both our governments have shared a unified policy when it comes to terrorism, wouldn't you agree?"

"I would."

"Like him or not, Valeri Volodin knows how to handle terrorism — he crushes it where he finds it. If you believe the Caucasus is troublesome now, imagine the region with someone other than Volodin at the helm. That is what keeps me up at night, Jack, as it should our leaders. Sadly, it does not."

Raymond Wellesley had in essence just admitted he had indeed gone rogue. Even so, the confession wouldn't be enough to indict him in the eyes of his government. While Wellesley was objectively right about Volodin's stance on terrorism, the man's larger national policies, dominated by blunt aggression, would eventually spill beyond the borders of the Russian Federation. If that happened, terrorism would be the least of everyone's worries.

"So, to directly answer your earlier question: Do you really imagine someone of my standing would betray Her Majesty's government?"

"You suggested Paul Gregory had done just that, and he had more years of service than you do. And he was a better man than you."

"You mean Paul Gregory, aka Boghos Grigorian? I am nothing like him. Tell me, Jack, how is Seth faring? Stable, rational?"

"Absolutely."

"Of course he is. Did he tell you where he got his father's coup manual? No, on second thought, he probably didn't."

Jack felt like he'd been punched in the stomach. It had been Wellesley. Via Oleg Pechkin, the SIS had given Seth the manual. He'd done his research on Seth, had found his weak spot, then planted the seed and nurtured it into an obsession. *Bastard*.

There was no telling how much of Seth's planning had been guided by Wellesley's deft hand — or how many of their own countermoves he and Pechkin had prepared. Wellesley was playing a chess game he might have already won.

Jack said, "You give yourself too much credit, Raymond."

"As you said, I guess we're going to find out. Jack, none of this needs to happen. You abort, we'll do the same, and we all go home, no harm done."

Jack was surprised Wellesley thought he'd buy such a blatant lie.

"That's a call way above my pay grade. I'm here for the duration."

Wellesley put down his fork and carefully folded his napkin. "Jack, I think it's time you come with me."

"That's not going to happen."

"Yes, it is. Stand up, Jack."

"What's your plan, Raymond, a gunfight right here?"

"No, we'll just walk you out to the car and drive away." Wellesley turned and nodded at his bodyguards. They stood and walked to the table.

"Time to go, Jack."

As if by magic, Dominic Caruso appeared and took up station to their left, his sight line to both them and Wellesley clear. Dom said cheerily, "Hi, guys."

In unison the bodyguards slid their hands into their jackets.

"Don't," Dom said.

Jack glanced sideways and saw Dom had his Ruger tucked behind his left leg, the muzzle just visible.

Jack told Wellesley, "Seth was right about you: You're too cocky for your own good."

Scowling, Wellesley stood up. "We'll see each other later, Jack."

Jack gave the SIS man a parting shot he hoped would shake the man's calm: "Come find us."

Back at the Opel, Jack first recounted the meeting for Ysabel, then called Gavin, who asked, "Did it go through?"

Going into the lunch date, Jack had one primary goal: to definitively sort out the two landline telephone numbers they'd collected from their Khasavyurt trip, Dobromir's contact for Wellesley and Helen's line to Pechkin, which was the same one Osin was to call after the raid.

"Yes," Jack answered. "Wellesley answered the two-twelve call."

"Okay, good. That's the number Dobromir had for him. Cocky bastard hasn't even bothered to change it."

"What did you text?"

"What you told me to: 'I'm Dobromir, I'm pissed, Helen's in a Scottish jail, and I want answers.' I don't see what good this is going to do us, though."

"It'll rattle Wellesley's confidence. By now they probably know Aminat's home safe, but as far as they're concerned Helen could be alive and talking to Scotland Yard. This is just one more thing for them to worry about."

"And waste time on. Got it. Okay, the other number: When it rang through I got that generic female voice asking for a text message. I put in, 'Khasavyurt raid negative. Umarov suspicious. Instructions?' I haven't heard back yet."

Jack now knew something about how Wellesley and Pechkin were operating in Makhachkala. Wellesley's cell, and probably Pechkin's as well, depending on whether Gavin got a response, were being routed through landlines, perhaps from inside Wellesley's Chirpoy Road apartment. If so, Jack might have identified their war room.

He asked, "What did Wellesley text back?"

"He told Dobromir to sit tight and he would find out what was going on."

"Let me know when you hear back from Pechkin."

Jack and Ysabel returned to the Tortoreto apartment. When they stepped off the elevator, Vasim and Anton were at their usual posts.

"Hi, guys," Jack said.

Anton nodded at him.

"I don't think I got a chance to say this, but you did good work back in Georgia. I was glad to have you along."

This seemed to break the ice. Vasim gave him the barest trace of a smile and said, "Thank you."

"Where did you two serve before joining the minister's detail?"

"Novolaksky district, near the Chechen border."

"Both of you?"

"Yes," said Anton.

"Pretty tough area," said Jack. "You sure as hell earned this posting, didn't you?"

Now Anton opened up a bit: "We have many years of service."

Jack got out his phone. "I just realized I don't have your mobiles. It would probably be a good idea."

"Ask Minister Medzhid."

"No problem, I understand," said Jack. "Anyway, thanks again."

He and Ysabel went through the door; as it closed behind them she said, "What was that all about?"

"Just making friends."

He texted Dom: STATUS?

AT CHIRPOY ROAD, came the reply. NO ACTIVITY.

THANKS FOR THE ASSIST EARLIER.

NO PROB. FUN TIMES.

I'LL RELIEVE YOU AT SEVEN.

They walked to the conference table, where Seth and Spellman were sitting.

"Where've you been?" asked Spellman.

"Having lunch with Raymond Wellesley."

Seth's head snapped around. "What? Why the hell did you do that?"

"To plant a few seeds," said Jack. "And I learned something: We've got them more nervous than we thought. He tried to snatch me from the restaurant."

"Ballsy fucker. Was Pechkin with him?"

"No, just a couple leather jackets."

One of Medzhid's pantsuited assistants came down the hallway. "Mr. Gregory, the minister would like to see you."

Seth told Jack, "We're doing radio and TV call-ins. They've started tossing him softballs now, so I think we've turned the corner."

Seth got up and followed the assistant back toward Medzhid's mini-suite. Once he was out of sight, Jack said, "We've got a problem, Matt. Wellesley's the one who gave Seth the coup manual. He's been playing Seth from the start."

"Ah, holy crap," Spellman said, and groaned. "Not that I doubted it, but man, Wellesley's good. I'd hate to play chess with the guy."

Ysabel replied, "I think we already are."

Looking at the CIA man's face, Jack

decided the frustrated expression he wore was genuine. Under the frequent hammering of John Clark's "Trust your gut" mantra, Jack had developed, he thought, solid instincts. His were now telling him Spellman was one of the good guys. This was a relief; they needed someone trustworthy in Medzhid's true inner circle.

While Wellesley's admission that he'd been jerking Seth's emotional strings removed any doubt for Jack about his friend's allegiance, he was more worried than ever about Seth's stability.

"Does this mean Wellesley has the whole plan?" asked Ysabel.

"Yes and no," replied Spellman. "Yeah, Paul Gregory's plan was ahead of its time, but it couldn't have taken into account things like social media, the Internet, how far propaganda methods have come, and so on. I'm sure Wellesley knows our plan will rely heavily on that stuff, but he doesn't know the nitty-gritty."

"Such as?" Jack asked.

"We've got the city rigged with satellite Internet and generators at coordination points in case Nabiyev shuts down the ISPs and the electrical grid, which I'm sure he will. For years we've been assembling mailing lists in the capital — about sixty

thousand people, most of them twentysome-
things who want big change, who'll get an
e-mail blast when our social media goes live.
We've got plenty of bandwidth and servers
prepped for the traffic. An hour after the
blast, pictures and vids of the protest will
be flooding Twitter, Instagram, Facebook,
and Tumblr. If Nabiyev orders in troops
from the garrison and it gets ugly, the whole
world will be watching it."

Could it really be that easy? Jack wondered.
The simple answer was no, of course not,
but the world had already seen the power of
the Internet in places like Tunisia, Iran,
Egypt, and Ukraine, where the governments
had initially discounted social media only to
find themselves playing catch-up as
hundreds of thousands of citizens marched
through the streets.

In and of itself this wasn't a new
phenomenon, but leaders who might
otherwise ignore, arrest, or brutalize peaceful protesters suddenly find their actions
and words scrutinized by the whole world.
Club a ten-year-old girl in Cairo and seven
minutes later a million people are seeing it
on YouTube, a *Boycott Egyptian Pistachios*
blog is up and running with twenty
thousand subscribers, and White Hat hack-
ers have turned the official government

website into a flashing orange mess of pop-up ads for mortgage refinancing and miracle face cream.

And Seth and Spellman were taking it even further. Not only would Makhachkala's streets be thronged with pro-democracy protesters, but they would have a camera-ready champion waiting just offstage. Their plan was solid, Jack thought, but none of it would be happening in a vacuum. Wellesley and Pechkin were no doubt preparing their own countermeasures, much of them based on the SIS man's knowledge of Seth's playbook.

Jack asked Spellman, "Are you running the whole thing from here?"

"Nah, we've got another place, a secure command center in the MOI building," Spellman replied. "Say, let's not push Seth on this Wellesley business. He's already figured it out. He's kicking himself better than we ever could."

"Yes, but is he dealing with it?" asked Ysabel. "Seth can get a little . . . obsessive."

"Really? I hadn't noticed. The answer is yeah, he's okay. He's also a tad passive-aggressive and —"

"Really? I hadn't noticed," Ysabel shot back with a smile.

"— and Wellesley's mind games are telling

him, 'You can't pull it off.' Seth's response is, 'Fuck you, watch me.' "

"That's the Seth I know. Matt, there's something else we need to talk to you about."

"Shoot."

Jack gave him the whole story about Khasavyurt, from their meeting with Dobromir to their being released by Major Umarov. He finished with the telephone trap he and Gavin had set for Wellesley and Pechkin. "We know Wellesley was Dobromir's contact, and as soon as Gavin hears back from the number Osin had, we could have Pechkin, too."

Spellman stared at the table, shaking his head. Jack guessed what he was feeling: An op like this was a juggling act writ large, with balls that were often invisible, and just as often on fire. And covered in thumbtacks.

"Hey, here's an idea," Spellman said. "How about the three of us get on a plane, head to Tahiti, and start a surf shop?"

Jack and Ysabel laughed.

"Seriously, though, you're sure it was just us in the truck that knew about your trip?"

Jack nodded. "We've decided it wasn't you —"

"Finally a little love for good ol' Matt."

"— and it wasn't Seth. As for Medzhid, I

can't imagine it's him, but who knows how many agendas he's got."

"So that leaves Anton and Vasim."

"And Medzhid's fiercely loyal to them," Ysabel said. "We'll need solid proof before he'll doubt them."

"You got that right. Just think about this: Two guys with guns who are never more than ten feet from Medzhid on the eve of a coup . . . We need to figure this out sooner rather than later."

30

MAKHACHKALA

Leaving Ysabel to keep an eye on things at the Tortoreto, Jack took off at six-thirty, swung past the now empty street outside the Ministry building, then drove the three miles to where Dom was staking out the Chirpoy Road apartment.

As Jack pulled to the curb, the sun was beginning to drop behind the Tarki-Tau hills west of the city. Already he could feel the air cooling.

"Go get some food and sleep," Jack said, walking up to Dom's window. Over the top of his car and through some trees Jack could see the apartment's gated entrance.

"Sleep I can use," Dom replied. "As for food, unless they've got a Jimmy John's stashed away around here, I'll pass for now. By the way, Ysabel's very pretty. Are you guys —"

"Shut up, Dom," Jack replied with a smile. "How's it look?"

"Eighteen rooms, each with a rear barred window and keycard locks on the doors. Whether they're opened by the gate key card, I don't know. Second-floor access is through a partially covered stairwell on the north end.

"Around the wall I've counted ten surveillance cameras hidden in the trees, one about every twelve feet, but we can assume the whole thing is ringed. One of the ground-floor apartments, number 102 at the far end, is occupied by some serious-looking dudes wearing jackets that hang like they're carrying bazookas in their armpits."

"Any of them look familiar from my lunch with Wellesley?"

"No."

"I asked Medzhid about this place. He doesn't know anything about it, so the guards aren't MOI *politsiya*. Maybe they're from the city's public safety office."

"Maybe, but I doubt it," replied Dom. "I had a cop car drive by about an hour ago. I ducked down and he kept going. Proactivity isn't on the police academy curriculum here.

"I've only seen two cars go in or out of the gate, but neither of them were Wellesley or Pechkin. The gate must trip some kind of alarm, because every time a car enters, the goon apartment door opens and one of them pokes his head out. The drivers flash some kind of permit and the guard waves, then goes back inside. Whatever that place is, Jack, it's sure as hell not making money as a commercial property."

"I've got Gavin looking into it."

"Okay, see you in four hours," Dom said, and pulled away from the curb.

Jack got back in his car and started his shift.

When night fell, rows of amber spotlights at the base of the apartment's wall came on, casting cones of light up the brick face.

At eight-fifteen a car pulled into the driveway. An arm emerged from the driver's window and swiped a key card, and the gate rose. The car pulled through, then into one of the parking spots. A woman got out, entered one of the ground-level apartments, then emerged a few minutes later. As she exited the gate, Jack zoomed in on the license plate and memorized it.

Shortly before nine, his phone rang.

"Jack, where are you?" Spellman asked.

"Sitting on an apartment. Why?"

"The men Medzhid has sitting on Koikov's house aren't answering. Can you get there?"

"Where?"

Spellman gave him the address, then said, "I'll steer you, just give me your cross streets."

"Wait one." Jack put Spellman on mute, switched apps, then texted Dom: GOTTA RUN. TAKE OVER HERE.

Dom answered immediately: EN ROUTE.

Jack started the Opel's engine and pulled away from the curb, then drove two blocks until he came to a cross street. He switched back to Spellman. "I'm coming up on Vaygach and Tuva. Headed east."

"Okay, hold on. You're three miles away. Head right on Vaygach."

For the next ten minutes, with Jack calling out streets or landmarks and Spellman responding with turns, he headed northward to Makhachkala's city limits.

"Okay, you're coming up on Kirovskiy district. Turn right at the next intersection."

Jack did so and found himself on a rundown residential street. At the end of it he took a left onto a dirt road bordered on one side by a barbed wire–enclosed pasture.

"I don't see any signs," Jack said. "There's a mile marker, though, with a twelve on it."

"Take the next right. It should be a driveway."

"Okay, I'm on it. I see a house directly ahead of me."

"Koikov's cabin is just west of it, maybe a quarter-mile. You should be coming up on another road, a small one, barely on the map."

"I see it."

Jack slowed, doused the Opel's headlights, then made the turn. To his left across the pasture he saw yellow lights filtering through a thicket of scrub trees.

Another hundred yards brought him to a T intersection. He turned left toward Koikov's cabin and slowly the trees thinned out until he could see a U-shaped clearing ahead. He let up on the accelerator and slowed the Opel to a walking pace. He rolled down the passenger window and listened. Save the buzzing of insects, all was quiet.

"Jack, you there?" asked Spellman.

"Call one of Medzhid's men."

Jack braked to a stop and shut off the engine.

Moments later he heard the ringing of a cell phone. After five rings, it went silent. Jack said, "Matt, hang on." He dialed Dom, looped him into the call, and then made quick introductions. "I need backup," he told Dom. "Matt's got my location."

Eyes fixed on the lighted windows of the

cabin, he crept down the road until the fence to his right formed a corner, which he followed, using the thicket to screen his approach to the cabin, now to his left front. He stopped, listened, then kept going until he was within ten paces of the front door, where he crouched. To his left in the driveway was a dark-colored SUV, thankfully not a Suburban, he saw. He had enough complications to deal with.

He heard a muffled male voice say something in Russian from inside the cabin, followed by a response. The tone sounded casual, but the exchange was too clipped, Jack thought, to be a friendly one. A silhouette moved past the curtained window, then out of view. The door opened and a man emerged. He walked a few steps to his right, then lit a cigarette.

Jack drew the Ruger from its holster and affixed the noise suppressor.

Jack's phone vibrated. He cupped his hand around the screen and read the text from Dom. TEN MINUTES OUT.

A voice in the darkness called out in Russian. Jack caught on two words: "car" and "there." They'd spotted his car.

The man who'd spoken walked up and joined his smoking partner, and they started talking quietly.

Suddenly from inside the cabin came a bang, then a shout and the slap of flesh against flesh. A shadowed figure crashed into the curtains, then was jerked away.

The smoking man said something and his partner laughed.

Gotta do something, Jack. Can't just sit here.

He rose from his crouch and started forward, placing each foot flat on the ground and getting it settled before taking the next step. The men to his right kept chatting. After ten paces and two minutes Jack drew even with the cabin's front door. He slipped left through the thicket, then followed the side wall around to the back, then down the opposite side until he reached the cabin's front corner. He poked his head out.

The two men were six feet away.

With the Ruger raised before him, he stepped out.

"Ruki vverh," he whispered.

Neither did as ordered. The smoking man spun left, his hand already reaching inside his coat, while his partner sprinted for the cabin door. Jack shot the first man twice in the chest, then shifted the Ruger and fired at the fleeing man. He missed. Before he could get off another shot the man was through the cabin door, shouting as he went.

Jack retreated to the corner, then adjusted

aim and put a round into each of the SUV's passenger-side tires. There was no pop, no explosive rush of air. Self-sealing tires. That said something.

The barrel of an assault rifle poked through the cabin door and swung toward Jack. He pulled back. The rifle began chattering, bullets tearing chunks from the wood and punching through the wall. He backpedaled, trying to get ahead of the piercing rounds as they kept pace with him. He turned left, shoved himself through some waist-high scrub, and then kept going, trying to put some distance between himself and the cabin.

After twenty feet he reached a woodpile. He ducked around it, peeked over the top. The SUV's front and rear doors were swinging shut.

The engine roared to life and the SUV accelerated out of the driveway and sped down the road.

Jack got out his phone and called Dom. "Where are you?"

"Passing mile marker twelve."

"Stop there and find a place to hide. In about sixty seconds a black SUV's going to be rounding the corner. Follow it."

"Sorry, guys, I lost 'em." Dom sat down on

his motel room's bed and tossed the keys onto the nightstand. He rubbed his hands through his hair. "Shit."

"We'll find them," said Spellman.

Jack made the introductions. They shook hands.

"Oh, yeah, the guy on the phone," Dom said. "You're CIA?"

"For however long that'll last," Spellman said, smiling. "By the time this is over I'll probably be working the tool counter at Home Depot. Did you get a license plate number?"

"There were none."

Ysabel went into the bathroom, filled a glass with water, then came back and handed it to Dom, who downed it. "Thanks."

"So," Jack said. "Tell us."

"I followed them for almost two hours, north up the coast, then lost them in this little village . . . Bakh-something?"

"Bakhtemir?" said Spellman.

"That's it. Just a speck of a place, but the streets were a mess and they seemed to know where they were going. Anyway, I backtracked south and sat on the road for a bit. They didn't come back my way."

"They didn't see you?" asked Spellman.

"No chance."

"Matt, what's up that way?" asked Jack.

"A whole lot of nothing. Mostly lowlands and a lot of open space. It's been drought conditions up there for a couple years, so it's probably desertlike by now. Bakhtemir's probably the largest settlement up there and it's only got a few hundred people in it."

"Why take Koikov up there?" asked Ysabel. "If they wanted to kill him, why not in his cabin? And they can't keep him hidden forever. He's going to have to appear before the panel."

"They had to have a reason," said Spellman. "If this is Wellesley —"

"It is," Jack replied.

"Then he's got a plan. He doesn't do anything spur-of-the-moment."

No one spoke for a while. Jack murmured, "What's good for the goose is good for the gander."

"What's that mean?" asked Spellman.

"We need to talk to Medzhid."

When they got to the Tortoreto apartment, Spellman woke up Seth, who in turn woke up Medzhid, who walked into the dimly lit conference area a few minutes later. His eyes were red-rimmed. "What's this about? You've found Sergeant Koikov?"

"No," Jack replied. He recounted the

shoot-out at the cabin.

"Puncture-proof tires," Medzhid repeated. "That has to be some kind of official government vehicle. I'll look into it."

"I think I have a hunch about what they have planned for Koikov."

"Does it even matter?" Seth said. "I mean, I feel for the guy, but he's lying about Almak and if he comes before the panel it'll come out. And if he doesn't show up, that's also proof he's lying. Win-win."

"Unless they kill him," said Ysabel. "That's a lose-lose for him."

"They won't."

"I think that's exactly what they're going to do," Jack replied. "Think about it: You've boxed yourself into a corner just like Wellesley did to himself. If they don't produce Koikov they lose, and if they do produce him they lose. The same applies to you: Medzhid's demanded proof that Koikov is safe and isn't being coerced, and you've got the media and the public screaming the same thing. If you suddenly let that go, everyone's going to wonder why. What have you got to hide?"

"Nothing," said Medzhid.

"The question will still be asked. Wellesley needs a way to keep Koikov away from the panel and make it look like you're guilty of

Almak."

"How?"

"Wellesley takes him to a remote place, somewhere connected to you, puts a bullet in his skull, then Nabiyev swoops in with Army troops. After a firefight Koikov is found dead, silenced by some of your loyal *politsiya* officers, who are themselves killed by Nabiyev's men." Jack paused. "Rebaz, in the space of an hour you'll be branded a murderer, not only of civilians in Almak, but of your own sergeant."

"Damn," Seth murmured. "He's right. Hell, they'll probably find Koikov in a shallow grave. Wellesley doesn't do anything half-assed."

"It wouldn't work," Medzhid said. He rapped his fist on the table. "I would eventually be vindicated."

"Maybe, but you sure as hell won't be keeping your job."

"And the coup is over before it starts," Spellman finished.

31

They had only one advantage, Jack knew, and it was Wellesley's own meticulous nature.

While the SIS man would want Koikov's place of execution to be traceable to Medzhid, if pressed for time or alerted they were onto him, Wellesley might bypass this element and simply kill Koikov and let the presence of dead pro-Medzhid officers serve as proof enough.

The surreality of the situation suddenly hit Jack: The possible success or failure of Dagestan's attempt to break free of Valeri Volodin and the Russian Federation now rested on the fate of a sickly, retired *politsiya* sergeant who was until a few days ago thought to be dead. Koikov probably had no idea that he'd become the most important man in the whole country.

Assuming Koikov's kidnappers had

continued north after Dom had lost them in Bakhtemir, Seth and Spellman began hunting for a location in Dagestan's northern lowlands that could be connected directly to Medzhid or at least to the MOI.

There were four possibilities, Spellman told Jack a few hours later: a currently unmanned training base for *politsiya* armored vehicle units outside Bakhtemir; the decommissioned Rybozavad Naval Base for Caspian flotilla patrol boats now under the guardianship of the Ministry; a two-hundred-acre stretch of tidal marshes outside Suyutkino that Medzhid's predecessor had appropriated as a private duck-hunting preserve; and an abandoned prison called Bamlag West, nicknamed after an infamous Siberian gulag. This, too, Medzhid said, was a throwback to Dagestan's Soviet era, when hundreds of enemies of the state had either served for decades or died from forced labor.

At first light Medzhid had a spotter plane in the air and headed north from Makhach-kala.

Jack and the others sat down at the conference table and waited.

"Jack, how long do you think Koikov's got?" Ysabel whispered.

"I've been thinking about that. Unless I'm missing something, Wellesley's got no reason to wait. It might already be done."

One of Medzhid's assistants appeared. She leaned down and whispered in Seth's ear. He picked up the remote control on the table and aimed it at the bank of televisions.

Medzhid, standing on the front steps of the Parliament Building, was speaking. ". . . It has come to my attention that another member of my team that was present at the Battle of Almak is still living. Upon hearing that Sergeant Koikov's demise had been misreported, I ordered my staff to begin scouring Ministry of the Interior personnel records, both electronic and hard copy, for similar errors.

"We did indeed find the name of another brave officer, a private named Shimko, who has been living in the town of Kula for the past ten years. Right now, this man is being escorted here and is prepared to give sworn testimony regarding the 1999 events in Almak."

Seth muted the television. "I'll be damned."

"Did you know about this, Seth?" asked Spellman. "Is it true?"

"No and no. Medzhid did have his people

review the records, but Koikov is the only surviving member from Almak."

Clever, Jack thought. With another possible witness coming forward at Medzhid's behest, having Pavel Koikov turn up dead would do Wellesley and Pechkin no good.

Medzhid had just bought them some time.

"But what happens when this Private Shimko doesn't show up or someone finds proof Medzhid is lying about him?" asked Ysabel.

"Then Koikov's dead," Spellman replied.

At one-fifteen came the first report from Medzhid's spotter plane: No activity at the Bakhtemir training base.

The next report came two hours later.

"Nothing at the hunting preserve," Seth said. "Two more to go: Rybozavad Naval Base and Bamlag West."

"How far away?" asked Jack.

"Rybozavad, a hundred kilometers or so from the plane's current position. It should be overhead within the hour. Bamlag's inland from there."

The hour came and went with no report.

Medzhid returned. He shrugged off his coat, tossed it onto the couch, then loosened his tie and strode to the conference area.

"That was brilliant, Rebaz," Spellman said.

"No, I am a fool. I shouldn't have used Shimko's name. One of my assistants got a call from the editor at *Pravda* asking for details — Shimko's dates of service, commendations, location and names of family members . . . By morning, all of Makhachkala will know I was lying about Shimko."

The phone rang again. Seth said, "Negative on Rybozavad Naval Base."

Have I got this wrong? Jack wondered. Had Wellesley simply killed Koikov and dumped him in a ditch somewhere?

At six-twenty the conference table phone rang again. Medzhid grabbed the receiver, listened for a few moments, then said, "No. No pictures. Tell them to get out of there and return to base." Medzhid hung up and said, "They spotted lights in one of the buildings at Bamlag. There should be no one there."

"That has to be it," Jack replied.

Wellesley's choice of location was both intentional and symbolic: the lone witness who could bring down Medzhid executed and buried in what Nabiyev would dub an "MOI Gulag."

Seth said, "Rebaz, how soon can your

ERF people get up there?"

"What are you talking about? I can't send them."

"Why?"

Jack answered. "Having the ERF descend on Bamlag could produce the result Nabiyev wants: Sergeant Koikov dead and Medzhid's people on the scene."

"We have to do it," Spellman said.

With Seth at the wheel of the Suburban, Jack, Spellman, and Ysabel headed up the coast road, then turned onto a gravel track leading to a wharf. Ahead was a wheeled fence gate emblazoned KEEP OUT in Cyrillic.

"We've picked up a tail," Seth announced.

"Describe it," Jack said from the backseat.

"Compact four-door, white."

"He's with me. Have the guard wave him through."

"Whatever you say," Seth muttered. "You and your damned secrets, Jack . . ."

Seth gave the guard his name and the gate rolled open. They pulled through and followed the curving road to a paved area between two warehouses lit by a caged bulb affixed to each of their walls.

As they climbed out, Dom walked up carrying his black duffel.

Jack said, "Seth, this is Dom; Dom, Seth."

"Another arbitrage buddy?"

"Something like that," said Dom.

Spellman asked Dom, "That your gear?"

"Yeah."

"I've got a spare rucksack. Come on, I'll help you sort it out."

Together they sorted and divided their loadout — three ARX assault rifles and Ruger pistols, comms headsets and portable radios, and binoculars.

"God bless," Dom said. "Somebody's modified these ARXs. Single shot, three-round burst, and full auto."

"You're welcome," Spellman said. "Ready?"

"Yep."

They secured the rucks and followed Seth toward the wharf.

"Let me guess," Ysabel said. "You want me to stay behind."

"Yes, but not why you think. I need you to —"

"Keep an eye on things at the Tortoreto. I'm fine with it. The truth is, this stuff isn't exactly my specialty. I'm betting that whoever's holding Koikov is above my skill set."

"You've done okay, Ysabel. Hell, you saved me at least once."

"At least twice."

"When's your birthday?" asked Jack.

"What? Um . . . June twenty-first."

"I'll buy you an assault rifle."

"That's so sweet, Jack. You know just what a girl wants."

She hugged him and whispered in his ear, "Come back safe."

As the terrain around Bamlag was either too swampy or too rugged for a fixed-wing plane to land, and he couldn't spare what few helicopters he had, Medzhid had arranged for their transport an Aviatik-Alliance seaplane, which would land near Bamlag on an unnamed lake.

The dual-engine parasol-winged craft was painted a mottled gray and brown; its tail and fuselage bore the Ministry's eagle emblem in matte black paint.

Jack climbed down the ladder and waited his turn to pile into the Aviatik's belly. Once they were seated, Seth leaned in the door and said, "Good hunting. Bring Koikov home and we'll stuff him down Nabiyev's throat."

He slammed the door shut.

The pilot climbed into the cockpit and began going through his preflight checklist. Out the windows the water of the harbor was flat and black; beyond the seawall, Jack could see the pulsing beacons of offshore oil platforms.

The engines coughed once, then turned over and started spooling up. Jack could feel the vibration in his feet.

Seated in the row behind the cockpit, Spellman leaned forward, asked the pilot a question, then shouted the answer over his shoulder to Jack and Dom: "Ninety minutes' flight time."

Dom leaned over to Jack and said, "Is this guy Spellman any good?"

"He saved my ass in Tehran. That's good enough for me."

Seventy minutes after they lifted off, the pilot turned west over Bakhtemir and headed inland for another twenty kilometers before putting the Aviatik into a gentle descent and bleeding off altitude until they were only a few hundred feet off the ground.

The pilot turned in his seat, got Spellman's attention, and pointed to the set of white headphones hanging from the bulkhead. Spellman donned them, listened, then said over his shoulder to Jack and Dom, "Nine miles out."

At four miles the pilot throttled back and kept descending until through the window

Jack could see the plane's barely perceptible shadow skimming over the rugged, boulder-strewn landscape.

The pilot held up two fingers: two miles.

Another minute passed. The pilot cut the engines. The sound faded until Jack could hear only the wind hissing through the door's gasket seal.

"Touching down," Spellman called.

The Aviatik's belly kissed the surface of the lake. The craft bounced one, twice, then settled, hissing over the water. The pilot brought the nose around until it was aimed at a curve of white beach, then let the plane's momentum carry it to within a hundred yards of the shoals, where he goosed the throttle until the keel scraped over the sand.

Spellman took off his headphones and returned them to the hook. "We're on foot from here."

32

The cloud cover was slow-moving and partial, leaving the moon a hazy disk that slid into and out of view as they walked. Jack would have preferred full dark but ops like this one were rarely served up perfectly to those involved.

A quarter-mile out they stopped and settled behind a cluster of chest-high boulders. Dom handed Jack one of the ARXs. Together they ran a weapons check, then attached the multipoint slings and draped the ARXs across their chests. Spellman was doing the same with his sniper rifle.

"Fucking Vietnam-era Dragunov," he muttered. "Is this the best they can do? At least the suppressor looks decent. Shit, I don't even know if it's sighted in."

"You'll have to do it on the fly," said Dom. "How long will our pilot wait?"

"As long as it takes. Or until he gets shot

431

at, I imagine."

Dom handed out the headsets and they ran a comms test, then switched channels and did the same with the Aviatik's pilot.

Jack said, "Let's check the ground." He poked his head over the boulders and raised his binoculars.

Though eight thousand miles from its Siberian namesake, Bamlag West Prison looked like all the other satellite images of gulags Jack had seen. Set on flat barren ground, the rectangular-shaped compound was enclosed by twelve-foot-high barbed-wire fencing, much of it half collapsed.

"Plenty of entrance points," Jack told them.

In the center of the camp stood a watchtower, which divided the compound into north and south sections, the former containing nine windowless, barracks-style prisoner huts arranged in a three-by-three square; the latter five wooden structures Jack assumed were administrative buildings. While these buildings sat close to the perimeter, none of the barracks sat closer than 150 feet from the fencing. This would be the no-go zone, Jack guessed. First the wayward prisoner would get a warning shot; after that, one through the head.

He relayed to Spellman and Dom what he

was seeing, then zoomed in on the admin buildings.

"No movement and no lights," he said. "And no sign of the SUV from Koikov's cabin."

He panned to the watchtower and dialed the binocular's focus wheel until the tower's hut became clear. Beneath the eaves of the slanted roof he saw a bank of windows, most of them broken.

"I've got movement in the tower," Jack reported. "Looks like one man."

"Armed?" asked Dom.

"Can't tell; he's just a silhouette."

"I'm not sure I can get him from here, not with this," Spellman said. "Let me take a look." He dropped to his belly and scooted sideways until he could see around the boulder pile. He pressed the Dragunov to his cheek and peered through the scope.

"Too risky," he said after a few moments. "If I miss the first shot, I doubt I'll get a second. Plus, with these subsonic rounds I'll need to be closer."

The approach was painstakingly slow. Spaced at twenty-foot intervals with Spellman on point, they belly-crawled from boulder to boulder, most of which were barely bigger than their heads. Soon Jack's elbows ached and he could feel the slickness of blood beneath his camouflage jacket.

Occasionally Spellman would signal a halt with a closed fist beside his thigh and they would stop and survey the compound through the Dragunov's scope before continuing forward.

After twenty more minutes Spellman stopped again.

Through his headset Jack heard, "Signs of life. Side door of the building on the far right. Call it Building One."

Slowly Jack brought up his binoculars and zoomed in on the building. Seeping from the edges of the side door was light. "I see it. What about the tower?"

"Wait one."

Jack watched as Spellman side-scooted until he reached a boulder ten feet to his right. "Clear shot," he whispered.

"On your time," Jack replied.

Dom called, "Hold. I've got movement. Building One side door opening. One man coming out. Door is shutting."

"I'm on him," Spellman said.

Through his binoculars Jack watched the man stride across their front from right to left. His figure was broken up by the barbed-wire fence.

"Shot doubtful," Spellman said.

The man raised a hand to his partner in the tower, then stopped at a building with a tall, corrugated garage door set into its front wall. He stepped though the pedestrian door and disappeared inside. The interior was dark.

"Calling that Garage," Dom said.

"Matt, how's the angle?" Jack asked.

"If I get him coming out the door the guy in the tower won't see him go down."

"Do it," Jack said.

Now we find out how good the Dragunov's suppressor is.

Five minutes passed. Then, from Spellman, "Garage door is opening."

"Take the shot," Jack ordered.

Spellman's Dragunov bucked. The rifle's report was no louder than a rock cracking against one of the boulders.

At the garage door, the man stumbled back across the threshold. As he fell Jack caught a glimpse of what looked like a vehicle's front quarter-panel.

"Heart shot," Dom called. "Nice shooting."

"I'm switching to the tower," Spellman replied. "He's looking around. You guys see any movement on the ground?"

"Negative."

"Negative."

"Firing."

Through his binoculars Jack saw the tower guard's head disappear in a cloud of dark spray.

"He's down," Dom reported, then chuckled softly. "Very down."

With the ground ahead clear of targets, Dom and Jack left Spellman on overwatch and sprinted ahead, slipped through a gap in the fence, then moved to the garage. Dom posted on the front right corner, ARX pointed at Building One. Jack nudged the dead man's legs off the threshold, then closed the door and proceeded to the building's opposite corner; he peeked around it.

"Clear on this side," he called. "Matt, come up."

"Moving."

"Hold!" Dom called.

Jack looked left and saw Building One's door open, casting a rectangle of light on the dirt. The man started walking toward the garage.

Dom said, "He'll have me in ten seconds."

Spellman called, "I've got more movement — past the guard tower near the barracks. Three men, all carrying SBRs," he said, referring to short-barreled rifles. "They're headed your way."

"I'm slinging," Dom said, simultaneously backing up and shifting his ARX so it was hidden behind his body. "Jack, can you —"

"Yep. Just stay out of my sight line."

The man kept coming.

He stopped. His posture stiffened.

Dom took a step to his right.

"A little more," Jack whispered.

Dom took another step, then raised his hand in greeting. The man waved back. His shoulders relaxed and he started forward again. Jack let him get to within six feet of Dom, then shot him in the forehead. As he went down, Dom asked Spellman, "Any reaction from your three?"

"No, but you'd better get that body clear. Wait until I tell you . . . Okay, go now."

Hunched over, Dom walked to the man's body, lifted it under the shoulders, then dragged it to the garage. Jack opened the side door, and Dom backed through and dumped the body beside Spellman's kill. The man was in desert camouflage identical to their own; Jack saw no insignias or patches.

"Matt, can you move?" he asked.

"Maybe. I'll lose sight of them, though."

Jack considered this. "We need to

consolidate. Move up when you can. I'll cover you."

Jack slid along the wall to the corner and looked around it. The three men were fifty yards away and passing through the tower's buttresses. Over his shoulder he heard the soft scuff of a boot in the dirt, then Spellman's voice: "Here."

"Into the garage."

Spellman stepped through and Jack followed, closing the door behind him.

"It's clear," Dom said. "There's another door at the back, but it's locked on our side. Hey, Jack, I'm pretty sure this is the SUV I tailed."

Jack knelt beside the vehicle's front tire and clicked on his penlight. In the sidewall was the depression from Jack's bullet at the cabin. "Yep. We're in the right place."

"It's better than that," Spellman replied with a smile. "That, gentlemen, is a Volvo XC90 — standard issue for Dagestani government officials. Let's see if we can get a VIN . . ." Spellman opened the Volvo's door. The dome light popped on. He climbed in and leaned over the dash, looking.

Near the back of the garage came the sliding thunk of a dead bolt.

33

Spellman froze. Jack stepped to the SUV and crouched beside the tire. Dom, who was standing beside the rear tire, showed Jack a closed fist, then a thumbs-up. With the ARX tucked into his shoulder, he poked his head around the Volvo's corner post, fired once, then moved forward.

Jack heard the back door's dead bolt slide back into place. Dom reappeared dragging a body. "We've got ourselves another ARX," he whispered.

"Looks like Seth and these guys share the same armorer," Jack replied.

"Doesn't mean anything," Spellman said from the Volvo's driver's seat. "Some of the city garrison troops are getting them from Moscow."

"Does that mean these are regular Russian Army?" asked Dom.

"Possibly. If so, Volodin might be more committed to keeping Nabiyev in power than we thought."

"Better find that out," said Jack. "If the garrison decides to march on your protesters it could be a bloodbath."

He and Dom frisked the bodies but found nothing.

Spellman hopped down. "Good news, bad news. The bad is there are no keys in the ignition and the hood lock is on remote."

"Fuckin' tank," Dom muttered.

"The good news is I've got a VIN. Any bets on who it belongs to?"

"I'm going with President Nabiyev himself," Jack replied with a smile.

"Always the optimist," Dom said.

"Let's get these guys in the back of the Volvo and keep moving. Somebody's going to notice they're short four men."

After Dom jerry-rigged a bar for the garage's back door, they went out the front and crossed to Building One, cleared its outer walls, then stacked up outside the door. Dom pressed his ear to it for a few moments, then pulled back. He made a quacking-duck gesture with his hand, then held up two fingers and shrugged.

At least two men inside, Jack thought.

Dom gestured again: *Bypass and keep moving.*

Jack nodded.

Spellman, with his Dragunov slung over his back and his Ruger held at the ready-low position, took point. Jack was in the middle with their spare ARX slung over his shoulder. Dom brought up the rear, turning slow circles and scanning for movement as he walked.

In turn, they cleared the remaining admin buildings. All were empty and appeared to have been unoccupied for years. There was no sign of Pavel Koikov. They paused in the last building to down some water.

"He's either in that first building or in one of the barracks," Jack said.

"Unless they're empty of furniture, clearing them is going to be a nightmare."

From somewhere outside there came the hiss of radio static.

It stopped.

Dom crept to the tarnished window next to the door and looked out.

"Four more men coming from the direction of the barracks. All have SBRs. Okay, looks like they're bypassing the garage and heading for Building One. They look relaxed."

"That won't last," said Spellman. "Once they're inside, somebody'll do a head count."

"How many bad guys does that make?" Jack asked. "Four we've downed plus at least two in Building One, then these four."

"Sounds about right," Dom replied. "That makes eleven, including Koikov. No way they all fit in that Volvo."

"There's another vehicle somewhere," said Spellman.

And as many as six more men, Jack thought.

While they covered him, Spellman climbed the tower.

"In place," he radioed. "I've got decent sight lines except for the alleys between the barracks and behind the last row."

"Roger," said Dom.

"Just for clarity's sake, what say we name them? From right to left, Bravo One, Two, and so on. Objections?"

"None," Jack replied.

"The guy up here had another ARX. You want it?"

"Keep it," said Jack. "In case you get rushed."

"There's a cheery thought," Spellman replied. "Okay, I'm set. Move when you want."

By mutual agreement, Jack and Dom had decided to simply spread apart and walk the remaining hundred yards to the barracks — bodies moving at speed were easier to spot in the darkness.

They had crossed a third of the distance when Spellman called, "Hold."

In unison, Dom and Jack froze, then slowly crouched.

"Side door opening on Bravo One."

The man trotted down the barracks' short steps, then started walking toward the tower.

"Hold . . ." Spellman whispered to them. "I want to put some distance between him and the barracks."

"Hold . . . Firing."

In mid-stride the man collapsed to his knees, then rolled onto his side, dead.

"You're clear," Spellman called.

"I'm going to check him," Dom said. He trotted over to the man, frisked him, then returned to where Jack was crouching.

"He had Volvo keys," Dom said.

"We're moving again, Matt."

"Roger."

They reached the first building and went around to the side steps. Dom signaled for Jack to wait, then headed to the barracks' rear corner. He returned a moment later and whispered, "No sign of a second vehicle. It's gotta be behind the last row."

"How's your Russian?" Jack whispered.

"Nonexistent."

Jack opened the door a few inches. Aside from the strip of light Jack had just created, the interior was black. A few feet away he saw the outline of a triple-tiered bunk and the corner of a rotting mattress. The air was so pungent it stung his eyes.

Jack put a rasp in his voice and called softly, *"Ey, drug!"* Hey, friend.

He got no response.

"Matt, we're entering Bravo Three."

"Roger. Nothing moving out. There's music coming from Building One. Sounds like they're having a party."

"With vodka, hopefully," Dom added.

Guided by their penlights, they moved down the barracks' center aisle, checking bunks as they went until they reached the next door.

"On our way out, moving to Bravo Two," Jack radioed.

"Hold position," Spellman replied.

There was thirty seconds of silence.

"Okay, you're clear to move. I heard a car door open and shut. Sounds like it came from behind Bravo Eight."

The middle barracks in the back row, Jack thought. "Moving."

Inside the next building they found a battery-powered lantern glowing beside the last bunk. On the mattress was a sleeping bag, still slightly warm from where Spellman's last kill had been sleeping.

"Heading to Bravo Four," Jack radioed.

In turn, they cleared the next three buildings. They had just walked up to the steps outside Bravo Nine when Jack heard a series of rapid clicks over his headset. It was their prearranged warning signal.

Jack whispered, "Movement?"

Spellman replied with a single click: *Yes.*

"Our end?"

Double click: *No.*

"Yours?"

There was a pause and then Spellman said, his voice barely a whisper, "Coming up the ladder."

Jack heard the double pop of a handgun, followed by one more.

"Shit!" Dom growled.

"Go put eyes on the other car," Jack ordered.

Dom hopped off the steps, sprinted to the corner of the building. After a moment he said, "Nothing."

"Hold there and keep me posted."

Jack went left and crossed the entrance of the alley to the front barracks, where he crouched down. He aimed his binoculars at the tower and zoomed in. There was no sign of Spellman.

"Matt," he called.

No response.

"Give me a click . . . something if you're alive."

Spellman came on the line, breathing heavily. "I'm alive. I got another dead one up here with me. Had to bash the fucker's head in. You guys okay?"

Before Jack could answer, Dom replied, "Nope. I got movement back here. Three guys coming out of Bravo Six and heading for an SUV, looks like another Volvo. They're pushing a fourth guy ahead of them. His head's covered by a blanket. Gotta be Koikov."

"Do you have a shot on the others?" Jack asked.

He heard the muffled crack of Dom's ARX. "Got one," he replied. "The rest are in the vehicle. It's moving away, coming around the other side of the building."

Jack radioed Spellman: "Matt, get ready to put some rounds in the engine block."

"Roger."

"Dom, come to me."

"Roger."

On the other side of the tower, Jack saw a

rectangle of light slant across the ground. "Matt, someone's coming out of Building One," he called.

"Try to keep 'em off me."

Jack raised his ARX, looking for a target. He heard the roar of the Volvo's engine. He glanced right. The SUV came around the corner of the first barracks, its tail end skidding, throwing up an impenetrable cloud of dust.

"I got no shot!" Spellman shouted.

A few seconds later, the Volvo charged from the cloud and accelerated toward the tower. The muzzle of Spellman's Dragunov flashed once, then again. A pair of holes appeared in the Volvo's hood and the vehicle began slaloming.

"Adjusting," said Spellman.

Dom came up behind Jack and together they sprinted after the Volvo.

The Dragunov flashed again. "Hit."

Steam gushed from the Volvo's grille, but it kept going, rapidly closing the gap to the tower and leaving Jack and Dom behind, enveloped in swirling dust.

Spellman called again, "Hit."

Jack heard overlapping gunfire erupt somewhere to their front and knew the men from Building One had opened up.

Spellman shouted, "Shit, shit, I'm taking fire!"

"Drop flat!"

"Fuck that!"

Spellman's ARX started chittering from the tower.

Jack heard a crash of steel against wood, then a grating shriek.

Spellman shouted over the gunfire, "Bastards just sideswiped my tower. I think they rammed the side of the garage, too."

Jack and Dom kept running. The dust cloud thinned. Looming before Jack's face were the tower's crisscrossed support beams. He dodged left. His shoulder slammed into a stanchion, knocking him sideways. From the corner of his eye he saw three muzzles flashing near Building One. The shots were directed at the tower.

"I'm running out of ammo," Spellman called.

Dom appeared at Jack's side and lifted him to his feet.

"Come on, Jack, let's light these fuckers up."

Jogging abreast of each other, they opened fire on the group. Jack's ARX ran dry. He ejected the magazine, inserted a new one, and kept firing until they reached the safety of the next building's wall.

A man lunged around the corner, his rifle coming up. Jack stepped forward, butt-stroked him across the jaw. As he fell, Jack shot him in the chest.

"Clear!" Dom called from somewhere up ahead. "All down. You good, Jack . . . Matt?"

Spellman replied, "The Volvo just went through the fence. It's limping, slowing down."

Jack and Dom took off running.

The Volvo had covered a couple hundred yards, having nearly reached the boulder pile where Jack and the others had scouted the compound.

"Matt, you have us covered?" Jack asked.

"Yeah, but just with the Dragunov. My ARX is dry."

Its tires bumping over rocks, the Volvo coasted to a stop. The engine revved, then sputtered and went silent.

Jack and Dom kept running, ARXs tucked into their shoulders.

"We're wide open out here, Jack. No cover."

"I know."

Simultaneously, the Volvo's front doors burst open. A man hopped out of the passenger side and, hunched over, rounded the door and knelt by the tire. He opened fire.

"Shot," Spellman called, and the top of the man's head disintegrated.

Now the driver emerged, but instead of taking cover he charged down the side of the Volvo, firing from the hip. As he passed the rear door it opened. Two men piled out, one in camouflage, the second in civilian clothes.

Koikov.

Spellman shot the man charging Jack and Dom.

At the Volvo, Koikov stumbled, almost pitched forward to the ground, but the second man grabbed him by the collar and jerked him back. He wrapped his arm around Koikov's neck and jammed the barrel of his pistol behind Koikov's earlobe.

Shocked, Jack realized he recognized the man holding Koikov. Black hair, long sideburns . . . This was Captain Salko, Medzhid's ERF commander.

With his face pressed tight against Koikov's, Salko began backing toward the front of the SUV.

Spellman called over the headset, "Jack, I'm losing any shot I've got . . ."

"Percentage?"

"Fifty-fifty and dropping fast."

Salko stepped left, and he and Koikov disappeared around the Volvo's bumper.

"Shot's gone, Jack," Spellman radioed.

"Stay on him. I'll see if I can get you an angle."

Jack released his grip on the ARX and let it dangle across his chest. He called, "Salko! Captain Salko, can you hear me?"

"I can hear you."

Jack started walking forward.

Dom warned over the headset, "Jack . . ."

"Find a spot. If Matt doesn't have a clear line, take your best shot."

A wounded Pavel Koikov is better than no Koikov at all, he thought.

"Salko, I'm coming around the right side of the vehicle," Jack called. "My weapon's down."

Jack didn't wait for a response, but kept walking. Hands raised, he passed down the Volvo's right side. When Salko and Koikov came into view, Jack stopped so that the SUV's hood was between himself and Salko.

Pavel Koikov's lip trembled and his eyes darted back and forth from Salko's gun hand to Jack's face. Jack ignored him and focused on Salko, whose own face was bathed in sweat, the muscles of his jaw pulsing.

"This is going to break Medzhid's heart," Jack said with a chuckle he hoped didn't sound as forced as it felt. "You're the best *politsiya* he has."

"What he's planning is treason," said Salko.

Jack had myriad questions he wanted to ask the man, the foremost of which was: Who ordered you to do this? But Salko wouldn't answer, and the longer this standoff went on, the greater the chance that he'd simply kill Koikov.

"Maybe so," Jack replied, "but what you're doing won't make any difference."

"What do you mean?"

Before Jack could answer, Dom's whispered voice came over Jack's headset: "I'm almost in place. Ten more seconds."

Jack said, "They didn't tell you? Medzhid found another witness to Almak, a private named Shimko. He's probably in the capital by now."

"There was no one else at Almak. Just this one."

"No, they missed Shimko. He's alive. The man you've got here is useless now. You might as well let him go."

In his ear, Jack heard Dom whisper, "Say when."

Salko said, "I want to call —"

"Go," Jack said.

Lying on his belly beneath the Volvo's rear bumper, Dom took the only shot he had.

The ARX's bullet slammed into Salko's right ankle, propelling the leg backward as though it had been jerked hard by a rope. As Salko pitched forward his weight shifted onto Koikov, who crumpled, his neck still clenched in the crook of Salko's forearm.

Salko's face slammed into the ground. Jack, his ARX already up and tucked into his shoulder, ran around the Volvo's bumper. Salko lifted his head, his eyes glassy, and saw Jack approaching. He tried to raise his pistol. Jack kicked it away.

Dom jogged up. He stared down at Salko, then said, "Well, what do you know? We got a live one."

Medzhid was waiting by the Tortoreto's private elevators when Seth steered the Suburban into the parking spot and shut off the engine. As Matt Spellman climbed out, Medzhid walked up with Anton a few paces behind. "Where is he?"

Which one? Jack thought. He hadn't told Medzhid about Captain Salko.

Jack reached back into the rear passenger seat and helped Pavel Koikov down. When he saw Medzhid, the old sergeant stiffened as though trying to come to attention. "Mr. Minister."

Medzhid cupped Koikov's face in his

hands. "Stop with that, Pavel." He wrapped Koikov in a hug. "I am sorry this happened to you. Are you injured?"

"No, just tired. And hungry."

"I can remedy both those things. Here, go with Anton and Seth. They'll get you settled upstairs." When the elevator doors closed behind the trio, Medzhid turned to Jack and Spellman and shook their hands. "Well done."

"You need to see something," Jack said.

He led Medzhid to the back of the Suburban and opened the gate. Captain Salko lay on his side in the SUV's cramped cargo well, his wrists and ankles bound and his mouth covered with a strip of silver duct tape.

When he saw Medzhid he started mumbling through the tape, his eyes angry.

"What is this?" Medzhid asked. "Why is he —"

"He was holding Koikov — with a gun to his head."

"That cannot be."

"It is," Spellman replied. "He thinks you're a traitor."

Medzhid stared at Salko for a few seconds, then leaned down and spat in his face. "I'm done looking at him."

Spellman shut the tailgate.

"I'll send Vasim down to take him away," said Medzhid.

"We've got a better idea," Jack said. "Aside from the five of us, nobody knows we have him. Let's keep it that way. For now, stash him someplace nobody will look."

If they didn't already, the opposition would soon know what had happened at Bamlag. Their lever was gone, along with their mole inside the ERF, a man Jack feared might have been a cancer. According to Seth, the ERF fielded four platoons of twenty-eight men each, along with armored personnel carriers and heavy weapons. It was the closest thing the MOI had to Special Forces. Medzhid needed to know if he could count on them.

"I'd start taking a hard look at your people, Rebaz. Did Salko know about the coup?"

"Not from me."

"Whoever told him to take Koikov does, and we should assume Salko told others in the ERF," said Spellman.

Jack said, "We've got some pictures for you to look at later — the other men at Bamlag — and a couple VINs for you to check."

Before they'd left the camp they'd jotted down the VIN of the second Volvo, then searched Building One and the remaining barracks, but came up with nothing save the cell phone in Salko's pocket and a collection of Beretta ARXs.

"Let's hope Captain Salko was an aberration. In the meantime, I have a safe house that will suit him."

"Call ahead and tell them we're coming," said Jack. "And, Rebaz, resist the impulse to pay Salko a personal visit, okay?"

Medzhid's expression turned hard. "Jack, since we don't know one another very well, I'll forgive you that comment. But only once. The last four men who held this job had no qualms about torture. I am not them. Captain Salko will be tried, and if he is found guilty he will be imprisoned. Do we understand one another?"

"We do."

34

MAKHACHKALA

For the first time in what felt like months, Jack slept soundly, for a full eight hours before Ysabel woke him. She held a steaming cup of coffee under his nose until he groaned and opened his eyes.

"What time is it?"

"Two o'clock," she replied. "Tuesday. The coup is over."

Jack sat up and took the mug. "Not funny. Have I missed anything?"

"Medzhid's called a press conference on the steps of the Parliament Building. He and Sergeant Koikov are testifying before Nabiyev's panel."

"How's the city?" he asked.

"Quiet. It's like the protests never happened."

"The calm before the storm."

"Then let's make the most of it," Ysabel replied with a sly smile.

She took the coffee mug from his hands

and put it on the nightstand.

After a shower and a second cup of coffee, Jack phoned Dom at his hotel to check that all was well, then he and Ysabel found Spellman sitting in the conference area. Medzhid's cadre of assistants was nowhere to be seen, as were Medzhid's bodyguards. The apartment was quiet, save the gurgle of the floor-to-ceiling fountain set into the wall.

"Where's Seth?" Jack asked.

"He went to visit Salko."

The stashing place Medzhid had sent them to had been an unremarkable two-story house in one of Makhachkala's southern neighborhoods. A middle-aged man and woman in civilian clothes directed them to pull into the garage, where they helped Salko out of the Suburban's cargo area, then escorted him into the house's back door. The entire exchange took less than a minute and not a word was spoken.

"Will he get anything out of him?" asked Ysabel.

"Probably not. I think Seth just wanted to look him in the eye. Seth told me he should've personally vetted Salko."

"It wasn't his job," Jack replied.

"By the way, I think Salko's phone is

probably a dead end," Spellman said. "It went to a landline — some cooking supply shop in Leninsky district. I'll check it out, but I suspect they paid some sap a few bucks to play operator. Salko's phone shows a call there at about the time the Volvo sideswiped my tower. I liked that tower, too."

"Let's call Gavin and see if he's got anything for us," Jack said. He dialed the number, then put the phone on speaker.

It took four rings before Gavin picked up. Groggily, he said, "Yeah, sorry, I fell asleep. I have something on the Chirpoy Road apartment. It belongs to the Office of the Mayor."

"So by default, President Nabiyev. According to Medzhid, they play racquetball twice a week."

"They use the place for visiting foreign VIPs, both political and business types, and a few local officials as well," said Gavin, "so I guess it makes sense that Wellesley's holed up there."

"Why?" asked Ysabel.

"Wellesley would want someplace secure, but President Nabiyev can't put them up in a state or federal government building," Jack replied. "He needs the same kind of deniability Volodin does, otherwise nobody will believe the coup failed because Dagestanis love good old Mother Russia and want to stay part of the Federation."

Spellman said, "We need to get into that apartment, Jack."

"Dom's going to poke around there tonight."

"Tell him not to bother," Gavin said. "The two plates he gave me came back to generic government lease cars, but the one you got is registered to a private citizen — a woman named Zoya Vetochkina in the city's Department of Culture. She looks on the up-and-up. If you're lucky, maybe she leaves her car unlocked and her key card in the visor. Jack, you said you don't know whether one key card works on both the gate and the doors, right?"

"Right. Is that a problem?"

Gavin laughed. "Hell, no. Chances are the locks are Quanix brand. All you gotta do is scan the thirty-two-bit key, feed it back to the lock, and you're in. You're going to have to do a little shopping, though. Matt, does Makhachkala have any Devpulse clubs?"

"I've got no idea what that is."

"Google it. It's an open-source hobby electronics thing."

Spellman typed the term into his laptop, then scrolled and clicked a few times. "I'll be damned. Yeah, there are four of them."

"E-mail the webmaster, tell him you're working on a school project for your son that's due tomorrow and you need an ATmega32u4 —"

"Whoa, slow down. Say that again."

"Just tell him you need a twenty-IO controller and a standard barrel jack. He'll know what you're talking about. Once you've got the stuff, I'll walk you through everything."

"Super. What exactly are we building?"

Jack said, "Don't encourage him, Matt. He'll talk your ear off. Gavin, call Dom with Zoya Vetochkina's details."

"Will do. Okay, I saved the best news for last: I got a text back from the number we have for Pechkin. He didn't identify himself, but he seemed to buy that I was Captain Osin. He asked for a meeting."

Almost there, Jack thought. They now knew that after he and Ysabel had left for Khasavyurt, either Vasim or Anton called Pechkin, who had in turn called Osin.

"We've got the son of a bitch," said Spellman. "That's the link we needed."

"Not quite. We have to find Pechkin's number on one of their cell phones, or in their call history. Without that, Medzhid won't make a move."

461

Ysabel said, "Gavin, you hijacked Dobromir's and Osin's numbers. Couldn't you do the same with Pechkin's? We get Anton and Vasim in the same room, dial their numbers, and see which one rings. Matt, you have them, don't you?"

"Sure."

"Dobromir's and Osin's were straight cell phones," Gavin explained. "Pechkin's is being routed through a landline cluster."

"I don't know what that means," said Ysabel.

"It's just another way to anonymize yourself, hiding your IP — Internet protocol — address with a proxy server, using disposable e-mail addresses, setting up a VPN — virtual private network. There are lots of ways; landline routing is pretty old-school, but it works. The point is, without Pechkin's cell phone in hand, I'd need to be in the room with whatever they're using as forwarder. Or one of you would need to be."

"Let's make it happen," said Spellman. "I doubt all they're using the place for is to route calls, anyway."

"Gavin, when did you set up the meeting with Pechkin?"

"Tomorrow morning at ten. Someplace called Anzhi Sady."

"*Sady* is Russian for 'gardens,' " said

462

Spellman. "I know the place. It's actually a children's playground. Pechkin's no dummy, I'll give him that. School hasn't started yet, so the place will be packed."

"What're you thinking, Jack?" Ysabel asked.

"Wellesley and Pechkin seem pretty fond of kidnapping. Let's play it their way."

Seth burst through the apartment door and strode toward them.

"It's starting! Medzhid's on!"

Spellman grabbed the remote control and turned on the television. Medzhid was already making his statement: ". . . by unanimous vote the panel chaired by our President Nabiyev has determined the story that appeared in *Dagestanskaia Pravda* two days ago was in fact false. As I knew he would, Sergeant Pavel Koikov supported the official report I filed following the Almak incident. I will take questions now."

Offscreen voices clamored until Medzhid pointed at one of the unseen reporters. "Mr. Minister, were representatives of *Pravda* present during the hearing?"

"No, they were not. But it is my understanding they were invited."

"What actions will you take now?"

"Personally, none. I have, however,

ordered my deputy, Mr. Alenin, to convene an independent panel to investigate this matter. Either someone at *Pravda* misquoted Sergeant Koikov, or he was never interviewed for the story, or he was coerced into giving a false account of what happened at Almak. Should this be the case, I fully expect criminal charges will be filed against those responsible."

"Where is Sergeant Koikov now?"

"He is in protective custody but will be made available to Deputy Alenin's panel — and to the press after all of this is over, should he so desire. Next question?"

"There have been reports that the man you mentioned yesterday, Private Shimko, is not alive. Would you care to comment?"

"Only to say this: From the moment this fallacious story appeared in *Pravda,* we have had reason to fear for Sergeant Koikov's safety. Beyond that I can say no more. But rest assured all will be made clear when Deputy Alenin's investigation is complete and made public."

"Minister Medzhid, there are also reports that a member of the *politsiya,* Captain Salko, is missing —"

"Thank you, no more questions . . ."

Spellman muted the television. "They sure didn't wait long to put Salko out there."

"They'll forget about it by the end of the day," Seth replied. "Is Medzhid slick or what? Wellesley and Pechkin just got bitch-slapped on live TV."

But not Nabiyev, Jack thought. Though it would've been easy for Medzhid to throw a barb or two at the president, he had instead made them partners in protecting the public good. Rebaz Medzhid was no dummy.

"Well, we're back on schedule," Seth said. "Another week and we're good to go."

Seven days, Jack thought.

Seven days to confirm the location of Wellesley and Pechkin's war room, find out how many moves ahead on the chessboard they were, make sure the multitude of parts and pieces of Seth's plan weren't unraveling, uncover which of Medzhid's personal bodyguards — and perhaps members of the Emergency Response Force — were playing for the other team, and figure out how far Valeri Volodin was willing to go to keep hold of Dagestan.

Not nearly enough time.

At eight p.m. he left the Tortoreto to relieve Dom at the Chirpoy apartment.

As he walked to the Lada, Dom rolled down the window. Jack handed him a white paper bag. "It's not Jimmy John's, but the place I got it from looked a lot like a Blimpie."

"Good enough, thanks. No sign of Pechkin or Wellesley. You know, the security inside that compound might be decent, but they've gone ostrich — heads all the way in the sand. I've been here three hours and nobody's even looked my way."

This was often the case with "secure compounds," Jack knew, especially ones that aren't tested frequently. Under those conditions it was easy to fall into a complacent mind-set: We're safe and secure behind these walls and cameras and no one bothers us, so what's to worry about?

This could work to their advantage when the time came.

Jack asked, "Did Gavin get ahold of you?"

"About the Vetochkina woman? Yeah, I followed her from her office to a house on Elista; it's covered by a fumigation tent. She talked to one of the workers, then went back to the office. She locked the car. I'm going to swing by there again on the way back to the motel."

"How goes Gavin's game of phone tag with Pechkin and Wellesley?"

"Pechkin's meeting fake Captain Osin tomorrow at a playground a few miles from here. Matt will call you with the details. As for Wellesley, Gavin —"

"Continuing his acclaimed role of Dobromir the Broker."

"Right. He's been stringing Wellesley along, demanding to know what's happened to Helen. As far as Gavin can tell, Wellesley hasn't figured out she's not in an Edinburgh jail. We're going to keep poking at him. Hell, maybe he'll fly off to Scotland and we can have Clark's Hereford friend pay him a visit."

"A man can dream. Jack, my boy, you're a devious son of a gun. I'm outta here. I'll call you if I catch up to Zoya. Otherwise, I'll see you in the morning."

35

MAKHACHKAL

"There must be hundreds of them, Jack," Dom said over the speakerphone.

"At least," Ysabel replied, then handed the binoculars to Jack, who watched the throngs of children as they scampered over jungle gyms and down slides, chased one another across sandpits, and bounced on vast stretches of raised trampolines.

Either it had slipped Spellman's mind or he himself didn't know, but Anzhi Gardens was massive, at least a hundred acres of green grass, flower beds, and wooden benches that formed a ring around the central play area.

Jack and Ysabel were parked on the street along the eastern edge of the park, Dom the northern. Spellman was in a third car at the park's main entrance, to the south. Since arriving ninety minutes early they had been swapping positions, lest Pechkin had arrived before them and was watching for the very trap they were trying to lay for him.

As they had no stand-in for Captain Osin that Pechkin would fall for, Jack had decided to play it by ear. If the SVR man gave them an opening, they would take it and hope for the best.

"You see the size of that ball pit?" Dom asked. "Where the hell was that when I was a kid?"

"Apparently, in Dagestan this whole time," Spellman replied.

Jack checked his watch: 10:09. "He's late."

"Did you expect anything else?" asked Dom.

"Hey, I think I've got something," Spellman called. "A guy in a yellow cardigan just got out of a taxi."

"And?" said Jack.

"He didn't pay the driver. Yeah, I think it's Pechkin. He's got a hat and sunglasses on, but I'm ninety percent certain. Dom, the taxi is turning north on Murom Street. It's red, with a bum front headlight."

"I see it. I'm on him."

Jack and Ysabel waited.

"He's just passed me," Dom reported. "Still headed north. I'm following. We're turning west onto a private drive. Heading uphill. I see some kind of statue ahead, a guy on a horse —"

"Imam Shamil monument," Spellman replied. "Jack, there's a clear sight line from there down to the park. Do you have eyes on Pechkin?"

Through the Opel's side window Jack aimed the binoculars at Pechkin and zoomed in. "I've got him. He's on the main path, headed to the playground. He's taking his time."

"Probably giving his backup time to get set. Dom?"

"He's pulling into a parking spot. He's got binoculars. I'm going to circle around, see if I can get a better look. Jack, you and Ysabel stay put."

"We're not going anywhere."

Two minutes passed, then Dom said simply, "Abort."

As planned, they cleared the area on separate rounds, then rendezvoused back at Dom's hotel. "The guy went to his trunk and pulled out a long box with a picture of a telescope on it. Trust me, that guy ain't no astronomer."

"Ruthless motherfucker, Pechkin," Spellman said. "He was going to gun down Osin right in front of the kiddies."

"Or whoever approached him," Jack

470

added. "Time for plan B."

Jack opened his laptop, connected it to his phone's built-in hotspot, then called Gavin and explained what he wanted him to do.

"Loop me into the exchange," Jack said.

"Okay, you should be up."

Jack opened his chat window. In the upper right-hand corner the words *Remote Connection* were slowly pulsing.

"I'm texting him now," said Gavin.

A moment later, the first message appeared:

OSIN
I WAS THERE. YOU WEREN'T ALONE. I AM NOT STUPID.

It took almost a minute for Pechkin to respond.

PECHKIN
IT WAS JUST A PRECAUTION.

OSIN
YOU WERE GOING TO KILL ME!

PECHKIN
THAT IS NOT TRUE. WHERE ARE YOU? I WILL COME THERE. ALONE.

OSIN
HOW DO I KNOW THAT?

PECHKIN
YOU CAN PICK THE LOCATION.

OSIN
I WANT MORE MONEY OR I TALK TO
MY COMMANDER AND TAKE MY
CHANCES.

PECHKIN
THAT CAN BE ARRANGED. YOU MUST
RELAX. TELL ME WHERE YOU ARE.

Over the phone, Gavin said, "Jack, what
do you want me to say?"

"Tell him you'll get back to him."

Jack disconnected and turned to Dom,
Ysabel, and Spellman. "We can either let
him go or try again. Votes?"

"Try again," Dom said.

"Definitely," said Ysabel.

Spellman nodded his agreement. "Our
odds of winning improve if we can take even
half the Pechkin-Wellesley duo out of the
picture."

"Jack, I can see the gears turning in your
brain," Dom said. "What's up?"

"How do you guys feel about a road trip?"

■ ■ ■ ■

Though Jack had asked the question with the vague kernel of a plan in his head, he also realized his last response to Pechkin had put them in a time crunch.

As Gavin had portrayed him, their version of Captain Osin was a panicked and money-hungry man on the edge of confessing everything to his boss. Someone in that frame of mind wouldn't wait days to reestablish contact with Pechkin, which meant they had to leave immediately and finalize the plan en route and pray they scared Pechkin enough that he would follow.

After briefing Seth on the plan, they left Makhachkala, Jack and Ysabel in the Opel, Spellman and Dom in the Lada. Knowing only that their plan had to happen within twenty-three miles of Khasavyurt, the range of Major Umarov's jurisdiction, Jack drove northwest up Highway M29, while Ysabel studied the map, looking for an area that fit their criteria.

Passing through Skalsoye, Jack had her dial Spellman in the Lada. "Guys, I think we've got our spot," he said. "Go ahead, Ysabel."

"There's a little town called Endirey about five miles outside Khasavyurt. Unless we give Pechkin enough time to take another route, it's got the only bridge across the Yaryksu tributary."

"Sharp girl," Dom said on speakerphone. "No offense, Ysabel."

"None taken."

"Jack, what makes you think Pechkin will even come? This has to smell fishy to him."

"Maybe so, but what choice does he have? As far as Pechkin knew, he was talking to Captain Osin. The last thing he needs is one of Medzhid's district commanders hunting for him for the murder of a Khasavyurt citizen."

"True," replied Spellman, "but who says he just won't send his telescope-loving friend?"

"We don't. We can only hope Pechkin wants to make damn sure it gets done right. Let's find a place to set up for the night."

In Endirey, a village of a few hundred, surrounded by black dirt farm fields and copses of willow trees, they found a youth hostel on the banks of the river that was empty, save the proprietor and a middle-aged hippie couple who spoke German. The woman who gave them their keys barely

474

looked up from what looked to Jack like a Russian version of *People* magazine.

Once they were settled in their room, a twelve-by-twelve-foot square with two double bunk beds, Jack briefed Spellman and Dom on the plan.

"We need to be smart about how we set this up, but not so smart Pechkin won't believe it's coming from Osin."

"It's your call," Spellman said. "You're the only guy that's met Osin. How sharp is he?"

"I wouldn't call it a meeting, but he is one of Umarov's, who is pretty sharp himself, so Pechkin might buy having to jump through some hoops."

Ysabel said, "Either way, this is an invitation Pechkin can't ignore. Having Osin as a loose cannon could be a disaster for him and Wellesley."

"She's right," said Jack. "You guys take the afternoon and drive the area. Put yourselves in Pechkin's head."

They were back two hours later. They walked into the room, and Ysabel went to the mini-fridge, a clattering avocado-colored box with no handle, and pulled out a couple of sandwiches Jack had scrounged at a nearby café.

"South of the highway is a no-go," Dom said. With the sandwich in one hand, he laid their map on the floor. "Too many hills and too few decent roads. It'd take him hours to reach the next river crossing and circle up to Khasavyurt."

"North of here is a little different," said Spellman. "Between us and Bavtugay to the east there are a few ways he could take into Khasavyurt that'd only add forty or so minutes to his trip."

"Then we've got to pick a spot between here and Bavtugay," replied Jack.

"And at a time that forces his hand," added Ysabel.

Doing both would, they hoped, keep Pechkin on the main highway and straight into their crosshairs.

"Jack, what's this twenty-three-miles-from-Khasavyurt stuff?" asked Dom. "It's a pretty odd number."

"I'm assuming Major Umarov is a stickler for jurisdictional range. We're going to hand Pechkin over to him."

"Shit, he'll be out before supper," said Spellman.

"I doubt it. As far as Umarov is concerned, Pechkin's a co-conspirator in Dobromir Stavin's death. Umarov's a law-and-order kinda guy, and it happened in his city. Unless Moscow is willing to spring Pechkin by force, the guy will be locked up at least until the coup is over."

Jack checked his watch. "Time to wake up Gavin."

Right on schedule, a few minutes past six the next morning, Gavin called. "He says he's coming."

"How'd he sound?" asked Jack. As soon as the words left his mouth he realized how silly they were.

"It was a text, Jack, so he sounded like he sounded. I put the pressure to him, told him I was very scared and I needed money to leave Dagestan."

"How much did you ask for?"

"The average MOI cop makes about four thousand U.S. a year. I demanded half of that. Pechkin didn't bat an eye."

Of course he didn't, Jack thought. It was money he never planned to pay.

"I told him eleven a.m. in Khasavyurt's main market square. I'll keep you posted."

Jack disconnected. "He's on his way," he told the others.

Assuming Pechkin would have left right after Gavin's message to him and knowing Makhachkala to Khasavyurt was at least a three-hour drive, Jack and the others waited until eight-thirty and then moved to their positions. If Pechkin was true to form he would want to reach the market in Khasavyurt as much before eleven as possible.

Outside, they found the air was cool, hovering around forty degrees, but the sky was cloudless, so the sun was already burning off the fog hovering over the fields. The tall grass along the roads shimmered with dew.

At Highway M29 they parted company, Jack and Ysabel heading east to Bavtugay, Spellman and Dom west through Endirey proper toward the Yaryksu Bridge.

When Jack reached Bavtugay's main intersection, he turned left and started driving, killing time and passing mile after mile of farm fields before they hit the branch road Dom had shown them on his map. Beside the stop sign, a sign read KHASAVYURT in Cyrillic, followed by a left-pointing arrow and 24 KM.

Jack made a U-turn and headed back to Bavtugay. As he reached the M29 intersection, he pulled onto the shoulder.

"What's wrong?" asked Ysabel.

"I don't like it. We're giving him too much wiggle room. And the traffic's heavier than I thought it'd be. We don't know what kind of car he's driving, and if we miss spotting him we're screwed. Let me see the map."

She handed it over and Jack laid it over the steering wheel, his finger tracing along the roads surrounding Khasavyurt. *The map ain't the territory,* Jack reminded himself. He should have driven more of the area. Seeing the various roads, turnarounds, and villages on a piece of paper wasn't the same as putting eyes on those features. He needed a way to further reduce the chance of Pechkin's taking the northern route into Khasavyurt.

"There, right there," he said, tapping the map. He dialed Gavin and said, "Contact Pechkin and change the meeting spot."

"To where?"

"Arkabash. It's a village about a mile south of the Yaryksu Bridge. Tell Pechkin to text you when he gets there."

"And if he asks why the change?"

"Uhm . . ."

Ysabel said, "Osin's got a dacha down there. He'd feel safer somewhere he knows, wouldn't he?"

"Yeah, tell him that."

"Okay, hold on." A minute later Gavin came back. "He says that's fine."

Jack disconnected, called Spellman and Dom and told them about the change. He heard crinkling over the speaker as they opened their own map. "Okay, we see it," said Dom. "He's gotta be pretty confident of his backup to agree on a location like that."

With a decent sniper, home-turf advantage can be easily turned into no advantage at all.

"Jack, I'm not fond of audibles like this," said Spellman.

"Me neither, but this guy makes me nervous."

"Well, any more changes and he'll get nervous and abort."

"I know. Get set up on the Arkabash Road and we'll take your spot at the bridge. Where is it?"

"A small maintenance driveway or something, right side."

"On our way."

Ten a.m. turned into eleven. Jack called Gavin. "Text him. Tell him he's late and ask why. Try to sound nervous. Use lots of caps and exclamation marks."

Gavin replied, "Okay . . . it's sent. Waiting . . ." Jack heard the ping of an incoming text message. "Okay, Pechkin says he's running late. There was an accident east of Bavtugay. He swears he's coming. Twenty more minutes at most."

"He's buying time," Ysabel said when Jack disconnected.

A few minutes later, Ysabel was proven right.

Through the thin line of trees to their left Jack saw a silver Kia Sorento cross the bridge and start slowing. The Sorento's left-hand turn signal came on.

"Everything's fine, Oleg," Jack muttered. "Keep going."

"You think he can see us?"

"We'll know in a few seconds."

The Sorento turned onto the Arkabash Road, then disappeared down a slight rise.

Jack called Dom. "Let's switch to headsets." Once the three of them were on the portable radios, Jack said to Ysabel, "Stay here."

He got out and jogged across the road until he could see just over the rise. The Sorento's taillights were bouncing as the SUV negotiated the muddy track. To the right was the river, its surging waters lapping at the bank; to the left, a short slope covered with thick grass.

The Sorento's brake lights came on and it coasted to a stop.

Jack returned to the Opel. "Dom, you got one coming your way. Silver Sorento."

"Roger. We're set up around the second bend a few hundred yards down. He won't see us until he's on us. Any sign of his overwatch?"

"Not yet —"

"Hold on, this might be him," Ysabel said, tapping the window glass.

The second car, a black Nissan sedan, appeared on the bridge, then slowed down and made the turn and disappeared from view as the Sorento had.

Once more Jack climbed out and jogged across the road. The Nissan had pulled to a stop behind the Sorento; its driver got out, reached back into the car, and came out with a canvas rifle case. He slung it over his shoulder and trudged up the grass slope.

Jack returned to the Opel and relayed what he'd seen to Dom. "Is there any high ground near you?" asked Jack.

"Yeah, a hill off to our right."

"That's where he'll be coming from. Get him before he's set up — both of you."

"What about —"

"Just block the road with your Lada, then go. No shooting unless you have to."

"On our way."

Jack turned to Ysabel. "Guns."

She reached for the duffel in the backseat and placed it on the floorboard between her feet. She handed Jack one of the Rugers, which he tucked between his seat and the center console.

He started the Opel, put it into gear, then crossed the road.

Without knowing how long it would take Pechkin's sniper to reach the hill overlooking Dom and Spellman's Lada, Jack had no choice but to spring the trap prematurely. Pechkin would almost certainly be armed, but if he and Ysabel could shut him down quickly enough he wouldn't have time to warn his sniper.

"Dom, we're moving."

"Roger."

Jack waited until the Opel's wheels bumped over the shoulder and the nose tipped down the rise on the other side, then jammed the accelerator to the floorboard.

He mistimed it.

The Opel's front bumper hit the slope, plowing into the soft earth and splattering the windshield with mud. Ysabel's head bumped against the roof and she yelped.

"I'm okay, I'm okay!"

The Opel's tires bit down again and thudded into a rut, jerking the hood toward the river. Jack let up on the gas, eased the steering wheel left, and brought the car back onto the center of the road.

He flipped on the wipers. As the windshield cleared he saw the brake lights of Pechkin's Sorento, now a quarter-mile ahead of them, flash once, and then a fan of mud erupted from the rear tires.

The Sorento disappeared around the next corner.

Jack accelerated again, fighting the wheel as the Opel lurched from side to side. Ysabel glanced out her window at the roiling water. "Looks deep, Jack."

"I know," he replied through gritted teeth. "Dom, where are you?"

"Moving north. We can't see him. We think he's in the high grass ahead of us."

Jack prayed the sniper hadn't already spotted them and was setting up.

"Just keep him boxed in, if that's the best you can do."

They approached the corner. Jack eased up on the accelerator, then aimed the hood at the slope until the grass was scraping down his window, then tapped the brakes. The Opel's tail slid toward the riverbank. Jack spun the wheel left, punched the accelerator, and the Opel's tail snapped back around until they were once again in the middle of the road.

Through his headset Jack heard Dom say, "Matt, he's on your right, coming your way."

"I see him. Get around him. I'll keep him busy."

Ysabel shouted, "Watch out!"

Jack glimpsed a flash of brake lights, saw the Sorento's rear bumper looming through their windshield. He jerked the wheel and the Opel scraped down the side of the Sorento, which swerved left, shoving Jack and Ysabel into the slope. Grass and dirt peppered the windshield. Jack felt his side canting upward as the Opel's tires were shoved sideways up the slope. Crushed between the two vehicles, Ysabel's side mirror tore away. The window bowed inward, then spiderwebbed, pelting her face with chunks of glass. The ARX she'd been holding across her lap slid between Jack's legs and onto the floorboard. He glanced sideways and saw blood on Ysabel's face.

"Are you —"

"I don't know!" she cried. "I can't see out of my right eye!"

"Fuck this," he muttered.

He reached out, pulled Ysabel down over his lap, then lifted the Ruger and fired four rounds out her window into the Sorento's door. He turned the wheel, driving the Opel's hood against the SUV, giving them half a foot of leeway, then stomped on the brake. The Sorento surged past them. The Opel dropped to the ground, once again level. Jack saw the Sorento's brake lights blink, then the nose veered left as Pechkin tried to again bulldoze them against the slope.

Jack stomped on the accelerator and spun the wheel right and rammed the Opel's nose into the Sorento's rear quarter-panel, shoving it sideways a couple of feet. The mud did the rest. The Sorento spun. As its hood came around to face them, the Opel raked down its side.

Jack saw water loom out the side window. The Opel tipped sideways and the tires slipped off the bank. The hood plunged into the river. Water crashed over the windshield and began gushing through Ysabel's shattered window and onto her lap. She screamed, her eyes caked with blood, then she started climbing through the window.

"No!" Jack shouted. "Not that way!"

The river's current would carry her away in seconds.

He clamped his hand on her forearm and pulled her against his body. Her window tilted downward, now fully immersed. Ysabel slipped back and slid beneath the surface. He lost his grip on her arm. Her hands reached for him. He grabbed her arm, pulled her back into the air, then brought her hand to his belt and shouted, "Grab on."

Jack fumbled between his legs until his hand touched the ARX; he lifted it and pointed the barrel at his window. He closed his eyes and turned his face away, then pulled the trigger. The window shattered outward.

"Just keep ahold of me and climb!" he shouted.

"I can't see!"

"Climb!"

Jack's window was now pointing straight up; through it he saw blue sky. Brown water surged over the door and into the Opel's interior. With his left hand Jack grabbed the door frame, pressed his right foot against the dashboard, then pushed and pulled at the same time. His head lifted clear of the window. Still gripping the ARX, he stuck his elbow out, braced it against the frame, then levered his torso free. Ysabel's fingers dug into the skin of his waist.

On the road the Sorento had come to a stop diagonally across the road. The door swung open. Pechkin climbed out, a revolver in his right hand. He half stumbled in the mud and fell to his side. His left pant leg was black with blood; one of the Ruger's bullets had struck home. Pechkin pushed himself to his knees. He spotted Jack. He raised the revolver.

In that moment Jack was struck by the absurdity of the situation: It was the first time he was seeing Oleg Pechkin in the flesh and the man was pointing a gun at his head. *Worst introduction in history,* he thought.

With the ARX still acting as a brace on the window frame, Jack swiveled the barrel toward Pechkin and pulled the trigger. His three-round burst went wide, peppering the Sorento's quarter-panel. Pechkin's gun bucked; the Opel's side mirror exploded. Pechkin fired again; the bullet smacked into the Opel's door frame. Jack rotated the ARX slightly left, thumbed the selector switch to full auto, and squeezed the trigger. The bullets walked sideways down the Sorento, shattering windows and punching holes in the side panels until the rounds reached Pechkin, stitching him diagonally from collarbone to ribs. Already dead, he tipped over backward into the mud with his legs bent beneath him.

Jack called into his headset, "Guys we

need help! Where are —"

Over the Sorento's roof, Jack saw Dom and Spellman skid to a halt at the top of the slope.

Whatever the Opel lacked in amenities or aesthetics was made up by the quality of its tempered glass. Though Ysabel's facial cuts were plentiful, they were all superficial, the safety glass having shattered into chunks no bigger than half-dollars. Once Jack had rinsed away the blood caked over her cheeks and eyebrows, he saw her eyes were undamaged.

Though she wasn't crying, she stared vacantly at the ground. Jack knew the look; he'd worn it himself. He put an arm around her shoulders.

As he and Ysabel looked on, Dom and Spellman first placed Pechkin's corpse inside the Sorento, then that of the sniper they'd killed on the hillside. Their guns went in next, and then they put the SUV in neutral and rolled it into the river, where it quickly disappeared beneath the roiling surface.

Whether Ysabel's reaction was from relief, adrenaline overload, the shock of what had just happened, or a mix of all three, Jack didn't blame her. His heart was still pounding and he was having trouble catching his breath. He tried to convince himself they would have gotten out of the Opel no matter what, but he knew it wasn't true. They'd almost died. If Pechkin's bullets hadn't done the job, the river would have.

He shouldn't have hurried the trap, he thought. Or better still, he shouldn't have gone after Pechkin at all. What good would his capture have done them, really? Had he expected Pechkin would break down and give them some secret code word that would make Wellesley throw his hands up? If anything, losing his Russian partner would only make the SIS man cagier.

He'd been too clever by half and it had almost gotten Ysabel, Dom, and Spellman killed. *Arrogance, Jack.* He should have just lured Pechkin to a remote spot outside Makhachkala and double-tapped him. Seeing this image in his head, Jack felt a chill. It would have been so simple — too simple to do, should the need arise again.

Careful, Jack. The world in which he worked was a gray one, where people often mistook the ability to do a thing with the righteousness of the thing itself.

Dom and Spellman walked up.

"Nothing in the guy's Nissan," Spellman said. "It's a rental. There are no serial numbers on their weapons, either." He handed Jack a pair of cell phones. "Maybe we can do something with those."

"Let's go home."

37

MAKHACHKALA

"I screwed up, John," he said over the phone. "I forgot the first rule: Keep it simple, stupid."

"It happens," Clark said.

After making sure they'd policed the crime scene as well as possible, the four of them got into Dom's Lada and drove back to Makhachkala. They found Seth sitting alone at the conference table. Medzhid and his bodyguards and assistants weren't around. "Nothing new," Seth had called, as Spellman joined him, and Ysabel and Jack walked back to their mini-suite. Ysabel went to sleep and Jack called home.

"John, I almost got them all killed — and I'm not talking about some kind of notional, 'Whew, that was close' bullshit. It's just dumb luck Ysabel's alive. What the hell was I thinking?"

"That's for you to sort out."

"How do I do that?"

"Learn the lesson. And give yourself a break. You made a choice, things went bad, and you're accountable."

"Isn't that a nice way of saying I'm to blame?"

"Call it what you want, I don't care, just don't play semantics with yourself. Christ, Jack, did you think you were going to get through your career without having this kind of close call?"

Jack considered this. "Yeah, I think I did, actually."

"Then you were lying to yourself. You gotta stop doing that — and right fucking now, before things get going there."

"I'm going to send Ysabel back to Tehran."

Clark chuckled. "Good luck with that. From what you've told me, you'd have better luck pissing up a rope. Don't insult her, Jack. She's an adult. If she wants to stay, don't try to talk her out of it. Plus, it sounds like she's not exactly a liability."

They talked for a few more minutes and then Jack had Clark transfer him to Gavin, who asked, "How'd it go with Pechkin?"

"Not so well. He's dead. We've got his cell phone."

And now we see which of Medzhid's bodyguards has turned, he thought. The idea of it gave him pause that he probably

494

wouldn't have felt eight hours ago. Even catching Anton and Vasim by surprise wouldn't be without its dangers. They'd have to choose the time and place carefully.

Jack said good-bye and hung up. Quietly he slipped into their bedroom and lay down beside Ysabel; she stirred and edged a bit closer, pressing her body against his.

"I want you to stop, Jack," she whispered.

"Stop what?"

"You're playing it in your head, over and over."

"It was too close. I'm sorry, Ysabel." Hearing himself say the words made them seem even more inadequate.

Ysabel reached across his body, gently grabbed his hand, and brought his fingertips to her face. "They're just scratches, Jack. They'll heal."

"It could be a lot worse."

"That's exactly my point."

"I got cocky," he replied. "With guys like Pechkin and Wellesley, you don't make things up as you go."

"Then call it a lesson learned and forgive yourself."

"Funny, I just got the same advice from someone else."

"I heard you talking on the phone out there. Is that who you mean?"

Jack nodded. "John."

"And what else did he tell you?" she asked.

"That I'm an idiot and you should go back to Tehran."

She slapped him lightly on the chest. "Liar."

"He said if I tried to send you home you wouldn't go, so don't bother. I think there was something about pissing up a rope in there, too."

"A very smart man, this John. Sorry, Jack, I'm here with you until the end."

They slept until Jack's watch woke him at six-thirty; then they walked out to the main room. Medzhid had returned and was sitting at the conference table with Seth and Spellman. A variety of steaming dishes and bowls were arrayed before them.

"Jack, we were just going to wake you," called Medzhid. "Come join us."

They sat down. Ysabel filled a plate for Jack, and then for herself.

"My goodness, Ysabel, what happened to your face?" asked Medzhid.

"Just a little accident."

"I'll call my —"

"I'm fine, really. Jack's not a half-bad nurse."

"Jack's a good man," Seth said.

He meant it, Jack decided.

"You could do a lot worse, Ysabel. He's a keeper."

Ysabel smiled at him. "Thank you for saying that, Seth."

Medzhid chuckled. "Jack in a nurse's uniform . . . That is something I would like to see."

"Seconded," Spellman replied.

"Never going to happen, guys. By the way, where are Anton and Vasim?"

"I gave them the evening off. They've had no time to themselves for several weeks now."

Jack and Spellman exchanged glances. The CIA man nodded, then asked, "When are they back on duty?"

"Tomorrow morning."

Seth said, "This feels weird, enjoying a pleasant meal right before all hell is about to break loose."

"Enjoy the eye while the eye watches you, Seth."

"Pardon?"

"It's an old Avar proverb. You see, right now we're in the eye of the hurricane. Relish this time before the trailing edge arrives. We've defeated our enemies, if only temporarily, and an old friend of mine is alive and safe. Tonight is for contentment."

"Well said," Jack replied. "In fact, do you mind if I invite a friend?" It didn't seem right that Dom was sitting alone in his motel room eating not–Jimmy John's.

"As long as it's not the kind of friend you brought me from Bamlag, then by all means. I will call down to the garage and tell the guard to expect him."

Dom arrived thirty minutes later. As he stepped into the suite, he looked around and let out a low whistle. "Well, Jack, seeing as you blew my cover for this, I'll forgive you."

Jack led him to the table and introduced him to Medzhid, who stood up, shook Dom's hand, and gestured to a seat. "Join us. Let me see, now . . . You look Italian, perhaps Greek. So, Domenico or Domenikos?"

"Right the first time."

"And how do you know —" Medzhid stopped and held up his hands, smiling. "Never mind. I don't actually know who Jack is, so why spoil a good thing? Where has he been keeping you, Dom?"

"In a crappy motel with cockroaches the size of hamsters."

"Not true," Jack said.

"Shame on you. Dom, you will stay here.

Jack and Ysabel will double up, won't you?" Medzhid asked with a half-smile.

"Of course," Ysabel replied.

Unexpectedly, Jack felt the tension draining from his body. It took a few moments to realize why. As bizarre as it was, this group had become not quite a family, but something similar to that, albeit a dysfunctional and temporary one that had been brought together for a deadly serious purpose. At least for right now, though, he could forget about that. The coup, Wellesley, Pechkin, and everything else would be there the next day. *Enjoy the eye while the eye watches you,* he thought.

They talked and ate and laughed, and Seth seemed almost like his old self, but still there was a sadness just beneath his smile. Jack wondered if Seth was even aware of it. He didn't blame his friend. Paul Gregory had been branded a traitor, tossed out like garbage, then hounded by the very government he'd served so loyally until finally he'd put a gun to his head. And he'd kept it all hidden from his only son. All things considered, Seth was bearing up pretty well, especially given the difficulty of what he and Spellman were trying to accomplish here.

Jack only hoped his friend wasn't secretly

unraveling, as his father had done before him.

Medzhid said across the table, "Jack, Matt tells me Pechkin slipped out of our grasp again."

Spellman caught Jack's eye and gave a slight shake of his head.

"Something like that. Listen, I hate to ruin the mood —"

"My mood is unruinable, Jack. Go ahead."

"Where are we with Captain Salko?"

"Nowhere. He is not talking, but I expected that. As for the ERF itself . . . I have confined them to barracks. They were told Salko was arrested for corruption and that his disgrace has unfortunately cast them in a bad light. I have people interviewing each and every one of them."

"I doubt that'll prove anything," said Seth.

"My people are very good at what they do. They know the questions to ask. If Salko had cohorts, we will find them. The ones who are shown to be loyal will receive a personal visit from me and my thanks. Stick first, then carrot. I know my troops. By morning, we'll have the bad ones culled."

They ate and talked for another hour before Dom checked his watch, then excused himself and gestured Jack and Matt off to the side. "I'm heading downtown.

Zoya Vetochkina is pulling an all-nighter. The Department of Culture is putting on some new exhibit tomorrow. Be ready to move if I call."

"Will do," said Jack.

"Ysabel, too. She and Zoya look a lot alike."

Dom called at ten. "I had to use a coat hanger on her car door, but I got the key card and permit. I'm heading over to Chirpoy now."

"We'll meet you there," Jack replied.

He, Ysabel, and Spellman took Seth's Suburban to Dom's stakeout spot. As they pulled to the curb he got out of the Lada and climbed into the backseat next to Spellman. He handed the key card and permit over the seat to Ysabel in the driver's seat.

"What do I do?" she asked.

"Just swipe and go through. There's no camera or guard at the gate."

"Does it matter that we're not in Zoya's car?"

"I don't think so. We'll find out."

"That sounds easy enough," said Ysabel. "Heads down, boys."

Jack crouched on the floorboard as Ysabel circled the block, then turned into the driveway. She rolled down her window, swiped the card, then pulled through.

"There's a door opening at the far end," she said.

"Wave that permit at him," Dom said. "If he doesn't wave and go back inside, or he comes back out with a rocket launcher, say so."

"What?"

"He's kidding," Jack said.

Ysabel stuck the permit out the window. "He's waving. He's going back inside. The door's closed."

Jack said, "Zoya's is the sixth stall on the right."

Ysabel turned into the spot, put the Suburban in park, and shut off the engine. "Now what?"

"Do what Zoya would do. Once you open the door, have a quick look around. If it's clear, we'll come in."

Ysabel opened her door and climbed out.

From across the parking lot, a male voice called, *"Privet, krasavitsa."*

Ysabel whispered, "Jack, it's one of the goons."

"He's saying hi."

"I know what a regular 'Hi' sounds like. He's hitting on me. He's coming this way."

"Just say, *'Spoki, mne nado idti,'* then point to your phone, raise it to your ear, and head for your door."

She did so, and the guard replied, *"Khorosho!"*

"Okay, he's going back into the apartment," Ysabel whispered. "You're clear. Come on."

The three of them climbed out the Suburban's passenger side, then entered Zoya's apartment. Ysabel locked the door behind them.

"Creepy guy," she said. "What did I say to him?"

"Oh, you don't wanna know," Dom said.

"Hush." She walked into the kitchen and turned on the overhead light.

Zoya Vetochkina's apartment was tiny, three hundred square feet of bedroom, bathroom, front room, and kitchenette, with white walls and furniture that might have actually looked better with some duct-tape adornment — not the decor a woman from the Department of Culture would choose for herself, Jack thought. She was probably counting the minutes until her house was finished being bug-bombed.

"Do we know which apartment belongs to Wellesley?" asked Ysabel.

"Let's find out," Jack said, and pulled out his phone. He punched in Pechkin's number and hit send. He wasn't even sure their ploy would work; depending on what kind of forwarding system Wellesley was using, incoming calls might be soundless.

"It's ringing."

He put his fingers to his lips and gestured for the others to spread out.

Posted in the room's four corners, the four of them listened.

Jack held up one finger . . . two fingers . . . three fingers . . .

Dom raised his hand and pointed above his head. "Second floor. Old-timey ringtone."

Jack ended the call. "Let's go to headsets."

He, Dom, and Spellman donned theirs. "Dom, you and Ysabel stay here. If one of the goons shows, give a holler."

Jack peeked out the front door. All was clear. With Spellman on his heels, he walked down the sidewalk to the stairwell, then took it to the second floor.

"Dom, call it again," Jack said.

"Sending it now."

Jack trotted down the balcony, hand resting on the rail until he reached the halfway point, then stopped and turned to face Spellman. They listened.

Faintly, Jack heard *brng-brng.* He turned his head, trying to localize the sound.

Brng-brng . . .

Spellman strode forward, hand cupped as he passed doors. He stopped beside apartment 206, gave Jack a thumbs-up, then pressed his ear against the door. He gave Jack another thumbs-up. "Okay, let's see if this thing of Gavin's works."

Jack knelt by the door and pulled from his pocket a thumb-sized circuit board taped to a nine-volt battery; jutting from the edge of the board was a brass-colored plug. Jack ran his index finger along the bottom of the lock, found the indentation, then inserted the plug.

The lock started flashing red. As Gavin had instructed, Jack waited until the light first turned amber, then started flashing faster. No alarm system. He removed the plug and then reinserted it. The lock flashed green and the dead bolt clicked open.

Spellman whispered, "I gotta tell our DS-and-T guys about this thing. Probably save the government millions."

Jack opened the door and they stepped through.

"Dom, we're in."

"Roger. All's quiet down here."

Jack immediately felt a chill envelop him. Above the window, cool air was gushing from a wall-mounted A/C unit. While the apartment was the same size as Zoya's, the walls here had been crudely ripped down, leaving studs but no drywall, save what chunks were still nailed to the two-by-fours. Taking up most of the space was a circular table in whose center sat a pyramid of six computer tower hard drives, each of which was attached to an LCD monitor whose swirling multicolored screen savers cast shadows on the apartment's walls. Dangling from the ceiling above all this was a bundle of zip-tied cables, from coaxial to standard phone and several Jack didn't recognize. He looked for cables connecting any of the towers but saw none.

"Sure looks like a nerve center, doesn't it?" Spellman whispered.

Jack nodded. "Start taking pictures."

He sat down before one of the monitors, put on his gloves, then tapped the keyboard to wake the monitor. An administrator log-in page appeared.

"No surprise there." Jack dialed Gavin and put him on speakerphone. Jack explained what he was seeing.

"Operating system?"

"Windows Vista."

"Fantastic. Don't worry about the password. We won't be able to brute-force it from your side of the screen. Are there USB ports?"

Jack checked the tower behind his monitor. "Yeah, but they've got plug locks."

"Optical drive?"

"Yes, and it's clear."

"Okay, let's see if these guys think small. Get out that CD I downloaded to you, the one called 'PoodleCrack,' then press and hold the computer's power button until it shuts down, and then power it up again. When you hear the start-up chime, insert the CD and tell me what you see."

Jack did all this and then said, "Admin log-in again."

"Okay. Repeat the process, but hold down the left mouse button to eject the CD, then stick in the one labeled 'Widgeon-Rescue,' then tell me what you see."

When the screen reappeared the log-in page was gone, replaced by a black screen with white block lettering.

"I'm in the command line screen," said Jack.

"Ha!" Gavin blurted. "You'd be surprised how many people don't reboot-protect their systems — even guys like Wellesley and Pechkin. Okay, now type in those commands I gave you and tell me if you get any 'Yes' answers."

Jack did so. "Nothing."

"That means there's no key-logger stuff

on there. Do that with every drive before you start digging into any files."

Jack disconnected. "Matt, you get started on the next one."

They concentrated on sorting folders by size, then files by extension type and whether or not they were encrypted. Aside from the standard folders and applications the systems were shipped with, they found nothing of interest on the first four computers. Whether they had missed anything, Jack didn't know, but short of cloning each hard drive and uploading it for Gavin to dissect, they could only keep moving.

Spellman said, "Jack, about Anton and Vasim: I can probably get their addresses. We can pay them a visit and use Pechkin's phone to nail whichever one has turned."

"It's tempting, but we need Medzhid in the room when it happens. Plus, who knows, maybe both their phones would ring."

At the fifth computer, neither the Poodle-Crack nor the WidgeonRescue got Jack to the command line. Jack rebooted, then inserted the final CD that Gavin had given him, labeled "GongShowItAll." This did the trick.

Spellman stood up from his monitor and leaned over Jack's shoulder. "You got something?"

"Yeah, I think so," Jack replied, his eyes scanning the directory names.

"There, try that one," Spellman said, tapping the screen.

Jack clicked on the file labeled "Khibiny-Borisoglebsk" and the text document opened. It was one page long and covered in thirty-four lines of characters, in almost identical formats:

Hepo5..38GZT.703971mE.4759623mN
Zore6.38GTZ.703408.62mE4759419
.87mN
Gaxy4..38GTZ.702170.47mE.4758546
.44mN
Gefo9..38GZT.706544.22mE.4757843
.69mN
Cuce4.38GZT.704959.76mE.4760436
.66mN
Xole8..38GZT.702999.03mE.4760085
.31mN
Juky6.38GZT.704430.97mE.4759664
.05mN
Hevu9,,38GZT.704185.57mE
.4760505.20mN

"What the hell is that?" Spellman whispered, squinting at the screen.

"I have no idea."

Jack dialed Gavin back and said, "You

need to see this."

"Go into network settings and give me your IP address." Jack did this, then waited as Gavin set himself up a remote access port. "Yeah, there's a lot of stuff here, but it'd take days to clone it all. I'll just grab whatever looks juicy."

"Great, bye."

Dom's voice came over Jack's headset. "We may have a problem down here. Somebody's at the door — Ysabel's new boyfriend, we think."

In the background, Jack could hear the man lightly tapping on the door with his finger. "*. . . vodka, krasavitsa.*" I have vodka, beautiful.

Jack thought for a moment. His grasp of Russian was being stretched. "Tell her to slap the door, shout *'ukhodi'* then *'otchet,'* followed by *'mer.'* "

Dom did this and Jack heard Ysabel shouting.

"Izvinite, izvinite . . ."

Dom said, "He's going away. She wants to know what she said."

"For him to go away or she'll report him to the mayor."

"You also suggested they were married," Spellman said.

"Oops. Dom, we're almost done up here."

"We'll meet you back at the Suburban."

38

MAKHACHKALA

The next morning after breakfast, as Medzhid was getting ready to go into the Ministry, Jack, Ysabel, Dom, Spellman, and Seth sat down at the conference table. Jack ran through the plan one more time. "I don't expect it to go bad, but assume it will." *Advice you should have taken with Pechkin,* he reminded himself. "Either way, Medzhid will want to find a way to dismiss it. We can't let him. This close to the coup, he needs to get his head right. Questions?"

Seth said, "I hope you're wrong about this."

"I'm not, but if I am we've got much bigger problems."

Now that Jack had already decided that Seth, Spellman, and Medzhid were innocent of burning him and Ysabel in Khasavyurt, only two suspects remained: Anton and Vasmin. But which one?

Followed by his personal assistant Albina,

Medzhid strode down the hallway from his suite, adjusting his tie and cuffs as he walked. "Good morning, everyone. I will be —"

"Rebaz, we need to chat."

"I am running late, Jack. Can we do it later?"

"No. Anton and Vasim should hear this, too."

Medzhid frowned. "Jack, I don't like the expression on your face. What is going on?"

"Just call them and I'll explain."

Medzhid sighed, then walked to the apartment door.

Dom got up and walked toward the windows while Spellman moved in the opposite direction until he was standing against the wall a few feet from the door. Ysabel stayed at the table within arm's reach of Albina.

Medzhid stepped back and Anton and Vasim entered.

"Now, Jack, what's this about?"

"It's about Pechkin."

On cue, Ysabel, holding Pechkin's phone behind her back, hit the send button.

"What about him?" asked Medzhid.

A phone started ringing.

"Pardon me, Minister," Anton said, and reached into his coat.

Medzhid said to Jack, "Have you found him?"

"No, but we just found out who he's been working with."

Ysabel held up the cell phone.

"That's Oleg Pechkin calling you, Anton," said Jack.

Anton glanced down at the phone, then shook his head. "I don't know who this is. I don't recognize the number."

"Show the minister your phone."

Anton narrowed his eyes at Jack. "You are setting me up. Why are you doing this?"

"Show him your phone," Jack repeated. "Do it."

"Anton, what is he talking about?"

"This isn't right, Minister. This man is lying to you. I am loyal. He's trying to turn you against me, please believe me."

Anton slipped the phone back into his jacket.

"Move, Rebaz!" Spellman shouted. He lunged for Medzhid. Vasim backpedaled out of his way, then reached out and snagged Spellman's sleeve; Spellman tried to shake it off, his arms extended toward Medzhid.

Startled, Anton backed away. His hand came out with a gun.

"Drop it, drop it!" Jack shouted.

Out of the corner of his eye he saw Dom

moving, his Ruger out as he sidestepped and tried to clear Medzhid from his sight line.

Anton pointed his gun at Spellman and fired. The bullet slashed across his neck. He stumbled sideways. Vasim wrapped his arm around Spellman's neck and they fell through the doorway to the ground.

Jack heard Ysabel shout, "Oh, God!"

He drew his Ruger, leveled the muzzle with Anton's chest. "Don't!"

Anton turned toward him, gun coming around. Jack fired. The bullet hit him in the chest, shoving him backward, but his gun was still up. Jack fired again, as did Dom, whose round struck Anton in the throat a split second after Jack's punched into Anton's belly. He went down.

Jack rushed forward and kicked his gun away.

On the other side of the door, Spellman and Vasim were wrestling, the latter trying to crawl from under the CIA agent to reach his fallen friend. "Anton! Anton!"

"Stop, Vasim, you don't —"

"Get off of me!"

Medzhid yelled, "Quiet! All of you, quiet!"

Vasim stopped struggling. Spellman rolled off him, then helped him to his feet. Vasim shrugged off his arm. He stared down at

Anton's body.

"Matt, you're bleeding," said Jack. "Your neck."

The CIA man touched the spot. "Ah, shit."

"Jack," Ysabel called, her voice barely a whisper, "it's Albina."

He turned. She was kneeling beside Medzhid's assistant. The woman had a bullet hole below her left eye.

"Oh my God, oh God, no . . ." Medzhid muttered, almost chanting as he backed away. His legs bumped against the back of the couch. He plopped down. His eyes were vacant.

"What have you done? What just happened? Someone tell me!"

Jack stooped over, reached inside Anton's coat, and tossed it to Medzhid. "Check his call history. The last number belongs to Pechkin. Ysabel, show him."

She walked over and handed Medzhid the phone. The minister studied each screen in turn. "This isn't . . . Are you sure?"

"We're sure," Dom replied.

Medzhid looked at Seth, who nodded. "Pechkin died yesterday outside Khasavyurt. That's his phone. I'm sorry, Rebaz, I really am."

"Anton called Pechkin after Ysabel and I

left you in Buynaksk," Jack added. "Pechkin then called Captain Osin and told him to raid Dobromir's house and kill him. He would have done the same to us if we'd given him the chance."

"Why?"

"Wellesley and Pechkin hired Dobromir to kidnap Aminat. They didn't want him talking to us."

"Anton and I have been together for almost nine years. I can't believe he would be a part of this."

"He did it for the same reason Salko snatched Koikov. He thinks you're a traitor."

"I'm not a traitor."

"We all know that, but they thought otherwise, and there might be others close to you who feel the same way. You need to wake up, Rebaz. This is the second time the bad guys have tried to stop what you're doing, first with Aminat, and then this. What's about to happen in Makhachkala is going to be bloody and people are going to die. You need to get your head around that. Either that or we call it off."

"That was pretty harsh, Jack," Seth whispered. "He didn't deserve that."

They were sitting at the conference table.

Medzhid had retreated to his suite. Grim-faced and avoiding eye contact with Jack and the others, Vasim had called in the rest of Medzhid's day-shift bodyguards, who were gently wrapping Anton's and Albina's bodies in blankets for removal. The carpet where Albina's head had lain was saturated with blood. Ysabel had found the bullet from Anton's gun in the wall behind the conference table.

"Maybe so," Jack replied, "but he needed to hear it. I learned a hard lesson yesterday and he's learned one today — actually, his third lesson, counting Aminat and Koikov. Wellesley's going to keep coming at us, probably even harder now that we've evened the odds a bit."

"Well, we're not calling it off, that's for damned sure. That's not your decision to make."

"I know it isn't."

Dom said, "Jack's right. The man needs to understand — really understand — what he's signed on for."

"You really don't think he knows that?"

"You know him better than anyone else. What do you think?"

"If he didn't get it before, he does now," said Spellman.

"I'm not so sure," Ysabel replied. "Has he

518

given any thought about what will happen to his wife and Aminat if this fails?"

"Of course he has," said Seth. "He'll be moving them both out of the capital the day after tomorrow. The MOI minister in Azerbaijan has agreed to take them in."

"Thank God for that."

Vasim walked up to the table. He handed Spellman a handkerchief. "You will need sutures to close that. I will take you to the minister's doctor later."

"Thanks."

"You weren't lying about Anton? You did not set him up?"

Jack shook his head. "And we didn't want it to happen this way."

"Did this Pechkin man say anything before he died, anything that might explain why Anton did this? Perhaps he was being forced into it."

"It's possible," Ysabel replied. "I don't think we'll ever know. We're very sorry, Vasim. We know you were friends."

"Yes, and for a long time, but he was the traitor, not the minister. You said Pechkin's partner is still out there, yes?"

"Raymond Wellesley."

"I hope you find him and kill him."

"We'll do our best."

39

MAKHACHKALA

The next afternoon Gavin called, having spent the previous fourteen hours sorting through the bits and pieces he'd cloned from Wellesley's computer. "John and Gerry are on the line, too."

"Are you alone, Jack?" asked Gerry.

"I'm with Ysabel, why?"

"That's fine. You need to be careful who you share this with," said Clark. "Gavin's found something — probably a game changer, and not in a good way."

"Well, hell, now you've got me worried. What's going on?"

Gavin said, "I've got a lot more of the hard drive to go through, but what we're mostly worried about is that text document you found, the one with the strings of numbers. Have you got it in front of you?"

Jack called up the screenshot of the doc he'd taken with his phone. The first one read *Hepo5..38GZT.703971mE.475962 3mN.*

"I'm looking at it," he said.

"I must be a little sleep-deprived to have not seen it right away. I don't know about the characters before the first decimal point — maybe a location identifier — but the next set of numbers is UTM," Gavin said, referring to the Universal Transverse Mercator coordinate system.

Jack knew UTM well, though using it had taken some getting used to. UTM was both simpler and more accurate than latitude and longitude, so much so that the U.S. military used a customized version of it, the Military Grid Reference System, or MGRS.

"Yeah, I see what you're talking about now," said Jack. "Don't feel bad, we both missed it. The way it's grouped is odd."

38GZT signified the UTM Grid Zone, which divides the earth into sixty zones each measuring six degrees of longitude in width. The rest of the characters denoted the "easting and northing" coordinates specific to the zone.

"Have you mapped them yet?"

"Just the first six," replied Gavin. "They're streets in Makhachkala — an apartment on Penza, a house on Ayon, some kind of warehouse by the harbor. Online maps for Makhachkala are either outdated or so Cyrillic-heavy it's going to take some time."

Ysabel said, "We know. We've switched to paper maps. They're the only ones that are trustworthy."

"Do any of these streets mean anything to you, Jack?" asked Gerry.

"No. Or at least I hope not."

"What's that mean?" Clark replied.

"One of the keys to Seth's plan is social media, which means Internet, and the first thing Volodin and Nabiyev are going to do is shut down all the service providers in the whole country. To counter this, Seth's set up satellite Internet hubs across the city. I don't know where they are but if these UTM coordinates are them, we've got a problem."

A fatal problem, Jack thought.

"If that's the case, why haven't they just raided the addresses and shut down the hubs?" asked Gavin.

"It's not enough for the coup to fail. The world has to watch it wither by itself, without Volodin dropping the hammer."

"Makes sense."

"What did you find out about the document's file name" — Jack checked his phone — "Khibiny-Borisoglebsk?"

"Both are place names, both in Russia," replied Gavin. "Khibiny is a mountain range on the Kola Peninsula and Borisoglebsk is

522

both a town in Voronezh oblast and an airbase for Su-25 Frogfoots and Su-24 Fencers."

"Those are ground attack birds and bombers," said Clark. "Volodin used both of them in Ukraine and Crimea."

"What the holy hell is going on?" said Gerry. "Those two places are how far from Makhachkala, thousands of miles —"

"Seventeen hundred miles and eight hundred miles, respectively," said Gavin. "And Russia's got airbases a whole lot closer to Dagestan than Borisoglebsk."

Jack asked, "Do any of the UTM coordinates match up to that or Khibiny?"

"Not so far, but I've got twenty more to go."

Clark replied, "Wellesley could be sending Jack and the others on a wild-goose chase. What choice do they have but to run down each and every one of these coordinates, then sit on them until the coup's over?"

"It wouldn't be a problem if we had a few dozen guys and a full week to plan and coordinate it," said Jack. "We've got neither."

"John, if you're right about this, then we need to treat everything Jack gathered from Wellesley's apartment as suspect," said Gavin. "Worse still, if it's all a red herring, that means Wellesley knew you were coming, Jack."

"Don't say that. I've played enough chess with this asshole to last me a lifetime. If Wellesley's playing us, then we may be back where we started: Somebody else on our side has turned."

"Who knew you were going to Chirpoy?" asked Clark.

"Everyone but Medzhid and his people."

"No way the recently departed Anton could have known?" Gerry asked.

"Am I a hundred percent on that? No, but close to it. Listen, we could go round and round with this until our ears are bleeding. It doesn't matter. John said it: We've got to chase down these coordinates. Gavin, how soon will you have them all mapped?"

"Eight hours, give or take."

"Gerry, how long since you had lunch with Mary Pat Foley?"

"Jack . . ."

"Buy her a piece of cheesecake and ask her to retask a satellite or two."

"Is that all?"

"Right now all I've got is Google Earth, which is fine for finding a coffee shop but lousy for what we're talking about. Plus, Spellman's not keen on calling Langley and pressing the panic button — not this close to the start. He's already stuck his neck out for Seth and he's liable to get it chopped off."

"What's that mean?"

"Spellman's bosses don't know Seth's working off his dad's manual, and they don't know where he got it in the first place. I, uh, forgot to tell you about that last part."

"Which is what, exactly?" said Gerry.

"Wellesley fed Seth the manual. The guy's a master manipulator. He did his homework, saw a wound he could salt, and did just that."

"Oh, shit," Clark murmured under his breath.

Gerry Hendley said nothing for a long ten seconds.

"Jack, if you ever forget another little detail like that again, I'll have you planted in a chair faster than you can say 'WTF.' You hear me?"

"I hear you, boss."

"Wellesley's in Seth's head," said Clark.

"Not anymore. I'll vouch for him."

"You might come to regret that."

"Possibly. Bottom line is, if Langley gets wind of all this, the coup is off."

"Doesn't sound like a half-bad idea," said Gerry. "I'm not even sure I want to be complicit in this. I'll give you sixty seconds to convince me otherwise."

"Their plan is solid. Period. You always say, trust the guy on the ground. They're on the ground, and so am I, and we think it's doable. Whether it will actually succeed I can't say."

"You're losing me, Jack."

"Then how about this: In all likelihood Wellesley's out here making policy against the wishes of his own government; if we derail this thing we'll be doing the same thing with U.S. policy."

"He's got a point," Clark said.

"Too damned good," Gerry muttered.

Jack said, "Like it or not, we're neck-deep in it."

Gerry chuckled. "You know, Jack, I might bench you anyway just for the principle of it. But not today. I'll give Mary Pat a call. What do you need?"

"First things first. We need eyes overhead Borisoglebsk. We need to know if those Frogfoots and Fencers are still there."

If the UTM coordinates they'd found on Wellesley's computer were not only locations within Makhachkala but also the sites of Seth and Spellman's satellite Internet hubs, then they may have already been marked as air strike targets.

"Say the names again, Jack," Seth said a

few minutes later. "Penza Street . . ."

Jack checked his notes and recited the locations.

Spellman said, "Yeah, those are all hub sites."

"Shit!"

Seth bolted from the conference table. His chair bumped against the wall. He paced, running his fingers through his hair. Jack watched him, looking for the slightest crack. Their situation had just gone from raining to pouring.

Seth took a deep breath and let it out. Nodding, he turned back to the table. "Okay, okay . . . Let's put it into perspective. We don't 'know' anything, right? We wait until Gavin's mapped all the coordinates, then we check them against our list."

"We're down to three days, Seth," said Spellman. "If —"

"Yeah, we're down to three days, so we're not playing the 'if' game. Jack, what else was on Wellesley's computer?"

"Gavin's working on it."

"Have him work faster. What about this airbase? When will we know if the planes are still there or if they've been moved, and if they have, where are they?"

"Slow down. Take a breath. You're giving

me a headache."

"Yeah, sorry," he replied with a sheepish grin. "Anybody got any Xanax?"

Dom replied, "No Xanax, but I'd be happy to dart you."

"I was kidding, Dom."

"I'm not."

Jack said, "Seth, we'll hear about Borisoglebsk when we hear about it. It's out of our hands."

"Yeah, okay. We should think about getting back into Wellesley's place, too. Maybe we missed something. In the meantime, we hit the streets. We visit each of those hubs, talk to our people, and see if anyone's been poking around. If so, we uproot 'em and move 'em."

By sundown all but one of the sites had been checked. None of the "Hub Captains," as Seth had dubbed them, had reported any strange activity. Seth was visibly relieved. Jack was growing more worried. The implications of what Gavin had found were starting to sink in.

Surgical or otherwise, if air strikes were launched against the capital's hub sites, Seth's plan wouldn't simply be gutted. It would also mean they'd gravely misread Volodin's resolve and that the man cared only about seeing the coup fail — organically or militarily, it didn't matter — and he didn't care if the whole world watched it happen. Unarmed protesters on Makhachkala's streets would be targets, terrorists. Anyone involved in orchestrating the insurrection would be put against the wall.

Dom walked into the apartment a half-hour after everyone else and said, "I walked every foot of those docks. Either the UTM coordinate I have is wrong or it's sitting at the bottom of the harbor."

"The other ones were dead-on," Spellman replied. "It doesn't sound like Wellesley to make that kind of mistake."

"We'll know more when Gavin gets back to us. He'll triple-check all the numbers. By the way, where's Rebaz?"

"He's staying the night in his official residence, with his wife, Marta, and Aminat. They're leaving for Baku in the morning."

"Good for him," Ysabel said. "And Miss Balloon Boobs, where is she?"

Spellman laughed, as did Dom and Jack. He said, "That's not very nice."

"You're right, my apologies. Miss Balloon Breasts. Is that better?"

"Much."

Seth, shaking his head, replied, "Niki has —"

"Does she dot the *i* with a heart?"

"A smiley face. She has her own place in Derbent. I'll have you know, she wants to be an actress or a —"

"Pop star," Ysabel guessed.

"Yep."

"Imagine that."

"Rebaz does love his wife, Ysabel, and they've got a good marriage. It's just a different culture here."

"I'm Iranian. I know about different culture. I'm not judging him, actually. It's just that he seems to be such a remarkable man; to have him be so banal with his love life is disappointing."

"Hold on, let me get a dictionary."

"Shush," she replied.

"Nobody's perfect. He'll be a better leader than Dagestan's seen in the last hundred years. Listen, if you really feel strongly about it, I'll talk to him about Niki. Maybe he can convince her to stop using the smiley faces."

"Funny man."

Seth reached across and gave her forearm a squeeze. "I've missed you, Ysabel."

"Careful, there, buddy," Jack said with a grin. "Don't get handsy."

"Sorry."

Ysabel said, "It's good to see you laugh, Seth."

"It feels good. So, does this mean we're friends again?"

Ysabel pursed her lips, thinking. "Not yet, but in time maybe. In the meantime, I should probably get that scorpion out of your bed."

"Funny girl." Seth paused, looked down at his hands. "Listen, guys, this ain't easy for me, but I'm sorry. I'm sorry for it all. I shouldn't —"

"It's okay, Seth," Jack said. He had no doubt Seth meant what he said, but he feared that until the coup was finished his friend would be vulnerable to the win-at-all-costs mind-set that had been driving him for three years.

"No, it's not, not even close," Seth replied. "I shouldn't have used you to flush Wellesley; I almost got you both killed — at Pardis and at the farmhouse. Truth is, I kinda feel like I've lost my way. I've done things in the past year I never thought I could. After this, I need to do some serious thinking." He chuckled. "Hell, maybe you guys can even set up some kind of intervention for me — a 'Hey, Seth, you've been a real asshole' type of thing?"

Both Ysabel and Jack laughed. "Deal," Jack said.

Jack awoke to the sound of rain pattering on their bedroom window. He got up and peeked through the curtain. It was still dark out and the streetlights were reflected in the puddles. He started getting dressed.

"Where are you going?" Ysabel asked groggily.

"To get coffee."

"Fabulous idea."

He walked out to the main room. Seth and Spellman were sitting at the conference table with a carafe of coffee between them. Newspapers were spread across the table before them and one of the wall televisions was tuned to a morning news show, the volume muted. President Nabiyev was displayed in the inset box beside the presenter's head.

Spellman looked up, gave him a wave, then returned to his paper.

"Morning, Jack," Seth said.

Jack poured himself a cup of coffee. "What's going on?"

"Matt and I decided to break the story a day early."

"What story?"

"It seems President Nabiyev has been selling city contracts to the highest bidder, then using the kickback money to buy up land outside Sulak."

"Is all that true?"

"Every word of it," Spellman replied.

"And it'll get worse as the day goes on," said Seth. "Turns out Nabiyev didn't even pay for the land, but instead used Dagestan's version of eminent domain to oust the owners. The kickback money is hidden in an account in Liechtenstein. To top it off, he was planning to sell the land back to the government at triple the going price."

"So this is your catalyst," said Jack. "This is what puts the people on the streets."

"More or less. Medzhid will step forward, share the people's outrage and disappointment, promise a full investigation, and tell them they deserve better from their leadership. From there the message will turn to freedom, national pride, the right to be heard, and so on. By this time tomorrow the story will have gone from worthless swampland in Sulak to the future of Dagestan."

Seth said these things in such a blasé way that Jack wondered whether his friend truly believed them or whether they were simply a propaganda tool, red meat for the masses he himself had primed. He hoped it was the former. And if it wasn't, what then? While the "means to an end" ideology was one he'd never been entirely comfortable with, he knew all too well that the real world wasn't all roses and puppies. If the stakes were high enough, were any methods justifiable? Who set those thresholds, and was morality scalable?

Questions like this made Jack happy he hadn't even the slightest trace of political ambition. Then again, neither had his dad, and look what that got him.

Jack's phone vibrated. It was a text from Gavin. HAVE INFO.

He took Ysabel a cup of coffee and then she joined them at the table. Jack dialed Gavin and put him on speakerphone. "We're all here."

"On this end also," Gerry said. "The BBC's talking about President Nabiyev. Is that your doing, Seth?"

"His own, actually," Spellman replied. "The story was going to get out eventually.

We just massaged the timeline a bit. It's high time for him to go."

Jack said, "What have you got for us?"

"We're still waiting on the overhead shots," said Clark. "She's working on it, but the retasking is a bit more complicated these days."

"Who's 'she'?" asked Spellman. "Never mind. I don't want to know."

"As for the UTM coordinates," Gavin said, "I've got them all mapped. All but five of them are in the city. I'm sending you all a Dropbox link right now."

Seth and Spellman crowded together before Spellman's laptop and started comparing the coordinates with their hub sites.

"Jack, I think Wellesley's Chirpoy apartment went dead. I installed a key-logger program on the main computer after you left. About an hour ago I got a flurry of activity — burst e-mail traffic, their landline forwarder pushing out a backlog of calls . . . that kind of stuff, like somebody had sent some kind of cyber 'bug-out' signal."

"Or a 'go' signal," Ysabel replied.

"That seems more likely," Clark agreed.

"Anyway, after that all six computers jumped on the apartment's broadband for about forty seconds, then, poof, lights out. I managed to snag some of the residual outbound messages before that happened, so I'll see if I can make anything of it."

"Wellesley's pulled up stakes and moved," Clark said. "He knows the Nabiyev story means you've started prepping."

"The question is, Where's he gone?" said Gerry.

And what will be his first countermove? Jack thought.

"They're all there," Seth said. "Every damn one of our hubs nailed down to a square meter. How the hell did they get this?"

"How many are there?" asked Jack.

"Twenty-six."

Jack opened Ysabel's MacBook and clicked on the Dropbox link Gavin had sent them. The map popped up, an overhead full-color view of Makhachkala covered in red dots labeled with their corresponding UTM coordinates. Ysabel and Dom watched over Jack's shoulder as he zoomed and panned the map.

"There's a total of thirty-two locations, but only twenty-six hubs," said Ysabel. "What are these other six? Do you guys have anything there?"

"No," said Spellman.

"Did you ever?"

He shook his head. "Four of those are in the Tarki-Taus west of the city. There's nothing up there but some hiking trails and a maintenance road. The fifth location is the one you couldn't find at the harbor, Dom."

"Yeah, I saw that. It's in the exact place I looked the first time. What about the sixth?"

"It's downtown somewhere, a building I don't recognize."

"Then these six are mistakes or red herrings," said Ysabel. She stared hard at the screen for a few moments, then said, "Jack, can you show me a list of the coordinates next to the map?"

"Sure."

He brought up the list, then split-screened it with the map. She traced her index finger over the screen, matching up locations and numbers. "This is interesting. Take a look."

She turned the laptop so everyone could see.

"The six spare locations have different coordinates . . ." She highlighted the ones in question:

Hepo5..38GZT.703971mE.4759623mN
Gaxy4..38GZT.703971mE.4759623mN
Gefo9..38GZT.703971mE.4759623mN
Xole8..38GZT.703971mE.4759623mN

Byma1.38GZT.703971mE.4759623mN
Hevu9,,38GZT.703971mE.4759623mN

"I don't see it," said Seth. "Different how?"

"Look at Hepo Five. See the double decimal points after it? The first four have that notation, the next one, Byma One — your site at the harbor, Dom — has a single decimal, and Hevu Nine has double commas."

"Input errors. Typos," Seth said. "Doesn't mean anything."

"I'm not convinced."

"Suit yourself. It still doesn't answer the real question, though. How the hell did Wellesley find out about the hubs?"

"Who else knows about them?" asked Jack.

"All of them? Just us at this table. Matt and I were real careful about compartmentalization. I mean, yeah, each hub captain knows what he or she is running, but they don't know there are others — or at least how many more there are and their locations."

"Do you run diagnostic tests on them?"

"About once a week," Spellman replied, "but it's just a blind-burst transmission that lasts all of two seconds."

Dom said, "How've you been keeping track of all this?"

"Nothing online, if that's what you're asking. It's all hand-to-hand between me and Seth, with password-protected flash drives. I always know where mine is."

"Same here," said Seth. "When we visit the hubs we don't use the same schedule or route, and we make damned sure we haven't picked up any tails. I'm telling you, our op sec is solid."

"Then I don't know what to tell you," Jack replied. "The truth is, right now it doesn't matter how Wellesley knows about them, it matters what he's got planned for them."

"We need to know about those planes," Spellman said.

They split up: Spellman and Dom went to find the unidentified building downtown while Jack and Ysabel took one of Medzhid's Suburbans into the Tarki-Taus.

By the time they reached the outskirts of Makhachkala, the rain was falling in sheets and slashing at the windshield while the wipers struggled to keep up. As they left the paved road for a gravel one, Jack switched the Suburban into four-wheel drive. The road narrowed and steepened into a series of switchbacks that wound up the northern flank of the escarpment before finally opening onto a maintenance road that ran north along a ridge overlooking the city.

The trees on either side of them swayed in the wind. Branches seemed to reach out, their tips scraping over the Suburban's roof.

Through the trees Jack caught glimpses of the city, still lit up by streetlights in the gloom. In the distance the Caspian Sea lay shrouded in fog.

"These are closer to mountains than they are to hills," Ysabel said.

"How far does this road go?"

"We're at the far southern end, so . . . about six miles."

"What's our first spot?"

"Hepo Five."

They'd decided the UTM's alphanumeric prefixes were indeed randomly generated place names. The building Dom and Spellman were checking out was Hevu9.

"It should be a half-mile in front of us."

They covered the distance at a near walking pace as the gravel beneath the Suburban's tires became more and more waterlogged.

"Just up here, on the right."

Jack braked to a stop. Ysabel rolled down her window. The interior filled with the sound of rain. Beside them, just over the edge of the road, was a treeless, flattened rectangle of earth roughly the size of a semi-truck. The far end looked down over the city.

"Those stumps look freshly cut," Ysabel said.

"Stay here."

Jack pulled up the hood of his poncho, climbed out, and walked into the clearing. The dirt was rutted with bulldozer tracks half full of water. He walked the perimeter, looking for anything that might explain the clearing's purpose. There was nothing.

He went back to the Suburban.

"Well?"

"It's just a flat patch of earth."

"It's more than that," Ysabel replied. "We just have to figure out what."

They continued on to the remainder of the sites — Gaxy4, Gefo9, and Xole8 — and found each one the same as the first: razed clearings overlooking Makhachkala. They were spread down the ridgeline at one-mile intervals, give or take a few yards.

"Well, I'm sure as hell not going to try to keep track of the code names," Jack said. "My brain is too full as it is."

"How about 'Ridge Sites'?" Ysabel offered.

"Works for me."

Jack's phone rang. He put it on speaker.

"Dom, what's up?"

"Nothing. We checked Hevu Nine —"

"We've decided we're not using those names anymore," said Ysabel.

"Thank God. Anyway, it's a two-story brick building on Lena Road; it looks like an old schoolhouse. There's a realtor's sign on the front. The doors are padlocked and the windows are boarded up. Want us to break in?"

"No, let's check out the realtor first."

"We're going to head back to Byma One — sorry, the docks — to check it out again. Meet you back at the apartment."

Frustrated, Jack and Ysabel drove up and down the maintenance road, half hoping they might spot someone nosing around the ridge sites. After an hour they gave up and headed back down into Makhachkala.

Despite the rain, the city seemed busier, the streets and sidewalks full of cars and pedestrians. Coffee shops and restaurants were packed. Jack sensed an undercurrent of agitation in gestures and body language. Patrons were clustered around tables, leaning in as they spoke to one another.

Ysabel said, "Do you feel it?"

"Yes."

Seth and Spellman's corruption story about President Nabiyev was gaining traction.

Back at the Tortoreto they found Medzhid seated on the couch, talking quietly with one of his assistants, Yana, whom Medzhid had promoted after Albina's death. The minister looked up and gave them a curt nod.

"He's got his game face on," Jack whispered to Ysabel.

"I don't blame him."

Medzhid gestured them over. "Thank you for what you said yesterday, Jack. You were right: I was asleep. But I'm awake now."

"Good."

Ysabel asked, "Marta and Aminat?"

"Safe in Baku. Whatever happens here in the coming days, they will be safe. I only hope they have a home to come back to. By the way, Aminat told me to give you a message."

"What?"

"And I quote: 'You better be taking your Keflex, mister.' "

Jack smiled. "Tell her I am. No oozing pus."

Dom and Spellman walked into the apartment, and the four of them settled around the conference table to compare notes.

"Where's Seth?" asked Jack.

"Driving around, taking the pulse of the city," Spellman replied. "Medzhid's starting our PR push later this morning. We pull the trigger in forty-eight hours. How did you guys fare?"

Jack explained what they'd found in the hills.

"How fresh were the sites?" asked Dom.

"No more than three weeks, I'd guess."

"Those are some pretty precise intervals," said Spellman. "Can't be an accident. I'll do some digging and see if there are any construction projects planned up there. As for the Lena Road building, we called the realtor. According to her, the building's already been leased. She just forgot to put up the 'Sold' sign. The buyer — she wouldn't give us a name — is due to move in this week."

"Well, we know who it is. Wellesley," said Ysabel.

"Matt, call Gavin with the particulars. Hacking a realtor's computer should be a nice change of pace for him. How'd you do with the docks?"

"The docks are pissing me off, that's how we did," Dom said. "The UTM we have is dead center in the water, about a hundred feet offshore. Maybe these assholes have a midget submarine."

Jack couldn't help but laugh. His friend was having a grudge match with Byma1. "Go get him, bud."

"What now?" asked Ysabel.

"We wait."

Until they got eyes on Borisoglebsk, they were in limbo.

The day wore on.

As planned, Medzhid was moving from interview to interview on every radio station and television channel in Makhachkala. He was never more than twenty minutes from being seen or heard by an increasingly attentive citizenry. Continuing the tone they had set after the debunking of the Almak massacre story, hosts lobbed him softball questions, which he deftly turned into mini-speeches that hammered at Seth's themes — dignity, self-determination, trust, and pride of nation.

Between spots, Medzhid and Seth conferred over the phone, reshaping and refining the minister's message and slowly but steadily turning up the rhetoric.

At ten-thirty that evening, he gave his final television interview of the day: "My fellow Dagestanis, I share your shock over today's news reports regarding our president Nabiyev. Of course, we must let the investigation into these allegations take its course, but Mr. Nabiyev's refusal to address this matter disappoints and surprises me, as I'm sure it does you.

"As never before it is critical we remember that we are one people, whether Avar or Tsakhur; Muslim or Orthodox; rich or poor. We are all Dagestanis with a long and proud heritage.

"I am also both heartened and saddened today. Heartened by the hope I saw in your faces as I walked our city's streets. Saddened because I can't help but feel I could have served you better. Corruption, wherever it is found, is a stain on our nation. You deserve better.

"I tell you this now, without reservation: I am reenergized by your devotion. I share your hope for a better life for yourselves, for your children, and for our future generations.

"While it is not my place to direct the path you choose, I am confident the coming days and weeks will be ones we will all remember with pride for decades to come. Tonight, as you go to sleep, ask yourselves what the future of Dagestan should be, and know that anything is possible if we stand together.

"Thank you for your time. I am, and

always will be, a proud Dagestani. Good night."

Spellman aimed the remote at the television and turned it off.

There was silence around the table.

Seth murmured, "If that doesn't drive them into the streets, nothing will."

41

MAKHACHKALA

The next morning the rain finally broke. The clouds drifted west over the Tarki-Taus, leaving behind the sun and white cotton-ball clouds. The weather had certainly tipped in Seth and Medzhid's favor as they began their final media blitz before the coup. There would always be a fraction of would-be protesters that hated standing in the rain, no matter how worthy the cause.

As he was the day before, Medzhid was out the door at first light, moving through the city, shaking hands with early-morning commuters and shop owners on the sidewalks, listening to people's concerns and assuaging their fears, and holding impromptu press conferences at carefully chosen spots throughout the city. At each venue the size of the crowds grew and took longer to disperse until intersections and entire streets were blocked. *Politsiya* from the Ministry of the Interior rerouted traffic.

Hand-painted signs appeared on the façades of government buildings. As Seth had predicted, the first messages were simple ones, reflections of the themes Medzhid had been pushing for the past twenty-four hours — hope, pride, unity. Protesters started gathering outside the Parliament Building, the signs calling for action: CHOOSE FREEDOM, STAND TOGETHER, THE FUTURE IS OURS TO MAKE. Seth's unwitting agents were there, videotaping every moment, uploading snippets to Facebook with captions like "Peaceful Dagestanis asking only for a better life," and sound-bite interviews with smiling twentysomething protesters appeared on Twitter. The local newspapers and radio stations picked them up and ran them instead of commercials between scheduled programming.

By noon reporters from BBC and Al-Jazeera were landing at Makhachkala's airport, where they were immediately granted temporary visas by Ministry of the Interior border-control officers and assigned a personal guide and a car.

Surrounded by microphones, Medzhid gave walking interviews while throngs followed him, jostling one another in hopes of getting a handshake or to pat Medzhid on the back.

The momentum was building.

While Jack, Dom, and Ysabel watched from the couch, Seth and Spellman paced the conference area, talking into Bluetooth headsets, while a retinue of MOI staff sat shoulder to shoulder at the table, working the phones and passing messages to Seth and Spellman. On the wall above them all three televisions were on.

Seth took off his headset and called, "It's on! Channel Fifteen. Everybody be quiet!"

One of the staff members unmuted the television in the middle. A woman with blond hair and a stern expression was saying, ". . . once again, we have reports that President Nabiyev has left the capital in the wake of the allegations raised by the Sulak land deal. A source close to Nabiyev claims the trip to a newly opened canning factory in Buynaksk has been on his schedule for several weeks. Channel Fifteen producers have tried to contact Mr. Nabiyev's press secretary for further comment but have received no response. We now take you to the Parliament Building, where crowds are rapidly growing . . ."

"That's enough, turn it down."

The assistant muted the television again.

Seth walked over to the couch. "What do you think? Clockwork. Did you notice they're using the term *president* a lot less? That's a big deal here, it's sort of like saying 'that guy Nabiyev.' "

"Nice touch with the 'in the wake of the allegations' bit," said Jack.

"That wasn't us. Channel Fifteen has never liked Nabiyev."

"Is that true about his trip?" asked Ysabel.

"Mostly. He went to the factory yesterday. The last part about the press secretary is slightly exaggerated. It'll come out later the trip was actually unscheduled. I'm sure Nabiyev is already on his way back. When he reaches the city limits there'll be crowds and cameras waiting for him. With any luck his limousine will hit someone. Relax, I'm kidding. I mean, if it happened it wouldn't hurt our cause, but we're not going to shove somebody under Nabiyev's wheels."

"That's nice of you," Ysabel said sarcastically.

"What can I say? I'm a sharing carer."

"So what happens next?" asked Dom.

"Nabiyev will go on radio and television and deny the allegations, but he'll be whispering in a wind tunnel. Medzhid's exposure ratio is climbing by the hour. Nabiyev will never catch up and the questions he'll get will be brutal. We'll be leaking bits and pieces of the Sulak story all day, then drop the bomb tonight."

"What bomb?"

"That some people in Sulak were forcefully ejected from their homes. One of them had a heart attack. And yes, before you ask, it's all true. We've got a couple of them — an elderly farmer and his wife — lined up with interviews before Medzhid goes on one last time. We're firing on all cylinders, guys. Tomorrow we dump the nitro in. Oh, and be packed up and ready to go by seven. We're moving to the command center."

Seth headed back toward the conference area, then stopped and turned back. "Anything from Gavin?"

"Not yet."

"Jack, before morning we need to know if Volodin's sending bombers our way. We'll have a hundred thousand people on the streets by nine. I'm not going to walk them into a slaughterhouse."

Seth walked away.

Jack dialed Gavin, who said, "Nothing yet. Mary Pat's got a Keyhole scheduled for retasking, but it's probably going to be another eight hours before it's overhead Borisoglebsk."

"What about the old schoolhouse

downtown?"

"I got into the realtor's system with no trouble. The building is being leased by something called Pacific Alliance Group. It stinks of something, but I don't know what yet. Hey, Gerry and John want to talk to you. I'll transfer you."

A few seconds passed, and then Gerry Hendley's voice came on the line. "Jack, CNN and MSNBC have picked up the Dagestan story — both the protests and the Nabiyev scandal. They're running them at the top of every hour and the news crawler's running full-time. They've probably got reporters headed your way, too. Looks like Seth knows what he's doing after all."

"It's red meat for the press," Jack replied. "Scandal, greed, and hope, with a hint of chaos on the streets that could turn ugly at any second."

"Could that happen?" asked Gerry.

"Anything can happen, but Medzhid's walking the tightrope pretty well. The streets are full, but there haven't been any reports of violence. It doesn't hurt that Medzhid's *politsiya* are standing back. We haven't heard anything here about Volodin. Has he made a statement yet?"

"No, but it probably won't be long now," replied Clark. "His tone will tell us a lot."

Dom said, "Like whether he's going with the 'organic failure' approach or the boot-on-the-throat approach."

"Exactly. What we don't know is if the Russian garrison troops in the border districts will turn and head for Makhach-kala. If that happens Medzhid's going to have a tough choice to make — tell the masses to go home or gamble that the garrison won't wade in with clubs swinging. Does Seth have any early-warning assets in place?"

"I expect so," Jack replied. "I'll check. He's more worried about the Frogfoots and Fencers. We're cutting it close with the satellite imagery."

"It's coming," Gerry promised.

Jack hung up. He stood, paced a bit, then sat back down and twirled his phone in his hands. "Let's get out of here."

"And go where?" asked Ysabel.

"Back to Chirpoy Road. I want to know why Wellesley's computer system went dark."

Dom said, "I'll give up Jimmy John's if the dickhead's standing there when we walk in."

With Ysabel at the wheel, they pulled out of the Tortoreto's garage and swung by the

Ministry of the Interior building a few blocks away. The street was quiet save a couple dozen people walking up and down the sidewalk, either chanting "Medzhid . . . Medzhid" or holding up signs bearing his official MOI photograph.

"They're campaigning for the guy," Dom said from the backseat.

"Nice signs," Ysabel replied with a smile. "Surprisingly sophisticated for an average Makhachkalan. Seth's covering a lot of bases, isn't he?"

She made a U-turn, then headed north toward Wellesley's apartment. Four times in the mile between the MOI building and Chirpoy Road, *politsiya* detoured them around intersections thronged with protesters. Through the Suburban's half-open windows Jack could hear bullhorn-amplified voices over the cacophony.

Ysabel turned onto the road Jack and Dom had been using as a stakeout spot and pulled to the curb. She rolled down her window so Jack could survey the complex through binoculars.

"Everything looks normal. I don't see Zoya's car."

After their last break-in here, they'd decided to take a risk and not return the woman's key card and permit. If she'd reported them missing they would soon know.

"Any sign of creepy vodka guy?" Ysabel said.

"No."

"He's probably got his eye pressed to the peephole, pining for your return," said Dom.

"Stop it."

"You broke the guy's heart, Ysabel."

Jack said, "Enough, kids. Let's go in and see what happens."

Nothing happened. Ysabel pulled through the gate, waved the permit at the goon — not creepy vodka guy — then parked in Zoya's spot. They waited until the man disappeared back into the apartment, then trotted to the stairwell and up to the second floor.

Jack knelt by the door and got out Gavin's Devpulse lockbuster. Dom drew his Ruger and nodded. Jack disengaged the lock, then scooted aside as Dom stepped through. "Clear," he whispered. Jack and Ysabel followed him in.

Aside from a bundle of cables dangling above the table, the apartment was stripped bare.

"Jack, I think this is for you," Ysabel said,

pointing at a yellow Post-it note on the table.

Jack picked it up.

Better luck next time, Jack.
By the way, I enjoyed your Dobromir impression.
So sad to learn his sweetheart is no longer with us.
Your doing, I assume?

— W.

"Son of a bitch."

He passed the note to Dom and Ysabel.

She said, "Seth's right: He is a cocky bastard."

"And slippery," said Dom.

Where is Raymond Wellesley? Jack wondered.

There was no way the SIS man had gone home, which meant he'd set up his nerve center elsewhere in anticipation of the coup. Surely he would have seen Medzhid's media blitz and the Nabiyev/Sulak story for what they were — Seth's softening-up barrage.

But had the SIS man left this apartment because he knew it had been broken into or because the move had been planned from the start? The Post-it note suggested the former, but Jack couldn't be certain, not with Wellesley.

"What's this mean?" asked Ysabel. "What about the UTM coordinates? Are they just a distraction?"

"Can't be," said Dom. "We know the ones for the Internet hub sites are right, and those clearings you found on the ridge are real enough, and so is the dodgy schoolhouse."

Jack nodded. "You're right. The ridge sites are at least three weeks old, which means they were created even before Wellesley knew I existed. The guy's smart, but he's not clairvoyant."

"It's gotta be the schoolhouse; that's his new nerve center. Where's a better spot than downtown Makhachkala in the middle of the action?"

"Agreed."

When will Wellesley make his first move? Jack wondered.

And what will it be?

42

MAKHACHKALA

Late afternoon, as Medzhid was winding down his interviews and his staff was preparing for the move to the command center in anticipation of Seth's husband-and-wife-farmer bombshell, Gerry Hendley called.

"We got the Keyhole images back. All the Frogfoots and Fencers are right where they should be at Borisoglebsk."

"Thank the Lord," Seth replied.

"Not quite yet. John, you tell them."

"Okay, guys, it's a bit complicated, so bear with me. Khibiny and Borisoglebsk are places in Russia, we know that. But they're also associated with something else — EW."

Jack leaned back and ran his hands through his hair. "Shit."

"EW?" Ysabel said.

"Electronic warfare," Clark replied. "Using directed energy to disrupt equipment — communications, radar, television signals . . . Essentially anything that uses the EM spectrum. Depending on the power of the weapon you can jam or fry whatever you're targeting."

"Like satellite Internet," Spellman said. "And cell towers."

"Right, those are easy. Your hubs are harder. That's why Wellesley has all of them mapped. They're queued up for EW attacks."

"This can't be happening!" Seth barked. "Hell, it *can't* be done. Ahmadinejad tried to do it in '09 and it didn't work."

"Yeah, well, he didn't have what Volodin has. Do you guys remember the USS *Donald Cook*?"

"No," said Dom.

"It's an *Arleigh Burke*–class guided missile destroyer. Top-of-the-line warship with latest-generation Aegis, Tomahawks, RIM surface-to-air missiles. In spring of 'fourteen it sailed into the Black Sea to give Volodin something else to worry about other than Ukraine and Crimea.

"Two days later the *Cook* gets buzzed by a Russian Su-24 Fencer. They never saw it coming. The *Cook*'s Aegis radar, fire control systems, comms, and data network went dead. The boat was essentially blind and deaf and defenseless. The Fencer repeated the process twelve more times and there was nothing the *Cook* could do."

Clark said, "The Fencer was carrying an EW pod nicknamed Khibiny."

"One plane did that?" asked Ysabel.

"Yes. In the space of a few seconds. Khibiny is part of a larger system called Borisoglebsk-2, along with something they call Zhitel. Rumor is, it's specifically designed to take down satellite and GPS systems."

"So, one plane flies over Makhachkala and our whole hub network goes down," said Seth. "Is that what you're telling us?"

Jack said, "Relax, Seth."

"Relax? How about you go fuck—" Seth took a breath, let it out. "Sorry, Jack."

Clark said, "To answer your question, no, one plane won't do it. The Fencer disabled the *Cook* because it was a single target, not a diffuse web like you've got there."

"Explain that," said Ysabel.

Gavin said, "We're just guessing here, but Wellesley probably doesn't know exactly how sophisticated your hubs are. For all he knows, after the first pass by a Fencer, you'll start moving your hubs, cycling the power, maybe rotating frequencies. What the Khibiny and Zhitel can't see they can't hit."

"Which means," Jack said, "unless Volodin commits a dozen planes and runs round-the-clock sorties, the attacks won't come from the air. They'll be land-based. Ground vehicles."

"Right."

"The sites on the ridge," Spellman said. "From up there they'd have a clear line of sight. They could cover the city from one end to the other."

"Yes and no," Clark said. "You guys have twenty-six hubs. From what we know about Borisoglebsk units, they're good at destroying but not so good at hunting. They're usually paired with tracking platforms."

"What size are we talking about?" asked Jack.

"For the hunter units, big. Our best guess is they'll use what's called a Krasukha. They're about the size of an articulated semi-truck: squat, boxy, powerful-looking, with a foldable parabolic dish on the back."

"They sound about the same size as the clearings," said Spellman. "Jack, you said the sites are spaced at, what, mile intervals?"

"About that."

Gavin said, "Well, Makhachkala's about a hundred-eighty square miles, so that'd be about right."

"Great," said Seth. "Let's find the fuckers and kill 'em. Tell us how to do it."

"It's not so tough to disable them," Clark

said. "The trick is to first find them, then get to them. You gotta understand: These things are eight-million-dollar vehicles stuffed to the gills with Russia's latest and greatest shit. They don't go anywhere without a built-in security team."

"How big?"

"Figure a light platoon per vehicle — a dozen guys with heavy weapons. Fifty men in total."

"We haven't got the firepower to handle that," said Spellman.

Gerry asked, "Jack, when was the last time you were up to the ridge?"

"Yesterday. There's no way Wellesley would risk sending the Krasukhas through the city, not with the streets as crowded as they are, and not with so many cameras rolling. If they're not already on the ridge, they'll be coming from somewhere else."

"Wellesley wouldn't wait until the last minute to bring them in country," said Spellman. "But maybe they'd stash them within quick driving distance. Either way, we need to get to them before they have a chance to dig in."

"Isn't that putting all our eggs in one basket?" asked Ysabel. "John, you said these Krasukhas use separate tracking platforms. What would one of those look like?"

"Smaller, more mobile — and they'd only need one of them."

"Take a guess," said Jack.

"Probably a Kvant SPN9. It's a converted radar jammer built on a BTR armored personnel carrier chassis. You could hide one in a standard-sized garage."

Gavin added, "Keep in mind, though, it'd need to be stationed away from the Krasukhas. The better the triangulation data they get, the tighter and more powerful the directed energy. With twenty-six hubs to kill they'll want to avoid hunting-and-pecking."

Dom murmured, "Byma One."

"Come again?" said Gerry.

"That's one of the UTM prefix codes we got from Wellesley's computer," said Jack. "Dom's checked it twice. The spot's located in the harbor. John, could they stick a Kvant on a ship?"

"Easy. It wouldn't even need to be visible."

As night fell, they split up again, Jack and Ysabel heading back to the ridge, Spellman and Dom to the harbor. Seth, Medzhid, and the remaining staff at the apartment piled into one of the Suburbans for the short drive to the Ministry of the Interior building.

So crowded were the streets that it took

Jack and Ysabel twice as long as it had on previous trips to reach the city limits and start up the switchback road to the ridge. At the top, Jack turned onto the maintenance road and doused his headlights, leaving on the yellow fog lights to guide them down the gravel track.

They stopped at the first clearing, then got out and started panning their flashlights over the ground.

"I've got tire tracks," Jack said.

"Footprints over here."

He joined her and together they followed the tracks to the edge of the clearing. The footprints stopped at a tree; there were fresh gouges in the bark.

"Climbing spurs," Jack said.

They shined their beams up the trunk until they saw a chunk of metal jutting from the tree.

"What is that?" Ysabel murmured.

"A hook. Let's spread out and look for others."

Once done they met back in the center of the clearing.

"Eight," Ysabel said.

"Six. It's just a hunch, but I'd say they're rigging for camouflage nets."

They checked the remaining three sites and found the same setup — recent tire tracks, footprints, and hooks affixed to the perimeter trees.

Jack made a K-turn in the last clearing and started back the way they'd come.

"Stop," Ysabel said. "I see something."

Jack did so and they both climbed out.

He followed her into the underbrush to a tree trunk. Standing beside it was a steel post set into a concrete ring three feet in diameter. Sitting on the ground was a pile of chain; the links were the size of Jack's fist.

"This wasn't here before," Ysabel said.

Jack walked across the road and found a second post. Someone was building a barrier.

"So we take the chain with us."

"It's five hundred pounds at least, Ysabel. Let's get out of here."

Halfway down the hill, Ysabel pointed through the windshield. "Did you see that?"

Jack pulled over.

Below them the lights of Makhachkala were blinking out in checkerboard sections from south to north.

Jack's phone rang. "Jack, where are you?" asked Spellman.

"On the ridge road. We see it. The whole city's dark."

"At the docks, too. Try to make your way —"

The lights began coming back on, marching across the city until everything was back to normal.

"Meet us at the docks, we may have something."

"On our way."

Jack disconnected. Ysabel asked, "What just happened?"

"A shot across our bow," he replied.

They pulled into the harbor parking lot an hour later. Spellman waved to them from the sidewalk leading to the docks. They walked over.

"Well, now we know Nabiyev knows where the off switch is," Spellman said. "If he thinks it'll do him any good he's got a surprise coming. Did you listen to the interview, the farmers from Sulak?"

"No," said Ysabel.

"They were perfect. You could almost see Nabiyev's people shoving them out their own door with nothing but the clothes on their backs. I'm sure it didn't happen exactly like that, but the imagery will resonate. A lot of people here live in the same home for generations. The thought of getting pushed out of the place where your great-great-great-grandparents lived and raised children is serious business to these people. Nabiyev's forgotten that."

"Then it seems he's due for a reminder," Ysabel replied.

"Well said. Come on, Dom's waiting."

Spellman led them down the winding walkway to the docks, then up another set of stairs to the harbormaster's office. It was closed for the night and lit only by a sconce fixed above a plexiglass-covered pegboard. Dom was leaning against the wall.

"You saw the un-light show?" he asked.

Ysabel nodded. "Are we sure it wasn't a hiccup in the grid?"

"No, it was deliberate," said Spellman. "We expected this. Sometime tomorrow he'll shut the grid down again — this time for the duration — then he'll order the city's ISPs offline. We'll let him savor the victory for a couple hours, then bring our hubs online."

"What've you got, Dom?" asked Jack.

His friend was wearing a smug smile.

Dom tapped the plexiglass. "The *Igarka*. She's a seventy-foot front-ramp hauler out of Astrakhan. She's due to put in tomorrow morning at pier four, mooring twelve. I'll give you one guess where that is."

Ysabel answered. "On top of Byma One."

"You got it. In fact, the *Igarka*'s already here — at anchor." He pointed out into the harbor. Jack could see the ship's masthead light winking in the darkness.

They drove back downtown. The city's streets were quieter, but only slightly less crowded as the hardier protesters settled in for the night in tents and folding chairs. Here and there Jack could see the glow of charcoal grills and LED lanterns.

Right now this was an adventure for them, he thought. Had Medzhid told them the truth during his speech the night before — that some of them may die along the way — would they be as enthusiastic about all this? Ideals like freedom and self-determination were powerful and worthy goals but right now these things existed only in the minds of the Dagestani people. Aside from having to stand in the rain they'd yet to feel the kind of suffering that usually goes hand-in-hand with gaining one's independence. Even if this coup was blood-less and Medzhid proved to be the leader they hoped for, breaking away from the Russian Federation would mean years of hardship and uncertainty and an economy that was as fragile as a sheet of rice paper.

Hated and feared as Stalin was, for

decades after his death there were tens of thousands of Russians who wanted him back because he made the trains run on time. How many Dagestanis might feel the same way about Valeri Volodin in a few years' time?

As Seth had instructed, Jack pulled up to the wrought-iron gate at the back of the Ministry of the Interior building and gave the guard their names. Jack pulled the Suburban through, followed by Spellman and Dom. They found a pair of parking spaces beside the rear entrance, where Seth was waiting.

"Any luck?"

"Some," said Jack.

Seth led them down a tiled corridor to an elevator, which took them to the building's top floor. When the doors opened, Jack heard the sounds of overlapping voices and telephones ringing. They followed Seth toward a pair of tall oak doors emblazoned with the MOI's yellow eagle emblem. An oil portrait of Medzhid looked down at them from the wall above.

Through the doors was an open office space with burgundy carpet and dark paneling covered in oil paintings of what Jack assumed were moments from Russian and

Dagestani history, most of them depicting either battles or the founding of settlements.

Sconces spaced at intervals along the walls cast the room in a soft glow. Four seating areas with couches, club chairs, and coffee tables occupied the center of the space. It felt to Jack like a hotel lobby.

Medzhid emerged from one of the side offices, walking fast and studying a file, with Yana and Vasim in tow. As Medzhid strode past them he glanced up and said, "Everyone is well? Good. Make yourselves at home. Seth will show you around," then disappeared into another office and closed the door behind him.

"Yana, get the ERF watch officer on the phone!"

Ysabel whispered to Jack, "Serious game face."

"It's almost game time."

Seth gave them a stationary tour, pointing at the various doors while describing their function: communications, bedrooms, kitchen, conference rooms one and two.

"Give me five minutes and I'll meet you in conference room two. The phones are secure in here, so go ahead and use them."

Seth went back through the main doors. Jack heard the clicking of his shoes fade down the hallway.

"Looks a bit like a bunker," Dom said. "Matt, do you guys know something we don't know?"

Spellman shook his head. "Just a precaution in case we've misread Volodin."

"If we've misread Volodin, an iron gate and some oak doors won't do us a damned bit of good."

"It won't come to that."

Jack said, "I need to call home."

They walked down the hallway and found the conference room. Jack dialed The Campus. As they always seemed to be when he called lately, Gerry, John, and Gavin were there. Jack gave them the latest.

"The *Igarka* out of Astrakhan," Gavin repeated. "Got it. Should be easy to check her registry."

"Unless it's a micro-micro-Kamsarmax," Clark said, "any cargo carrier would have no trouble accommodating a Kvant. The fact that this one's a ramp loader should tell us something. It's kinda dicey to swing a fifteen-ton APC aboard with a crane. One more thing you should keep in mind: Just because the *Igarka*'s slated for a pier doesn't mean she's going to put in."

"What do you mean?" asked Dom.

"In most ports you need to have paid for a mooring to get an anchorage. Some vessels use one, some both. It depends on the reason for the visit. How far out into the harbor was she?"

"A quarter-mile, maybe less," said Jack.

"That's plenty close. If there's a Kvant aboard, it can do its tracking from the anchorage. Hell, if I was there and about twenty years younger I'd take a swim and see what's what. As it stands, you might have to do it yourselves."

Gerry asked, "Jack, did you ask Seth about the outlying garrisons?"

"I did. He doesn't have anything in place. He's working on something, but his assets are spread thin. Medzhid, too."

Spellman said, "It's a calculated risk we had to take, Gerry."

"We get that, but if Volodin's going to actively oppose this thing, those garrisons will be the first ones to move. You'll only get about ten hours' notice before you've got twelve thousand troops on your doorstep."

"Troops that've been fighting Chechen and Georgian terrorists for the past two years," John Clark added.

"We know the numbers and we know the risks. If push comes to shove, Medzhid will back down before there's any bloodshed."

"His call," Gerry said. "Just be damned

sure you guys have an exit plan in place. Four Americans and one Iranian in Medzhid's inner circle . . . Volodin would probably reopen Bamlag West specially for you, then drop you in a hole."

Jack awoke to a buzzing sensation against his cheek. He forced open his eyes and fumbled around until his hand touched his vibrating phone. He read the screen: Ysabel. He looked to her side of the bed. It was empty.

"Where are you?" he asked.

"In conference room two. Wake up the others and come in here."

Jack, Seth, Dom, and Spellman shuffled in a few minutes later. Ysabel gestured to a carafe on the table and said, "Fresh coffee."

"Are we going to be awake long enough to need coffee?" asked Jack. The clock on the wall read 11:20.

"That depends on whether you want to find Wellesley's Krasukhas."

This got everyone's attention. They sat down and Spellman poured the coffee.

"I couldn't sleep," Ysabel said, "so I thought I'd do a little snooping in Pechkin's phone. He was pretty good at keeping his call history cleared, but he forgot one. About an hour before he got to Khasavyurt the other day, he called a local Makhachkala number. I just called it. I got an answering machine."

Ysabel stopped and smiled as though savoring the moment.

"Oh, come on," Dom said. "Put us out of our misery."

"The number belongs to a branch of Hamrah Engineering."

Seth sat forward. "Where?"

"Agachaul."

"Where the hell is that?" asked Dom.

Spellman answered: "It's about three miles from here on the other side of the Tarki-Taus."

"You're shitting me."

Ysabel shook her head. "According to Hamrah's main website, it's called the Agachaul Logistics Center, whatever that is."

"It's a fancy name for storage warehouses," Seth replied.

Jack asked, "You didn't know about this place?"

"No. I was too busy playing surveyor on the railway's main lines."

"Well, clearly Pechkin knew about the place," said Spellman. "Ysabel, what about the route between Agachaul and here? Is there a road that —"

"Leads up to the ridge? Yes. Right up the northern slope, onto the maintenance road, then past the clearings."

Jack smiled. "Ysabel, I could kiss —"

"You bet you will. Later. What are we going to do with this?"

Seth said, "Well, provided I haven't been fired from my old job, I can probably get us in there."

43

At dusk, dark swollen clouds had begun to roll over the city, and now, as Jack and the others pulled out of the Interior Ministry parking lot, the rain was starting to fall.

Following Ysabel's directions Jack took the coast road south, then followed the Yargog-M29 highway as it looped out of the city and into a narrow valley tucked against the reverse slope of the Tarki-Tau hills. After two river crossings they pulled into Agachaul. Save a few lighted windows off the main road, the village was dark.

"Seems like an unlikely place for a logistics center," Ysabel said.

"According to Seth, the Parsabad–Artezian project ran on a shoestring budget for a while. I'm sure land was cheaper outside Makhachkala."

Behind them, the headlights of Seth's Suburban blinked. Jack pulled onto the shoulder, then rolled down his window as

Seth pulled alongside.

"I'll take us in from here," Seth called through his window. "The warehouse is on the northern edge of the town on the left side. Let's switch to headsets."

Seth pulled away and Jack fell in behind him.

A few minutes later they passed the warehouse. There was no mistaking it, two aircraft hangar–sized structures fronted by rolling garage doors and separated by a smaller, tin-roofed breezeway. Like Agachaul itself, the complex was dark.

"Is this place still in use?" Jack asked Ysabel. "I don't see any vehicles in the parking lot."

"The website didn't say. It sure doesn't look active, does it?"

Seth called over the headset, "We're going to pull in, Jack. Drive past me, then pull over up ahead and wait."

"Roger."

Seth slowed the Suburban, doused the headlights, then turned off the road and pulled up to the gate. He leaned from his window and punched the keypad box. The gate started rolling open.

"Still gainfully employed, I guess," Seth called. "Sit tight. We'll take a spin around the lot and see if we draw any attention."

Jack and Ysabel watched as the Suburban disappeared around the side of the southernmost warehouse. When it emerged around the opposite end, Seth said, "We're good, Jack. Nothing's moving. The keypad code is 77426."

Jack did a U-turn, pulled up to the gate, typed in the code, then drove to where Seth was parked before the breezeway entrance, a double-doored glass alcove.

Jack and Ysabel got out and joined the others at the back of Seth's Suburban. Dom handed out the Ruger pistols, then the ARXs. Jack gave Ysabel a quick run through the assault rifle's operation. He hoped none of them had cause to use the weapons. If the Krasukhas were inside, their security teams probably wouldn't be far away. Fifty against five was impossible odds.

"What's the plan, Seth?" asked Dom.

"Jack's call," replied Seth. "The only thing I know about the place is the entry code."

Jack mentally flipped a coin and decided on the simple approach. He walked to the front door and waited while Seth punched his code into the keypad. With a soft buzz the lock disengaged. With Jack and Dom in the lead, the group stepped through and into a wide concrete corridor lit only by the light coming through the doors and from a humming soda machine standing beside a potted fake palm.

Four office doors, two on each side, lined the corridor. At the halfway point a pair of hallways branched off, one leading to the south warehouse, the other to the north warehouse.

Jack pointed left. Dom led them down the hallway to a steel door. He tried the knob, then gave them a thumbs-up. He opened the door a crack; through it Jack saw darkness. Jack nodded and Dom went through, followed by the others with Jack bringing up the rear.

Sitting in the middle of the hangar in a staggered line abreast were four Krasukhas painted in a dark green forest camouflage pattern. Clark hadn't been kidding. These were beasts, impossible to mistake for anything but high-tech military vehicles. The flanks were lined with square and rectangular pods Jack assumed were part of the onboard EW suite. Folded snugly against the top was a ten-foot-wide parabolic energy director. At the back of each vehicle was what looked like a draw-bridge-style ramp. Folded lengthwise along the length of each Krasukha was a heavy green canvas tarpaulin with fixed ratchet straps; while these wouldn't disguise the

Krasukha under close scrutiny, in passing they might be mistaken for standard semitrailer trucks.

Spellman said, "Nicely done, Ysabel. You found the needle in the haystack."

"Thank you."

Jack gestured to the others and made a twirling motion with his index finger. They split up, made a circuit of the interior, then regrouped. "All clear," Dom whispered.

Jack stared at the Krasukhas. Part of him hadn't expected to find them here. Now that they had, he wasn't sure of their next move. They had no way of destroying the Krasukhas, or even disabling them; the exteriors were armored, as were the tires and probably any vital system. They were built for the battlefield.

Jack felt powerless.

"What now?" Seth asked. "Pop the tires, put sugar in the gas tanks, call Daddy Volodin and tell him the kids are off joyriding again?"

Dom laughed softly. "Fuckin' hell, Seth."

Jack walked to the nearest Krasukha, stepped onto the running board, and tried the door. It was open. He leaned in, then hopped back down. "No keys."

"Something like that you'd expect to at

least have push-button ignition," muttered Seth.

"You're on fire tonight, man. Jack, what're you thinking?"

Behind them came the clicking of boots on concrete. A male voice started humming.

"Cover," Jack whispered.

They moved to the wall and stacked up on the hinge side of the door. Jack drew his Ruger. The footsteps stopped. They heard the tinkling of coins followed by the thunk of a soda can tumbling down the machine's chute. A few seconds later a door banged shut.

"One road," Ysabel whispered. "There's only one way up to the ridge."

"She's right," Spellman said. "We shut that down, we shut them down."

Nothing short of cratering the road would do that, Jack knew, but every minute they could delay the Krasukhas was another minute Seth's hubs could be broadcasting.

"Let's get out of here," Jack said.

He led them back through the main corridor and out the main doors to the Suburbans. A half-mile down the highway, he pulled over. He and Ysabel walked back to the other Suburban.

"Seth, when do things kick off?"

He checked his watch. "Six hours. Our

first e-mail/text blast goes out at eight. The first wave of protesters should be at their rally points by nine."

If Seth's previous estimates were correct or even close, Makhachkala's streets would go from crowded to standing room only, especially outside the government buildings and President Nabiyev's private residence. Nabiyev would immediately order the ISPs shut down. And in response, Seth would order their satellite Internet hubs powered up. None of this would come as a surprise to Wellesley; he and Pechkin had had a year or more to hone their counter-coup plan.

These Krasukhas would need to be in place on the ridge and operational before dawn.

"Dom, you're with me. Grab everything. Seth: You, Matt, and Ysabel go back to the city. Convince Medzhid to send us some of his ERF troops — threaten him, bribe him, whatever it takes."

Ysabel said, "Jack, I thought we agreed we were never having this conversation again."

"It's not a conversation, Ysabel."

"Why are you doing this?"

He'd half hoped she would go along with his request. He didn't know how to answer her question. Why was he doing this? It certainly wasn't because he couldn't count on her, or that she hadn't earned her place on their thrown-together team. He could, and she had. That one obvious reason for his decision: He didn't want her to get hurt; the thought left a hollow feeling in his belly. He didn't want Dom to get hurt, either, or Matt, or Seth, but that was different, wasn't it? He knew why that was, of course, but he didn't want to think about that right now. He couldn't think about that right now.

"Matt, drag her if you have to."

"You got it."

"Jack, please, don't —"

Jack turned around and walked back to his Suburban.

44

"Time isn't on our side, Jack," Dom said.

"We're almost there."

Although Agachaul was no farther from the ridge road than Makhachkala, the rear approach up the escarpment had taken more than an hour to traverse, partially because the roads were steeper and the hairpins more plentiful and partially because of the quickly deteriorating weather. The intervening day of sun since the previous rainstorm had done little to dry the gravel roads, and rainwater streamed over them in rivulets. And while this was enough to often slow the Suburban to a walking pace, Jack doubted the Krasukhas' massive off-road tires and powerful diesel engines would have trouble negotiating the grade.

Finally, they rounded the last bend before the entrance to the maintenance road. Jack's headlights flashed over something dull and metallic. He braked hard and the Suburban skidded to a stop.

The barrier chain was up, its thick links drooping between the steel posts and completely blocking the road.

They got out.

The wind was stronger up there, driving the rain so hard against their ponchos it was as though handfuls of sand were being hurled at them. Jack could feel the chill seeping up his legs. He suppressed a shiver.

"Jack, over here."

Dom played his flashlight over the steel post. "Padlocked. Big bastard, too. We'd need a fifty-cal to break it."

They stepped over the chain and walked to the first clearing. Jack shined his flashlight upward. Thirty feet above him a camouflage net drooped between the trees.

"Thorough bastards," Dom said.

Jack's phone rang. He stuck it under his hood and bent double to dampen the wind. "Yeah, Seth, what's happening?"

"We're back safe. Ysabel's pretty pissed, though."

"She'll get over it."

"She's using curse words I've never even heard before."

"Tell me about ERF," Jack said. "We could use some help up here."

"Medzhid said no. He's sorry, but he can't

spare anyone."

"God damn it, Seth —"

"Jack, Volodin's ordered the border garrisons to move. They'll be here by evening at the latest."

They now had the answer to their big question: Volodin wasn't going to let Dagestan go without a fight. The ERF wouldn't be nearly enough, Jack knew. Twelve thousand hardened Russian troops against a few hundred Medzhid *politsiya*. With luck, they could fight a delaying action long enough to give Seth and Medzhid time to clear the streets of civilians.

"What about the city garrison?"

"They're still sitting inside their barracks. The commander isn't taking Medzhid's calls. At best, they're going to sit it out. At worst, we'll have sixteen thousand marching through the city rather than twelve."

"If that happens, document it all," Jack replied. "Fire up your hubs."

"It's already started, Jack. We sent out the e-mail blast about a half-hour ago. We should start seeing the next wave of protesters joining the first wave outside the Parliament Building. Whether we can show the world depends on you and Dom. I'm not going to risk the hubs until I know they won't be fried by the Krasukhas."

"We'll do our best. If you can spare Matt, send him down to the docks and see what he can do about the *Igarka.*"

"I can do that."

"Seth, I want you to get Ysabel out. Put her on a plane or a boat or in a taxi, whatever you've got."

"She won't go."

"Make her go."

"I'll try, Jack."

"Do better than that."

Jack disconnected. He looked around and saw Dom standing beside the Suburban's open passenger door, a pair of binoculars raised to his eyes.

"Dom?"

"They're coming up, Jack, all four of them. We've got a half-hour at most."

"Either we head back to the city, try to shanghai some ERF guys and come back, or we stand and fight," Dom said.

"There's no ERF to be had," Jack replied, then told him about Seth's report. "It's unraveling down there. I vote we stay."

"Fine by me, bud. What's the plan?"

"We're going to have to part ways with our Suburban."

Jack explained what he had in mind.

■ ■ ■ ■

Moving fast, Jack first shattered the Suburban's dome light, then turned the vehicle around so the nose was facing downhill. Dom found a heavy stone and placed it in front of the rear tire.

They removed their weapons and ammunition from the Suburban, stacked all of it in the trees on the other side of the chain, and did an inventory: four ARXs, two Rugers, and two hundred twenty rounds of ammunition.

"We need steel ones," Jack said.

Dom checked one of the Ruger clips, said, "Lead hollow-points," then examined an ARX magazine. "Bingo. Full metal jackets."

"Hold on," Jack said.

He walked the road, panning his flashlight over the ground. The rain was coming harder now, raking at the trees along the road. Leaves swirled around Jack's feet. He stooped over, picked up a flat rock, and carried it back to where Dom was standing.

"Go."

Dom lifted the ARX to his shoulder and pulled the trigger.

A spark leapt from the rock's surface.

"We've got a winner," Dom said.

Next they turned their attention to the Suburban. Using the combo car jack/ crowbar, they shredded the interior, from the seat covers to the carpet to the roof liner. Finally they tore free all of the material and piled it into the front seat.

"Looks like a tiger got trapped inside for a couple days," Dom said.

"Perfect. Where are they?"

Dom grabbed the binoculars from the dashboard and aimed them down the road. "About halfway up. The hairpins are slowing them down. I'd say another fifteen minutes."

Jack checked his watch. It was three forty-five. They had about an hour before sunrise. Good. They could make the darkness work in their favor.

He leaned into the driver's seat and tugged at the seat cover until he had an armful of cloth. He stuffed this into the cargo area, then added some of the roof liner. Finally he placed the flat rock at the base of the pile.

"What are the odds this'll work?" asked Dom.

"Depends on how you define *work*," Jack replied with a grin. "It'll go up, no doubt about it. Whether it'll do us any good we're going to find out. We'll need to rig the steer-

591

ing wheel."

"I'll handle that. You check on our friends."

Jack grabbed the binoculars and tracked them down the road until he saw the lead Krasukha's slitted headlights. The three trailing vehicles were spread down the road at fifty-foot intervals. This, too, might work to their advantage.

"Ten minutes," Jack called.

After Jack adjusted the Suburban's tires so they were pointed straight down the road, Dom tied the Suburban's steering wheel with a length of wire he'd ripped from under the dashboard.

"Let's walk it," Jack said.

They hopped over the chain barrier and split up, each of them pushing through the underbrush for a few minutes before meeting back at the Suburban.

"I've got a few good trees on my side, but not much room to maneuver," said Dom.

"Same here. If we can get them stopped and out of their vehicles, they'll have to come straight up the middle with no cover."

"And if we don't get them stopped, they're going to plow right over us. We haven't talked GTFO," said Dom, referring to the Get the Fuck Out plan.

"We run like hell."

"You know what they say about a bear chasing you, right?"

"Huh-uh."

Dom grinned. "You don't have to be faster than the bear, you just have to be faster than the guy running beside you."

"Fuck you, Dom."

"Love you too, man."

Faintly in the distance they heard the groan of diesel engines.

"Time for the gas," Jack said.

45

Using the crowbar, Jack punched a hole in the gas tank. Fuel started gushing, splashing on the ground and mixing with the rainwater sluicing down the hill. The stench filled Jack's nostrils.

Dom began handing him material from inside the Suburban and then, once it was saturated, threw it into the backseat and fed Jack another chunk.

"Headlights coming around the bend," Dom said, grabbing and tossing material.

Jack resisted the urge to look. The sound of the Krasukhas' diesel engines grew louder. Jack could feel the ground trembling beneath his feet.

They kept up their daisy chain until every shred of material they could lay their hands on was dripping with gasoline. Finally, Jack stuffed a chunk of foam into the tank's hole.

Down the hill, the first Krasukha was a hundred yards away, its thick knurled tires churning up the wet gravel. The headlights were climbing up the slope, slowly edging closer to the nose of the Suburban.

Jack opened the driver's-side door, started the ignition, and shifted the transmission into neutral. The Suburban's tires rolled up the stone wheel blocks, then rolled down them. Jack returned to the tailgate. Dom handed Jack a pair of ARXs and one of the Rugers in a paddle holster, which Jack clipped to his belt. He slung one of the ARXs across his chest, the other over his back.

"You look like a bandito," Dom said.

"What do you make the distance, about two hundred feet?"

"About that," Dom replied.

"Let's send it."

Dom knelt and jerked the stone free.

The Suburban started rolling.

They turned, hurdled the chain, and took up their positions on either side of the road.

It hadn't covered ten feet when it hit a soft spot in the gravel. The nose veered left toward the drop-off. The tires hit the shoulder berm and the Suburban veered back into the middle of the road and started picking up speed.

"Do it," Dom said.

Jack raised his ARX and peered through the scope; in the compressed view the Suburban was a jittery blur. Jack placed the lighted green reticle on the pile of material in the cargo area and pulled the trigger.

Miss.

He fired again.

Another miss.

Come on, Jack, shoot straight, damn it.

"You're two inches high right," Dom shouted.

A hundred feet away, the lead Krasukha skidded to a stop, its brakes screeching. Jack heard the grinding of gears and the vehicle started backing up. Horns started honking.

Jack adjusted his aim again. He thumbed the selector to three-round burst, took a breath, let it out, and squeezed the trigger.

Inside the tailgate, the rock sparked.

With an audible whoosh the material burst into flame, immediately engulfing the rear and middle seats. Fire streamed from the half-open windows, blooming as the Suburban picked up speed and oxygen was funneled through the interior.

The lead Krasukha was still reversing. Behind it, the second vehicle sped up and veered toward the shoulder, trying to avoid the collision. As they slid past each other, the left-hand Krasukha's wheels slipped off the edge and the vehicle began tipping sideways with the sound of groaning steel.

Fully engulfed now, the Suburban slammed into the lead Krasukha, and its push bumper crushed the Suburban's hood beneath it. Fire shot from the Suburban's side windows and splashed across the Krasukha's windshield, over the roof, then down the sides.

The second truck rolled onto its side, teetered there for a moment, then began barrel-rolling down the slope, its engine revving and headlights spiraling. Jack heard shouting, barked orders in Russian. There wasn't a trace of panic in the voices.

Men came running up the side of the first Krasukha, dodging flames and firing from the hip. Jack counted four of them, then five, then eight charging past the engulfed Krasukha and up the hill toward them.

"So much for the shock factor," Dom shouted from his tree across the road.

Jack took aim on the lead soldier and pulled the trigger. The man went down. Dom opened up, firing in tight three-round bursts, dropping two more.

The others spread apart, making themselves harder targets, then went prone and began returning fire.

Jack heard a snap beside his head, then a

second. Bullets thudded into his tree and peppered the soil beside his foot.

Four more soldiers joined the first group, and together they began leapfrogging up the road, two prone and laying down suppressing fire while two others advanced. They were thirty yards away and rapidly closing the distance.

These men were disciplined and well trained, Jack realized. It had taken them less than a minute to recover from the suddenness of the ambush, then to regroup and attack. This had never been a fight he and Dom were going to win; the best they could hope for was to hold these soldiers off for more than another couple of minutes, by which time they'd be within hand-to-hand range — if they survived that long.

From down the road came the roar of a diesel engine at high revolutions. Jack saw the glare of headlights, and then the third Krasukha emerged from the flames, scraping down the length of the first one and shoving it sideways as it chugged its way up the slope. More men came charging around the side of the vehicle, firing as they went.

Dom shouted, "Jack, time to GTFO!"

"Yep. Let's get their heads down first!"

Simultaneously they peeked out from behind their trees, braced the ARXs on the trunks, and opened fire on full auto. The soldiers scattered.

Jack and Dom turned and started running.

Twelve minutes later, Jack turned left off the trail, then over a rise, then lost his footing in the mud and started sliding. He clawed at the passing branches and jerked to a stop. Only a few feet behind, Dom tried to leap over him but fell short. He landed hard on his back and his head smacked into Jack's sternum. Dom rolled over and started crawling. Jack followed him until he felt pavement under his palms, then stopped. His heart thundered. His ears pulsed with rushing blood.

Where were they?

He saw white lines on the asphalt. A parking lot. It was empty. At the lot's entrance was a green-and-white sign with a pine tree emblem on it. A nature reserve or hiking area, Jack decided.

Dom gasped, "Do you see them?"

"What? I can't hear you."

"Are . . . they . . . following . . . us?"

Jack pushed himself to his knees and looked around, trying to get his bearings. He glanced back the way they'd come. It was getting lighter out and the wind had died away, but the sky was still full of leaden clouds. In the distance, barely visible through the rain, he could see the ridge road winding up the slope. He saw no headlights. Somewhere up there the two Krasukhas they'd failed to stop were probably in place and spooling up.

"No, we're fine," Jack said. "I'm not exactly sure where we are, though."

"We're off that damned ridge, that's good enough for me. How many did we take out?"

"Bad guys or Krasukhas?"

"Krasukhas."

"Two, the one that went over the side and the first one. It might be operational, but there's no way they're getting it up that hill."

"Fifty percent. Not bad," said Dom.

"Are you hurt?"

"I hurt everywhere. How far do you think that was?"

"Two miles, at least."

"I've never run that fast in my life."

Jack got to his feet; his legs were rubber. He helped Dom up, then Jack patted his pockets until he found his phone. He was down to fifteen-percent battery life.

He dialed Ysabel and got no answer, then tried Seth and Spellman with the same result. He dialed the Ministry of the Interior's main switchboard and got a busy signal. Cell towers were down, either shut down locally or fried remotely by the Krasukhas.

Jack dialed The Campus and explained to John and Gerry what had just happened. Gerry said, "We don't know about cell service, but the whole of Dagestan's Internet went dark about an hour ago. Nothing's getting out."

"Nabiyev and Volodin have shut down the ISPs, and probably the power grid, too. Seth won't bring his hubs online with the Krasukhas still operational."

"Well, you sure as hell can't go back up to that ridge, Jack. You gotta go after the *Igarka*," said Clark.

Jack disconnected. He said to Dom, "We need to find a way back. We need to find out what's going on."

"Whatever's happening, that can't be good," Dom said, pointing.

To the east, Makhachkala's skyline was cloaked in roiling black smoke.

They followed the canyon's narrow road to a rural neighborhood, then turned west and started picking their way into Makhachkala proper. Soon they caught the stench of burning rubber. Tires, Jack guessed. He wondered if Seth's protesters had gone from peaceful to violent.

The fringe neighborhoods appeared normal, if a little quiet, with no protesters in sight, but the closer to the city center they got, the more crowds they saw, first in small clusters, then in the dozens on street corners, and then in the hundreds in intersections. Gone was the chanting and singing from the day before, replaced with something Jack couldn't put his finger on. Discouragement? Worry? Faces tracked them as they passed. He felt eyes on his back.

"Jack," Dom whispered. "Our guns."

They tucked their ARXs beneath their

ponchos and kept walking.

Finally, they reached Amet Road, a major north-south thoroughfare. The traffic was heavy, with almost bumper-to-bumper traffic, but eerily, Jack heard little honking. He saw the black smoke now, hovering over the northern end of the city.

"All the cars are headed south," Dom said.

Jack wasn't sure if this was a good sign or a bad sign. Seth's plan called for the bulk of the protests to take place in the northern third of Makhachkala, where most of the government institutions were located. This southbound exodus suggested that's exactly what was happening; it also suggested these citizens wanted to be far from the action.

"They know the border garrisons are coming," said Dom.

"Probably so."

People liked the idea of freedom, but not the prospect of being clubbed or shot.

Jack got out his phone and tried Ysabel and the others again, and again got no answer. The MOI switchboard was still busy.

"Where do you want to go?" asked Dom.

Jack assumed — hoped — his lack of contact with the others was simply a communications glitch and that they were still safe within Medzhid's war room.

"The docks," he said. "Maybe Matt was

able to get there."

"Maybe he's already sunk the *Igarka*," Dom replied.

Jack glanced sideways at him.

"What, Jack? A man can dream."

They kept walking until they hit Gamidova, where they were able to hail a taxi. The driver agreed to take them to the docks, but at triple the going rate. They agreed.

Unsurprisingly, the docks were also strangely quiet. Roughly two-thirds of the vessels that had been tied up the last time Jack was here were gone.

They made their way to the harbormaster's shack.

Matt Spellman was sitting down, his back against the wall, eyes closed. As they approached he cracked an eyelid and said, "Hi, guys. Whatchya been up to?"

Jack and Dom laughed.

"A little of this, a little of that," Dom said. "We only got two of the Krasukhas."

"Doesn't matter." Spellman got to his feet and they shook hands.

"You look like shit, Matt," Dom said, nodding at Spellman's face.

The CIA man's left eye was almost swollen shut and his bottom lip was split.

"I got ambushed on the way here. My phone got smashed."

"I've been trying to reach the Ministry," Jack said.

"Yeah, when I left, Medzhid was sending everyone into the basement. It was a bit crazy."

Jack felt his heart lurch. "Why the move?"

"Ysabel's okay, Jack, don't worry. Rebaz is just playing it safe. Last night we started getting reports of gangs roaming the government district, bashing heads, looting stores, and setting cars on fire."

"And videotaping it all, no doubt," Jack said.

Volodin and Nabiyev's opening moves had been to shut down the Internet and the power grid; flooding the streets with provocateurs was Wellesley's.

Until Seth's hub system was up and running, the only images the outside world would see wouldn't be ones of a peaceful, grassroots uprising, but rather ones of violence and chaos. Why rally behind a country whose citizens had no qualms about turning on one another?

The world would watch, of course, and news outlets would play the images over and over until something nastier and juicier came along, and then Dagestan would be forgotten.

"Medzhid's sending in his *politsiya* to find them, but he's got to play it right," said Spellman. "Videos of club-wielding cops in riot masks will only give Wellesley exactly what he wants."

Jack said, "Seth should have used the hubs. Now he's playing catch-up."

"You didn't hear? No, I guess you wouldn't have," replied Spellman. "After you talked to Seth, Medzhid convinced him to change his mind. He said if the world wasn't seeing the truth of what they were trying to do here, Volodin was going to roll right over them.

"So Seth sent out the first e-mail blast and fired up the hubs. Five minutes after they came online, the Krasukhas started frying them. We lost half of them before we figured out what was happening. No way in hell did we think the Krasukhas would be that fast.

"Medzhid ordered Seth to pull the plug. Jack, there were five thousand people with five thousand cell phones standing outside the Parliament Building with no way to get the videos and pictures out to the world. It's falling apart even before it got started."

"We've got half the hubs left," Jack replied. "Is the *Igarka* still at anchor?"

"Yep. When most of the other boats were

running for the breakwater, she stayed put. She did circle on her anchor chain, though. Her stern is pointed inland now — against the tide."

So the Kvant has a clear view of the city, Jack knew.

"Show us," Dom said.

They followed Spellman down to the pier. The fog thickened around them until Jack felt as though he were suspended in midair. They reached the end of the planking. Spellman handed him a pair of binoculars.

"She's moved a bit closer since you last saw her. Look at about two o'clock. If the fog parts, you should be able to just make out her masthead light."

"I see it," Jack said. "How long until the border garrisons get here?"

"Last I heard, five."

Unless they had the Internet hubs online by then, Volodin could crush Makhachkala and there wouldn't be a single live recording to contradict his version of events.

Jack said, "We need to find a boat we can borrow."

Surprisingly, they had little trouble finding a boat perfect for their needs, a blunt-prowed twenty-eight-foot crew boat with navigation radar and an enclosed forecastle cabin that not only was unlocked but also had keys jutting from the ignition.

While Jack started up the engines, Dom and Spellman cast off the lines then hopped onto the afterdeck and joined him in the cabin.

Jack said, "Just so you know, I haven't got much of a plan, so let me know if you've got something."

"Let's hear yours," Spellman said.

"Pull alongside the *Igarka,* board her, shoot anyone who points a gun at us, then drive the Kvant over the side."

"Works for me."

"Me, too," said Dom.

"Fire up that radar, will you?"

Having taken a rough bearing on where they'd last seen the *Igarka*'s masthead light, Jack pulled away from the dock and pointed the bow into the harbor. Immediately the fog enveloped the cabin until the bowsprit was just a hazy vertical line floating ahead of them.

"She should be just up ahead," Spellman said.

Leaning over the tiny radar scope set into the helm console, Dom replied, "I've got something, but it's moving away from us. Two hundred yards off the starboard bow and picking up speed."

"Is there anything else around?"

"Astern of us in the harbor, but out here it's just us and this one."

"Why would she be moving?" Spellman asked.

Then it hit Jack: "Wellesley. The Krasukha crews would have called in the ambush. It's not a big leap for him to guess it was us — and what we're up to."

Jack pushed the throttle to its stops and the boat surged ahead, but slowly and steadily the *Igarka* began pulling away from them until finally, after ten minutes, she disappeared from Dom's scope.

"Last bearing I had on it was about one-three-zero degrees, heading south along the coast."

Jack eased the wheel over until the binnacle compass read 130.

"She has to stop sometime," Spellman said. "Any farther south and the Kvant won't be able to triangulate for the Krasukhas."

"Unless they already put the thing ashore and we missed it."

"Not on my watch," Spellman said. "She never left her anchorage."

They kept going.

■ ■ ■ ■

"I got a blip," Dom called out a few minutes later. "Dead on our nose, about half a mile."

"Still moving?"

"Yeah, but it's . . . Jack, she's turning to starboard, heading toward shore. She's slowing down."

Spellman began rifling through the cabinets above their heads, then the drawers beneath the console. "Come on, where are you?" He pulled out a chart. "Dom, where is she?"

Dom tapped the scope face. Spellman held the chart next to the screen, rotating it until he found a landmark on shore he recognized.

"She's heading for the Akgel Inlet," he said.

"Which leads where?" asked Jack.

"A reservoir about a hundred yards inland. It's a recreational boat area."

"Docks? Road access?"

"Uh . . . lemme think. Yeah. Nasrudinova Street, it heads north toward downtown."

"Dom, I can't see a thing. You're going to have to steer me."

"You got it." Dom leaned closer to the scope face. "Keep going . . . Okay, start easing to starboard. Keep coming around until you hit two-two-three degrees, then straight ahead."

Jack did so, his eyes darting between the rotating compass and the windscreen. The fog was thinning. Off the bow he could make out fuzzy geometric shapes; slowly they began to resolve into buildings.

When the compass hit 223, Jack let the wheel spin back to center.

"I see lights ahead," he said. "Off the port and starboard bow."

"Those'll be the inlet markers," replied Spellman.

Jack eased back on the throttle until they were moving at eight knots.

"Keep it steady, Jack. This thing looks real narrow."

"Forty feet, I'd guess," Spellman added. "Tight fit for the *Igarka*."

Dom said, "She's dead ahead, maybe a hundred yards and still slowing."

Out both windows Jack saw gray shadows gliding down the hull as they entered the inlet.

"Almost through," Dom muttered. "*Igarka*'s still slowing . . ."

Spellman said, "Don't crowd her, Jack."

He eased back on the throttle again. Six knots.

"We're through," Dom said. "*Igarka*'s fifty yards off."

Jack throttled the engines back to idle and let momentum carry them forward. Through the haze a pair of headlights flashed twice, then twice more. Still invisible in the fog, the *Igarka*'s diesels revved up.

"Moving again," Dom said.

The *Igarka*'s engines faded and they heard the scraping of steel on sand.

Jack said to Dom, "Get Matt one of the ARXs. Same thing as before, guys: If somebody's holding a gun, they're a target. No gun, they better be on their bellies. Sound good?"

Both Dom and Spellman nodded.

"I'm going to get us alongside as quick as possible, so hold on to something. Once we're stopped, get aboard and start clearing the decks. Dom, you're up high, Matt and I are heading forward along the deck."

Jack shoved the throttle forward and the boat plowed ahead.

"Come to starboard a bit," Dom called. "A little more. Good. Fifty feet . . . forty feet. Now to port . . . a little less. We should see her any —"

A black shape loomed before the windscreen. Jack thought, *Davit,* then shouted, "Get down!"

Spellman and Dom dropped to their bellies, Jack only a split second behind them. The *Igarka*'s boat davit clotheslined the cabin, shattering the windscreen and peeling the roof back like the top of a tin can.

Dom pushed open the cabin door and crawled out with Spellman and Jack on his heels. Jack stood up, looked right. The side of the *Igarka* was there, a few feet above them. Jack placed his foot on the gunwale, hopped up and snagged the *Igarka*'s gunwale, then boosted himself up. He brought the ARX to his shoulder and aimed it down the deck. Nothing moved.

Dom and Spellman climbed up and crouched next to him.

"Dom, go."

Dom jogged to a ladder affixed to the aft superstructure and started climbing. The fog enveloped him.

"Ready?" Jack said.

"Yep."

He and Spellman headed toward the bow, Jack taking the starboard side, Spellman the port.

As Jack passed the first hatch, it swung open, shoving him sideways into the railing. Jack spun, his ARX coming up. A man was standing in the hatchway. He was unarmed.

"Back inside!" Jack shouted. He kicked

the hatch shut and kept going.

From somewhere above came the dull pop, pop, of Dom's ARX, then, "You two, down! Get down! Jack, you're clear to the bow!"

Jack sprinted past the front edge of the superstructure and onto the forecastle until he reached the bow railing. Below he saw the broad outline of a flatbed truck cab.

He shouted over his shoulder, "Dom, you and Matt clear belowdecks."

"Got it!"

Jack lifted his legs over the railing, let himself hang free, then dropped to the sand below. ARX raised, he sprinted toward the truck, which began backing away, its tires spewing sand. On the other side of the windshield, a lone figure was behind the wheel.

Jack pointed the ARX at him. "Shut off the engine!"

The driver ignored him and kept backing up, until the truck's cab disappeared into the fog. Jack sprinted forward until the cab reappeared; then he fired a round into the passenger-side windshield. The truck braked to a stop.

"Engine off, hands out the window!"

The man complied.

Jack ordered him down from the cab, then

onto his belly.

Dom ran up.

"Clear it for me," Jack said.

Dom was back in ten seconds. "Nobody else."

They found Spellman standing on the sand before the *Igarka*'s bow. "Three crew in total," he reported. "All scared shitless, but unhurt. I've got them locked in the chart room. I don't think they know anything about the Kvant."

Jack prodded the driver of the truck forward. "Add him to the collection. We'll send some of Medzhid's ERF for them."

As Spellman took the man away, Dom asked, "Now what?"

Jack scratched his head. "Do you know how to sink a ship?"

47

MAKHACHKALA

Jack's unease grew stronger each block they drew closer to the Ministry of the Interior building. The streets were eerily empty. Shops and restaurants were closed. Buses and cars sat empty in the middle of intersections. It was, Jack thought, as though the whole of the government district had been transformed into a massive, post-apocalyptic movie set. The rain clouds had begun to break up, letting through intermittent patches of sun that warmed the still-slick streets enough that the pavement was shrouded in a thin layer of almost imperceptible fog. Another special effect, Jack thought.

The residents that hadn't fled to the city's southernmost neighborhoods were now behind locked apartment and house doors with curtains drawn, save a gap through which the owners could watch the streets.

Volodin's ordering of the border garrison

troops into Makhachkala hadn't been announced on the radio or the television, for those, like the Internet and the power grid, had been shut down shortly after dawn. The news had instead traveled by word of mouth, as had the protesters' heartbreaking realization that no one outside Makhachkala was seeing or even knew that Dagestanis were trying to take their first steps toward independence.

Jack pulled the truck to the curb outside the MOI's rear entrance and they climbed out. The guard let them through the gate and they took the elevator up to Medzhid's offices.

Jack found Seth leaning forward in one of the club chairs, his head in his hands.

"Why the hell aren't you answering your phone?" Jack said.

Seth looked up. "What?"

"The Kvant is sitting at the bottom of the Akgel Reservoir. Without that, the two Krasukhas should be easy to keep ahead of."

"It's too late, Jack. Medzhid's not going to send people back into the streets with the border garrisons on their way. It's over."

"It's not over. Get him in here."

"Okay. I'll be right back."

Jack said, "Hey, where's Ysabel —"

617

He saw her emerge from the nearby adjoining hallway. She stopped and stared at him. She crossed her arms. Her eyes were wet.

Jack walked over to her. "I'm sorry." He folded her in his arms. "I just couldn't let —"

"I know, it's okay," she whispered. "Jack, you need to listen to me, okay?" The tone in her voice was deadly serious. "Just keep hugging me."

"Okay . . ." he replied.

"There was something about Anton's face when you accused him of betraying Medzhid. He seemed genuinely shocked. Heartbroken. This morning I decided to go through his phone. Aside from Pechkin's number, there was only one other in his call history. It was labeled 'Mamochka' — mother. I called it. The woman who answered said, 'Vasim, where have you been?' "

Jack felt like he'd been punched in the stomach. Vasim had covertly swapped phones with Anton.

"I'm sure about this, Jack. It was Vasim. He was the one working with Pechkin, not Anton."

Oh, God, Jack thought. He'd killed the wrong man. He replayed the scene in his head and realized Anton had never actually pointed his gun at Medzhid, but instead had drawn it on instinct when Spellman had charged him.

Worst of all, Anton may have died thinking Rebaz Medzhid hated him.

"How did Vasim know we were onto one of them?" Jack asked.

"I don't know, and it doesn't matter. You need to get to Rebaz and —"

"Jack!" Medzhid called. "Dom . . . Matt!"

Jack whispered to Ysabel, "Get to Dom or Matt and tell them what's happening. I'll try to get Medzhid and Vasim separated. Watch the muzzles and stay out of the line of fire."

"Be careful, Jack."

He turned to face Medzhid, who was striding across the carpet. Vasim was two paces behind and to his left. Seth stood to Medzhid's right.

Jack shook the minister's extended hand. "Rebaz."

Out of the corner of his eye Jack saw Ysabel standing beside Dom. He glanced that way. Dom gave him a wink.

"Glad to have you all back safe," said Medzhid. "Seth said you want to talk to me. If it's about asking people to go back into the streets —"

"No, it's not that. Let's go in your office and I'll explain."

"Here is fine, Jack. I have staff in my office. And to be honest, I could use a break from commotion."

"Okay, then. Let's sit down." Jack gestured to the couch area.

"Dom, what're you doing?" Seth blurted.

Dom, who had been maneuvering himself behind Jack for a clear shot on Vasim, stopped. "What?"

"Why do you have a gun?"

Medzhid turned around. "Dom?"

Jack kept his eyes fixed on Vasim. Rather than moving to put himself between the principal and the threat, Vasim was staring at Dom. His eyes flicked toward Jack, then to Medzhid.

Vasim's hand shot into his coat.

"Rebaz, down!" Jack shouted, and raised his Ruger.

Vasim was moving sideways, using Medzhid's body to block Jack's firing angle.

Seth shouted, "Jack, what the hell is —"

Suddenly he seemed to notice Vasim's gun was out. "Hey, what are you —"

"Out of the way, Seth!" yelled Dom.

Time seemed to both slow down and speed up in Jack's mind, a stop-motion blur he felt strangely disconnected from.

He ducked down, leaned sideways, fired a round past Medzhid's leg. Vasim took the bullet in his thigh. To Jack's left, Dom was trying to maneuver for his own shot, but Seth was also turning, his eyes wide, as though trying to make sense of what was happening.

Vasim raised his gun and took aim on Medzhid.

"No!" Seth shouted.

He lunged forward. Vasim fired. Seth seemed to freeze in mid-step. His body convulsed and he dropped to his knees, then rolled onto his side. Jack, already charging, shoved Medzhid aside, raised his Ruger, and put a bullet in Vasim's throat, then another in his chest as he slumped back against the paneled wall.

Somewhere a woman screamed.

Jack was frozen in place, the Ruger still extended before him. His eyesight fluttered at the edges. Sounds seemed to fade in and out.

Seth is dead.

Seth is dead. He knew it in his gut.

"Jack." Spellman's voice. "Jack, let me have that. Let it go."

He pried the Ruger from Jack's grip.

Dom strode forward, knelt down to check Vasim's pulse. He glanced over to Spellman and shook his head, then started toward Seth's body, which was curled into an almost fetal position.

"Leave him alone," Jack murmured.

Dom stopped, gave a slight nod, moved off to the side.

Jack stepped around Medzhid, who was trying to sit up. The sleeve of his white shirt was bright with blood.

"Check him," Jack ordered, and kept moving until he reached Seth. He knelt down. He placed his palm on Seth's side. His friend's body felt somehow flat, deflated, missing whatever it was that made Seth Seth.

Jack bent forward at the waist, pressed his forehead against Seth's shoulder, and squeezed his eyes shut.

48

After a while he opened his eyes again.

There was activity all around him, voices, people rushing, phones ringing.

He lifted Seth's body off the ground.

"Jack," Ysabel whispered at his side, her hand on his biceps. "Let's put him in our room. Come on, I'll take you."

Ysabel led him down the hallway and opened the door to their bedroom. She shoved one of the pillows out of the way and smoothed the comforter.

"Here, put him here."

Jack laid him down.

Seth's eyes were open and staring. The front of his shirt was a mass of blood. There was a perfectly round hole a couple of inches below his chin and an exit hole at the nape of his neck. Vasim's bullet had punched into the soft tissue of Seth's throat and blasted through his spine, right below his brain stem. There was probably some life left in Seth, but there was nothing to be done. He was as good as dead.

He felt Ysabel's arms around his waist. She pressed her head against his back. "I'm so sorry, Jack. I wish there was something I could do for you."

"Is Rebaz okay?" he asked.

"The doctor's with him now, but it could be bad. He was hit somewhere in the chest. Dom thinks the bullet went through Seth."

He nodded.

"I don't know what to do, Ysabel."

"I know."

"He asked for my help," he said.

"You did help him."

"No."

Later he wandered out to the main room. Dom and Spellman were sitting on the couch, heads together as they talked. Jack took one of the club chairs across from them. Neither of them told him "Sorry"; they didn't need to.

"Rebaz?" Jack asked.

"He took the round in the right lung. Sucking chest wound. We got a piece of cellophane on it quick, but his lung was already collapsed," Spellman said. "We should know more in the next hour. He wants to see you."

"Why?"

"He didn't say," Dom replied.

"It's over," said Jack. "We're going home. Medzhid can't be a beacon of hope from a hospital bed, not with troops in his city."

"That's his decision to make," said Spellman.

Jack shrugged. "I need to find Raymond Wellesley."

"Well, Medzhid must have your mind," said Dom. "Yana told me that while we were chasing the *Igarka,* Medzhid sent a couple ERF guys to the schoolhouse on Lena Road. They found computers, monitors, cables . . . the same setup we found at the Chirpoy apartment. There was nothing left but a melted pile of junk. They found traces of white phosphorus."

Spellman added, "We figured that once he saw the hubs were getting fried by the Krasukhas, the protesters were dispersing, and Volodin was sending in the border garrisons, he decided his job was done."

"He was right."

"Jack, I can see it in your eyes," Dom said. "I know what you're planning."

"No, you don't."

"It's a raw wound right now — and a shitty time to be making big decisions."

"As far as I'm concerned, it's an easy

decision."

Medzhid's doctor walked in. "Are you Jack?"

"Yes."

"The minister would like to see you. Follow me."

He led Jack out into the tiled hallway. They took the elevator down to the basement and then went through a white door with a red medical cross on it. Medzhid was lying on a hospital bed with an IV in his arm. Behind him a monitor chirped softly. His face was very pale and his eyes were sunken. A square transparent bandage was taped to his chest; through it, Jack could see a ragged hole. The bandage bulged slightly each time Medzhid took a labored breath.

"Jack," he said. "Thank you for coming. I am sorry about Seth. I feel responsible."

"I'm the one who got it wrong. I killed Anton instead of Vasim."

"It's a forgivable mistake. Seth loved you like a brother, you know. Even before we met I felt like I knew you, he talked about you so much. He was a good man."

Jack simply nodded. "How're you feeling?"

"Lucky. Seth saved me, my doctor tells me. Had he not . . ."

"Slowed the bullet down?"

"Yes. I would be dead right now. I need surgery to repair the lung. I told him he can do whatever he likes with me, but not immediately. Jack, I know you want Wellesley. I can help you find him, but I need your help first. Don't misunderstand. I'm not bargaining with you. I will help you regardless of whether you agree to help me."

"Go ahead," Jack said.

"Soon I am going to get out of this bed and go meet with the Makhachkala garrison troop commander. He has pledged his support to me but there is one more thing we must do —"

"It's over, Rebaz. If you're lucky, you'll get out of this alive. If you do, step out of the spotlight, wait a few years, then test the wind again."

"In other words, live to fight another day."

"Or take Aminat and your wife and move someplace warm."

"There won't be another day, Jack. Seth and I spent the last three years putting this plan into place. The strategy is sound, as are the tactics. The networks and infrastructure are largely intact. Most importantly, Dagestanis are still out there and they're hungry for freedom. The only things we've lost are the element of surprise and some of our satellite Internet hubs —"

"And Seth."

"Yes, and Seth. Believe me, I'm not trying to diminish him, but Matt knows the plan as well as Seth did. He would want us to go —"

"Don't," Jack said. "Don't use him."

"He wanted this to work and he still does. I truly believe that."

Jack sat down on the bedside chair. He palmed his eyes and ran his hands through his hair. He was so tired.

"Rebaz, I can't decide if you're a truly great man or truly full of shit."

Medzhid smiled. "Mostly the former, with a dash of the latter. Will you help me?"

"Why do you need me? You have the entire MOI at your disposal."

"Let's examine the situation: Both my closest bodyguards are dead, one of them a traitor who framed the other one to be killed; the leader of my ERF, also a traitor; and Seth is gone. And then there is you: a man who risked his life to save my daughter, a complete stranger to him. I trust you, and I trust Ysabel, and Dom, and Matt. They look to you as a leader. I need people like the four of you by my side if I am to have any chance of succeeding. Plus, do you really want to miss the endgame, whatever the outcome?"

Jack thought about it. "You'll help me find Wellesley? Your word on it?"

Medzhid nodded. "Yes. Whether you help me or not."

"Okay. What's your plan?"

"To buy my country some time."

49
VATAN

It would be only later that Jack would fully realize how well crafted Medzhid's gambit was. As it was, he was having trouble focusing on anything more than putting one foot in front of the other.

Seth's gone, Jack thought. In various combinations the phrase kept popping into his head as though on some kind of subconscious timer. *Seth's dead.*

The rugged serpentine valley west of Vatan that Medzhid had chosen to confront the approaching border garrison was not only ideal ground for a smaller force to hold off a larger one. It was also, Medzhid had told Jack, the site of one of Dagestan's most famous battles, Lemmes Nok, where six hundred Avar, Kumyk, and Tsakhur tribesmen had banded together to repel Tahmāsp Qoli invaders.

Having secured the local garrison commander's commitment that morning, Medzhid had to make only a single call to get the four-thousand-man force moving northeast out of the city toward Vatan.

By the time the Ural truck in which Medzhid, Jack, Ysabel, Dom, and Spellman were riding reached the entrance of the canyon, the troops were already in position, standing at attention and formed into eight phalanxes of five hundred men each that blocked the mouth of the canyon, from rock face to rock face. None of them was armed.

It was an impressive spectacle, Jack thought, but useless on a modern battlefield. Of course, Medzhid knew this, as did the city's garrison commander, and probably every one of the four thousand men. If whatever military vehicles were about to come down this road decided to open fire, many hundreds would be dead within minutes.

Dressed in his formal Ministry of the Interior *politsiya* uniform, Medzhid climbed down from the truck with his doctor's help, then made his way up the road, passing through the phalanxes' ranks as he went. He looked straight ahead, his gait steady. Jack saw no trace of pain on his face, no small feat, given what he must be feeling. His lung was working at half capacity at best, the doctor had told Jack in the truck. And not until they got him into surgery would they know whether there was any hemorrhaging.

Jack and the others followed behind Medzhid until he reached the front of the formation. He stopped to exchange salutes with the garrison commander, then continued on until he was twenty feet ahead of the first rank and standing in the middle of the road.

Jack checked his watch: 5:20.

An earlier reconnaissance report from one of Medzhid's ERF units had put the lead units of the border garrison three miles away.

Jack felt the approach of the armored personnel carriers at first as shivering of the ground beneath his feet, then as a rumbling as the first vehicles came around the bend three hundred yards up the road.

Jack said to Ysabel, "If they start shooting, I want you to go —"

"You'll never learn, will you, Jack?" she said, and gave his hand a squeeze.

Upon seeing Medzhid's blocking force, the leading APC eased left, making room for the trailing vehicles until four of them were moving down the road in a line abreast. One by one, the APCs' thirty-millimeter cannons swiveled about until they were aimed at Medzhid's force. They closed to a hundred yards and then ground to a halt.

After a minute or so a GAZ Tigr — the Russian Army's version of the Humvee — rumbled down the shoulder past the APCs, then eased left into the middle of the road. The Tigr kept coming, its diesel engine echoing off the canyon walls, until it was thirty feet away. It slowly coasted to a stop, and a man in camouflage coveralls and a maroon beret climbed out of the passenger seat and walked forward.

"Good morning, Minister Medzhid," the man said, saluting.

Medzhid returned the salute. "Colonel Lobanov."

"May I ask what this is about, Minister? Why are these men blocking the road into the city?"

"The city is quiet, Colonel. There is no need for you to enter."

"I have orders to the contrary."

"I have orders from the people of Makhachkala," Medzhid replied. "You are an Avar Muslim, aren't you?"

"Pardon me?" Medzhid repeated the

question and Colonel Lobanov nodded. "I am."

"I'm also Avar, but Russian Orthodox. The city's garrison commander is of mixed heritage, Lak and Chechen. His wife is Azerbaijani."

"I don't understand, sir."

"There are thirteen different ethnicities that call Dagestan home, Colonel. We all speak Russian and probably a mixture of other dialects. We know one another's foods and drinks, our various marriage and funeral customs, our religious holidays and festivals. We are Russians, but we are also Dagestanis — Avars, Laks, Chechens, Tsakhurs . . .

"What you have been sent here to stop isn't a violent uprising of three million thugs. The only damage that's been done to Makhachkala has been done by covert forces sent here by President Volodin. The reports of violence you've received were not acts committed by people who call Makhachkala home.

"Earlier today, Colonel, I was shot by my own trusted bodyguard, a man working for Moscow. He is also responsible for the deaths of two dear friends. Another man, a sergeant named Pavel Koikov, with whom I served during my early days in the *politsiya*, was kidnapped from his home. This, too, was done at the behest of Moscow. Three days ago I was accused of having killed sixty-two fellow Dagestanis, burning them alive in a mosque at Almak in 1999."

Lobanov said, "I know Almak. My father talked about you. I remember reading the news stories. You killed only terrorists."

"Terrorists who had beheaded nine Russian soldiers," Medzhid added. "Agents from Moscow took and tried to kill Sergeant Koikov for fear he would tell the truth about Almak.

"My own daughter was kidnapped, Colonel, taken from the university where she is studying to become a doctor. You remember Aminat. You met her four years ago at my birthday party."

"I remember."

"They threatened to send her back to my wife and me in pieces."

"Minister, I am truly sorry that these terrible things have happened, but I have my orders."

"Orders from where? Moscow? From whom? The same people who ordered done all the things I just told about?"

"I have no choice —"

"You have discretion!" Medzhid shot back. "You're Dagestan's military governor. You live here, Colonel, along with your wife and two sons. You've called Dagestan home your entire life. Colonel, you're Russian, you're Dagestani, you're Avar, and you're Muslim, and you live and work beside people who are the same as you, and yet different from you. These are the people Moscow has told you are militants and thugs. That's the story they want you to believe. But what do you think?"

"Minister, what would you have me do?"

"Turn around, return to the border districts, and tell Moscow all is quiet in Makhachkala." Medzhid offered Lobanov a smile. "If later you hear otherwise, call me and you can come down and see for yourself."

Lobanov held Medzhid's gaze for a long ten seconds, then shook his head and smiled. "Good day, Minister Medzhid."

"And to you, Colonel. Safe travels."

EPILOGUE
BAKU, AZERBAIJAN

Jack wasn't sure it qualified for the strict definition of irony, but in the end Raymond Wellesley's obsession over derailing the coup, which was matched only by Seth's obsession to see it succeed, would be the SIS man's downfall.

The fact that Wellesley had chosen to use the Four Seasons Baku as his bolt-hole after leaving Makhachkala made Jack wonder if there was something to Jung's theory of synchronicity after all.

"I love it when a plan comes together," Ysabel said, taking a sip from her coffee cup.

"I'm not celebrating until I see him step off that elevator," Jack replied.

From their position in one of the lobby's seating areas, they had a perfect view of where Wellesley was to emerge.

Jack only hoped that wherever Seth Gregory had gone, he was watching what was about to unfold — especially since it was

Seth who'd made it possible. His seemingly trivial act of making off with the coup's operational funds had been the final nail in Wellesley's coffin.

Having invested so much time and effort in trying to stop the coup, Wellesley had chosen to tap into his own private operational war chest, funds that were themselves suspect. Gavin Biery and Matt Spellman, working in conjunction with a recovering but still hospitalized Medzhid, and Medzhid's counterpart in Azerbaijan's own Ministry of the Interior, had managed to penetrate Pacific Alliance Group, the front company Wellesley had used to lease his nerve center schoolhouse in downtown Makhachkala. From there, the rest of the dominoes had fallen in rapid succession — through Pacific Alliance Group, Wellesley had not only hired the *Igarka* to transport the Kvant to Makhachkala, but also paid, in person, the owner of the flatbed truck that was to take the Kvant to yet another PAG-leased building from which the Kvant was to track Seth's hubs for the Krasukhas on the ridge above Makhachkala. Finally, Wellesley had used funds from Pacific Alliance Group to rent the only available property outside the village of Keshar-e Sofla, a cabin at the end of the lonely dirt road where Ysabel had ambushed Jack's kidnappers.

At Gerry Hendley's request, Mary Pat Foley had presented this evidence to the chief of Britain's Secret Intelligence Service, who, as it turned out, had recently initiated a covert probe into Wellesley's extracurricular financial activities.

While Gavin and the others had found no proof that Wellesley had received compensation from the Russian SVR, Jack suspected that evidence would eventually be found. In men like Raymond Wellesley, hubris always trumped hypocrisy.

"Are you sure we can't shoot him?" Ysabel asked. "Even just a little bit?"

Jack smiled. "Tempting as it is, no. I'm already on thin ice with my boss."

"There he is," Ysabel murmured, nodding toward the bank of elevators.

Dressed in khaki trousers and a blue oxford shirt and carrying a leather valise draped over his shoulder, Wellesley looked more like a visiting businessman than an intelligence operative who may or may not be on the run. Though Gavin had been able to pin down the front end of Wellesley's travel arrangements, his destination was a mystery. However, unless they'd missed some detail, it appeared the SIS man assumed he was in the clear.

Wellesley strode past them, pushed through the revolving doors, and headed to the waiting black ZiL limousine. The driver opened the rear door, shut it behind Wellesley, then walked around to the driver's side.

Jack's phone chimed with a text message: READY WHENEVER YOU ARE.

Jack and Ysabel stood up and walked out of the lobby. Jack opened the ZiL's rear door and leaned in. "Morning, Raymond."

Wellesley's face went pale. "Jack, what are you —"

"Do you mind if we join you? Ysabel, after you."

Ysabel climbed in and took the seat opposite Wellesley. Jack did the same and shut the door. He asked, "Are you carrying?"

Wellesley seemed to have regained his composure. His shocked expression was gone, replaced by the smug half-smile Jack had seen many times since meeting the SIS man. "No, Jack, I'm not armed."

"That's good, because our driver is."

"I see. What's your plan, then? Take me out into the countryside, shoot me, then bury me?"

"It worked for Oleg Pechkin." *Sort of.*

"Who?"

Ysabel said, "You know, Mr. Wellesley, Seth was right about you: You're too arrogant for your own good."

"Ah . . . How is Seth, by the way?"

"Dead," Jack replied. *But already on his way home,* he thought. He and Ysabel would be back in Virginia in time for the funeral.

"Sorry to hear that. I actually liked Seth. He reminded me of a younger, more crass, less intelligent version of myself. Come to think of it, he was nothing like me. But the man had vision, I will say that."

Jack clenched his jaw, but was careful to keep his face impassive. "Things have a way of working out, Raymond," he said, then called out, "Dom, we're ready."

"On our way," Dom replied.

They sat in silence, Jack's eyes never leaving Wellesley's. By the time they reached Heydar Aliyev International Airport's charter terminal, the SIS man was shifting nervously in his seat.

Dom pulled through the rolling gate, then turned right through an open garage door and into a dimly lit hangar. Through the window Jack could see a gleaming white Gulfstream 650 jet with its folding stairs extended. Standing at the bottom of the steps were a pair of trim, broad-shouldered men in navy blue suits.

Wellesley glanced out the window. "What are you playing at, Jack?"

Ysabel replied, "This is your plane, isn't it?"

"It is. This is perhaps the worst kidnapping in history, you know that, don't you?"

Jack ignored him. He checked his watch: 8:20 a.m.

"Raymond, five minutes ago, e-mail and text messages went out to forty-two thousand Makhachkala citizens. In an hour, they're going to be on the streets, surrounding every government building; in ninety minutes, President Nabiyev will be announcing his resignation. In two hours, Rebaz Medzhid will be on every radio and television network in the country. In six hours, every major network and social media site in the world will be streaming the coup, live and in color."

"Good Lord, Jack, you're not a very fast learner, are you? Volodin will simply order the border garrisons back in —"

"He may indeed. It won't matter. Those garrisons will never come within fifty miles of Makhachkala. Medzhid and the military governor have come to an understanding. If Volodin wants to put boots on the ground in Dagestan, he'll have to fly them in — an order which has gotten a little stickier."

"What does that mean?"

"Over the last twenty-four hours Volodin's foreign minister has been visited by or has heard from ambassadors from the United States, the United Kingdom, France, Germany, and China. I'm paraphrasing, but the message was simple: You've had your fun in Crimea, Ukraine, and Estonia. Don't push your luck."

"That won't scare him."

"Probably not, but he's no idiot, either. He's going to have to make a choice: let Dagestan go and hopefully maintain a cordial relationship — something I think Medzhid will be open to — and easy access to Caspian oil, or march in, crush yet another republic that simply wants freedom, and take his chances with the backlash he'll get from a new crop of Dagestani insurgent groups, not to mention the nasty ones already in Chechnya and Georgia — as well as the non-Federation Caspian governments who'll like the idea of another free country sitting beside the basin's deposits. My guess is Volodin will make the smart move and keep the crude flowing."

"That's a big gamble, Jack."

"The Dagestani people are willing to roll the dice."

Wellesley shook his head sadly. "You have no idea what you've done. You've turned this whole region into a terrorist incubator."

"That may be," Jack replied. "If so, we'll hunt them where they are — just like we always do. You've got no faith, Raymond. The West doesn't need Volodin, and it never will."

Jack scooted forward and opened Wellesley's door. "Time to go home, Raymond."

Wellesley climbed out, followed by Jack and Ysabel, who said, "Travel safe, Mr. Wellesley."

The SIS man gave them a puzzled expression, then turned to head toward the plane. Blocking his way were the two blue-suited men. The older of the two said, "Mr. Raymond Wellesley, I'm placing you in custody for suspicion of violating the Official Secrets Act."

"Pardon me?"

"Turn around, sir, and surrender your bag."

The younger man placed his hands on Wellesley's shoulders and jerked him around so he was facing Jack and Ysabel. As the SIS man felt the handcuffs ratchet into place, his face went blank. "What the bloody hell is this, Ryan?"

"You were careless with your money," Jack replied. "You wrote one too many checks on your Pacific Alliance Group account."

"You bastard!"

With one hand on each of Wellesley's biceps, the two SIS men frog-marched him to the Gulfstream, up the steps, and through the door, which closed a few moments later. As the gap closed, Jack heard Wellesley cry, ". . . bloody fools, don't you —"

Dom called, "Anybody for breakfast?"

"Yes, absolutely," Ysabel replied.

Dom climbed back into the driver's seat.

Ysabel said to Jack, "Have you decided where we're going?"

"I'm going to leave it up to you. I've got two weeks' vacation and I'm taking every second of it."

Ysabel nodded, pursed her lips as she thought. "Matt's suggestion of Tahiti works for me."

Jack smiled. "Me, too."

ABOUT THE AUTHORS

Tom Clancy was the author of more than eighteen #1 *New York Times* bestselling novels. His first effort, *The Hunt for Red October*, sold briskly as a result of rave reviews, then catapulted to the bestseller list after President Reagan pronounced it "the perfect yarn." Clancy was the undisputed master at blending exceptional realism and authenticity, intricate plotting, and razor-sharp suspense. He died in October 2013.

The *New York Times* bestselling author of the Briggs Tanner series (*End of Enemies*, *Wall of Night*, and *Echo War*), **Grant Blackwood** is also the co-author of the Fargo Adventure Series (*Spartan Gold*, *Lost Empire*, and *The Kingdom*) with Clive Cussler, as well as the co-author of the #1 *New York Times* bestseller, *Dead or Alive*, with Tom Clancy, and *The Kill Switch*, with James Rollins. A U.S. Navy veteran, Blackwood spent three years aboard a guided missile frigate as an Operations Specialist and a Pilot Rescue Swimmer. He lives in Colorado, where he is working on his own stand-alone series starring a new hero.

M   7/15

Blackwood, Grant
Tom Clancy, Under
Fire